Saint Peter's University Library
Withdrawn

A TERRIBLE BEAUTY

"All changed, changed utterly:
A terrible beauty is born."

A
TERRIBLE
BEAUTY

Arthur J. Roth

FARRAR, STRAUS AND CUDAHY

George F. Johnson Library
St. Peter's College
Jersey City 6, N. J.

Copyright © 1958 by Arthur J. Roth
Library of Congress catalog card number 58-5186
First Printing, 1958

Acknowledgment is made to Mrs. W. B. Yeats,
the Macmillan Company of Canada, Ltd., and The
Macmillan Company (New York) for permision to
quote from "Easter, 1916" by William Butler Yeats.

Published simultaneously in Canada by
Ambassador Books, Ltd., Toronto. Manufactured
in the United States of America
by H. Wolff, New York. Design: Betty Crumley

9/20

F
R 74

NOV 2 1960

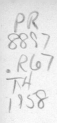
PR
8897
.R67
TH
1958

To Carrie and Leo,
who were mother and father to me,
and to my "sister" and "brothers"—
Rena, Gregory and Sean.

8661

A TERRIBLE BEAUTY

ONE

The news traveled quickly around the crowded dance hall as little groups formed to discuss the event. On the stage the members of the band had laid aside their instruments and were huddled together in a knot, smoking and talking. Two rows of girls were seated, facing each other, on the benches that ran the length of each side wall. Most of the men were gathered in clusters at the back of the building. A slight haze of cigarette smoke drifted upward and softened the glare of the light thrown out by the naked electric bulbs that hung from the ceiling. The six blacked-out windows stolidly kept the light and music from spilling out into the night.

On the stage a chair scraped, a fiddle threw out a tentative note, another joined it, an accordion barged in and the drummer welded the sounds into a fast reel. The music swung out over the crowd, reaching into the back corners and drawing the men up to the front of the hall. The master of ceremonies stepped to the center of the stage and called, "Take your partners for the Sixteen Hand Reel."

Dermot O'Neill looked up and down the two rows of girls. He caught the eye of a girl and nodded to her. She nodded back. He let several couples go out on the floor before he walked over and said, "I haven't danced with you tonight, Neeve."

The girl was dressed in a dark blue skirt and a light blue sweater. Black hair and eyebrows framed and arched an oval face. Her hair was drawn back, revealing a small pair of silhouette-less ears that lay in snug to her head. She had a large mouth and underneath her right eye a tiny black mole dramatically drew attention to gray-green eyes—the kind of giveaway eyes that quickly show anger or pain. Her figure had a voluptuous stockiness, making her appear smaller than her actual five feet, three inches.

The eyes revealed a little more than ordinary interest as she looked up and replied, "No you haven't danced with me. And tonight's my birthday."

"Happy birthday Neeve," Dermot said. He reached down, caught her hand and helped her to rise. They walked to the center of the hall and joined the other couples who were waiting for the M.C. to complete the set.

She laid her hand on his arm. "Tell me then, Dermot, what's the big fuss about tonight?"

A quick flare came into his blue eyes and a grin pulled at the corners of his mouth. "The I.R.A. raided an ordnance depot in Derry City," he replied. "They got away, clean as a whistle, with a hundred rifles and a couple of thousand rounds of ammunition."

"When was this?"

"Tonight. It was on the twelve o'clock news. Terry McNally heard it on the wireless just before he came to the dance."

"What can the I.R.A. do with a hundred rifles against the British Army?"

"What they did in 1916," he answered. "Chase them the bloody hell out of the country. Like Hitler chased them out of France. There never was a better time. England's beat. The old lion is down. When Germany jumps the channel the I.R.A. goes out. They'll clear every British uniform out of the Six Counties."

The conversation ended as the music started for the dance. The eight couples circled to the right and back to the left. Two opposing couples advanced to the middle of the circle and retreated. Again they advanced and boisterously swung around each other before taking their places in the ring of dancers. A chain was formed, the girls going one way and the boys the other, until each boy met his partner. The third movement started and Dermot and Neeve danced out and formed a bridge with their arms and the opposite couple danced under. Both couples then danced back to their places in the ring. The dance was executed in a wild exuberance, heels drumming, toes tapping and heads thrown back.

The dance ended and Dermot and Neeve went over to the side of the hall and sat down. She turned to him, "When did the I.R.A. start up again?"

"I don't know," he answered, "probably a couple of months ago."

"Are you in it?"

"I wish I were, but I suppose they don't want lads," he replied in a chagrined voice.

She looked at him for a few seconds, wondering whether or not to believe his remark. At twenty he was more than a lad. The tweed jacket he wore failed to hide the powerful set of his shoulders and the heavy work-developed arms. He was tall with large bones and a broad face. His eyes were blue. His dark brown hair was disarranged with the exertions of the dance and the ends of several strands were curling. When his hair got damp it riotously tightened up into hundreds of curls and from his grade-school days he had learned to detest curly hair. He always carried a black beret to wear when it rained.

"You're the queer old-fashioned lad," she said. "Your father was in the I.R.A. wasn't he—the time of the troubles?"

"Aye he was; and my Uncle Vincent too, Lord have mercy on him."

"Who was Vincent?"

"Vincent was brother to my father. You know the gate at the foot of the lane? He was shot at that gate one night by the Tans in 1920."

"I didn't know that."

"That was before you were born," Dermot smiled indulgently.

He looked down at her and ran his tongue over his upper lip. "If I take you home tonight will you give me nineteen kisses?"

"You big omadaun! If you want to take me home then ask straight out like a man—no putting ifs and ands to it."

Dermot laughed, revealing one slightly crooked tooth that edged over its neighbor. "If ifs and ands were pots and pans— what a merry world for tinkers," he recited.

Neeve put a small slender hand against his chest and pushed, "Away out of that with you. You're an old cod."

Dermot pretended seriousness, "Ah my wee pet, if you can't find anyone else to take you home, why I will."

"I'd be hard up to wait on you," she snapped.

He reached over and touched her gently on the cheek, "Be good, wee angel," he said as he stood up and left her.

He walked down to the end of the hall and mingled with the young men who had gathered there. The M.C. called out the next dance and the men started drifting to the top of the hall. Dermot was about to go up when he was approached by two of his friends. Don McGinnis, the taller of the two, was dark complexioned with a thin, El Greco face. Black bushy eyebrows complemented a head of thick hair that rode in graceful waves. Almost black eyes and a small mouth gave his face a stern impression. A congenital clubfoot caused him to limp when walking. Sean Reilly, his companion, was stockier with sandy-fair hair and blue eyes. A laugh continually lurked around the corners of his mouth and a scattering of freckles spotted his forehead.

"What do you think of the raid tonight?" McGinnis asked.

"Proper medicine," Dermot replied. "A few more like that and we could fly the tricolor instead of that cow's afterbirth that Britain calls a flag."

McGinnis nodded to Sean, "Let's take a dander up the road." Turning to Dermot he asked, "Coming with us?"

"Are you batty man?" Dermot protested. "It's freezing out there. What for?"

"Isn't that just like him," Reilly remarked to McGinnis. "He has to know the what for of everything. We want a chat with you," he explained. Dermot scented intrigue and, in a sudden flash of understanding, knew what they wanted. "Wait till I get my coat," he said.

They started walking up the road away from the town. The frost had already whitened the fields and the road rang metallic under their heels. McGinnis spoke, the words attached to cloudy white puffs, "You're not to repeat anything we might tell you tonight."

"I'm not a sieve," Dermot protested.

"The I.R.A.'s forming a company in Duncrana," McGinnis continued. "Would you think of joining it?"

Dermot stopped. "It's not just a Duncrana thing is it? Is it connected with the boys in Derry?"

"It is then," Reilly answered, "connected with Derry and Belfast. It's a new I.R.A. modeled on the old one, with headquarters in Dublin. It covers the whole country."

The three men formed a tight little circle in the middle of the road. From the town came the faint strains of the music and the barely audible tapping and drumming of the dancers' feet.

"I'm your man," Dermot answered, "and damn the better you'll find. The O'Neills have fought England for five hundred years. There never was a generation of us that didn't have its rebel."

"That's grand talk," McGinnis drily said, "and if talk could free us we'd be along with the South tomorrow. It's action we need. It's the gun and the bullet and the bomb. Let you think it over. If you're still of the one mind, come to the shop next Tuesday about seven-thirty."

From a field to the right of them broke the harsh bray of a donkey. The rhythmic rasping of the sound savaged the tranquillity of the night. Sean laughed nervously. "It's Rafferty's ass. Let's turn back."

The three men walked back to the dance hall. McGinnis stopped at the door. "I'll not be going in," he said. "We'll see you on Tuesday?"

"Right as rain," Dermot answered.

McGinnis walked down the street. Dermot and Sean watched the figure with its limping shuffle disappear into the dark. They listened to the firm impact of his right foot and the dragging whisper of his left as the sounds receded and were lost.

"There walks a strange man," Sean commented.

"Aye, he's another Patrick Pearse," Dermot thoughtfully replied. "I often wonder why Don didn't become a priest. He doesn't chase the lassies or drink or smoke."

"His people never had the money to send him on," Sean answered.

They re-entered the hall and Dermot looked around for Neeve. She was sitting on one of the benches and as she noticed him she frowned. He walked up and sat down beside her. "Now what was that for?" he asked.

She cocked her head to one side and looked up shrewdly.

"Where were you?" she asked. "There was a ladies' choice called and I wanted to ask you but you were gone."

"I went outside for a few minutes."

"What for?" she asked, wondering if he had been out with another girl.

Guessing the reason for her curiosity, he smiled and replied, "I went out to make my water."

She looked around quickly to see if anyone had heard. "What in under heaven makes you say a thing like that?" she protested. "You've got a shocking tongue."

"You had to know, didn't you?"

"You might have said, 'I went out to the convenience,'" she suggested.

"'Convenience,'" he mimicked her, "I don't know what's convenient about a hedge. Let a girl leave this town and go to the city for a few years and you wouldn't know a word she's saying."

"The city didn't change me," Neeve said emphatically.

"Deed it did. When you went away you were just a homely wee slip of a thing. By the way," he said, adroitly changing the subject, "how's your business?"

"It's a little slow right now. Most of the women still go to the Rathgiven hairdressers. But to have been started only two months, I'm not doing bad."

"It must be grand to have your own wee business."

"Deed it is. And you, when are you going to start up something?"

"This town is dead. What can I do? The only work is at the British airdrome they're building at Lough Neagh and the old one won't hear of me working for the British. They won't hear of me going to England either. I'll have to content myself with helping Ned on the land, and hope that things will change. I'd like to go to America, but that would be when the war's over."

"Aye that would be nice. Do you have ever a relative there at all?"

"I have an Aunt Carrie; sister to the father. We get a letter from her once in a while."

"You could go out to her," she said.

A brief handclap interrupted their conversation. The M.C. stood up and announced, "Ladies and gentlemen, Mr. Tommy Ryan has kindly consented to sing a song." The M.C. walked over to the edge of the stage and called down, *sotto voce*, "Here Annie, find out what in the hell he's going to sing." A girl detached herself from the crowd at the head of the hall and self-consciously walked down to where a young boy sat. A brief conversation ensued. Annie came back and whispered to the M.C. The M.C. straightened and clapped once again, "Mr. Tommy Ryan will now sing 'The Foggy Dew,'" he announced.

A desultory round of handclapping broke out and then receded. A low murmur of conversation filled the hall. There were several indignant cries of "whist," and the conversations stopped. Finally an almost dead silence reigned. The boy continued to sit with his shoulders bowed, his hands thrust between his knees and his eyes fixed on a point in the middle of the floor. Then giving an exploratory cough he started, his voice curiously flat and lonely after the rollicking music of the band.

"As down the glen one Easter morn,
To a city fair rode I . . ."

At the end of the first stanza he paused and glanced up nervously. There were several shouts of encouragement:

"That's the spirit, Tommy."

"Ach you're in grand voice, Tommy lad."

"There's a song that'll never die."

Reassured, he started into the second stanza. At the end of each stanza there were the cries of encouragement, the hopeful look of the singer and the vigorous nods of approval. The song ended and a tumultuous handclapping broke out and lasted half a minute. Mr. Tommy Ryan permitted himself a pained smile. The conversations were continued.

"Well, am I leaving you home or not?" Dermot asked.

"You can if you want," Neeve answered.

"Let's leave now," he suggested.

"No." She shook her head warningly. "Wait till the next dance is started. Then we won't be noticed."

The next dance was called and couples moved out to the center of the hall. Dermot and Neeve stood up, got their coats and left.

Outside the hall, Dermot slipped his arm around Neeve's waist. They walked across the street and down the town.

"It'll snow," Dermot remarked, "I can smell it."

"Aye and you can see the wind too," Neeve mocked him.

"And court my way through a townland of widows," Dermot added.

They laughed together, richly, the way young people laugh in the darkness; he with a deep masculine tone and she with a bubble in her throat. They walked down the middle of the town, past the church and turned into the back entrance of Neeve's house. Neeve took a key from her coat pocket and quietly inserted it in the lock of the back door. Half turning, she said to Dermot, "Good night my warrior bold."

He caught her arm and complained, "You wouldn't send me home like this and the snow coming and the wind cutting the ears off me?"

"What would you be wanting then?" she asked.

"It's not a cup of tea," he replied as he pulled her in close with his right arm and tilted her head back with his free hand. He stooped quickly, awkwardly, and kissed her. "Be good," he whispered.

At the street he paused and looked down at the only light visible in the town: a small yellow bulb outside the door of the police barracks. He grunted derisively and started walking home. As he walked he softly whistled "The Foggy Dew." The thin flutiness of the tune climbed up into the sky and lost itself in the night.

TWO

The O'Neill farm was situated a mile and a half from the town of Duncrana. The mortared-stone farmhouse poked its backside in against the flank of a hill. Normally the house seemed a natural outgrowth of the rocky land but when it was newly whitewashed it stood out glaringly and the mountain appeared to withdraw, as if ashamed of the strange white lump on its side. Gradually, with the wind and the rain, the whitewash discolored until the mountain and house again became reconciled in a stringy, slate-gray color.

Standing under the eave one could count the different coats of thatch the house wore, from the golden yellow of the latest one to the rotting blackness of the first roof.

In front of the house a cobbled yard looked out over gently sloping land that dipped into a valley and then climbed until it met the town. The town was visible from the O'Neills'; a huddled jumble of dwellings that crowned the hill, each house dragging an untidy garden behind it, the whole brooded over by the steeple of the Catholic Church that thrust up above neighboring slated roofs. Sometimes in the early morning the valley floor was covered with a mist that wraithed and filtered through the fields. As the day advanced patches of mist arose and necklaced and earringed the hilly town. At other times the mist flowed up past the O'Neill farm, gently rising until it combed through the whin bushes that spotted the mountain behind the house.

In winter, when the wind blew fierce and strong, everything about the place rattled: the chain on the gate, the byre door, the windows of the house and if by oversight a bucket were left out, it danced all over the cobbled yard and like as not wound up in a hedge.

The farm was all the more treasured for being a poor one, only half of the forty-six acres being suitable for crops. The rest was rough mountainy land, useful only for grazing and as a refuge for foxes and badgers.

In addition to the usual complement of livestock, cows and calves, a horse and chickens, there was also a cat called Tippy and a dog named Tone.

The oblong house was made up of four square rooms in a row: the kitchen, the scullery or storeroom and two bedrooms. The house was bracketed on one side by the byre and on the other by the turfshed. In addition to turf, the latter structure contained a yellow and black two-wheeled farm cart. The walls of the turfshed were festooned with chains and ropes, rakes and pitchforks, the mare's harness and a faded poster that patriotically appealed in yellow and green letters to support the Balinderry Drum and Pipe Band.

A short lane ran from the county road into the farmyard. The yard itself was enclosed with a low stone wall. Opposite the byre was the doughal or dungheap, which was neatly built up during the autumn and winter until spring came and the fields were manured. Behind the house was a small garden for vegetables. In the corner of the garden grew two apple trees, a plum tree and timidly apart, as befitted a poor relation of the plum family, stood a damson tree.

Also behind the house was the haggard with the haystacks. In proportion as the hay decreased in the haggard, the doughal grew and the byre was the agent of the metamorphosis. It was a natural cycle with the byproduct of milk. The hay fed the cows which gave milk and manure, the milk fed people and the manure fed the land which grew the hay.

Inside the house were Dermot, his mother and the dog, Tone, named after an Irish patriot. The dog was mature and honorable and Dermot spoke respectfully to him. "Tone, it's time you went out for the cows."

Tone began to whimper and got up hurriedly and went over to the door. Dermot let him out and Tone turned for another look. "Away out with you," Dermot said.

Tone went tearing down the lane, squirmed through the bars of a gate and went racing across a field.

Dermot's mother, a tall lath of a woman with almost white hair, combed back and coiled in a bun, said to him, "Aren't you early tonight? A nice evening like that, they should be left out till dark."

"I want them milked early. I have to be in town by seven-thirty."

"Sure Patrick could milk them if you want to get away."

"Aye he could," Dermot answered, "and I'd never hear the end of it. I'll do it myself rather than listen to him." Dermot liked to give no one, least of all his father, cause to complain.

Meanwhile Tone had rounded up the cows and driven them down to the gate. Dermot came down and opened the gate and the cows came through sedately, their hindquarters swaying, and started up the yard in single file. The black cow crowded a little too close behind the brawny one and the latter swung her head back and swiped with her horns. The brawny cow always led the procession and was uneasy if another cow tried to get ahead of her. Dermot, watching her, said, "Oh! but that's the bad-tempered old tinker."

Tone showed his agreement by dashing in and pretending to nip the cow's leg. The brawny cow lashed out with her hoof, barely missing the dog, and Tone discreetly skipped back. For Dermot's benefit he gave a low growl to show that he'd stand for no further capers.

Dermot followed the cows into the byre and tied each one to its headpost. He went into the house and got the milking bucket and scalded it with hot water from the kettle. Returning to the byre he pulled the stool out from a corner, placed it beside the black cow, sat down and leaned his head against the cow's flank. His broad hand reached down and gently wiped the udder several times to clean off any dust or pieces of dirt that might later fall into the bucket. Then he directed three squirts of milk from each teat to the floor of the byre. The "little people" propitiated, he placed the bucket between his legs and with both hands started milking. The milk came spurting out and hit the bottom of the bucket with sharp little pings until the noise gradually changed to a deep hiss as the liquid plooshed up in a froth.

Dermot's father Patrick, and his older brother Ned, had returned from their work in the fields and were seated at the fire. Patrick was in his sixties and a smaller man than either of his sons. He had a wrinkled reddy face, large ears from which grew straggly tufts of hair, a small nose and yellow irregular teeth. His arms were still powerful, the veins standing out like dead ivy roots on the trunk of a tree. His hands were nicked and scarred with the stigmata of fifty years' work. Over his bushy eyebrows a faint white scar ran diagonally across his forehead, the result of a fall from a horse in his youth. His hair was white, thick around the sides but thin and scarce on top.

Ned was in his late twenties and the same height as Dermot,

though he appeared smaller because he walked with the shoulders slightly hunched. Like Dermot his eyes were blue but deeper set. His nose had a slight ridge across it and gave the impression of having been broken. His hair was black and a fast growing beard gave him the appearance of habitually needing a shave. He walked in a lumbering way and his movements were not as graceful as those of his brother.

Both men had drawn their chairs up close to the hearth fire and the steam was rising from the bottom half of their trousers which were wet from walking through the fields. Patrick looked over at Dermot and said, "Turn on the wireless, it's nearly news time."

Dermot went over to the table and turned on the wireless set.

In a few moments the sound of Big Ben came belling out followed by the suave voice of the radio announcer: "This is the B.B.C. Home Service and now for the news. The Admiralty reports today that H.M.S. Godiva, a light cruiser, has been sunk in the North Sea as a result of enemy action. There were four hundred and thirty casualties in the crew of over two thousand."

Patrick looked up excitedly, "Whist do you hear that man! Another cruiser. Get the book Dermot and write that down."

Dermot picked up a blue book from the table and opened it. The first page was headed, "Battleships," the second page, "Heavy Cruisers," then came "Light Cruisers," "Destroyers" and "Miscellaneous." Dermot wrote H.M.S. Godiva on the Light Cruiser page. Then he asked, "How many were lost did he say?"

"Four hundred and thirty," Ned answered.

"Boys-a-boys, but them Germans is lovely fellows," Patrick said as he got up and walked over to the table. Pointing to the book he asked, "How many cruisers is that now?"

"Seven altogether," Dermot answered.

"Oh lovely, lovely. England can't build new cruisers that

fast. Mind now the war won't last much longer if this keeps up. And there's no America this time." Patrick walked back to the fire and rubbed his hands together. Dermot's mother came in from the scullery where she had been straining the milk. Patrick said to her, "Kathleen did you hear the great news that's after being on the wireless?"

"Aye I heard it all right. It's great news it'll be for the mothers of them that went down," she replied as she lifted the bottom of her apron and dried her hands.

Patrick rumbled, "Proper bloody stuff for them. They didn't think of my mother when they shot poor Vincent, God be good to him, at the head of the lane and him dying without a priest and there not as much harm in the man as would hurt a fly."

"Aw give over about Vincent," Ned said and added, "Sure to hear all the talk about this house, you'd think it was yourself that shot him."

Patrick's brow furrowed as a quick anger came upon him. "What in under God are you saying? Was it my fault he was shot?" His voice rose slightly as he continued, "Was it my fault the Tans were looking for me? Is it me you're blaming?"

"Nobody's blaming you," Ned answered shortly. "Sit down and give us peace."

"I'll sit down but I'll have my say first. Vincent was a man. Do you hear that now?" The last sentence was almost shouted, "A man, and he didn't have his lip stuck around the edge of a bottle every time he set foot out of the house."

Ned got up slowly and walked out of the kitchen and into the yard. The sky was clouded over and the night had crept silently down from the mountain. A little wind was rising and worrying the branches of the trees.

Inside the house Patrick sat down, a little ashamed of his outburst. Dermot was washing his hands and face in a tin basin in the scullery. He came out with the towel around his neck and said, referring to his sister, "When's Bella coming back from Moran's?"

"She'll not be back until ten or so," his mother replied.

"Is Mrs. Moran any better?" Patrick asked.

Kathleen looked over at him sharply and then ignored his question as she said to Dermot, "Let you not be staying out late tonight. You didn't come home Sunday until four in the morning."

"I had some heavy courting to do," Dermot answered.

Patrick's voice came irritably from the corner, "Is Mrs. Moran any better, I asked?"

"She's a wee bit improved but Bella will have to go over for the rest of the week. She's not fit to get around much," Kathleen answered.

Dermot put on his trench coat and asked, "Do you want anything from town?"

"I'll be going in tomorrow morning myself," Kathleen replied.

Dermot started to leave but his mother's voice stopped him at the door, "Bless yourself!"

Dermot came back to the small holy water fount that hung on the wall, dipped his forefinger and hurriedly crossed himself. Then he opened the door and stepped outside. "Ned?" he called softly.

"Aye?" his brother answered from across the yard.

"He's a shocking man sometimes. You might have known better than to get him stirred up over Vincent. I'm heading into town. Do you want anything?"

"Ne'er a thing."

Dermot walked up to the turfshed and got his bicycle.

THREE

The village of Duncrana was built on a sharp hill that rose above the surrounding tableland. Its two streets were unpretentiously called Main Street and Back Street. The former was a continuation of the main road that ran from Belfast to Londonderry. The road came from the east, snaking its way through a plateau of low rolling hills until, half a mile from the town, it spied the cluster of buildings that crowned the peak of the hill. Then the road braced itself and marched straight for the last half mile, driving through a small wood and on up the town, splitting the houses into two outraged lines. Halfway through the town it rested for a moment, where the peak of the hill flattened out to form a small square. In the middle of the square stood the Catholic Church, a cut-stone building with a single tower. The road investigated the church, sneaking around the back of it and out to the front again, before it headed on through the town and down a gentle slope. Here, tired of its disciplined effort, it meandered away in looping twists to the north.

Leading from the rear of the Catholic Church was another road that formed the Back Street. Not being an important artery it was much more undisciplined and it slid and skidded down the town in a shocking manner, careless of its course or gradient. But those who lived in the Back Street loved this little road and in the winter, when the snow came, the sleds of the children flew down the hill and there were snowball fights and wet boys and girls and heart-scalded mothers.

Duncrana had everything that its four hundred inhabitants might want. For the thirsty there were eight pubs. There were shops both large and small that dealt in all commodities. There was a newsagent's store where both the Dublin and Belfast, that is to say the Catholic and Protestant papers, could be bought.

For those who liked rhetoric and high drama there was a courthouse with a petty sessions every fair day—the second Thursday of the month. For the old cranks who loved to persecute their neighbors there was a police barracks where all kinds of complaints could be sworn out, from using foul and indecent language to attempted manslaughter.

The town even had a hotel with nine rooms although it was rare that a person stayed overnight in Duncrana. For those fortunate enough to possess a car, there was a garage. The town did not have, nor did it seem to need, a cinema. It had a barber and a hairdresser although the latter had just opened her business. For the sick there were two physicians, one Protestant and one Catholic, thereby assuring that each inhabitant was eased into and helped out of this world by a theologically approved doctor.

For those with a toothache there was a dentist who came from a neighboring town every fair day, though it should be

SAINT PETER'S COLLEGE LIBRARY
JERSEY CITY, NEW JERSEY 07306

noted that most people preferred the traditional cure—a wee spit of whiskey. There is no end to the wild and wonderful evenings that started with a faint twinge in a tooth, followed by the traditional cure.

For the young lads of the town there were steep gardens that clung to the sides of the hill, an ideal place for re-enacting military battles; the Protestant boys restaging the Battle of the Boyne and the little papists again defending Limerick.

There was a shady walk, known somewhat unromantically as Buttermilk Lane, where young couples could hold hands, make or break undying promises, defend honor or seduce virtue.

And at the head of the town stood McGinnis' bicycle shop. It had a front window with several new bicycles, bicycle accessories and advertising placards. Inside the shop there were rows of spare parts, bicycle wheels, tires hanging from the ceiling and an ever-present smell of oil and rubber. Leading off from the shop proper was a little workshop where McGinnis could usually be found at his work, mending punctures, fixing chains or replacing broken spokes.

It was a little past seven-thirty when Dermot opened the front door and walked through the store and into the workshop. There were twenty men present, all of whom he knew. He walked over and sat down on one of the benches and listened to the conversations that were going on.

Ten minutes later McGinnis locked the front door of the store and came back into the workshop. Pulling out a wooden box, he placed it against the wall and stood on it. From his makeshift platform he began to address the gathering. "You all know why we're here tonight. The I.R.A. has started up again. Never had we a better chance to free the North. You've all heard of the grand work the boys are doing in Derry and Belfast, but a handful of men in the cities isn't enough. We need a brigade in every village, a company in every townland." He paused and looked around at the men. Satisfied that they were giving him their full attention, he continued, "The headquarters is in Dublin and each province forms a division. We men of the North will be known as the First Northern Division. County Tyrone is divided into two brigades, an Eastern Brigade and a Western one. We'll be known as the Number One Duncrana Company, West Tyrone Brigade, First Northern Division."

A low knock came to the door. McGinnis nodded to Reilly, "Go out Sean and see who it is."

Reilly left and from the workshop the men could hear a whispered conversation. The shop door opened and Reilly and another man entered the workshop.

"I thought I said seven-thirty," McGinnis curtly remarked.

"Ah sure I had a puncture coming in the road and had to foot it the rest of the way," the newcomer answered.

A ripple of laughter greeted the remark and McGinnis waited for it to subside before he resumed, "Brigade headquarters has appointed me as commanding officer of this company and Sean Reilly as adjutant. Other officers will be appointed later. Only one man here has had military training." He nodded to a young man in a corner, "Charlie Malone there who spent three years in the Free State Army. He will probably be named training officer. We will not be soldiers in the regular sense. You will not be given arms except to carry out specific assignments and neither will you wear a uniform. It will not be an easy task but I know that all of you want to prove your devotion to Ireland. You'll many times be given jobs that will keep you out all night. You'll be asked to risk your life on occasion. You may be asked to go to England and carry on the work there. You may be caught and given prison terms and even executed. But patriots have always faced these dangers and Irishmen have always answered the call of their native land. Our generation must do the same. I am pointing out the risks so that if any man has second thoughts—now is the time to speak up. We must have wholehearted men."

A murmur of cries answered him:

"We're with you Don."

"Here's one man who's waited years for this day!"

"Up the rebels!"

A slight tic began jumping on McGinnis' cheek. He slumped a little, resting his bad leg, and continued, "You'll be asked to take an oath before you leave tonight. Not until we are better trained will we take part in any direct action against the government. As we have just started it will be some time yet before we're asked to do anything like the Derry raid. In the meantime one of our most important tasks will be the gathering of information about the enemy."

It was the first time he had used the word "enemy" in referring to the Northern government and in Dermot's mind the word had a pleasant ring. He turned it over once or twice, "the enemy," "enemy forces," and smiled.

"Every week an intelligence report will be sent to Brigade headquarters," McGinnis continued. "This report will eventually reach our ally, the German government. As soon as an intelligence officer is appointed I want each of you to report to him any military news such as lorry convoys passing through, names of regiments posted in the North, new airdromes to be built and types of planes that will use them. You will later be told what other information is needed."

McGinnis straightened himself and pulled a piece of paper out of his pocket. "I have here the oath of the volunteer Irish Republican Army. I am going to read it out, sentence by sentence, and you'll all repeat it after me."

Dermot slid off the bench and stood up. He looked around at his companions and noted that the festive air had disappeared. Suddenly he felt a warm burst of enthusiasm and comradeship as he realized that he was now becoming a member of the legendary I.R.A. He drew himself up and looked sternly at the opposite wall. A pretty girl on a bicycle calendar smiled back at him and his eyes slid hurriedly over to

McGinnis who had started to read the oath. "I swear allegiance to Ireland and promise to obey the orders of my superior officers in the Irish Republican Army . . ."

The men droned the sentences until the oath was finished.

For a few moments the men looked self-consciously at each other as a dead hush fell on the group.

"You are now members of the Irish Republican Army," McGinnis said, breaking the silence. "The next meeting will be on Friday night at eight o'clock in Corr's barn. Sean, see them out and no more than two at a time."

The men filed out and waited in the darkened store as Sean quietly opened the outer door and two men slipped out. A few seconds passed and another pair left. Presently Dermot and a companion were let out. They walked down the town, each man busy with his own thoughts. At the church they said good night to each other and parted. The other youth went around the back of the church and down the Back Street.

Dermot was still full of excitement and did not want to go home. He walked on down the street and irresolutely slowed at Neeve's shop, wondering if he should stop in for a moment. He decided against it and continued down the street. As he drew opposite the police barracks a voice called, "Night, Dermot."

"Good night sergeant," Dermot replied and crossed over to where the sergeant stood in the doorway.

Sergeant Crawley was forty-five and had been a member of the Royal Ulster Constabulary for twenty years. He had been a soldier in World War One and still retained a military bearing. He had a full, kind face with red, slightly mottled cheeks, a broad strong nose and shrewd gray eyes.

"That's a brave night," he said, nodding to Dermot.

"It is that," Dermot agreed and then asked about the sergeant's son, "Any word of Derek?"

"We get an odd letter from him."

"Is he still in North Africa?"

"He is. You know you remind me of him in certain ways. What height are you now?" the sergeant asked.

"Just a hair under six feet."

"Derek would be that now. He was five ten when he left and still growing. He was about your weight too, but I'm sure the army sliced some of it off."

"Aye and it might add a bit too. I hope he comes out of it all right," Dermot said.

"I hope so. I was wounded myself in the First War. I wouldn't like anything to happen to Derek."

The sergeant shifted his bulk and took off his cap. He ran his hand through a head of short grizzled hair. Dermot looked at the circular badge on the cap, a small Irish harp surmounted by a royal crown. "I'd better be getting home," he said to the sergeant.

"Good night Dermot. Keep out of trouble."

Dermot laughed. "The only trouble I have is women trouble."

"Aye with that ugly clock of yours it would be the sort of trouble you'd have," the sergeant replied.

They both laughed and the sergeant turned and went into the barracks. Dermot walked back up the street, thinking of the badge, of the harp surmounted by a crown.

FOUR

In the following weeks Duncrana Company of the I.R.A. went through a training period. A training officer was appointed and a program of close-order foot drill instituted. The training sessions were held in secluded fields on the outskirts of the town. Those sessions that did not require drilling took place in different barns, the meeting place being changed frequently to avoid the possibility of a surprise visit by the police. The company adjutant drew up a system of fines for being late or absent from meetings and the money thus gathered was used as the company treasury.

The men learned quickly. Brigade headquarters sent down an old 303 Lee-Enfield rifle and classes were started in the handling of the weapon. Rifle practice was held with dummy cartridges. The men were taught to sight a rifle, to judge distance to targets, to remove the bolt and render the gun useless if they were forced to abandon it and how to carry a rifle inside their clothes without it being seen or noticed.

An intelligence report was sent to Brigade each week. Specific intelligence tasks were handed out to various members. Several men were encouraged to work at a British airdrome some ten miles from the town, both to gain information and to have men positioned for sabotage when the need arose.

The men were taught how to effectively sabotage, how to stall a military truck by removing the distributor arm or stuffing the exhaust pipes, how to fell trees across a road to make a road block and how to cut telephone lines. They were shown the most effective use of explosives in cutting railway tracks, destroying bridges and starting fires. For some of these lessons an officer was sent from Brigade but usually the men learned from British Army training manuals that had been procured.

The art of the ambush was explained to them. They were taught to recognize good positions, how to place men, how to feint an attack and thus draw reinforcements into an ambush and how to withdraw from one.

More arms were gradually procured until all the officers had at least one side arm. There were now a total of three rifles available. An inventory was made of shotguns belonging to members of the company and to those farmers who, although not members, could be listed as sympathetic to the I.R.A.

There were no ranks as such in the company. The O.C. with the assistance of the adjutant had final authority in most matters, the other officers having authority only in their respective fields. With the exception of the O.C. all officers were considered as soldiers for training purposes. Thus, the intelligence officer and supply officer were ordinary members when rifle practice was given by the training officer. All officers and men, in so far as possible, attended all lectures and training sessions.

The men were gathered together one evening in Corr's barn when McGinnis came in and called the roll. He then addressed the group, "There'll be no training this evening. The T.O. had to attend a Brigade meeting. However, before we leave I have a few words to say. The first part of our training is over. Some of you may already have guessed that a rising is timed to take place when the Germans invade England. When this occurs our most important tasks will be sabotage and the disruption of communications. For this purpose it is planned to seize and destroy certain communications centers. We will try to close both Derry and Belfast harbors to shipping and prevent the troops in the North from going to England. Our best hope for a successful rising lies in a German victory in England. If Germany is victorious, then part of the peace settlement will be the handing over of the North to Ireland. This is in return for the aid that the I.R.A. will furnish."

"How do we know that Germany won't take Ireland too?" a voice interrupted.

"She'll have no need to," McGinnis replied. "It will cause her enough trouble to garrison England without having a hostile Ireland on her flank. With England defeated it is useless as a base against her. We don't have any raw materials or big industries that Germany might need. Germany realizes the nature of the Irish people, that we would never submit to a foreign government, and that a friendly Ireland is of more value than a hostile Ireland."

"A lesson England never learned," another voice added.

"She'll learn it soon," McGinnis replied and added, "I want O'Neill and Corrigan. The rest of you are dismissed."

The men buttoned their overcoats and put out their cigarettes. One or two said good night to McGinnis but for the most part they left silently. In a few minutes the barn was empty except for the three men. The wind moaned and tugged at the barn door and in the piled up hay the mice stirred restlessly. McGinnis walked over and sat on a box. "I want two men for an intelligence job. Can you both get away this coming Monday?"

"I can," Corrigan replied and Demot gave an affirmative nod of his head.

"Good. Brigade has assigned a wee job for us. There's a new airdrome being built at Termantown. This Monday they'll be taking on men to work there. I want both of you to go down and snoop around. So far nothing has been built except a small headquarters building. They'll probably see you in the building about going to work. Somewhere in this building, on one of the walls, will be a plan of the airdrome. It will probably be in the surveyor's office. Either steal this plan or draw a copy of it and bring it back. If either of you need the bus fare to Termantown, you'll get it from the supply officer."

"I have enough money," Dermot answered.

"Me too," Corrigan added.

"Good. Bring the plan to me when you come back."

"That's all you want—the plan?" Dermot asked.

"You'll do well to bring that much back," McGinnis replied.

McGinnis got up and lifted down the oil lamp. He pushed up the glass globe and blew out the flame. The three men left the barn, the two younger men in front and McGinnis behind, his bad leg making scrapey noises on the ground.

Later that evening Dermot went around to Hannafin's the cobbler. It was the only cobbler shop in the town and was halfway down the Back Street. Jimmy Hannafin was middle-aged and a wee butt of a man. He had almost black eyes, a puckered leathery face and the top of his head was completely bald. His shop consisted of a counter in front and shelves behind, upon which were rows of shoes either repaired or waiting to be. From a somewhat askew calendar, St. Anne de Beaupré piously contemplated a small buffing machine that sat against the opposite wall.

Hannafin sat on a small stool surrounded by tin boxes containing different kinds of nails and sparables. On the counter in front of him were half a dozen bends of leather of varying thicknesses and several patches of black kid leather. He had an iron last on his knee and close to his hand, on an upturned orange crate, were his implements: two cobbler's hammers, a pliers, an awl, a ball of thread, a rasp, black and brown sealing wax, several bottles of leather dye and the half-burned stub of a candle which he used for heating the wax. The floor around his feet was littered with leather shavings, several old soles that had been ripped off shoes, a couple of tiny heels and short pieces of waxed thread.

He wore a black cloth apron that was flecked with tiny holes, a light blue work shirt open at the neck and a pair of household slippers. His shop was the social center of the town for the young men. They mostly came in the evenings and filled the kitchen and overflowed into the shop: farm laborers, shop boys, lorry drivers, students and even the unemployed. When a young man left Duncrana for England or the Free State, Hannafin's was the last house he called at and the first on his return home. It was in Hannafin's that most of the deviltry in town was planned and past deviltries remembered and rejoiced in. The Hannafins had no children.

Sometimes Hannafin grew tired of the boisterous laughter and locked the front door. When the visitors came and found the door locked, they just went home again. Hannafin referred to himself during these antisocial periods, which never lasted more than two days, as being "on retreat."

The door of the shop opened and Dermot stepped inside. Hannafin looked up, put his hammer down and said, "The hard and the wild Dermot. You're getting uglier every day."

"You old goat, you should be talking about anybody being ugly and you with not two hairs on your head to keep each other company."

"Oh deed then, I'm ugly too. But I tell you Dermot, all Irishmen are ugly."

"And Irishwomen?" Dermot asked.

Hannafin smiled, "There are no ugly Irishwomen: only Irishwomen who are beautiful and Irishwomen who are not beautiful—but no ugly ones."

A seven-year-old boy came into the shop, talking excitedly. "Jimmy I just saw them at the foot of the town." The boy waited eagerly.

"Now who did you see at the foot of the town," Hannafin asked, his dark eyes humorous.

" 'The Boys of Wexford,' " the lad shouted, giving the name of a song that was popular at the moment. Then he squealed with laughter. Hannafin flung a small piece of scrap leather and it bounced on the door just as the boy scooted out and into the street.

"Why do you let those cubs make a cod of you like that?" Dermot asked.

Hannafin pondered the question for a moment. "It does me no harm and gives them some enjoyment," he answered. "I have found out that we usually act the way people expect us to. With the young boys I'm a fierce old man who'd sned their peckers off if I got the chance. With the young girls of the town I'm the one who somehow knows all their secrets and who knows how to keep them too. With some people I'm expected to talk seriously. With Sergeant Crawley I'm an expert on Irish folklore, and with the curate a student of Irish history. With each one I play a different role."

"I'm the same with everyone," Dermot said.

"I don't think you are. You don't talk or act the same with me as you do with Neeve."

"How do you know about Neeve?"

"The whole town knows it. She's a nice, levelheaded lassie. A bit too good for you. Do you know of Yeats's, 'The Wanderings of Usheen'?"

"Never heard of it."

"It's an old Celtic epic about a man who is bewitched by a beautiful young maiden whose name is Neeve. But you wouldn't know that. You're like the rest of the Irishmen in this town. The only way you can show your patriotism is by taking up the gun and shooting someone—yet you couldn't be troubled to learn something of your past."

"You're a terrible old blather, Jimmy."

"Aye, I'm an old blather, there's no doubt of that." He lifted the hammer and pounded in a few nails. He held a dozen nails in his mouth and as quick as the eye could follow, a nail would be spat into the hand and driven into the shoe. From the kitchen, to the left of the shop, came a sudden burst of raucous laughter.

"Do you hear the roars of that bull Gallagher in there?" he complained.

The shop door opened and a thin raky woman came in. "Do you have my shoes ready yet?" she asked.

"Friday, Mrs. Kerr."

"Ach Jimmy, you're shocking slow," she said mournfully.

Hannafin stood up and brushed his apron off. He leaned over the counter and looked down at the woman's feet. "Those pair you've on look like they'll last till Friday."

"Well mind that they're done by then," the woman replied sharply and then left the shop.

"Dermot," Hannafin said. "Irishwomen may not be ugly but there's some that have ugly hearts."

Dermot laughed and said good night to his friend.

FIVE

The following Monday Dermot and Corrigan took the bus for Termantown. It was raining, a persistent drizzle that fogged the windows of the bus and turned the countryside into a wet blur. Dermot rubbed a circle in his window and looked out. Cattle were standing behind stone walls, their heads down and backs humped against the driving rain. From farmhouses smoke peeked slyly from the chimneys and was whipped away flat by the angry wind. Here and there in the farmyards disconsolate hens scrabbled under the thatched eaves of the houses while roosters half-heartedly attempted to patrol them.

The bus threw out arcing wings of water as it hit rain puddles on the highway and the tires hummed wetly in a rising whine. Inside the bus it was cold and the conductor warmed his feet by stamping up and down the aisle. He blew into his cupped hands and looked around at the huddled passengers.

"Boys, but that's the raw day," he informed them.

"A great day for young ducks," Corrigan answered.

"Or a wake," Dermot said. "There's a day any poor soul would be glad to leave this world." He added, "I hear they're taking on men for a new airdrome."

"Aye and good money too. Three shillings an hour," the conductor answered.

"Where's the office?"

"It's about half a mile from town. You go out the Gortavoy Road. You can't miss it."

"Any men working there yet?"

"Not yet. They're not starting anyone until some lorries and a bulldozer come from Derry City. They're expecting them any day and as soon as they arrive they'll start hiring."

The bus stopped and some passengers got on. The conductor hit the bell and the vehicle started again. An old woman settled herself gingerly on the seat, looked searchingly across at Dermot and asked, "Would you be a son of Patrick O'Neill of Duncrana?"

"That's right," Dermot answered.

"I know the face. You're the spitting image of your father." She gave a tug at the black shawl she was wearing, pulling it tighter around the lower half of her face.

"I don't know you now. Who might you be?" Dermot asked.

"I'm Lily Groogan, wife of Tommy Groogan. I'm one of the Tullyodonnel Burkes. I mind your father well at the dances in Tullyodonnel. That would be over thirty years ago. He was a great man for the dancing. He's rightly?"

"He's grand. And he was a great man for the dancing? And if I set foot inside a dance hall the roars of him can be heard from here to Belfast."

"Ach pay him no mind." She sniffled several times. "When we get old we do be a bit jealous of the young ones disporting themselves."

The bus slowed and stopped as it pulled into Termantown. Dermot and Corrigan alighted and stood for a moment on the pavement. They pulled up the collars of their trench coats and distastefully surveyed the sleeting drizzle.

"Might as well start," Dermot said.

They walked on out the Gortavoy Road. After they had walked a short distance the rain eased off. Dermot shook his head and a shower of raindrops fell on his coat.

"I don't know what kind of an idiotic job this is to give a body," he said irritably.

"Know what I think?" Corrigan asked and continued without waiting for an answer, "I think it's a test. They want to see how well we can do this sort of thing. What was the sense of sending Rafferty and Flynn to watch the barracks for three hours last Sunday night and make a report of everybody who left it?"

"I don't know," Dermot answered. He stopped, took out a packet of cigarettes and offered his companion one. Holding the lit cigarettes inside their cupped palms, they continued their journey. Presently they came to a lane that was all torn up with the thick tires of construction lorries.

"This must be it," Dermot said.

"I think I see a building off there in the field," Corrigan agreed.

They followed the lane until it turned off into a field. In the middle of the field stood a long, low, wooden house. Three lorries were parked in front of it and leaning against one of the walls were a dozen or so bicycles.

Off to their left the surface of Lough Neagh was erupting in thousands of whitecaps. Several squalls, foggy gray pillars of wind and rain, were moving slowly across the lake.

They walked into the building and saw a line of young men standing in a hall.

"Is this where they're hiring?" Dermot asked.

"Aye, you have to wait in line here," he was told.

Dermot looked at the line that stretched the length of the hall and disappeared around a corner. He motioned to Corrigan and they both went outside. "Listen," Dermot said. "I'll keep our places in the line and you dander around and try to see if you can find the plan. Go outside and look in all the windows. I'll wait for you in the queue."

Corrigan left and Dermot re-entered the building. He looked at his neighbor and remarked, "That's a brave day."

"Aye. Tell me, how are they going to build an airdrome here? How could planes light down on this sort of mucky land?" the man asked.

"They'll make runways. They'll put in a good solid foundation of rock and tar it over—much the same as a road," Dermot replied.

The other man grunted. "I wouldn't trust one of my ducks to come down in these fields."

Dermot smiled and asked, "Is the airdrome for fighter planes or bombers?"

"Damn the particle I know about it."

Corrigan came back and joined Dermot in the line. Dermot turned and asked, "Did you find it?"

"It's in the room we're headed for. You'll get a gawk at it in a minute."

The line kept moving until Dermot could see into the room. In the middle of the room two men were seated behind desks. In one corner a stove was glowing and crackling. Desks had been built into the wall along both sides of the room and on top of the desks were scattered ledgers, books and papers. On the wall behind the two officials hung an architectural drawing of the proposed airdrome.

Dermot's turn came and the hiring boss, a red-faced man wearing leggings and cordoroy pants asked, "What was your last job?"

"I've been working on my father's land all my life," Dermot answered.

The man leaned back in the chair. "This work is hard. You'll be wheeling and carrying rocks for the runway. Think you can do it?"

A quick hint of anger came into Dermot's eyes. He folded his arms and said coldly, "There isn't a job in the county too hard for me."

The man looked up at the broad shoulders and the wide squat hands with their stubby fingers. "You'll do," he said. He nodded his head in the direction of the clerk and called out, "Next!"

Dermot moved over to the adjoining desk.

"Name?" the clerk asked.

"Dermot O'Neill."

"Address?"

"Duncrana."

"Age?"

"Twenty."

"Education?"

"Grammar school. One year at the Christian Brothers School in Rathgiven."

"Do you have a card from the Labor Exchange?"

"No."

"You'll have to get one before you start. Tell them that you're going to work here. The pay's three bob an hour and time and a half for overtime. Be here at eight on Monday morning."

Dermot stepped away and walked around behind the two desks. For a few seconds he stood with his back to the stove.

Corrigan went through the interview and joined him. Dermot whispered to him, "I'm going to stand at one of the desks and copy the plan. Stand you in front of me so that yon birds won't see what I'm at."

Dermot walked over to the wall desk and Corrigan stood in front of him. Pulling a pencil and envelope out of his pocket he started to sketch in the features of the drawing. He worked swiftly and in a few minutes had copied all the runways, buildings and different shaded areas. As soon as he had finished, he slipped the envelope into his pocket and nodded to Corrigan. The two men left the room and went outside the building. They walked in silence until they reached the lane. Dermot stopped, pulled the envelope out of his pocket and showed it to Corrigan, "I think I've got everything. How does it look to you?"

Corrigan took the envelope. "It looks all right except you forgot to put the scale in. There was a scale on the bottom right-hand corner of the map."

"Well fluke it," Dermot answered shortly. "Do you think we need it?"

"I don't know. Whatever you say," Corrigan replied.

Dermot pondered a moment, "I'll have to go back. If they say anything I'll tell them I lost something. What could I lose?"

"Your gloves. Say you left a pair of gloves behind."

"Good man, you wait here."

Dermot walked back into the building. There were still four men waiting to be interviewed. He moved past them and over to the stove and looked up at the drawing. He noted the scale and started to memorize it. He was interrupted by a loud voice, "What the bloody hell are you doing?"

Dermot swung around and looked at the supervisor. "I lost my gloves," he lamely explained.

"And do you think it's on the wall they'll be hanging?"

Dermot, his wits collected, answered. "I just saw yon map on the wall and looked at it."

The supervisor cast a quick glance around at the desks and floor.

"There's no gloves here," he said. "Did you look in the hall?"

"I'll look there now," Dermot replied and walked out of the room. He dallied a second or so in the hall and then left the building, rejoining Corrigan in the lane. He related the incident to him and wrote the scale down on the envelope and replaced it in his pocket. "We didn't do bad," he said. "It would have been better to take the plan but I don't see how we could have managed it. It was too big to carry under our coats and they would have seen us if we tried to lift it."

"Man I'm foundered," Corrigan said.

"When we're back in town we'll stop and have a cup of tea."

"I could do with a drop of something a wee bit stronger than tea," Corrigan replied.

"Whatever you like. I'll go in with you but I can't drink anything. I'm a Pioneer."

"You Pioneers would sicken a body," Corrigan said jokingly. "You'd think it was a mortal sin to drink a bottle of stout."

"I've got nothing against it," Dermot explained. "One day in the eighth grade the master came around with these wee cards to sign saying we'd never touch a drop of drink. You mind Jim Shea? He wouldn't sign his and the master gave him an unmerciful flaking. After that I signed my wee card and when I was sixteen I was given a Pioneer pin to make it official. Anyway I've never had the urge to drink."

"Does your father drink any?"

"Oh aye, he'll take a drop at a wedding or a wake but he's not what you'd call a drinking man. But Ned's a terror. He doesn't drink often but when he does, he's a regular dullally tap. He got stocious the fair day last."

They reached the town again and after checking at the bus depot they turned into a pub. Inside it was dark but warm with a good fire burning in the grate. A man came out of an inner room and asked, "What'll be?"

"I'll have a half-un of Bushmills," Corrigan answered.

"Nothing for me," Dermot added.

The man reached behind the counter and took down a bottle of Bushmills. He filled a shot glass and pushed it across to Corrigan. Corrigan reached into his pocket and produced a handful of change.

"Where might you boys be from?" the bar owner asked.

"Duncrana," Corrigan answered.

"Mountainy men?" the man affirmed.

"We're down to see about getting a start on the new airdrome," Dermot said. "Who's building it?"

"Leeds and Patrick is the name of the builders."

"Is it for bombers or what?" Dermot asked.

"I don't know. It's supposed to be the biggest in the North when it's finished. It would hardly be a fighter base."

"Odd place for an airdrome—right beside the Lough," Corrigan remarked.

The man walked out from behind the counter and poked at the fire in the grate. "The land's flat all around it and I hear that seaplanes of the Coastal Command are going to use the base," he said. "They could land on the Lough."

The men fell silent, warming themselves at the fire. The barman left, telling them to shout if they needed more.

"Well, we're none the wiser," Dermot said. "Is it a seaplane base, a fighter base or a bomber base?"

"That's not our worry," Corrigan replied. "Come on, it's time for the bus."

They buttoned up their trench coats and left the bar.

SIX

At the O'Neill farm the last chores of the day had been finished. Inside the house Patrick, Ned and Dermot were seated around the fire. At the kitchen table Kathleen was doing her monthly accounts. In front of her was an old cracked teapot, four or five receipts, several pound notes and a handful of change. A loose piece of paper was covered with a scattering of figures.

Bella sat at the opposite end of the table darning a pair of Ned's socks. Inside one sock had been thrust a shoe brush and the hole was tightly stretched over the back of the brush. Periodically Bella would glance over at the fire where a soda-bread loaf was baking in a round three-legged pot. The pot was set in close to the fire and live coals had been heaped on top of the lid. Underneath, between the cast-iron legs, other coals had been placed.

Tone was stretched out on the floor, his head resting on his front paws and his eyes sleepily watching Tippy the cat. Tippy was sitting under the table, wrapped in feline dignity and gazing at the fire, her thoughts on some distant dogless heaven. Tone's tail thumped once, lightly, on the stone floor of the kitchen. The cat's tail flickered and she delicately stepped over the low crossbar of the table and disappeared into the scullery. Exhausted with the byplay, Tone closed his eyes.

At the table, Kathleen laboriously made a few more calculations. She looked up. "Four pounds twelve and sixpence this month from the hens and the feeding stuff came to two pounds five."

"I need a new dress," Bella stated, her gray eyes wide and innocent.

"Oh I'll have a new dress to see my Johnny O!" Dermot sang mockingly, trying to needle Bella about her current boy friend.

Bella's eyes tightened, her large laughing mouth fell into a thin line and two furrows across her forehead threw into relief a handful of freckles. "You hold your tongue," she said sharply.

Dermot stretched out a pair of long legs, slid backward on the chair and stared upward at the accordion that hung over the mantlepiece. He said quietly, easily, to his sister, "Oh he's a lovely lad. Sure he has the hands of a priest. And the nice quiet wee walk of him coming from the rails every Sunday."

"It's a sight better than the clodhops of you—the twice a year you do manage to get to communion," Bella retorted.

"Last month it was Cokely the racing cyclist, before that it was Fitzpatrick who plays football for the county. You've made a rare about-turn taking a wee lad that's only fit for a seminary."

"Dermot!" his mother warned sharply and then said to Bella, "You've enough dresses for the moment. Dermot needs a new coat and Ned could do with a pair of boots and your father, that is if he has any respect for the house, should get a new suit."

Patrick leaned over and spat in the fire, making a black spot in the embers, "The one I have is good enough. I've got it twelve years and to look at it you'd think the tailor left it yesterday."

"To look at it you'd think a threshing machine left it," his wife retorted.

"Well now," Patrick gave a sly look over at the table, "I might need a new suit at that. It would have to come out of the egg and milk money though."

"You'd like that," Kathleen complained, "I'm supposed to feed and clothe the whole townland on a wheen of shillings that I get from the milk and eggs. You sold a calf the fair day last, there's at least the price of a suit in that."

"Aye there is," Patrick agreed. "And there's the tax money to pay and I'll soon have to order fertilizer for the spring."

"Before you get that lump anything," Bella spoke up nodding her head at Dermot, "you'd better make him get a haircut. He's got a head on him like a whin bush. But maybe he's letting it grow so he can jaunt in to the hairdressers and get a quif or two put in."

Dermot laughed, "It's not me that's ashamed of my company." He straightened in the chair and began to examine the minute lines in his palm. "I heard in town last Sunday that my sister was an awful poor court."

"That's not true!" Bella said emphatically.

"Then you're a good court?" Dermot asked.

Bella saw the trap and evaded it. "It's no news to you what kind of a court I am." She added spitefully, "I'm sure you're the cold old customer though."

Dermot closed his hand and began to examine the knuckles. "I'm a holy terror," he boasted, "ask any of them."

"Old Widower Foy could court more on one leg before Mass than you could in a fortnight," Bella scornfully replied.

"You'll go over no more of that talk Bella," her mother warned.

Ned got off his chair and reached up to the mantlepiece and took down the accordion. He went over to Bella and handed it to her. "Here, pay no heed to Dermot and play us a wee tune."

Kathleen folded the bank notes and placed them, along with the change and receipts, back in the teapot. She put the teapot behind a platter on the top shelf of the china closet. Patrick reached down with the tongs and caught a small coal, blew on it until it was red and lit his pipe.

Dermot sang softly, "Oh dear, what can the matter be, Johnny's not home from the fair."

Bella stood up. "Not a note till that clod shuts up."

Dermot fell silent and Bella fitted the straps around her shoulders. She gave a few squeezes on the bellows of the instrument. Her face softened, she bent her head in a listening attitude and a wealth of red hair came tumbling down over one shoulder. She played the scale, stopped and looked up, "What would you like to hear?"

" 'If I Were a Blackbird,' " Ned answered.

"You'd make the elegant blackbird," Dermot remarked.

Ned grinned, "You'll get no rise out of me."

"That's true enough," Dermot ruefully agreed. "The only one in the house with a bit of spirit is Bella."

"Play a good Fenian song," Patrick suggested.

Bella started playing "The Bold Fenian Men." Slowly she played it and Dermot accompanied her with the words. The air stole out, hauntingly sad—a lament for the dead. Daniel O'Connell must have thought of it when he asked to write the songs of a nation and not its laws. But no one wrote this song. It started before the time of Patrick. Deidre of the Sorrows wailed it for her Naoise. Cuchulain sang it mourning the death of Ferdia. Through the centuries it has been sung in different languages and often the words have changed, but the air remained the same, held the same power of expressing centuries of Celtic despair, all the blackness of hope deferred, all the bitterness of a nation enslaved.

"As down by the glenside I met an old woman,
A-plucking young nettles she ne'er saw me coming,
I listened a while to the song she was humming,
Glory O! Glory O! to the Bold Fenian Men."

It was a litany of racial heroes to the bards who strummed it in the ancient strongholds of the Celtic chiefs. The Danes, walled up in their sea-girt towns, heard it, feared, and as time passed sang it themselves. The few survivors of Drogheda—Oliver Cromwell's Lidice—keened it as a dirge while they buried their dead. And sometimes the melody was briefly lost; the failing strings of the harp grew cold, the notes quivered away with the wind and only in the wild mountain cabins was the air remembered. Then the land was peaceful and Englishmen could speak of a miserable peasantry.

"'Tis fifty long years since I saw the moon beaming,
On proud manly forms and in eyes that were gleaming,
I see them again sure through all my daydreaming,
Glory O! Glory O! to the Bold Fenian Men."

But it always came back. From the mountains it stole down, brought from home to home by wandering fiddlers. In the "Big Houses" the landlords noted a change in the people and blamed it on too much meat or too much idleness. The air grew stronger, was heard at wakes, keened at funerals, and old men hearing it became a little younger and young men a little fiercer. The tune grew, swelled in volume, became the raging soul-cry of a race and the people rebelled—and were defeated.

"When I was a young girl their marching and drilling,
Awoke in the glenside sounds awesome and thrilling,

They loved the dark daughter of Kathleen ni Houlihan,
Glory O! Glory O! to the Bold Fenian Men."

And it traveled over the sea, accompanied the Wild Geese to continental armies, the immigrants to Yankeeland, the felon-patriots to Australia, the adventurers to South America. The Irish Brigade hummed it around their campfires the night before Fontenoy. The song was sung in the armies of Bolivar as he liberated a continent. Mad Anthony Wayne's men grimly chorused it as they fought for an infant republic.

"Some died by the wayside, some died with the stranger,
And wise men have judged that their cause was a failure,
They fought for their freedom and never feared danger,
Glory O! Glory O! to the Bold Fenian Men."

It was nearly lost during the genocidal period of the 1846 Famine, only to flare again in 1916; the *De Profundis* of a poet-led rag-tag rabble, who issued a proclamation, laid down their lives and sired a republic.

"I passed on my way, God be praised that I met her,
Be life long or short sure I'll never forget her,
We may have good men but we'll never have better,
Glory O! Glory O! to the Bold Fenian Men."

Patrick sighed, "Ah but that's the lovely song and you play it just the way Vincent did."

Kathleen went over to the fire and lifted the lid from the baking pot. She pushed a knife through the crust and withdrew it, looking to see if any dough adhered to the blade. She replaced the lid and piled fresh coals on top.

Dermot stood up and said, "I'm going to town for a while."

Bella looked over at him, "Give her my regards and tell her to stay away from Byrne's hayshed."

Patrick complained from the corner, "I don't know what's worse about a house—a nesting hen or a lad that's mad for the women.When I was a lad if I got out once a month I was delirious."

"Lord but you were the quiet one," Dermot answered. "I was told the other day by Lily Burke of Tullyodonnel that you were the dancingest man in the county."

Patrick grunted and the rest laughed. Bella started another air and the strains of it followed Dermot as he left the house and cycled down the lane.

Neeve was standing in the shop door when Dermot arrived. He left his bicycle against the wall and asked her, "Any customers?"

"None now. I had a few during the day."

"Where will we go tonight, wee pet?"

"Out the Rathgiven Road."

She buttoned her overcoat, slipped an arm through his and they both started walking down the street. "Where did you go last Monday?" she asked.

"This place would grow years on a body," Dermot complained, "A cat couldn't kitten in Duncrana without the whole town knowing it."

"Somebody told me they saw you going away on the bus early Monday morning. I was just wondering."

"I went to see about work on the new airdrome they're starting at Termantown."

"It would be good if you could get a start with them."

"I can but the old one won't let me."

As they were passing the door of the police barracks, the sergeant called to them, "You want to be careful down that road. It's shocking the number of ghosts that have been seen on it."

"If you'd catch the boys that are running off the poteen, there'd be less ghosts seen in this country," Dermot replied.

The sergeant laughed at the sally, "If all I had to worry about was an odd run of poteen, I'd be the happy man."

The air was cold and clear and against the sky were pinned a thousand stars. Behind them the town stretched upward, the road shining dully between two lines of black boxy shadows. At the peak of the hill the steeple of the Catholic Church lanced at the sky. The stillness of the night carried the hobnailed clinks of Petey McFlynn as he crossed the square on his nightly pilgrimage to Hannafin's. From one of the back gardens a cat wailed, her voice scratching at the night, informing all and sundry of an Irish willingness to either court or fight.

The road was bordered by head-high hedges, interrupted at intervals by barred iron gates hung from monolithic stone pillars—fat pillars, squat and phallic, remnants of a Celtic past.

"The sergeant seems a nice enough man," Neeve remarked.

"He does. But he wears a British uniform."

"Ach now the poor fellow has a job to do. Do you know he used to be studying for the ministry?"

"Was he now? Come to think of it, it's not so surprising."

"You know the new constable, McVey?" Neeve asked. "His wife was in the shop yesterday and she told me that one night old Allen was on B-man patrol and the sergeant wouldn't let him go out because he had a brave drop of drink on him. You wouldn't think the sergeant would care what the B-men did," she said, referring to the special constabulary, Protestant Orangemen who patrolled the roads at night to prevent I.R.A. activity.

"He's bad enough," Dermot said, "having our hatred, without getting on the wrong side of the Orangemen. Mind now if the Orange Lodge took a notion he'd be in for a lot of trouble."

"He's the sort of man it would be hard to be angry with. I've yet to hear a bad word about him and he's in the town over two years."

They walked over to the side of the road and stood under a large oak tree. Dermot put his arms around Neeve and drew her in. "A penny for them," he said.

"I was thinking what a pity it was that you didn't get work at the new airdrome."

"Why are you so concerned about me getting work?" Dermot asked.

"I'd like to think the man I'm going with has something steady."

He pulled away from her and reaching out broke off a leaf from a holly bush and carefully tried to split it down the stem. "Aye and I'd like to think I had something steady too. But what can I do? Ned will fall in for the land. There's nothing in the town either. The only thing is go away for a few years, save up and then come back. I can't go to England. You know what my father's like. He wouldn't hear of it. Bella's in the same boat. She wants to go to England and go through nursing school but they won't let her. My father says he'd rather see us in the grave than working in England. The only thing is to wait till the war's over and go to America."

"Why can't you go to England anyway?" Neeve asked impatiently. "The wages are terrific and in a year or so you could come back and open a wee business in town here. God knows I don't want to see you away but if we're ever going to get married we'd need to think of these things now. You surely don't want to spend your life feutering around on a few acres of land that will fall to Ned?"

"I'm supposed to get a bit of money from the farm when Ned marries."

"Marry how-are-ye," Neeve answered scornfully. "Ned hardly looks at a woman as it is. You know he wouldn't think of taking a strange woman into the house while your mother's still fit to work."

"Well, what am I to do?" Dermot said defensively.

"You could still go to England," Neeve replied. "God-of-Mercy, you're as bad as my brother Jim and him away in the Free State Army, not doing a thing to help out at home. My father wasn't right in the grave till my bold brother skips away to serve his country." Neeve laid sarcasm on the last three words. She continued, "The little bit of business I do in the shop along with what Donal brings home from his job at the creamery is barely enough to keep us going. You know there are five of us."

"If it was myself, I'd go in the morning," Dermot said. "But you don't know what the old one's like. He'd have my head. If I left for England I might never plan on coming back. He wouldn't let my foot inside the door."

"What are you going to do then? Hang around Duncrana and hope that someone wills you a legacy?"

Dermot broke off another leaf. "Ah now, wee dear, don't talk like that. The way the war's going it'll be over in a year and then I can go to America. A few years there and I'll be back a rich man and we'll both be set."

"Aye, we'll be set all right. I'll be an old woman by then."

Dermot reached out and pulled her in close. He kissed her and said, "You'll make a lovely old woman. It's early you're talking about old age and you not twenty yet. Sure we've tucks of time."

"That's the old story around this town," Neeve protested. "Sure we've plenty of time. Like Minnie Boyce who went with Johnny Coleman fourteen years and they broke it off and neither of them ever married. I don't want that sort of thing."

"Let's wait a wee while. Maybe I can still finagle the old one into letting me work at the airdrome."

They stayed under the oak tree another half hour before going back to town. Dermot left Neeve at her door and went over to Hannafin's. Several young men were in the shop and Dermot listened a while to their conversation. Presently Sean Reilly came out of the kitchen and noticed Dermot. He walked over and whispered to him, "McGinnis wants to see you. Drop in at the shop on your way home."

Dermot hung around another few minutes and then left and went up the street. The shop was still open and McGinnis was in the back fixing a bicycle. Dermot stood and watched him work. McGinnis fitted the bicycle chain and turned the pedal several times, noting the slackness of the chain. He lifted the bicycle right side up and stood it against the wall. "Another five bob," he said.

"What kind of money do you make at this?" Dermot asked.

"I make wages," McGinnis answered curtly.

"I wish I had something like it. You've got a steady business here and people will always be using bicycles."

McGinnis limped over to a radio that sat on the window ledge and turned it on. He hoisted himself up on the workbench and his clubfoot dangled awkwardly, bulging at the ankle. He noticed Dermot looking at it and he folded his legs, putting the other foot over it.

"Brigade H.Q. wants two men from Duncrana," he said. "I'm sending you and Reilly. This is voluntary. You're not supposed to know but they're planning some sort of raid. I only want men who want to go. I don't want Duncrana let down by somebody who hasn't the heart for the job."

"You know me, Don. I'm not halfhearted about this. Anything or anywhere, I'm ready."

"Good man. Shsssh, here comes the news."

The announcer of the Irish radio station, Athlone, gave out the news of the day. There was little change in the progress of the war. British and German armies were deadlocked in North Africa. German Heinkels had raided Sheffield the night before. A German submarine had been sunk off the coast of Scotland.

The news report ended and Dermot said, "Get the B.B.C. and see what they have to say. We can still catch some of it."

"I never listen to those lying buggers!" McGinnis said as he switched off the wireless.

"Where do you think Athlone gets its news from?" Dermot protested.

"They listen to the German broadcasts and give their claims too."

"Well I won't argue with you. When are we supposed to go up to Brigade?"

"Sunday night. There's a dance there and one of the Brigade men will get in touch with you at it."

"How will he know us?" Dermot asked.

"They know Sean, he's been to enough H.Q. meetings."

"And how do we get up there?"

"There's a carload going from Dunorana. Sean has arranged seats for the both of you. If there's anything else you need to know, ask him."

"Right," Dermot replied.

"I have to go in and get a drop of tea. Why don't you come in and sit at the fire a while? There's nobody in except my mother and Philomena."

"I'd better be getting on home," Dermot answered.

McGinnis let Dermot out and locked the front door. He turned out the light in the repair shop and walked down a short connecting hallway that led into the kitchen. Inside the kitchen his mother and sister had their chairs pulled up close to the fire.

"Is the tea ready?" he asked.

"In a minute," his mother answered. "Would you like a boiled egg with it?"

"An egg'll do grand," McGinnis said. He walked over to the table, picked up a book and sat down, holding the book out in front of him. He looked at the book jacket. A big brawny man with thick legs and a barrel chest stood with his arms folded, a bandolier across his trench coat and a forty-five hanging from a holster. The title read, "*My Fight for Irish Freedom*, by Dan Breen." McGinnis opened the book and started reading.

SEVEN

Dermot and Sean stood at the back of the dance hall in Applebridge.

"Do you fancy anything here tonight?" Dermot asked his companion.

"I never went to a dance yet but I fancied something," Sean answered. "You know what my system is? I say to myself, 'Now my bold Sean, who's the best-looking lassie here?' Then I take her out for two or three dances in a row and ask to leave her home. Usually she says no. I go back to my spot, look around and pick out the next best-looking one. I go through the same business again. Once I reached the seventeenth best-looking one before I got a woman. But in two years of going to the dances my system's never failed. I get a woman every time."

"You mean ask enough and you're sure to find one?"

"Aye, look at them!" Sean waved his hand in the direction of the dancers. "Hundreds of them and they're all here for a man and I'm a man who could court grandmothers and dance with a corpse. How about yourself? Do you see anything you'd like?"

"I see plenty I like but none I dare go with or it would be the end of Neeve and I. There's a right-looking one in the yellow dress, with her hair done up in a ribbon. She hasn't what you'd call a beautiful face but there's something about her."

"Pay no heed to the face. I never look up at the mantlepiece when I'm poking the fire," Sean explained.

"It's little poking you'll do at that fire," Dermot said derisively.

"That's Annie McCafferty," Sean remarked, gesturing to a girl that danced past. "That one would breed well—look at the hips on her."

"Aye right enough," Dermot agreed. "She looks fit to mother a race."

A young man wearing the gold circular pin of a Gaelic speaker came up to them and nodded. "Hello, Sean."

Sean punched him on the arm. "The hard Terence. Terence, this is Dermot O'Neill who's come up with me."

Terence reached out and the two men shook hands. "We might as well leave now," he told them.

They left the hall and walked out into the street. Terence led the way through various side streets and alleys. The town was in darkness and the three men stuck close together. They crossed a railway track, went down a side street, turned into an alley, recrossed the tracks and arrived in a small square. Terence whispered to his companions, "Wait here. I'll be back in a tick."

He disappeared down a narrow street. Sean and Dermot talked in whispers. Instinctively, in tune with the night and their errand, they had flattened themselves against the side wall of a building. Presently Terence returned and beckoned to them. The two Duncrana men were led down a narrow alley and into a doorway. With Terence in the lead they climbed two flights of stairs and were ushered into a large room.

There were six men inside the room. Two men were leaning against a dresser and the rest were sitting on a big double bed that had been pushed in against a wall. At the other end of the room, propped against the wall and sitting on a chair, a small blackboard had been set up. A middle-aged man, wearing an open trench coat and a scarf, was standing in front of the blackboard.

"The Duncrana men," Terence told him.

"Sit down and take the weight off your legs," the man greeted them.

Dermot and Sean walked over to the bed and the seated men made room for them. The room was sparsely furnished; a double bed, a dresser and an old wooden chair. The floor had no covering and long wooden slivers were beginning to lift from it. A small electric bulb hung from the ceiling. One wall had a damp green blotch of mildew and on the other wall, slightly awry and filmed with dust, hung a picture of the Sacred Heart. The sole window was covered with an army blanket that was nailed at top and bottom. The blanket billowed and quivered with stray slaps of wind that came in a broken pane. There was no heating of any kind and the room was cold.

The leader's voice interrupted the quiet conversations. "All right men—we're all here." The leader waited until the men fell silent and added, "Our Brigade's been given instructions to raid an ordnance barracks."

He paused again and a man sat forward on the edge of the bed. One coughed, another cleared his throat and a third ground out a cigarette under his foot. The leader turned to the blackboard and drew a rectangle on it. "This is the shape of the barracks." He quickly sketched two tiny squares. "The entrance marked 'A' is the main gate, and 'B' is the back gate." He pointed to a third square in the middle of the rectangle and said, "This is the armory. It's situated inside a locked compound."

His finger indicated the square marked B. "The military policeman on gate duty locks this gate at one and then walks to the guardhouse at the main gate and leaves the keys with the sergeant of the guard. It takes the M.P. about five minutes to make the journey but sometimes he stops at the N.C.O's mess to have a bottle of stout. We can assume that it will be at least half an hour before the sergeant of the guard starts looking for the back gate keys. We should be able to get into the armory, load up and get out again in fifteen minutes. We'll drive up in a lorry to the back gate of the barracks at five minutes to one. The military policeman will come out to open the gate. One of our men, dressed as a sergeant of the South Staffordshire Regiment, will tell the M.P. that the lorry has come to move some tentage equipment. The M.P. will not be suspicious as the ordnance barracks does tent-repair work for all British Army regiments in the North. Our man will go to the gate house with the M.P. to sign the vehicle register book. Once inside, the M.P. will be covered and we'll drive through to the armory."

The silence in the room was complete. None of the men had been on a raid before. They sat stiffly, as if poised for flight or action. The men leaning against the dresser had straightened out.

"We have obtained a full set of keys," the leader continued. "Keys for both the armory gate and the storehouses. Once inside the armory compound, we'll be fairly safe. It's surrounded by high stone walls and there's no one around on Saturday afternoons. I will be dressed as a sergeant of the South Staffordshires and the rest of you will wear fatigue trousers and black army boots. You'll be supplied with these clothes on the morning of the raid."

The leader put the chalk into his pocket, took a few steps closer to the men and folded his arms. "It's intended to take boxes of grenades, three-o-three ammo and several boxes of Bren guns. Once the lorry is loaded, we drive out, lock the armory gate, pick up Tim at the back gate and skidoo as quick as we can. Now to detail the different jobs."

Dermot reached down and cracked two of his knuckles. Sean, hearing the snaps, looked over and grinned.

"I'm in command of the raid," the leader continued. "I'm also the sergeant in charge of the loading detail. Tim there," he nodded his head in the direction of a tall youth who stood against the dresser, "will be the other sergeant—the one who'll stay with the M.P. at the back gate. Johnny, raise your hand Johnny." A blocky muscular man on the bed raised his hand and grinned sheepishly. "Johnny will be the driver of the lorry and the only one dressed in civilian clothes. The rest of you will be the loading detail. After we leave the barracks we'll drive about three miles to a place where we'll have a van waiting. We'll transfer the load to the van, abandon the lorry and continue the journey. We'll drop the Loughbeg man in Cushendin and the Duncrana men near Rathgiven. You men will have to get a bus home. The rest of us will stay in the van to dispose of the load. There isn't much more to tell you. When we're inside the armory, the men on the loading detail will have to work rapidly, but not too fast, in case some officer looks into the compound. The Officer's Mess is a four-story building and the compound is visible from the top two stories. When you're walking across the compound to the lorry you don't want to give the impression of men in a desperate hurry. You wouldn't look like soldiers then."

Several chuckles greeted the last remark. "There's one more thing," the leader continued. "We'll take very few weapons. Tim and I will carry side arms and Hugh will take a Bren gun. The rest will be unarmed. We don't anticipate any difficulty and extra weapons would only be a nuisance. If we do get into trouble it will probably be in the armory and there are enough weapons there for everyone. If this job is carried out right, we shouldn't even have to cock one revolver. Now is there anything troubling anyone?"

"When will the raid be?" a man asked.

"Two weeks from this coming Saturday. However, you'll receive definite word of this from your commanding officers."

"At what time and where will we meet here in town that morning?" Sean asked.

"Be in town here at eleven-thirty and go around to the back of the Foresters Hall. You'll see the lorry there. It's possible that the meeting place will be changed but in the meantime, it's the back of the Foresters Hall at eleven-thirty."

"What military barracks are we going to raid?" another man asked.

The leader smiled. "I'm sorry but we can't tell you yet. When definite word reaches you to mobilize, you'll be told the destination."

"In case some of us are captured, what should our conduct be?"

A laugh greeted the question and Sean remarked, "Old long-face has us in the clink already."

The leader again smiled. "You will, of course, give no information whatsoever about your companies or about the raid. If you are tried you will follow the usual custom of refusing to recognize the sovereignty of Great Britain and therefore of its court."

"Suppose the raid is discovered a few minutes after we leave. Won't they have roadblocks up and be searching everything?" Dermot asked.

"Yes, they probably will. However, it may be anywhere up to an hour before the M.P. is discovered at the back gate. Should his discovery come soon after we leave, they'll be looking for a green lorry. They won't have time to throw up road-blocks before we reach the van. Once in the van we'll stick to the side roads and we'll have the men dropped off and the stuff hidden inside half an hour. It will take the police and military at least an hour to set up roadblocks and patrols on all the small roads. We'll be home by then and the stuff hidden. Most of the police activity will come that night. A few homes will be raided but they shouldn't find anything."

There were no more questions from the men. The leader started buttoning his trench coat. "I want to see the Duncrana men before they leave," he said. "The rest are dismissed."

Dermot and Sean lingered behind until all the men were gone. The leader came over and said to them, "Sean I know, and you," he nodded to Dermot, "are Dermot O'Neill."

Dermot looked with new interest at the man. He was somewhere in his early forties, he decided. He looked like a schoolmaster; a soft pleasant face and innocuous blue eyes. His hair was well shot with gray and he was clean shaven, with just the beginning of a jowl.

"That's right," Dermot replied.

"You're the man who got the plans of the Termantown airdrome for us?"

"Myself and another Duncrana man."

"That was a good job." Turning to Sean, he asked, "How many men do you have in the company now?"

"Sixteen," Sean answered.

"It's a little on the small side."

"Aye it is. It isn't that we can't get more. We can't take care of any more right now. The men lose interest. Attendance at drill meetings has fallen off this past month."

"If this raid goes off it will perk them up a bit. Especially when they realize that two of their company took part in it." The leader walked over with them to the door. He put one arm lightly on Dermot's shoulder. "We need more men like Dermot and yourself. Men who know how to wait. We could get half the men in the North to go out tomorrow and fight for Ireland but we're having a time getting them to wait a wee bit for their country. That's the hardest part—the waiting. Please God this summer the Germans will invade and we'll see plenty of action then. In the meantime we have to keep up the spirits of the men."

He opened the door and motioned them out. Sean and Dermot walked out on the landing and down the stairs. Just before they left, Dermot turned around and saw the leader standing in a square patch of light that spilled out from the room. He was pulling up the collar of his coat. Dermot waved to him and the wave was returned. Then he and Sean stepped out into the clean night air, leaving behind them the musty mildewed smell of the building.

EIGHT

Dermot and Sean sat in a small café in Applebridge. It was eleven o'clock and they still had half an hour to kill before going to the Foresters Hall. The waitress came over and poured two cups of tea. As she was leaving, Sean tapped her lightly on the backside and said, "Ah but you've the lovely way of walking. I'll hold money you're a lively one in a hayshed."

The girl stopped and gave Sean a withering look. "If I'd go into a hayshed," she said, "it'd be with a better man than you."

Sean laughed and said to Dermot, "She has sauce enough."

Dermot nodded but his mind wasn't following the byplay. He was thinking of a conversation he had had with McGinnis the previous day. "You know, Sean," he said, "our man McGinnis didn't take it well about not being able to go on this raid."

"I know," Sean agreed. "He cribbed to me about it too. It's the leg."

"Aye, he thinks Brigade doesn't want him because of the limp."

"Well, what could Brigade do?" Sean asked. "We're supposed to be British soldiers and I've never seen a soldier with a clubfoot. I told him that Brigade would never take a commanding officer to go on a raid. That they wouldn't risk losing too valuable a man."

"What did he think about that?" Dermot asked.

"Ah you know McGinnis. You can never tell what he's thinking."

The men lapsed into silence and Sean concentrated on watching the waitress walk back and forth from the tables to the counter. He sighed and said to Dermot, "Lord to lay with that one of a warm summer night and hear the soft honey of her voice running in your ear."

Dermot laughed. "How can you think of women at a time like this? We'd better dander over or we'll miss the lorry."

They left the café and walked around to the back of the Foresters Hall. A green Transport Board lorry, with high sideboards and covered with a canvas tarp was parked in the yard. On looking into the lorry they found that several of the men had already arrived.

The leader, dressed in a British Army sergeant's uniform, greeted them in Gaelic.

They answered in kind and climbed up into the lorry.

"Good lads," the leader said, reverting to English. "You'll find the fatigue trousers and tunics in the bag but don't put them on till later. We have ten minutes yet. Dermot, sit near the tailboard and keep an eye out for the rest. There are still three more."

Dermot sat at the back of the truck and looked out. They were in a small yard surrounded on three sides by a corrugated iron fence. The fourth side was open and led into a lane. It was a dull morning with low clouds that dropped layers of brume and gave everything a glistening film of dew. From a house on the opposite side of the lane a window creaked up and a woman's voice shouted querulously, "Johnny, you come back here this minute, you wee gat—in with you now." The window creaked shut. Dermot heard from the distance the rattle of cart wheels going over cobblestones and then a motor horn. A truant gust of wind came wandering into the yard and set a loose piece of corrugated iron squeaking against its neighbor.

A man walked into the yard, wheeling a bicycle. Dermot tensed and then recognized him as their driver. The man leaned the bicycle against the fence, walked over to the lorry and looked up at Dermot. "Is the gaffer inside?" he asked.

"Aye," Dermot answered.

The newcomer swung nimbly into the back of the lorry and asked the leader, "We all here yet?"

"No. The Loughbeg man has to come and Fitz hasn't arrived yet with the Bren. I'm worried about Fitz."

"He'll get here," the driver said.

A few minutes passed and another man stepped into the yard, carrying over his shoulder an old sack. He walked slowly, unconcerned, a cigarette stuck in the corner of his mouth. He walked over to the back of the lorry and carefully handed the sack up to Dermot. "Careful, Jonathan's loaded," he said.

He climbed into the lorry and took the sack from Dermot. He sat down and took out a long object, well wrapped in rags, and laid it to one side. He placed the empty sack over it and asked, "How much time is left?"

"Still five minutes, plus an extra fifteen I allowed in case anyone was late," the leader answered.

The Loughbeg man came into the yard, walking hard. He came over to the lorry and clambered in. "Thought I was going to be late," he said breathlessly. "I got a ride into town with an old farmer and he had to stop and yarn with everyone he met. Anybody got a cigarette?"

Hugh took out a pack of cigarettes and offered them around.
Each man took one.

"You couldn't have picked a worse time to flash cigarettes,"
Sean remarked.

"That's all right," Hugh answered, looking ruefully at the
depleted package. "I'll bill Brigade for incidental expenses."

Several of the men laughed. The leader looked at his watch
and said, "Johnny, we might as well start. Listen, drive slowly.
We have plenty of time. Try to arrive in Rathgiven about
twelve o'clock and Cushendin about twelve-thirty. It's about a
fifteen minute drive from Cushendin to the barracks. You
should pull up to the back gate of the barracks about five to
one. What time do you have now?"

"Eleven thirty-three."

"That's about right," the leader said, checking his own watch.
"When you come to the back gate, blow the horn several times
until the M.P. comes out to open it."

The leader looked across at the other man who was dressed
in British Army uniform. "Tim, you know what to do. As soon
as we're through the gate, Johnny will stop the lorry for several seconds and I'll hop out and help you with the M.P. Keep
the M.P. on the floor and the door of the hut closed. That way
anyone passing will think the M.P's gone to the main gate. If
anything happens and you're discovered, fire several shots in
the air and try to keep the back gate open till we get out.
Right, let's start."

The driver and Tim got out of the back of the lorry. In a
few seconds the lorry started up and began backing out of the
yard. It swung around in the lane and headed for the main
road.

The canvas roof billowed and flapped explosively in the
wind and Dermot thought of the canvas tarp that covered the
big haystack in the haggard. The wind drove the cold in
through a dozen cracks and the men sat hunched, their knees

drawn up and their heads tucked down inside the collars of their coats. Several abortive attempts at conversation were made but for the most part the men remained silent. Hugh had his legs outstretched, the covered Bren gun gripped tightly between his knees. Dermot reached up once to wipe his mouth and noted with surprise that his hands were sweating. He felt a desperate need to talk and he nudged Sean and asked, "What did you tell them at home?"

Sean stretched his lips wide in a grin and tapped one of his front teeth with his little finger. "I'm supposed to be getting this boyo filled," he explained.

"I told the old one that I was going to get a driving license and he said it was the first he had heard of a license needed to drive a horse."

Sean laughed. Dermot began to think of the raid, of the unknown factors that could lead to its failure: men working overtime in the armory, someone discovering the M.P. at the gate while they were inside the barracks, the lorry failing to start or breaking down while they were in the compound.

Shortly after they passed through Rathgiven, the leader drew out the sack full of clothes and told them, "Here are the fatigue pants and jackets. You'd better start putting them on."

The talk sprang up again as the men tried on the clothing. One man joked about finally being in the uniform of the king and another jauntily sang an Orange song, "The Boyne Water," until his comrades indignantly hushed him up. Dermot had trouble buttoning up his trousers and he wondered if his hands shook from the cold or from fear.

Hugh unwrapped the Bren gun and checked the mechanism to see that it was working properly. He grinned drily, his round black eyes sliding across to the leader. "Let's hope some one tries to stop Jonathan," he said, motioning with the gun.

The leader rebuked him. "Let's hope this thing goes off without a hitch. I'd far rather there was no shooting at all."

He then warned the rest of the men. "Remember once we're

inside the armory, we have to work swiftly but not in panic. Keep in mind that you're just a bunch of soldiers, browned off because you're working on a Saturday afternoon. I'll be watching everything so don't get the wind up."

They passed through Cushendin and the lorry drove slowly out the road to the ordnance barracks. It arrived at the back gate of the barracks at ten minutes to one. The driver parked and came around to the back of the lorry.

"We still have five minutes," he said. "You want me to stay here or drive around for a while?"

"Better to stay here," the leader answered. "Keep the engine running and put the bonnet up and pretend you're adjusting something with the motor."

"Right," the driver answered and walked around to the front of the lorry.

The men sat on the floor and waited. Dermot looked out at the big iron gate. The bottom half was covered with sheet iron and the top was a grille of thick round bars. The minutes slid by slowly. A door slammed and the lorry turned around and started up the ramp. The men braced themselves against the sideboards and Hugh laid the wrapped Bren gun across his knees. Dermot pushed himself up and sat on his heels. The horn of the lorry broke out with several impatient blasts. Dermot heard a long creak as the gate opened. The lorry drove slowly through. Dermot felt the leader brush past him and saw him swing out over the tailboard and drop to the ground. Dermot looked through the small window of the hut and saw the M.P. against one wall, a puzzled look on his face. The leader opened the door and closed it behind him.

"They've got the M.P.," Dermot whispered to the men.

A few seconds later the door of the hut opened and the leader came walking over to the front of the lorry. The lorry started moving again. It drove past several small barracks, across a wide concrete square, swung around between two buildings, went down a small incline and stopped in front of a stone wall. A gate was opened and the lorry moved through. The leader closed the gate of the compound, came around to the back of the lorry and called to the men, "Stay where you are till I shout."

Inside the compound there were six small buildings, all well separated from each other. The leader walked over to one and inserted a key in a heavy steel door. For several seconds he tried the key before the door swung open. The leader called to the men in the lorry, "All right, out, all of you."

The men came leaping out of the lorry as it started slowly backing to the open door of the storehouse.

"O'Neill," the leader called and Dermot went over to him. "I'm going to stay here and see that this stuff is loaded. Do you see that building across from us? Take these keys and find the one that fits and get the door open. When you get inside, you'll see about fifty boxes. Those are the Bren guns. Take four, no take six, and pile them close to the door the way they'll be ready when we come."

Dermot took the keys and walked across the compound to the other building. He felt a curious unreality as he heard, from beyond the compound wall, the harsh drawn-out command of a drill sergeant and the rapid drumming of heels as a platoon of soldiers carried out an order. His throat felt dry and he kept running the tip of his tongue over his upper lip. He reached the steel door and picked one of the keys and inserted it in the lock. He twisted the key several times and then tried another key. He looked anxiously up at the tall, ivy-covered building that was the officers' mess. Again the key failed to work. On withdrawing it from the lock he dropped the bunch of keys. For a second he stared stupidly at them. Then stooping quickly he picked a key at random, aware that he was probably taking a key he had already tried. Once again the key refused to work. He picked another one and this time felt the lock giving. He eased the key around and the lock slipped over with a dry click. He pushed open the door and went inside. In the light that spilled through the wide open door he saw a square pile of boxes neatly stacked in the middle of the floor. He picked one up and brought it over to the door and laid it down. He repeated the procedure until four boxes were piled up. He was carrying over the fifth box when a dark shape loomed athwart the door and for a moment he felt panic. Then he recognized the voice of the leader, "Good man! Now the grenades."

The leader pointed out another building and told him to open it. Dermot brushed against the wall and a small wall thermometer, used for checking the humidity and temperature of the building, fell to the ground. The crash startled Dermot. When he saw what had caused the noise, his relief came flooding out, "Good suffering Jesus, I thought the roof fell in." He laughed nervously.

The leader put out his arm and stopped him. "The job's half done and we've only been here five minutes," he said kindly. Dermot nodded and started across the compound. The leader walked out of the building and shouted to the three men, "Shake a leg there, you fellas."

Dermot opened the door of the last building. He did not know how many boxes to take but decided to pile up six near the door. He carried the boxes carefully, his ears straining for the sound of the lorry. After what seemed an age, he heard it backing up.

Sean came in and whispered urgently, "There's an officer watching from the window of the Officers' Club. We're to take four boxes. After the last box is out, you're to lock the door again."

Dermot nodded and Sean picked up one of the boxes of grenades. The other two men entered. Dermot looked out through the door and saw the leader standing beside the back of the lorry, his thumbs hooked around the buttons of his tunic pockets, his foot idly scuffing the ground. The last box was taken and Dermot swung the door shut and started to lock it. He forced himself to be calm as he turned the key and he went to the extent of giving the door a push to make sure it was locked. When he turned around, the tailboard was up and the men were climbing over it. He walked over quickly and lifted himself up. The lorry drove slowly across the compound and stopped at the gate. Dermot heard the leader get out of the front and seconds later the squeak as the gate swung open. The leader closed the gate, glanced briefly into the back of the lorry and went around to the front again. The men were all silent and Dermot, at his post near the tailgate, looked out over the parade ground of the barracks. Several platoons of soldiers, stepping smartly and carrying mugs and plates, were being marched back from the mess hall. The lorry passed close to a group of N.C.O's and a young corporal looked idly at the men in the back. His eyes caught Dermot and he raised his fist, all fingers clenched except the middle one, in a derisive army gesture. Dermot shook his head and grinned back at him.

Sean, who had been watching, whispered to Dermot, "If yon bird only knew who was gretting screwed!"

Dermot gave a quick laugh. "Aye, screwed, blued and tattooed. And his wee fart of a king too."

The lorry started slowing down and Dermot sensed that they were at the back gate. Again they heard a gate open and Dermot saw Tim walking quickly over from the gatehouse. The lorry drove through and stopped at the other side. Dermot looked out and saw the leader unhurriedly bring the two halves of the gate together. Then he noticed that the leader was having trouble keeping the gate closed. It could only be shut with a sliding bar that was operated from the inside. Dermot glanced around and saw a white barrel that was used as a marker at night, standing a short distance from the gate. He leaped down from the lorry, picked up the barrel and brought it over to the gate. Together he and the leader arranged it in such a way that it propped against the gate and prevented it from swinging open. They turned and clambered over the tailgate into the lorry. A shout and the lorry moved off. The last Dermot saw of the barracks was a small boy curiously looking at the white barrel.

The blackberry hedges whipped past as the lorry turned off the main road and bounced along a narrow dirt road.

"That's the trouble about the North," Sean broke the silence. "There's never a thing to do for excitement." The men laughed and one added, referring to the seat of the Northern government, "Excitement how-are-ye. Wait till Stormont gets the news."

"Not only do we steal a load of government explosives," Sean continued, "but one of our Fenian heroes has to do a bit of sabotage."

"What happened Sean?" Hugh asked.

"O'Neill here destroyed a beautiful government thermometer," Sean grabbed Dermot by the neck and forced his head down between his knees. "Oh but you're the likely rogue," he cried.

Dermot shook himself free. "The damn thing put the wits crossways in me when it dropped off the wall."

A general round of laughter greeted the remark. The men were full of a jubilant excitement and found it hard to believe that anything could now go wrong.

"We're not out of it yet," the leader cautioned. "First thing is to get out of the uniforms." He peeled off his tunic as he continued, "We overlooked one important thing. We should have brought a charge of explosives and set it with a fifteen minute fuse in the grenade house. That would have given us enough time to get away and still have been an effective bit of sabotage."

"Sure we couldn't do that," Dermot protested. "What will we do for grenades when we run out of this lot?" Another round of laughter broke out.

The lorry jounced along and the men continued to strip off their fatigues. Presently the lorry stopped at a lane and the men piled out as it backed up until the tailgate was facing the open doors of a black van. They quickly transferred the load and the lorry was driven out. The van followed it and drove up the road a piece. The driver turned the lorry, leaving it parked straight across the road. He got out of the cab and lifted the bonnet and removed the distributor arm. His hand wheeled and the part went flying out across a meadow field. He ran back and climbed in as the van lurched off, its gears grinding.

Fifteen minutes later they stopped a mile outside Rathgiven and Dermot and Sean got out. They shouted to the driver and the van sped off. A brisk walk brought them into Rathgiven where they entered a pub and Sean ordered a glass of whiskey. He grinned at Dermot and said, "Pioneer or no, you'd better have a good dose of this. You look sick."

Dermot sat down on a bench along the wall. "I'm all right. Just the excitement. Here, give me a wee sip of that!"

He took the glass from Sean and let a few drops trickle down his throat. He coughed and ruefully looked at Sean. "I've broke my pledge!"

Sean laughed. "You couldn't have broken it for a better cause."

That night the Minister for Home Affairs began preparing a Special Powers Act to be passed by the Northern government. The police and B-men set up roadblocks and sent flying patrols on all the main and secondary roads. In an old bog in the northeast corner of the county, fourteen boxes nestled inside the heart of a rick of peat.

The following day, from I.R.A. headquarters in Dublin, an order went out to division commanding officers instructing them to step up recruiting of new members.

NINE

The Catholic rectory stood at the head of the town, set back twenty yards from the county road. A high laurel hedge enclosed a lawn that sloped gently upward to where it was supposed to meet but actually invaded the flowered garden that bordered the house. A pebbled path shot straight up through the center of the lawn. Just outside the large front door two dwarf pine trees, like toy soldiers, self-consciously stood guard. On one side of the lawn a driveway curved up and around to end in a garage at the back of the dwelling. The house itself had two stories, and was rather ugly being square and boxlike with a steeply pitched slated roof. It was the sort of house that frowned on flower gardens.

Inside the rectory lived two priests. Father Sheehy, the parish priest, had been in the parish nine years and felt he knew it inside out. The curate, Father McCory, had been there two years and felt that he would never know it. In this regard their feelings were typical of parish priests and curates in general.

One morning, several weeks after the I.R.A. raid on the ordnance barracks, Father McCory sat in the study, reading one of the works of Cardinal Newman. Father McCory, when parish business was not pressing, had the habit of reading both Aquinas and Newman, whom he considered the philosophical pillars of Catholicism. He was seated close to the fire, his long legs stretched out, his blond hair mussed as his head scrooged down on the back of the armchair. Martha, the housekeeper, always complained that Father McCory did not sit "like a priest at all," and Father McCory usually sat up with a little more dignity for a while. With the passage of time, however, he slid down further in the chair, his square chin digging into his chest.

Although Father McCory realized the dignity of his calling, he refused to recognize the dignity of his person. In this he was a bit of a heart-scald to Martha.

The room was paneled with wood and had a gleaming wood floor that Martha polished every Monday. There was a rug in front of the fire and three armchairs grouped around it. A bare round table stood in the middle of the room and along one wall was a full bookshelf that reached to the ceiling. The books were mainly theological, with the exception of one shelf devoted to Zane Grey. These latter books had been left in the rectory on the death of a previous priest who had been a Zane Grey addict. Sometimes Father McCory read a chapter or two of *The Hashknife Outfit* or *Spirit of the Border,* but always with the uneasy feeling that someone would catch him at it.

There were two large windows giving light to the room and throwing a sheen on the highly waxed floor. Heavy red drapes, tied in the middle and hanging from brass rings, added to the formality of the room. Father McCory complained that the room was too much like a museum but Father Sheehy maintained that the parishioners expected the rectory to have a little dignity, a veiled reference to Father McCory's undignified habits, which included playing football with the village team.

On the walls hung two poorly printed reproductions. One was of Murillo's "The Immaculate Conception" and the other of Millet's "The Angelus." Father Sheehy talked at times of getting a picture of St. Brendan, the patron saint of the parish, but somehow it never went any further.

The hall door opened and Father Sheehy walked in. Father Sheehy was in his late sixties and also tall. He had a large nose and nearly white hair. White bushy eyebrows exploded over a pair of pale blue eyes and a mouth that was firm and reproving. Father Sheehy was a great searcher out of evil and his face, even in repose, seemed as if it were ready to storm up at any moment in an angry denunciation. He frowned when he noticed Father McCory in the chair. The latter self-consciously straightened a little. The parish priest stopped in the middle of the room, picked up an envelope from the table and walked over to the hatstand. He reached into an inside pocket, pulled out a pair of steel-rimmed spectacles and sternly examined the seal on the envelope.

"Letter from the bishop," he growled. Though a conscientious man, Father Sheehy sometimes had the attitude toward his bishop that a sergeant usually has toward his company captain.

"Probably an appeal of some kind," Father McCory answered.

The parish priest walked over to the fire, pulled up a chair and sat down. He peered over at Father McCory. "What's that you're reading now?" he asked.

"Newman."

"Do you never tire of reading Newman? Was he ever a parish priest? Answer me that."

"Reading Newman is a hobby with me," Father McCory replied good-naturedly.

"Wonder you wouldn't take up fishing. I'm not saying it's bad to read the Church Fathers, but you'd give a body the creeps the way you've always got your nose stuck in a book."

Father Sheehy ripped off the top of the envelope and proceeded to read the letter. Halfway through he snorted, and Father McCory smiled. The curate was well versed in the meanings of the twenty different snorts by means of which the parish priest could nearly carry on a conversation. The last snort was a clear portent of trouble.

Father Sheehy finished the letter and handed it to his co-worker. "What do you think of that?" he asked. "It's to be read off the altar."

Father McCory straightened in the chair and started reading the letter:

The following statement was issued on behalf of the archbishops and bishops of Ireland by the Standing Committee of the Hierarchy on Wednesday night and is to be read at all Masses in Ireland on Sunday, February 17, 1941.

We, the archbishops and bishops of Ireland, feel it is our duty to warn all Catholics against erroneous ideas and claims which are being advanced in regard to the raising of military forces and the waging of war.

Catholic moral teaching lays down the precise conditions in order that war be at all lawful.

War is the cause of very grave evils, physical, moral and social. It is not lawful unless it be declared and waged by the supreme authority of the State.

No private citizen or group or organization of citizens has the right to bear arms or to use them against another State, its soldiers or citizens.

Just as no private citizen has the right to inflict capital punishment, so he has not the right to wage war.

Sacred Scripture gives the right to bear the sword and use it against evildoers to the supreme authority and to it alone.

If individuals could arrogate to themselves the right to use military force, there would be disorder and chaos, leading inevitably to tyranny and oppression.

The second condition for a lawful war is that there be a just cause.

It must be certain that all peaceful means have been tried and found unavailing, that the matter at issue far outweighs the havoc that war brings and that it is reasonably certain that war will not make things worse.

No private individual has authority to judge these issues, or to involve the people from whom he has received no mandate, in the serious loss inevitable in hostilities.

But of all wars, a civil war between the people of one nation causes greatest injury and is most to be avoided.

Acting, then, in the virtue of the authority conferred on us by our sacred office, we declare that it is a mortal sin for a Catholic to become or remain a member of an organization or society which arrogates to itself the right to bear arms and use them against its own or another State; that it is also sinful for a Catholic to co-operate with, express approval of, or otherwise assist any such organization or society; and that if the cooperation is notable the sin committed is mortal.

With paternal insistence, we warn young men to be on their guard against any such organization or society, and not to be induced by false notions of patriotism to become members of it.

We appeal to the general body of the people to avoid violence, cherish peace and, as a Christian nation, give an example to the world of order, forbearance, concord and good-will.

> *Signed:*
> BISHOP OF RAPHOE.
> BISHOP OF ACHONRY.

"It's about time," Father McCory commented as he handed back the letter.

"Aye but you're the great Irishman," the parish priest said bitterly.

"I'm a priest in the Holy, Catholic and Apostolic Church.

My first concern is to safeguard the practice and morals of my parishioners. I have no quarrel with the Northern government concerning these two points. The practice of the Catholic religion is free in the North and the Northern government has done nothing to undermine the moral standards of the people."

"That's the way to a bishop's ring. Show more love for Rome than for your own country," Father Sheehy protested.

"It's not a question of showing love. To me it's not of paramount importance what government rules what people, provided that the Church is allowed to carry on its work without restraint on the part of the state."

"Why don't you read Suarez sometime and see what he says about the justice of revolution?" Father Sheehy asked.

"Yes, the I.R.A. is always quoting Suarez. They forget several important points. Suarez was a sixteenth-century Jesuit, and like most Jesuits he was opposing something—in his case the Machiavellian philosophy of an amoral state. Suarez sought to bring morality to the declaring of war and revolution, primarily to oppose the ideas of Machiavelli and also to justify Spain's expansion in the New World. Suarez states that sedition is just, provided the state or monarch is tyrannical and that—his first prerequisite for a just war—the potential harm created by the proposed war is not as great as the harm which aggraves it. Does this hold true in the North of Ireland? Can the I.R.A. honestly say that plunging the North into civil war is a lesser evil than accepting minor undemocratic practices on the part of the Northern government, such as gerrymandering and discrimination against Catholics in employment and in the letting of government housing? The I.R.A. refuses to see their sedition in the light of a possible civil war. The Protestants and Orangemen won't give up the North without fighting. We have a population which is sixty percent Protestant and forty percent Catholic. The I.R.A. is not fighting against an alien government. They are fighting against a people who firmly believe they have every right to remain in Northern Ireland and be a part of the United Kingdom. A rebellion on the part of the Catholics in the North would mean nothing less than civil war with our Protestant neighbors."

"They don't belong here," Father Sheehy protested. "You know as well as I do that their forefathers hunted the native Irish off the best farming land here in the North and stole it. The Catholics were left with nothing but poor mountainy land. This land, this North is ours, it's Catholic and Irish, and we should have the means of governing it."

Father McCory shook his head. "Who belongs anywhere? We are concerned with the present—not the historical migrations of peoples. One can trace this argument back to the dawn of time. Who did the Celts push out of Ireland when they came? The Fomorians. And the Fomorians defeated the Firbolgs. We can bring this to a *reductio ad absurdum* by claiming that animals should own the land because they were on it before we were."

Father Sheehy leaned forward in his chair. "None of your old twisting with me now! Answer me straight. Did the Catholics have the right to wage war against the planters when they came?"

"I would say yes, because the planters deprived them of their land and homes by force of arms."

"Right then," Father Sheehy continued. "Because the Catholics did not wage war, because they could not, does not deprive them of the right to do so. Right?"

"I suppose so," Father McCory answered cautiously as his mind nimbly turned over the arguments that the parish priest might possibly use.

"Well then, the Catholics waited. Waited until they were strong enough to wage war—which is today. What difference does it make if they waited a year or three hundred years? The principle is the same."

Father McCory threw back his head and gave a short dry

laugh. "Ah you're becoming the great Jesuit yourself. The difference is that today the people who own the land are not responsible for the fact that the land was taken by force—hundreds of years ago."

"I say they are responsible. And we should clear them out of the country and back to England. They're not Irish and you know it. They're neither fish nor fowl; neither Irish nor English. They have no racial memory, no racial culture. Here in the North they beat their breasts and proclaim themselves English, but when they go to England they want to be known as Irish. But they're not Irish. They swear allegiance to the king of England and they're proud of it. They don't learn the Irish language, nor the Irish customs. Religiously they're not Irish. What they're trying to do is to make the North another little corner of England. They're imperialists, holding the North by force."

"There's a certain amount of truth in what you say," Father McCory agreed. "But the Catholics are to blame for much of this. As long as we feel that they don't belong here, they themselves will feel the same and be drawn closer to Britain as a result."

"You're the way you are from reading English philosophers," Father Sheehy complained. "Are there no Irish philosophers you can read?"

"I could read Berkeley but I'm sure he's on the Index."

Father Sheehy grunted. "I've never seen a good Irish priest come out of Maynooth yet. That seminary was run by British money for so long that it might as well be a Protestant one."

"Not at all. We're Catholic in the fullest meaning of the word—universally Catholic. But St. Patrick's in Carlow. That place is a hotbed of Gallicanism," the curate answered, referring to the parish priest's seminary.

"Gallicanism? No, just plain patriotism."

"And patriotism is often an extension, or a more sophisticated form, of personal pride—the greatest of the seven deadly sins."

The parish priest gave a discussion-ending snort. Father Mc-Cory waited several seconds and then asked, "Will you give a sermon in it when you read the letter?"

Father Sheehy lowered his eyebrows and squinted. "I will not then. Their holy and apostolic graces said nothing about a sermon."

Father McCory reached down and picked up a couple of lumps of coal from the scuttle and threw them on the fire. He looked distastefully at the black smudge on his hand and went over and surreptitiously wiped his fingers on the drapes that covered one of the windows.

Father Sheehy leaned his head back on the chair, closed his eyes and sighed. "Old Widow McCafferty is bad again," he said. "Every winter about this time she takes into the dying. Since I've been in the parish she's been dying every February. Two sick calls last week and one this week."

"Was that her again, last night?"

"Aye."

"I'll take her sick call any time you like," Father McCory offered. "There's no need for you to be running out there all the time."

"Ach you know what the old people in the parish are like. They're afraid you'll get mixed up and say the wrong prayers and they'll wind up in purgatory, instead of being piped and drummed straight into the Lord's presence."

"You haven't forgotten there's a meeting of the Gaelic League tonight?"

"No. I went to see old Barney Brophy about buying a new football field. I thought he'd give us the railway field a little cheap because it's for the team. He wants six hundred and it's not worth a quid more than four hundred and fifty. He seems to think it's a great old chance to get back some of the dues he's paid—and a wee bit of profit. By jingo I'll fix him if he isn't more reasonable. Won't be the first time I've read a man off the altar."

"He'll come down with the price. He knows you're expecting it a little cheap so he threw on a couple of hundred pounds to give himself room. He'll come down all right," Father McCory assured him.

"He'd better," Father Sheehy subsided, grumbling. In his mind he began to compose a sermon along the lines of—what does it profit a man . . . ? He'd throw in a bit about Christ chasing the money-changers from the temple and if the bold Barney didn't get the hint after that, he'd come straight out about the exorbitant price he was asking. There were more paths than one out of a bog.

That evening Father Sheehy went to the parish hall to attend the Gaelic League meeting. There were some twenty young men present when he entered. He walked up to the stage and sat down at a small table that had been placed in readiness. He looked around the gathering and said, "We'd just as well start. Has our financial report been sent to the League in Armagh yet?"

"Yes Father, we sent it yesterday," a young man replied.

"What other business is there?" the priest asked.

Dermot, who played on the town football team and was an ardent supporter of the Gaelic League asked, "Any news about the football field, Father?"

"I'm afraid we'll have to rent the old field for another year. Barney Brophy's looking too much for the railway field. He's a shocking poor man and the only thing between him and the workhouse is the letting of that field every year."

There was a chuckle or two from the group who well knew that Barney Brophy was one of the wealthier men in the town.

"How much did we take in on the last dance?" the priest asked.

"We cleared ten pounds, fifteen shillings," the treasurer reported.

"Very good," the priest commented and added, "I'd like to warn you again about the aims of the League. You know it's the purpose of the League to bring back a Gaelic Ireland. One of the ways is through learning the Gaelic language and playing the Gaelic games. Several things have come to my notice. Not only is it forbidden to play any foreign games but it's also forbidden to support them in any way and this includes going to watch them or listening to them on the wireless. Last Sunday, certain members of the League, and I thinking they were staunch members, listened to the international rugby match between Ireland and Wales. I hope this sort of thing won't occur again. It's a disgrace!"

The priest sat up a little straighter in the chair and his nostrils flared as he continued, "Rugby is one of the decadent games introduced in Ireland by the conqueror. Far too many centuries we've aped the manners of the Saxon. It's past time to show them that we have an older culture, a more advanced and a more Catholic culture."

Dermot nudged Sean and whispered, "He's off again."

Sean grinned and whispered back. "Boys but wouldn't he have made the great politician?"

"I hope that this support of foreign games does not continue," the priest added. "Another thing—the attendance at the Gaelic language classes has fallen off. When we started last September there were over forty pupils. Now there are less than half. There's no excuse for this. If it were harvest time, I might see why some of you couldn't come in the evenings, but there's nothing to do on the land now."

The men stirred uneasily in their chairs. Dermot and Sean stood leaning against a wall and were engaged in a game they had played together since grade school days. They were methodically cracking their knuckles. Sean had reached eight and Dermot nine. Dermot was vainly involved in trying to crack the knuckle of his left thumb even though he knew he had never cracked it before and probably never would. Sean was working on one of his thumbs, trying to get even with Dermot. Thumb knuckles are notoriously hard to crack.

"Last Sunday night there was a dance in Rathgiven for the county hospital," the priest continued. "Several Gaelic League members from Duncrana were at that dance. I hope you're aware that going to English dances is breaking the regulations of the Gaelic League. They are foreign dances and cannot be tolerated. Because Catholics as well as Protestants use the hospital, I see no harm in supporting the dance, but this can be done by buying a ticket and not going. Another thing occurred which pained me very much. At the conclusion of the dance, 'God Save the King' was played. Those Duncrana members at the dance got to their feet for the anthem. This is disgraceful. They should have left the hall immediately they realized that the anthem was going to be played."

Dermot stopped fooling with his knuckles and folded his arms over his chest. He interrupted the priest, "There would have been a riot with the Orangemen if they had done that, Father."

The priest looked at Dermot and caustically asked, "And since when has a Gaelic League member been afraid of Orangemen?"

"You say they should not have been there. If they shouldn't have been there, they shouldn't have been there—without advertising the fact with a row. Anyway I don't think they knew that the British anthem was going to be played."

"You might have known that a Protestant band would play 'God Save the King,'" the priest shrewdly remarked.

"I wasn't at the dance, Father," Dermot replied.

"Then by jingo, why are you so concerned?"

"I was just thinking of what I would have done if I was there."

The priest leaned forward. "You're not meaning to say that you're afraid of an Orangeman?"

"I mean nothing of the sort," Dermot drily answered. "You know me better than that. And while we're on the subject of foreign games, can poker, which I understand comes from America, be considered a foreign game?"

Sean drew his breath in sharply and the rest of the men, astonished, stared at Dermot. It was well known that Father Sheehy went to the house of a local cattle dealer every Friday night and played poker for rather heavy stakes.

Father Sheehy's face tightened and his eyebrows pulled down as he angrily replied, "You know rightly that card games, not being physical exercise, are not subject to the jurisdiction of the League. I hope you're not trying to be imper tinent."

Dermot gave the priest an innocent look as he replied, "Deed then I'm not, Father. As a good member of the League I'd like to know all the rules."

The priest snorted. "Aye but you're the great scholar all of a sudden."

The treasurer asked, "Would the raid on the ordnance barracks be a foreign game, Father?" The men laughed and the remark helped to ease the tension.

The priest chuckled and replied, "No. That's an old Irish game if ever there was one. It's a pity it isn't played more often. Boys but that was the lovely day's work."

The men smiled at the enthusiasm of the parish priest. Father Sheehy suddenly remembered the bishops' letter and added, "It's a great pity that everyone doesn't realize the necessity of raids like that. Anyway it's a blessing no one was hurt." The priest temporarily forgot the presence of the men and shook his head, "No by jingo that was great work. A grand blow struck for Ireland."

Sean looked over at Dermot and they smiled at each other.

The priest stood up as he said, "Well, if we've taken care of everything, we might as well go home."

The men began to leave the hall. Outside, on the way down the town, Sean said, "Man that was hironious, that dig about poker. What in under God possessed you?"

"For a few seconds I lost my temper," Dermot explained. "Neeve was at that dance and she's very annoyed about the whole thing. A lot of people have been throwing it up to her. What could she do? I told her not to mind the old rips. Sure a body would never have peace if they listened to all that was said about them."

"I thought the P.P. was going to throw a fit."

"I wouldn't mind, but it's always them who do nothing but sit on their backsides that criticize other people for not being Irish enough. I consider Neeve to be as Irish-minded as anybody else and I know I've done a damn sight more for Ireland than most of the people in the town," Dermot concluded self-righteously.

"How many did you finally get?" Sean asked.

"How many what?"

"Knuckles."

"Nine."

"Well, you beat me again."

TEN

Sergeant Crawley wheeled his bicycle up the lane to the O'Neill house. It was a dull day with a feeling of rain and a hint of growth in the air. The harshness of winter had been temporarily left behind and the air was warmer than usual for March. The sergeant was whistling a waltzy piece from a Tchaikowsky symphony. He invariably whistled Tchaikowsky when he was cycling or walking, just as he usually whistled *The Sorcerer's Apprentice* when he was compiling reports or filling out forms in the barracks. The sergeant loved to whistle and rationalized that a whistling policeman showed that the law was part of humanity and not above it.

Halfway up the lane he ran across Ned who was working with a wheelbarrow full of stones. Ned was filling in the small potholes that came in the lane every winter as a result of the frost. The sergeant watched unobserved for several seconds. Ned drew a shovelful of gravel from the wheelbarrow, emptied it in a hole and then methodically tamped the small stones down with the end of the shovel.

"Well, there's one man doing a day's work around here," the sergeant called.

Ned straightened and casually tossed the shovel against the hedge. It landed upright, the handle supported by the bushes. Ned smiled in self-satisfaction and nodded to the policeman. "Anything wrong sergeant?" he asked.

"Not a thing Ned. Just here to check your blackout curtains."

Ned picked up his coat from the hedge and slipped it around his shoulders. "Between you and me sergeant," he said, "these blackout regulations are a cod. What good would it do a German bomber to see a light from our kitchen?"

"No good at all. But it's my job to enforce the laws and regulations."

Ned took a pipe out of his pocket and stuck it in his mouth. He extracted a plug of tobacco from his waistcoat pocket and cut a chunk from one corner with his pocketknife. Intently he rolled the piece in his palm, breaking it up into little flakes. The ceremony over, he looked at the sergeant and asked, "Any word of them catching the boyos that raided the ordnance barracks?"

The sergeant knew that Ned was interested mainly in a talk and was not particularly concerned about getting information. He smiled as he replied, "No word yet, but it's the last raid they'll get away so soft with. The commanding officer of the ordnance barracks is being court-martialed for negligence."

Ned tilted the loose tobacco from his palm into the pipe. He tapped it down in the bowl with his thumb, dusted off his hands and lit the pipe. "Sure they're taking all the glory of it away from the boys—calling it negligence."

The sergeant chuckled. "Your boys will see plenty of glory

yet if they're not careful. The government is going to pass a Special Powers Act that will give the police authority to arrest without warrant and to intern a man solely on suspicion for the duration of the war. There'll be a wholesale jailing of suspects if another raid happens."

"You'd never jail me sergeant?"

The sergeant paused briefly before replying. He couldn't say they would because Ned would know it for a lie and he couldn't say they wouldn't because it was another way of saying that Ned wasn't a very good Irishman—that the government had nothing to fear from him. He temporized, "You never can tell, though I'd say it's more likely your brother would be picked up."

"Who—that strip of a lad?" Ned scoffed. "The government has little to fear then."

Ned's protest was too sincere, too natural, to confirm a suspicion that had been taking shape in the sergeant's mind for the past several weeks. He had a shrewd idea that a company of the I.R.A. had been formed in the town. There had been many indications: a subtle change in the atmosphere, a certain evasiveness, a new-found insolence on the part of the younger men. The sergeant knew that if such a company had been recruited the members would come from the Gaelic League, the sons of old I.R.A. men, the players on the football team, the single men without wives and responsibilities. And Dermot fitted all these categories.

Ned interrupted the sergeant's thoughts. "I'll walk up to the house with you sergeant. They'll ask you to have a cup of tea and like a decent man say you'll take a cup. That way I'll get some myself. Course I could go in and ask for it but I'd rather get it this way."

"You're a rare turn, Ned," the sergeant said.

They entered the house, Ned going in front and declaring, "The sergeant's here to check the blackout curtains."

Kathleen came out of the scullery drying her hands on her

apron. She went over to the fire and set the kettle on to boil. "That's a nice day sergeant," she said.

"Deed then it is mam," the sergeant replied.

"Here sit down sergeant." She pulled a chair up to the fire. "You'll have a cup of tea?"

"Do you make a strong cup, mam?"

"Aye strong enough."

"You could trot horses over it," Ned said.

"There's nothing like a strong cup of tea," the sergeant added.

"Any word from your boy?" Kathleen asked.

"Aye we hear from him quite often. He's doing well or says so anyway."

"God spare him, the poor wee fella, miles away from his home." Kathleen's hand went up and patrolled the back of her head for a stray wisp of hair. Her face softened as she continued, "Will there never be an end to all this killing, sergeant?"

"I don't know but I'm afraid not," the sergeant answered.

Kathleen got the teapot and measured three spoons of tea into it. She tilted the kettle on the crook and a jet of boiling water hissed into the teapot. She set it close to the fire to draw and went over to the cupboard and set out a cup and saucer.

"Will you have an egg, sergeant?"

"Ah thank you no. I had breakfast a wee while ago."

"Patrick and Dermot are out in the barn, cutting seed potatoes. Do you want to see them?"

"I'll stop in to see them on the way out," the sergeant answered.

"Whatever you like now, sergeant. Ned why don't you go out and tell Patrick that the sergeant's here."

Ned left the kitchen. Kathleen poured out three cups of tea and handed one to the sergeant. "A wee slice of bread sergeant?"

"No, this is grand. I'm not hungry at all. This wee drop of tea will do the best."

Patrick, Dermot and Bella came into the kitchen. They greeted the sergeant and Patrick drew up a chair to the fire and sat down. "The wireless is licensed and the dog's licensed and there's not a drop of poteen in the house," he said to the sergeant. "Afraid you've wasted a trip."

The sergeant smiled. "It's nothing important, I came to check the blackout curtains."

"Somebody complaining?" Patrick asked.

"No," the sergeant replied. He looked over at Bella and smiled. "There's a fine looking lassie you've got, Patrick. Tell me. Is she courting yet?"

Bella blushed as her father answered, "Deed then she is. There's not a hayrick in the country she doesn't know the geography of. I'm thinking of tying her up on the week ends."

"Let her sport herself a wee while, Patrick. She'll be soon enough old and with responsibilities. Many's the time I wouldn't let our Derek out to a dance, or away for a day to the shore, thinking it better that he stick to the books—but it's little pleasure he's known this past year."

The sergeant got up and placed his cup and saucer on the table. "That was a grand cup of tea," he said to Kathleen.

Kathleen smiled. "It's little enough. It's not often we have your company, sergeant."

"More's the pity," the sergeant replied. He automatically tugged at the bottom of his tunic, straightening it and walked over to the window. He looked at the rolled up blackout curtain that was sitting on two nails driven into the top of the wood framing.

"You've curtains for all the windows?" he asked.

"Aye we have. Do you want to see the bedroom ones?" Kathleen asked.

"Not at all. I'm sure they're all right." He looked across at

Dermot who stood leaning against the wall. "You're rightly, Dermot?" he asked.

Something in the sergeant's tone put everyone on guard. Patrick shifted on the chair as his son answered, "Can't complain, sergeant."

The sergeant looked away from Dermot and out through the window. In the field facing the house he saw a young calf put down its head and dunt at the side of a cow. The cow, imperturbable, continued cropping at the short grass. The calf backed away and then went tearing around to the front of the cow and halted, trembling, its legs stiff and its ears speared forward. The sergeant spoke, the words coming out slow and measured. "Dermot, where were you the morning the ordnance barracks was raided?"

Dermot nervously ran his tongue over his upper lip and answered in a hesitating voice, "Why I suppose I was in the house here. I'm sure I was."

The sergeant continued looking out the window. The calf trotted away a few steps and then half turned, looking back. Its head lowered to the ground and it gave a spring, landing stiff-legged and again facing the cow.

"Think back a little bit," the sergeant said. "It was three weeks ago last Saturday."

"Three weeks ago?" Dermot repeated. "I must have been here. I never go anywhere on Saturday mornings." Everyone in the house except the sergeant was intently watching Dermot.

The sergeant noted that the calf had given up trying to annoy the cow and was now following the cow's example and quietly eating grass. He turned and looked at Dermot. "You got off the three o'clock bus from Rathgiven," he stated.

"Oh aye! Now I mind," Dermot said hurriedly. "I went into Rathgiven with Sean Reilly. We went in to visit his sister. Her that's married to the foreman on the county council."

The sergeant picked up his cap from the table and carefully

put it on. "Well I must be going now," he said as he left the kitchen. Ned was the only one to call a good-by after him.

Kathleen came over to Dermot. Silently she looked at him for several moments. Then she asked, her voice high and strained, "Why did you lie to the sergeant?"

"I didn't lie," Dermot replied evasively. "I was in Rathgiven that morning."

"You left here for Applebridge. You said you were going up for a driver's license."

"I went to Applebridge and then I went to Rathgiven."

"Answer me the truth now. Did you have anything to do with that raid?"

Dermot looked at his mother and then walked over to the fire.

"Answer me!" she insisted.

"He did. He was on the raid," his sister said.

Dermot turned on Bella. "You hold your flaming tongue!"

"Don't tell me to hold my tongue," she retorted. "You were on the raid and I know it. I was told by one of my friends."

Kathleen went over to the table and sat down. She put her hands up to her head and said softly, "It's a curse on the country. This continual shooting and killing and now my own son is mixed up in it." She turned to her husband, "This is your fault." Her voice rose, "All you do is blather and whinge about dear old Ireland."

Patrick leaned forward and spat into the fire. "Good for the lad. It's time the present generation woke up and did something for their country. I did my share and Vincent, God be good to him, did his."

Kathleen got up, her voice shaking and shouted at Dermot, "You'll stay away from that gang of blackguards. I'll not have my son coming home some night with his body riddled or rotting in a prison ship for twenty years. It wasn't for that I bore you and brought you up."

"Be quiet," Dermot said soothingly. "You're making a fuss

over nothing." He turned to Bella, "You're making her worse," he accused.

"It's you that's causing the trouble," Bella replied. "You with your grand ideas of freeing Ireland. You've gotten mixed up with a gang of lunatics in town and they've driven you astray."

Patrick stood up excitedly, knocking the chair over as he did so. They all looked over at him apprehensively. "Leave the lad alone," he said angrily. "I'm proud of him that's willing to do his share for Ireland. If we had more like him, the damned border wouldn't last long." He walked over and put his hand on Dermot's shoulder. "There'll not be a word said against you as long as I'm the man of this house." He looked over at his wife. "You're a woman. All you care is that a man do his work and lead a peaceful life but as long as there's a British soldier in the North there'll be men like Dermot and Vincent, God rest his soul, who'll not count the cost nor duck their heads when Ireland calls. You ought to be proud of your son."

Tone, excited by the loud conversation, raised his head and ambled over to where Ned was sitting on a stool. He laid his head on the knees of Ned and looked up solemnly at him. Ned reached down and scratched the dog behind the ears. He spoke quietly to the rest, "We might as well get back to work. The potatoes won't cut themselves."

Dermot was grateful for the remark and turned and left the kitchen. The others followed him, leaving Kathleen at the table. A hen came timidly in through the open door. With mincing steps it made its way to the dresser and pecked at a few crumbs that lay on the floor. Kathleen heard the digs of the hen and taking a broom she whooshed it out, scolding as she did so, "Away out of that with you. You've my heart scalded, coming in and dirtying up the kitchen."

She walked over to the window and looked out. She realized that it wasn't the blackout curtains that had brought the sergeant. She would have to get Dermot away out of Duncrana while there was still time. Either that or he'd end up like Vincent or her own brother, Johnny.

She looked down at the table and saw the blue book in which were listed the sunken ships of the British Navy. In a sudden fury she picked it up and tore it in two. She strode over and dropped the two halves of the book on the fire. Lifting the tongs she pushed the book deep into the heart of the flames and raked fresh coals over it. She started talking to herself, her voice a low whisper, punctuated by vigorous thrusts of the tongs at the now burning notebook. "That's part of it, this hatred of England, until we don't know what's right or what's wrong. I'll send him away. I'll send him to my sister's place in Donegal."

Inside the turfshed, Patrick, Bella and Dermot sat around a heap of seed potatoes. Each had a paring knife and beside each one was a bag of whole potatoes.

Dermot looked across at Bella. "Who told you about me being on the raid?" he asked.

"Never mind that. Neeve knows about it too." Bella's hand expertly snapped off several tiny buds from a potato and her knife whipped cleanly. She dropped the two halves on the pile.

"My God, the whole town knows it," Dermot complained.

Patrick picked a potato out of the bag. He cut twice and three pieces fell into his apron. In a low voice he started singing, "If I Were a Blackbird." Once when he was young, he had gone to a small seaside town in County Donegal. He had stared, fascinated, at the heavy rollers coming in and the spray exploding off the rocks and into the air. Ever since he had felt a wistfulness for the sea and it expressed itself in sea songs. Be there the slightest nautical reference in a song and Patrick immediately liked it. He sang his songs, "Galway Bay," "The Queen of Connemara," and "Harbor Lights," giving special emphasis to the lines that contained words concerning the sea and merely humming the other lines. His voice lilted out the words softly, "If I were a blackbird, I'd whistle and sing; I'd fly to the ship da de dum dum de da." He hummed the words, "That my true love lies in." Patrick didn't want words about love in his sea songs. He continued, his voice growing strong on the word "rigging." "And on the top rigging, I'd there dum de dum." He looked over at his son and asked, "Were you on the raid?"

Dermot replied shortly, "What difference does it make?"

"You know that Neeve knows all about it?" Bella asked. "Who told her?"

"I don't know. It was her that told me and she doesn't like it one bit."

"I won't have my life run by women," Dermot said crossly.

"Proper bloody order," Patrick agreed and started to sing, "Dum dum dum lies over the ocean."

"Daddy, why can't I go to England and be a nurse?" Bella asked.

"I won't have any of my children in that country," Patrick answered simply.

"When I'm twenty-one I'll go anyway and there's ne'er a thing you can do about it," Bella threatened.

"Twenty-one or forty-one, you'll do what you're told. There's no gratitude in children nowdays. You're all spoiled. What in the name of God is taking you over there? Have you not a home here?"

"Aye I've a home here and it's a home I'll have for the rest of my life. I'll be like too many of the women in this country. I'll probably never get a man and if I do it'll be some old farmer with one foot in the grave and the other trembling after it, and me spooning porridge into him three times a day."

Patrick listened to the heresy thunderstruck. Then shaking his head sadly he complained, "It's these American pictures that's ruining the country."

Bella laughed, "Oh deed it is and me that hasn't been to but three or four pictures in my life." She stood up and shook the tiny buds off her apron. "Do you want a mug of buttermilk?" she asked her father.

"No," Patrick answered crossly.

"Ah Daddy dear, don't be so cranky. Declare to God but you're getting old."

Patrick drew his hand back and threatened his daughter. "I'll have no impertinence from you, young lady."

Bella skipped away and said to Dermot, "Isn't he the saintly old man now? A bit of a beard and a staff and he'd pass for Saint Patrick."

Dermot grinned at his sister and told her, "Bring me a mug when you're coming back."

Bella left the shed and went into the kitchen. Her mother was sitting at the table, her head resting on her folded arms.

"This is the queer time to be taking a nap," Bella said.

Kathleen raised her head and Bella saw that her eyes were red. She went quickly over to the table and put a protective arm around her mother. "Listen now, don't be paying any heed to Dermot. Sure they're nothing but a bunch of lads."

Kathleen gave a weak smile at the idea of Bella referring to older men as a bunch of lads. Then in spite of herself the tears came again. She wiped quickly at her eyes with the end of the apron. "There was Johnny, a big strong man with a heart of gold," she said. "I can mind him in the fields, plowing, and there wasn't a better man with a plow or harrow in the county. I'd bring his tea out to him and always he let me crack the top off the boiled egg. In the evenings I'd go out and he'd sit me up on Sally, an old white mare we had, and he'd call me Queen Maeve. When the trouble came he went on the run with the I.R.A. Night after night he lay out on the wet mountains with the rain and fog beating into him. My mother, God rest her soul, never knew the minute he'd be brought back with a bullet in him. When the treaty was signed he came off the mountains with a cough and a year later he was dead of T.B."

Her eyes turned inward and her mind slipped back a quarter of a century. "And there was your Uncle Vincent, God be good to his soul. There wasn't a dance or a party in the county that he didn't play the accordion for. He was always smiling, Vincent. I didn't know him well, but I can mind the big smile of him and the foot tapping away to the music. And he was shot at the foot of the lane one night. I was at his wake in this very house. His mother died a year later and I was at that wake too. It was then I started courting your father. He's a good man. He's always been good to me and God forgive me for saying anything against him, but I don't want to see Dermot go the same way that Vincent did."

Bella walked over to the fire and picked up the teapot. She poured out a cup of tea and handed it to her mother. "Pay no mind to them. Sure it's nothing. Here, drink this."

Kathleen stirred the sugar in the cup and continued, "It wasn't only our ones. I mind Bob Allen and him high up in the Orange Lodge. He was coming back from a fair in Toberclare and he picked up our Johnny on the road. He took him home and they made him a feed and gave him clean clothes. And Johnny on the run and the police hunting up hill and down vale for him. Bob Allen, God be merciful to him, took Johnny the next day in the car up to Donegal and Johnny got to friends there and was safe for a while. It wasn't a month later that Bob was killed by the I.R.A. one night, coming home from a meeting in the Orange Lodge."

"Hush, forget about those times," Bella said soothingly.

"I'd hate to see him leave, but I'd far rather he'd go away to Australia or America than see him mixed up in these troubles. There's no good can come of it. What freedom are they looking for? We can go to church without hindrance. What more freedom do they want?"

A picking sound drew her attention. She looked around and saw that the hen had returned through the door that Bella had left open. "Chase that hen out, like a good girl," she said to her daughter.

ELEVEN

Neeve Donnelly sighed and looked around her hairdressing establishment. The paint was cracking and peeling on the wall that bordered the kitchen. The floor was wooden and partially covered with a threadbare gray rug. Two hair-drying machines grimly surveyed their eggheaded reflections in a wall-length mirror. A round table, covered with magazines, had four armchairs ranged behind it. A turf fire was dying in the fireplace, the half-burned clods frosted with a layer of ashes. The mantlepiece held a pile of hair curlers, a photograph of herself taken the day she made her first communion, a snap of her brother Jim in his Free State Army uniform and an advertisement for a hair shampoo. Sandwiched between the photographs were assorted bottles of hair lotion. Above the mantlepiece hung a huge mirror that rose to the ceiling. Halfway down the mirror,

running from one edge to the other, were large green letters
that spelled out BUSHMILLS WHISKEY. In the corners of
the mirror emblematic shields represented the four provinces
of Ireland; the Red Hand for Ulster, a round tower for Leins-
ter, a greyhound for Connaught and a harp for Munster.

Neeve in her more optimistic moments talked about redeco-
rating the place: painting the walls a light cream, putting in a
new carpet that covered the whole floor, knocking out the wall
that faced the street and putting in a broad plate glass window
instead of the square eight-paned one. She also planned on
replacing the leering whiskey mirror with something a little
more feminine.

She sighed again and lowered herself slightly, so that she
could look in the bottom half of the mirror, below the whiskey
lettering. With the back of her hand she brushed up the front
of her hair. Then she looked anxiously at the tiny mole under
her right eye. She considered it ugly and to hide her true feelings, referred to it jokingly as her trade-mark. She put her right
hand up and covered the mole with the tip of her finger and
again surveyed herself. Mouth a trifle too large, she thought,
and eyebrows that met in the middle, reminding her of an old
saying "Beware of those whose eyebrows meet," she recited
gravely.

She closed her eyes and a slightly pained, slightly comic expression came over her face. She spoke to the mirror, shaking
her head slowly, "Please Dermot, you know I love you but I
can't give you that. No Dermot, it isn't right. When we're married but not before." She gave a quick shake of her head and
ruefully admitted to herself that so far he hadn't asked for
"that." Still it was pleasant to pretend that he had. Her face
became stern as she continued, "Dermot, you're forgetting
yourself. And it the feast day of Saint Dominic!" Not that that
would bother him, the big pagan. She didn't like the way his
hands wandered sometimes or maybe she did like it and it was
done so innocently that she didn't know whether or not he had

evil intentions. Around her waist was all right, she knew, but sometimes his hands slid down too far. She liked the feel of his hands. They were strong, square and honest hands.

She wondered if it were true about him being on the ordnance raid. It would be like him, she knew. He'd come to the door some night, silent and uncomplaining, the blood seeping out of his shirt and she'd make him lie down and she'd get hot water to wash his wound and she'd stroke his forehead and bandage up his chest. Did he have hair on his chest? She would have to clip it off to dress the wound properly. And never a word would he say, but just reach up and kiss her fingertips.

She opened her eyes and looked in the mirror. "Neeve Donnelly, you're the greatest old cod," she reproved herself sternly.

With a determined burst of energy she exchanged her white apron for an old colored one and briskly began to sweep from around the machines. When she had finished, she swept the dirt into the fire and for a second it blazed and crackled furiously. Giving a last look around she switched off the light and went through a door and into the kitchen. At the kitchen table were seated her two younger sisters, Briege and Mary, halfheartedly doing their homework. Neeve's mother, a round ball of a woman, sat close to the kitchen range.

"You'll finish all that homework before you go to bed," Neeve admonished her sisters. "I've been hearing bad reports from Mrs. Kelly about the pair of you." She asked her mother, "Where's Donal?"

Her mother lowered the paper she was reading. "I think he went over to Hannafin's."

Neeve had a sudden suspicion that Donal might be mixed up with the I.R.A. She would need to keep an eye on him, she thought. It was bad enough keeping the house going without anything happening to Donal and the three pounds a week he brought home from the creamery. She decided to go over to Hannafin's a little later and see if he was actually there. She pulled a chair up to the range and sat down.

"Do you want your tea now?" Mrs. Donnelly asked.

"No. I'm going over to Hannafin's for a few minutes. I'll take it when I come back," Neeve answered.

"Put your coat on. It's very cold out," her mother warned.

Neeve got up and put on her overcoat and a scarf. She glanced over at the table and said to her mother, "I won't be gone more than half an hour. See that those two keep at the books."

"They'll need to be getting to bed soon," her mother replied.

Neeve walked out through the shop and closed the front door behind her. She stood for a moment looking down the town. As she watched, a milk lorry came rumbling up the street, empty creamery cans bouncing around the platform. The draft of its passing made her shiver and she turned up the collar of her coat as she stepped out into the street.

Hannafin was seated on his stool, methodically hammering studs into the sole of a boot when she entered. He looked up at her and said, "He's in the kitchen."

Neeve smiled at him. "Is he now? And how would you know who I'm looking?"

"You're either looking your brother or Dermot and they're both in the kitchen. Tell me Neeve, when are you going to give us the big day?" Hannafin looked up at her slyly.

"I'm too cold a woman to ever marry," Neeve retorted.

"There are no cold women—only women with cold moments," Hannafin answered.

Neeve laughed delightedly. Then she turned serious and said, "If I had my way, I'd marry tomorrow."

"Aye I know. The men around this town are fierce slow about putting the yoke around their necks."

"I like that," Neeve pouted. "You were quick enough getting yoked yourself."

"I was that. But I badly needed tying down. I wasn't worth a damn before I got married. I'm still not worth a tinker's damn and everybody in the town knows it except my wife. But she thinks she's made a man of me and she's happy about it."

He dropped a boot to the floor and picked up its mate. He looked in distaste at the hole that penetrated several layers in the sole and at the heel that was worn down through the steel protector.

"It was hardly worth while bringing that pair in," Neeve commented.

"When they reach this stage, I'm a bootmaker, not a cobbler." He ripped the sole off the boot with a pair of pliers. "I can tell a power about people just by their boots. There are two kinds who'd bring in a boot like this. The careless ones, who never look to see if their boots are worn at all and the misers, who keep putting it off. There's one difference. Usually the heel wears quicker than the sole and the careless ones eventually notice that the heel is going and they get it fixed. Then when the sole goes too far they bring in the boots but the heel's still in fair condition. "This one," he nodded to the boot on the last, "belongs to the miser type. The heels wear down to a certain point and then stop while the sole keeps wearing out. When they bring the boot in, both sole and heel are shot."

"What else can you tell?" Neeve asked.

"Well, there's the football player and sometimes he's over seventy. That one can't pass a stone on the road but has to have a kick at it. The toes give out first. The toe protector's gone and the leather wears down at the toe more than the rest of the sole. The top leather is cut and nicked where they've been kicking at stones. Fat people wear the outside edge of the sole more than the center or the inside edge. And if a fat person wears low shoes, like as not the stitches are broken at the heel seams. Then there's the cornerboy, the buckos who stand outside the chapel when Mass is over and on the steps of Devlin's pub on fair days. The top of the toe is lightly scarred and the surface all roughed up from crossing the legs and resting one boot on top of the other."

"My goodness, I don't know if I'd fancy bringing my shoes here any more. God only knows what you'd make of them."

Hannafin smiled at her. "Your shoes wear more on the soles than the heels. You're usually bending over someone in your business, throwing the weight of the body onto the ball of the foot. The heels get very little wear. Next time you bring your shoes look at them and tell me if I'm right."

He reached behind him and took a bag of caramels out of a cubbyhole. He handed the bag up to Neeve and said, "Here, have a sweet." She took one and Hannafin continued, "I can almost tell what kind of a housekeeper a woman is by the shoes and boots she brings in. Sometimes the boots are washed and polished and sometimes I get a pair that have waded through a doughal that morning and the dung hardly dry on them yet. And there's always the suspicious old woman who won't leave the leather thongs in the boots for fear I'd steal them." He chuckled. "For all that it's a grand job. Old farmers are the best to cobble for. They'll come in and I'll give them the boots and they'll turn them over in their fists and say, 'Ah that's a lovely job, Jimmy. A lovely job.' And they'll run their hands over the studs in the soles and along the sealing wax I use on the heels. Sometimes when I see this I think I know what the monks must have felt when they finally finished the Book of Kells."

"Next time I get a pair of shoes soled, I must remember to admire them," Neeve said teasingly.

"It's no cod," Hannafin protested. "For most people the thing they do for a living has more satisfaction when other people can see it. What farmer doesn't pride himself on how straight his furrow is? Did you ever notice the way the banks are cut in the bog? The banks nearest the road are the neatest, a nice straight cut and you never see a step that isn't cut down to the bog floor though sometimes it means cutting more than the farmer needs. But go into the middle of the bog where the banks can't be seen from the road. There'll be half-cut steps and crooked edges and sloppy drains. The further you go into the bog, the sloppier the banks. That's because the cutters next to the road know that their work will be seen and they want other people to admire it. If all the people in the world were blind I don't think I'd take half the trouble cobbling boots. There wouldn't be the same satisfaction if only myself could see the finished job."

"Aye right enough, when I give a permanent it does my heart good to know I've done a good job. But I get far more pleasure when someone looks in the mirror and compliments me on it."

From the kitchen came the subdued murmur of voices. A young man pushed open the door and entered the shop. He nodded to Neeve and said to Hannafin, "Did you hear about Anne Reedy of Cornamaddy?"

"Is she dead?"

"Aye, she died this evening about an hour ago."

"God be good to her soul. She was a grand old woman," Hannafin said.

"She must have been over eighty," the newcomer remarked.

"Aye that she was and till this winter she used to walk the two miles into town every Friday to collect her old age pension. There weren't many like Anne."

Neeve turned to the youth and asked, "Are you going into the kitchen?" She herself would never go into the kitchen during the evenings. It was a male sanctuary and she knew that the presence of a single girl would throw a brake on the ribald talk that often flew. She also feared the barrage of witticisms she would be subjected to; remarks about past, present and potential boy friends, her business and even her appearance.

"Aye," the newcomer asked.

"Will you tell Dermot that I want to see him?"

The young man grinned, opened the door and shouted into the crowded kitchen, "Dermot O'Neill! Neeve Donnelly's in a terrible way looking you."

Neeve blushed furiously at the quick burst of laughter that followed the speaker's remark. Dermot got up and gave the youth a black look as he came through the door. He said to Neeve, "That's the half-witted idiot if ever I heard one!" Hannafin smiled and with his leather knife began paring out a new sole from the corner of a bend of leather.

"Anne Reedy's dead," Neeve said. "Will you be going to the wake?"

"I suppose so. What night do you want to go?"

"I'd just as soon go tonight."

"I'll see you then at the wake," Dermot said.

"All right. Tell that brother of mine if he wants any tea he'd better be coming soon."

Dermot watched as Neeve left the shop. He turned to Hannafin, "I suppose you'll be going?"

"I'll have to pay my respects to the dead," Hannafin answered piously.

"You sanctimonious old goat. You can smell the porter from here."

Hannafin rubbed his chin on his shoulder, brushed off the leather chips from his apron and replied, "It ought to be the great old wake. There's no one really close. I suppose the niece from Glencross will come down to make the arrangements."

"Deed then it shouldn't be a quiet wake. If I know the boys around this town, there'll be brave crack before the night's out."

Dermot returned to the kitchen. Hannafin placed the rough-shaped sole over the boot and pared off the overlapping edges with sure and easy strokes. He pounded two nails into the new sole and placed the boot on a shelf behind him. Standing up, he stretched, gave a hitch to his trousers, put his hand up to his face and scratched his beard. He rubbed his chin contemplatively, debating whether or not to shave. He looked at the shelf of old shoes and the shelf of repaired ones and said aloud, "Fluke it, I've done enough."

He untied his apron, folded it neatly and placed it on top of the counter. He snapped his fingers once or twice and did a little jig step on the floor. "Ho!" he sang, "for she looked so neat in her snow-white feet."

He went into the kitchen and told his wife, "I'm for Anne Reedy's wake tonight. Put on the kettle. I'll be needing a sup of tea and I have to shave yet."

TWELVE

The wake house was two miles from the town. It lay in a fold of land, nearly hidden by the tall alder trees that ringed the yard. The night was frosty cold with brief spurts of wind sweeping over the land. The stars gleamed through a million peepholes and a small, smoke-puff cloud slid across the face of the moon. From beyond the house came the solemn hoot of an owl, a mournful complaint about things particular and nights in general.

Dermot and his father came wheeling their bicycles into the yard. They placed them along one wall of the house, in company with another twenty or so bikes that had been set there.

"I'll not be staying long," Patrick said. Dermot, realizing that his father would probably stay until the dawn was breaking, smiled to himself in the darkness.

Patrick pushed open the door and both men stepped into the kitchen. The room was packed with seated men, radiating out in semicircles from the hearth. Several teapots were brewing in front of the fire and a large kettle was hanging on the crook. The quiet hum of scattered conversations filled the room. Patrick and Dermot waited at the entrance to the kitchen until a woman dressed in black came over and said, "You're welcome. It was good of you to come."

"I'm sorry for your troubles, mam," Patrick replied.

"Ah well, she had a happy death, Lord have mercy on her, and the priest with her not an hour before she died."

"She'll be missed. There wasn't an ounce of harm in Anne. A decent wee woman if ever I knew one." Patrick thought about the squabble he had had with her some ten years previous when she had accused him of throwing a sick hen into her fowlhouse and had threatened to go to the police. "Aye," he answered, "a decenter woman never lived than Anne. We were great friends."

"She often spoke of you," the woman, a niece of the deceased, replied.

Patrick squinted suspiciously at her and searched for a hidden meaning. He breathed easier when the woman added, "She was forever praising the O'Neills."

"Where is she, mam?" Patrick asked.

The woman motioned to a door that led off the kitchen. "Just go on through. It's the second room."

Patrick and Dermot pushed through the crowd in the kitchen, went on through the parlor and into the room where the corpse was laid out. The room was illuminated with a dozen flickering candles. Three of them, sitting on saucers, had been placed on a small bedside table. The bed itself had a candle on each post and the running wax had guttered down and collected in frozen splashes on top of the posts. A small kneeling rug had been laid on the floor, alongside the bed. Against the head wall was a low dressing cabinet covered with a white cloth, on which had been placed two more candles in golden candlesticks. Beside the cabinet three old women sat in chairs, their black shawls drawn up over their heads, their voices rising and falling as they recited the rosary.

The corpse lay on the bed. Several pillows had been propped under the head, leaving it slightly raised. The eyes were closed and two small pieces of cotton wool had been stuffed into the nostrils. A white shroud covered the body and came to the dead woman's neck. The arms were lying on top of the sheet, the hands folded and a rosary entwined in the fingers.

Patrick knelt down on the rug and whispered to his son, "She's shocking thin."

"Aye," Dermot answered. "She's been ailing since the harvest and she's badly failed."

Patrick took out his beads and started saying a decade for the repose of the dead woman's soul. Dermot lowered his head to his chest. He had forgotten his beads and said a decade from memory. When he finished he looked up at the corpse. He examined it carefully: the waxen sheen of the face, the sunken eyes, the ridge sharp nose and the thin bloodless lips. He kept expecting some sign of life from it. He had never before seen a face stay as still and he had an unreasonable urge to reach over and slap it. It must be alive, he thought. No one could stay still that long. For some reason he started to wonder how Neeve would look, laid out as a corpse. Then he imagined Bella laying on the bed although that was harder than Neeve. He couldn't picture Bella's mobile, continually changing face, set in the grim eternal lines of the face on the bed. Suddenly he felt ashamed of his thoughts and began the Hail Holy Queen.

Patrick looked over at his son and nodded. They both got to their feet, left the wake room and went into the parlor. Around a big table ten people were seated at their tea. Dermot noticed Bella at a side table with a basin full of dirty dishes and her rag going furiously. She looked over at him and crinkled up her nose and he wondered who was chasing her now and whether or not she was looking for a man at the wake.

In the kitchen, the general conversation had died and an old man was quietly relating a tale. ". . . that was a wake to sing songs about. The boys were out in the yard and they'd filled a big tub of water and dragged in a harrow from the fields and they were arguing whether they should place the tub or the harrow first, in front of the door. Some argued it'd be better for Jimmy to trip over the tub and fall into the harrow and others wanted him to trip over the harrow and fall into the tub. They could hear him inside, ranting away, and little Red McDonald opened the door . . ."

The niece of the deceased came over to them.

"She looks grand," Patrick said to her. "She's at peace now."

"Come on Patrick," the woman replied. "You too Dermot. There's room on a bench here at the back of the kitchen. When the next sitting goes in for tea you can move up closer to the fire."

"Now don't be bothering yourself about us. Sure we're not a bit cold," Patrick answered as he moved toward the back of the kitchen.

Dermot looked around and saw McGinnis talking quietly with several other men. He made his way over to the group and squatted down on his hunkers.

"Will you be staying long?" McGinnis asked.

"Depends on the crack," Dermot answered.

"I want to see you about a wee thing before you leave."

"Right."

The woman in black came over to Dermot and bending down, whispered to him, "Will you have a wee drop of something?"

Dermot looked up and shook his head. "Thank you mam, but no. I'm a Pioneer." Dermot felt a twinge of conscience as he remembered that he had broken his pledge the day of the ordnance raid. He still wore his Pioneer pin, however, as he dreaded the explanations he would have to give if he took it down.

Jimmy Hannafin sat close to the fire, smoking a pipe. Someone finished a story and a rattle of loud laughter came from the men. Hannafin looked over at Dermot and started. "Aye, but that was a town lad. I knew once of a country lad, a big lump of a cub, thirteen or so."

Dermot inwardly groaned. Here goes the old bastard with that goat story again, he thought. How was he to know then that a goat wasn't the same as a cow?

Hannafin continued, ". . . brought a goat home from the fair. It hadn't been long after kidding and needed to be milked. The old man says to the cub, 'Here take a bucket and go down and milk that goat I bought today.' Well the lad, and a smart enough lad he was," Hannafin looked over at Dermot and gave a dry laugh, "the lad starts off for the byre. He's gone a brave few minutes and then comes flying back in a terrible way and says to the father, 'I had the wildest time. Where's the other two teats?'"

A quick flurry of laughs followed the story and in spite of himself, Dermot smiled. He looked over at Hannafin and silently mouthed the words, "Screw you!"

The woman in black passed around a plate full of cigarettes and a small box of loose tobacco. The men helped themselves to the cigarettes and tobacco and the talk continued.

"At the price of these, it doesn't pay to hand them around," a man remarked, inviting comment.

"Aye, they say that a war always brings good times but I have my doubts," Patrick answered from the back. "I mind years ago when an ounce of tobacco cost twopence and a dozen eggs sold for sixpence. Mind you there was a happy balance— three ounces of tobacco for a dozen eggs. Now eggs are two shillings a dozen and tobacco three shillings an ounce. What kind of government is that?"

"There's a man who buys his tobacco from the egg money. I wish my woman was that soft!" someone commented.

Patrick defended himself. "She buys an ounce a week from the egg money. The rest I buy myself."

Several derisive laughs greeted the remark and Patrick lapsed into silence.

A young girl came into the kitchen and asked different men to go into the parlor for tea. Patrick left with the group but Dermot had not been asked. Being younger, he had to wait until the older men had all been served.

The outside door opened and several girls, including Neeve, came in. Dermot gave her a barely perceptible wink and she smiled back at him before going into the wake room.

Presently Dermot and Don McGinnis were asked to go in and have tea. They left the kitchen and went into the parlor. Bella had been relieved of her dishwashing and was now in the other bedroom where all the women were gathered. In the parlor, ten places were set and in the center of the table were three plates piled high with different kinds of bread. Two more plates contained cold sliced ham and on another plate were thin slices of cake.

As they sat down to their places, Neeve began pouring the tea. She started with McGinnis and some of the tea spilled over the lip of his cup and into the saucer.

"She's terrible nervous tonight," McGinnis remarked drily.

"Aye, I'm that nervous I might send it down the back of your neck," Neeve replied.

"You'd better save it for your man. It's him that needs cooling off, or is it heating up?"

Neeve blushed and Dermot stared at the wall, hoping that the raillery would pass. As Neeve was pouring for another youth, he sconced, "She'll be all right once she gets that wee tremble out of her hand. Now if she had someone like Dermot to hold that hand."

"That hand could warm your ear, young man," Neeve answered sharply as she moved on to Dermot. Everyone looked over at her and offered advice:

"Lean your arm on his shoulder. It'll help steady you."

"Don't look in his eyes. That's what's giving you the trembles."

"A darling couple."

Dermot glared fiercely around at his companions and the men fell silent and began to eat, while Neeve and another girl waited on them, bringing more bread and tea as required.

After the tea, a youth lit a cigarette and remarked philosophically, "I'd rather get a woman at a wake than at a dance or anywhere else. There's something about a wake that makes a woman easier to handle. I've seen women I couldn't get my arm around, normal times, and coming home from a wake there'd be no end to the courting with them."

"It's the sight of the corpse that does it," another volunteered. "They look at the corpse and think that in a few years they'll be the same and why not kifuffle around a bit while they have time?"

"By chance a woman will sometimes go home from a dance on her lone but she'll never go home alone from a wake," Mc-Ginnis remarked.

Having completed their theorizing about women and wakes, the men moved into the kitchen to make room for another serving. Dermot noticed that his brother had arrived and he wondered if Ned would get tight before the night was over. In the kitchen another story was in progress, one that Dermot had not previously heard. He sat down and listened as an old man unfolded his tale, punctuating it with long juicy spits into the fire and employing emphatic nods of his head for exclamation marks. ". . . and they were both stocious. They finally got old Mickey to bed but the son dug up a bottle of poteen and the boys helped him drink it. They danced around in the kitchen a while and finally, with all the drink, the son passed out. The boys thought to bring him out to the asses' shed and put him to sleep there for the surprise he'd get the next morning and for the crack they'd have of telling how he went to sleep with the donkey. Some of the sober ones decided it wouldn't be safe— the ass might take a notion to kick his brains out and the one kick would have done it—so instead they put him to sleep in the asses' shed and locked the ass in the kitchen."

The old man stopped, lifted the tongs and reached into the fire for a live coal. He relit the pipe and continued, "Old Mickey gets up in the wee hours of the morning for a drink. You know the wild druth whiskey will put on a man, and he wanders out to the kitchen. It's black dark and he stumbles over the ass as he's walking across the floor. Thinking it the son, he draws back his foot, kicks the ass and roars at him, 'You drunken old sot! Have you no shame, going to sleep there on the floor!' The ass isn't used to having his rest disturbed so he lashes out and kicks back. Mickey goes hopping around the kitchen, holding his leg and moaning about the bad beast of a son he had. He comes over again and delivers a good hearty kick with the leg that isn't hurting. The ass kicks back again and this time Mickey goes down. He crawls over to the wall, starts to sniffle and moans, 'Ah dear God, but that's the bad brute I've raised that would kick his own father!' "

The kitchen exploded into laughter, the somberness of the occasion forgotten in the humor of the story and the warm feeling that the drinks had given the men. The old man smiled delightedly at the response. Puffing contentedly on his relit pipe, he leaned back on the stool and benignly surveyed his neighbors.

The hours of the long evening passed. Now and then someone came in and a draft of cold air swept into the kitchen and drove away the men's drowsiness. The fire was kept raging on the hearth and the bottles, both porter and whiskey, circulated freely.

And now the sconcing had started in earnest. Sconcing was a method of telling a story about someone who was present but telling it in such a way that the audience was left guessing as to whom it might be. A good sconcer was very subtle. A hint of a physical characteristic, a slight reference to an incident in the past, a personal idiosyncrasy, and the listeners pieced together the clues and made the identity. Sometimes sconcing dug too deep, was remembered, and weeks later erupted in a savage brawl at a public house. But a wake house was sacrosanct and for that reason sconcing was always more needling and satirical at a wake than at any other function. Sconcing was traditionally confined to the older men and served as an effective method of social criticism as well as a means of conserving the established cultural patterns. Generally, all males were considered lads until they married or reached the age of forty, both events usually occurring within a year or two of each other.

Dermot listened with interest as Hannafin started out on a sconce. "He was a rouser, no doubt about that," Hannafin said. "A good man, full of thunder and lightning. It was his first dance and he stood at the back of the hall like a proper young buck, casually looking over the lassies. The music would set the heels of a corpse to dancing." The words were no sooner out than Hannafin glanced in the direction of the wake room, smiled weakly, and continued, "Well anyway, it was grand music. Our warrior has a shine on his shoes that'd do a minister credit. There's an edge to his pants that'd cut short barley and the waves in his curly hair would make a sailor seasick."

Dermot looked around at the young men still in the kitchen. There were only two with curly hair and one of them had a bored look on his face and was elaborately feigning disinterest. Hannafin continued, "While our boyo is standing there, a lassie he knows well comes along and asks, 'Is there anything here that tickles your fancy?' Our hero looks carefully around the hall at the different girls and tells her, like he's been going to dances all his life, 'There's one sitting over there in a blue dress.' The lassie goes over to the girl, whispers something and

comes back to our man and tells him, 'It's all set. You're to
take her out for the next dance.' Our fella takes her out for
the dance and mind he's not the best dancer in the world but
he gives a few whirls and twirls and when the dance is over,
back he goes to the foot of the hall. Some of the boys start pulling his leg about getting a woman and he remarks that he's got
the one in the blue dress all lined up. He's really feeling himself a dandy and when the boys scoff at him, he takes the girl
in the blue dress out for another dance and asks to leave her
home. The lassie says yes and our hero starts walking around
the hall, feeling his oats and thinking what a hell of a man he
is with the women. As the evening wears on he gets to thinking
about taking her home and this starts to trouble him a wee bit.
He's never been out with a girl before. The more he thinks
about it the more of a stew he gets into. He considers leaving
the dance and going on home and letting the girl fend for herself. He'd have done it too, only for fear the rest of the crowd
would find out. Squaring a woman and then running off isn't
the best way to start going with women, he realizes. He's really got the wind up though. He doesn't know how to talk to
the girl or what to do with her. Finally he decides to confide in
Big Peter McGuckin. He goes to Big Peter in a corner of the
hall and says to him, 'Peter, I've got a wee problem.' Peter cods
him along by answering, 'Sure a man like you should have no
problems at all.' 'Wait till I tell you Peter. You know the
young Murphy girl, Teesie?' 'A right looking girl,' Peter answers. 'I'm leaving her home from the dance,' our man tells
Peter. 'Good for you,' says Big Peter. Our lad says to Peter,
'The matter is that, er, I know all about the women of course,
but this one's a wee bit different. How do you think I should
handle her?' Big Peter's beginning to tape on and he plays
canny by saying, 'Just stick to your usual old style.' 'The usual
style,' our boyo mutters to himself. That leaves him as far forward as ever. He stutters around a wee bit and then asks, 'Yes,
but what should I do?' Big Peter puts an innocent look on his

face and says, 'Do? Why leave her home of course.' Our man's desperate by this time and he grabs Peter by the arm and says, 'Peter I'm in a fierce way. I've never been out with a girl before. WHAT DO I DO?' Well Big Peter took into the laughing and he told it all over the country and from that day to this our warrior never asks to leave a girl home from a dance but she's bound to ask back, 'You're sure you know what to do?' "

The men in the kitchen started laughing. A young man with black curly hair got off his stool and went over to the dresser. He took down a mug and dipped it into a pail of well water. The others watched him closely. He drank the water slowly and walked out of the kitchen.

"You've sconced him home, Jimmy," one of the men remarked.

"Damn the that," Hannafin answered. "He'll be back as soon as he cools off."

To sconce a man home was the ultimate victory and an outcome that Hannafin never wanted. He knew that the young fellow would rage around in the yard for a few minutes and then come back.

Another hour passed in tales and sconces and quiet conversation. Presently Don McGinnis came into the kitchen from the wake room and came over to Dermot. Speaking quietly, he told him, "There's a meeting this Friday. It's an important one —so don't miss it. McAleer's barn."

"Right," Dermot answered.

"You should go into the wake room," McGinnis continued. "There's rare sport in there. Your brother has a good jag on."

"What are they doing?"

"Go in and see."

"I hope he's not making an idiot of himself."

"No, nothing like that. Go on in and see, I tell you," McGinnis insisted.

Dermot got off his chair and walked into the parlor. The table had been cleared. Everyone who had come to the wake had been given tea at least once and Neeve, another young girl and an older woman were redding up the place. Dermot called to Neeve, "Going home soon?"

The older woman pushed Neeve and said, "Go on home wee dear. You must be dead. We'll finish up here."

"I'm not a bit tired," Neeve protested strenuously. "I'll stay until the dishes are done." She pushed back a stray wisp of hair that had fallen down over her forehead and smiled at Dermot, "Go on," she told him. "I'll let you know when I'm ready to go home."

Dermot walked into the wake room and stopped, astonished at the scene. Four men were gathered around the corpse, two of them sitting on the bed and two sitting on chairs that were drawn up alongside. Old Anne was sitting up in the bed. The rosary had been taken out of her hands and her arms were stretched out straight on the white sheet. A man was dealing out five hands of poker, one each for the four players and one for the corpse. Dermot watched for several seconds and asked, "What in the name of God are you doing?"

The dealer, a middle-aged man with a beefy moon face, looked over at Dermot and replied, "We're having a wee game."

Dermot noticed a nearly empty bottle of whiskey sitting on the floor and two mugs on the bed. "Where did you find the whiskey?" he asked his brother.

Ned looked up with a drunken canniness at Dermot. "Get out, you lemonade drinking pissant."

Dermot laughed. One of the men pointed to a small dresser against the opposite wall. A drawer had been pulled open and lying inside were two bottles of whisky. Apparently three bottles had been set aside for the following night's wake.

"Doesn't she know?" Dermot asked and nodded his head in the direction of the parlor. Ned studied his cards with great deliberation. "I'll open," he said and threw three cards into the middle. He pushed out a penny and replied to his brother, "She was in and said we were a disgrace and that she was going to tell the parish priest tomorrow."

"If I know Father Sheehy, he'd take a hand himself," the dealer said.

"Aye, him and old Anne would make a great pair. Trouble is that you wouldn't know which one's dead and which one's alive," a young fellow remarked. He threw his hand in and picked up Anne's. "Anne bumps it a penny," he remarked jovially as he threw twopence into the pot. "Don't we Anne?" he asked, patting her hand. There was a small pile of pennies and a shilling piece laying between Anne's hands on the bed.

"Do you play her hand all the time, Jim?" Dermot asked.

"Whoever doesn't stay, takes care of Anne." He looked over at the dealer and said emphatically, "Anne needs one card."

"Oh, she's a terror," the dealer complained as he threw a card over. "The luck she has!" He pointed to her and declared, "Look at the wee smile of that face. That's the face of a saint."

Ned shivered. "Damn the saint. Who ever heard of a saint playing poker."

"Check," the dealer said.

"Check," Ned echoed.

The third man threw in his hand and Jim, who was playing Anne's hand, placed two pennies in the pot. "Anne bets tuppence," he said slyly.

The dealer groaned and threw in his cards. Ned studied a pair of kings and complained, "If I see her—she has them. If I don't—she's bluffing. She started out with sixpence I lent her and she's paid that back and now I'm losing ninepence." He peered over at Jim and warned, "It wouldn't be right to play tricks on the dead."

Jim looked again at his hand and smiled enigmatically. Ned suddenly made up his mind and threw twopence in the pot. Jim turned over Anne's hand, revealing a pair of queens and a pair of sixes.

"Take it," Ned said disgustedly.

The young fellow gathered in the pot and placed it on top of Anne's pile. "She'll soon have enough to pay for her own offerings," he remarked.

The fourth player, a dark saturnine man, lowered his head to his chest and lugubriously intoned, "The . . . dead . . . shall . . . arise . . . again. There . . . shall . . . be . . . weeping . . . and . . . gnashing . . . of . . . teeth."

"For God's sake stop saying that," the dealer complained irritably. He looked at Dermot and added, "He's been at this dead rising again all night."

The man raised his chin and challenged, "You're fusty!"

"Who's fusty?" the dealer asked.

"You're fusty. You and Anne are both fusty." His head sank to his chin again.

The dealer gave him a disgusted look and picked up his mug. Shoving it in front of Ned, he said, "Here, pour me another snort."

Ned lifted the bottle and made several grand gestures and impressively made the whiskey splash, making sure however that little of the liquid actually went into the mug.

"Don't drown us all," the man said sarcastically.

Ned, fearing the man would ask for more, lifted the bottle and said to the corpse, "Will you have a wee drop, Anne?" He shook his head mournfully, "She won't touch it. Another damn Pioneer like my brother here."

Jim picked up the thin, blue-veined hand and replied, "No, she's no Pioneer. A good scout Anne is. A darling woman." He dropped the stiff hand and continued, "You see she doesn't want to have a hangover." He leaned over confidentially to the others and whispered, "She has to go to a funeral soon!" He burst out laughing and the others followed suit. In spite of himself, Dermot smiled.

"No, she won't join our celebration because I know Anne,"

Ned said. He lowered his head and leaned over the bed, following Jim's example with the previous remark. The dealer and Jim also leaned forward in conspiratorial attitudes. "She won't, because she's a very stiff woman!" Ned finished. The others broke out laughing and Ned sat back, feeling pleased with himself.

The dark man lowered his head again and solemnly said, "The . . . dead . . . shall . . . arise . . ."

The dealer interrupted him by appealing to the others, "For God's sake, won't he ever shut up about the dead arising?"

The dark man curled one lip back and sneered, "Fusty!"

The dealer picked up his mug to hit his tormentor with and then noticed there were still a few drops of whiskey in it. He drained the mug and leaned over the bed and held it menacingly over the man's head. "Say I'm fusty again and I'll cleave your head open!"

The dark man ignored him and mumbled, "weeping . . . and . . . gnashing . . ."

Jim pulled the dealer's arm back. "Listen, let's get back to the game. Anne will never make enough for her coffin at this rate."

Ned picked up the cards and started dealing. Dermot heard a light step behind him and felt a pair of arms encircle his waist. Neeve stood on tiptoes and leaned her head over his shoulder. "Aren't they a terror?" she asked.

Dermot appealed to the men, "Listen, why don't you pack it up and all go home?"

"Do you think I'm batty?" the dealer protested. "After playing cards half the night with a corpse, I'll not set foot on the road till the sun's up a good hour. I want no wee men following me home."

"Fusty!" came the challenge from the dark man.

Dermot turned to Neeve. She was wearing her overcoat but

had not yet buttoned it. He started to button the coat for her. "Penny for them," he said.

She pursed her lips and blew softly in his face. "It's time to go home," she replied.

THIRTEEN

The priest and altar boys came out in a file from the sacristy and the congregation stood up.

"Introibo ad altare Dei," the priest intoned, his head bowed.

"Ad Deum qui laetificat juventutem meam," the altar boys responded.

In the gallery the girl's choir stood up and their high angelic voices spread, mantling the congregation with the Kyrie Eleison. A few latecomers took advantage of the hymn to slide quietly in and join the regulars who always stood at the back of the church.

Patrick and Dermot were seated in one of the back pews. Patrick was wondering if two bushels of grass seed would be enough to sow the well field. He decided that it would and began to calculate how much potato manure he would need for the eight-acre field.

Dermot was mechanically saying the rosary while his eyes searched the ladies' side for Neeve. Finally he located the furry white beret she usually wore to Mass. He settled down to a steady stretch of the favorite Sunday pastime of the younger men—girl friend watching.

On the woman's side, Dermot's mother was also saying her rosary. Kathleen took a mathematical attitude toward the Mass. She had long ago established that one could, during a Sunday Mass, say ten decades of the rosary. She kept a mental running account of her debit and credit balances with the Savior. If her attention wandered during Mass and she only managed nine decades, she carried the other one until the next Mass and tried to say a total of eleven. She had even established a numerical scale for the different religious functions: ten decades for a Sunday Mass, five for a weekday Mass, five for evening devotions and twelve for a Holy Hour. Sometimes she had as many as five or six decades to her credit and when this happened she felt very pious, indeed felt that somehow the Savior was a little bit indebted to her. This is not to say that Kathleen wasn't religious. She liked to know exactly what her obligations were and to adhere to them rigidly. She was, on this particular Sunday, two decades behind and therefore her hands steadily worked the beads.

Up front, Neeve dallied with her rosary. She made a determined effort, said five or six Hail Marys and then her eyes wandered and she noticed an altar boy with a hole in the sole of one shoe. That made her think of Hannafin and the night of Anne Reedy's wake which in turn made her think of Dermot and marriage. She made a mental effort and said the rest of the Hail Marys in the decade. In the middle of the next decade she noticed that one of the Loughran girls had a new coat. For a few minutes she gave herself over to the problem of the coat before again recalling her mind to her prayers.

Hannafin sat halfway down the church, his missal accidentally open at the Litany of the Saints. His eyes ran down the list of names. Seeing St. Dominic brought to his mind the Dominican priest in Drumcar. He smiled, thinking of the way the priest used to sing the names of the saints in an ordinary monotone: "Sancte Antoni" and the choir would answer, "Ora pro nobis"; again in an ordinary tone, "Sancte Benedicte" and again the choir's normal response, "Ora pro nobis"; but when the priest reached Saint Dominic, the founder of the order, his voice thundered out—"SANCTE DOMINICE" and the choir, taking its cue, came back loud and strong with the "ORA PRO NOBIS." Having startled the congregation and rendered homage to his patron, the priest would return with a quiet "Sancte Francisce." Hannafin wondered if a Franciscan, with his vow of humility, would single out his patron's name for special attention. Or the Jesuits—how would they sing Saint Ignatius? His mind started probing the composition of the Litany. Who determined the listing of the saints? Was the Litany the same in all countries? What happened when a change was made in the Litany? Was it handed to a special group in the Vatican, perhaps a committee for the composition of the Litany? Did the cardinals have discretion to add or drop saints for their particular dioceses? Why were there no Irish saints in the Litany?

Father Sheehy came down to the foot of the altar, the congregation stood up and the priest read the Gospel. After the Gospel everyone contentedly settled back into their seats.

Father Sheehy folded his arms, looked at the back of the chapel, frowned and testily remarked, "There are plenty of seats at the front here. We have some Catholics whose idea of attending Mass is to gather with their neighbors for a wee chat at the back of the church."

A group of men sheepishly made their way up the center aisle and shuffled into the empty seats at the head of the chapel. Father Sheehy glared at them and they in turn wondered what had gotten into the parish priest. The priest cleared his throat and announced, "Before the sermon there is a letter from the archbishop."

He read the letter referring to the activities of the I.R.A. and the attitude of the Church that such activities were incompatible with the obligations of Catholics. The letter came as no surprise to the older people of the parish. They remembered that during the troubles a similar letter had been read in the Catholic churches.

Patrick O'Neill was indignant and wondered what the Church was coming to. His wife, Kathleen, heard the letter with a vast sense of relief and viewed it as the clinching argument to get Dermot away from the I.R.A.

Hannafin murmured *"Roma locuta est"* and thought that at the least sign of trouble, old mother Church was sure to tuck up her vestments and head for the nearest dogma.

Neeve Donnelly thought that the letter would mean the end of the I.R.A. in Duncrana and for that she was grateful.

Dermot cautiously began to examine some of the letter's phrases: ". . . mortal sin to . . . remain a member of the organization." That meant that he could not go to confession and stay in the I.R.A. If he confessed to being in the I.R.A. and of having no intention of leaving it, the priest would have to refuse absolution. And what was that business about a civil war? They weren't fighting the Orangemen or the Protestants. They were fighting against the British Army that occupied the North. He wondered how the I.R.A. would take the letter and if it would make any difference in their plans.

The congregation waited for Father Sheehy to elaborate on the letter but to everyone's surprise he made no further mention of it and his sermon concerned the means of attaining grace through prayer.

Mass ended and the people streamed out of the church. The young men gathered on the road outside and watched the parishioners coming out. Dermot circulated from one group to another and found that no one was taking the letter very seriously. He got hold of Sean Reilly and together they walked up the town.

"What do you make of the letter from the bishop?" Dermot asked.

"I don't know what to think," Sean confessed. "I do know it won't make any difference to us."

"It means that we can't go to confession any more. The priests will refuse absolution."

"I don't care what the priests say. It takes more than patriotism to put a body in hell. Anyway the letter has no effect on our policies. We're still the I.R.A. and we still have to free Ireland. You can go to confession when our work's all finished."

"In the meantime," Dermot protested, "I stand in danger of losing my immortal soul."

Sean laughed, "You're the rare turn. You're always in danger of losing your immortal soul but you don't always have the opportunity of serving Ireland."

"I don't mind serving Ireland but I don't know if I want to go to hell for her."

"Listen, the true Irishman should be able to give up his life and his soul for the cause."

Dermot could find no argument to answer this. The two men parted at the head of the town and Dermot cycled home.

The following Thursday night Dermot went to Corr's barn where the company had assembled. McGinnis called for attention and began to address the men. "Brigade has planned another raid and this time they've asked for three men from Duncrana. Two of these men have already been picked. I know that all of you would like to be the third member but this man will be chosen for his attendance at meetings and the quality of his work in the company." McGinnis hesitated a moment while he looked over the men. "If this forthcoming raid is a success," he continued, "Brigade has promised to let us carry out raids on our own, subject to their approval. They believe that with three men already tested in raids, we'll have enough experience to carry out our own operations."

A buzz of excitement whipsawed through the barn as the men started whispering to each other. Dermot walked over to Sean and said in a low voice, "We're going on another raid?"

Sean nodded. The rest of the men were covertly watching Sean and Dermot. It was common knowledge that they had taken part in the ordnance raid.

McGinnis called for attention and the men again fell silent. "There'll be a lecture by the intelligence officer on recognition of British Army regimental insignia," he told them.

Donagh Quinn, the intelligence officer, was a young boy still in his teens. He had a triangular face and a broad high forehead that narrowed down to a sharp pointed chin. He was still a student at the Christian Brothers School in Rathgiven and took his intelligence job seriously. He felt a burning sense of shame for the wrongs his country had suffered and he wrote dark and solemn poems about the villainy of Britain and the intransigence of Ireland's allies. In ten years he would achieve the destiny of his country's idealists: he would either be a dead hero or a mildly cynical clerk, filling a comfortable position in Britain's Civil Service.

He pointed to the chart on the wall and began to explain the significance of the different insignia seen on trucks and tanks. When the lecture was over and all the questions answered, McGinnis dismissed the company. As the men were leaving the barn he called to Reilly and Dermot to stay behind.

"Brigade has asked for you again," he told them. "You'll be contacted at the football match next Sunday in Applebridge. I don't know yet who the other man will be—probably Corrigan."

Dermot felt pleased at the possibility of Corrigan going. He knew Corrigan's worth whereas the others were question marks. Dermot remembered the bishop's letter and asked, "What do you think of the letter that was read Sunday?"

McGinnis frowned before answering. "It makes no difference. The Church can't tell us what to do. Anyway, they're only playing politics."

"Yes but what does it mean?" Dermot objected. "Does it mean that we can't get absolution any more? When I joined the I.R.A. I didn't think it would mean giving up my religion."

McGinnis looked hard at Dermot. A tic began jumping on his left cheek and he crossed his legs and leaned against the barn wall. "No one's asking you to give up your religion," he answered, his lips thin and tight against his teeth. "We're not sure what the priests will do. They may not refuse absolution. Anyway, you can give up your religion for a while, but you can't give up the I.R.A."

"What do you mean?" Dermot asked sharply.

"Exactly what I said," McGinnis answered angrily. "You can't resign from the I.R.A. This isn't the Boy Scouts. We can't have somebody sliding around who knows all about us. We'd have to make sure he wouldn't tell anything."

Dermot stared at McGinnis and then walked over close to him and quietly asked, "Are you threatening me by any chance? Because if you are, I don't take threats from anybody. The I.R.A. or the king of England or the Pope himself doesn't threaten an O'Neill."

McGinnis' voice took on a conciliatory tone, "No one's threatening you. I was trying to explain the position of the I.R.A."

Sean broke in quickly, "Aw for God's sake calm down. What's coming over you, Dermot? You're arguing with everybody." He threw an arm over Dermot's shoulder. "This isn't the time to get contrary, just when the excitement's starting. We've got more thermometers to break."

The tension eased and Dermot slapped McGinnis on the

arm and said, "Nothing meant, Don. I'm a wee bit quick tempered sometimes."

"You're a soldier in an army and you have to take orders," McGinnis curtly answered. "No one's threatening you."

The three men left the barn but in spite of the amiable settlement of the dispute a certain coldness developed between McGinnis and Dermot. As they walked into the town, McGinnis addressed all his remarks to Sean. A growing anger had come upon him and he saw himself losing control of the company and his work negated by the Church and Dermot's insubordination. And the fact that Brigade had again refused to let him take part in the coming raid had added fuel to his feelings. When Brigade finally gave permission for company-size raids he would make sure that he would lead as well as plan the operations.

They said good night to McGinnis at his door and Sean and Dermot walked over to Hannafin's. Sean went on into the kitchen and Dermot stopped for a moment to talk to Jimmy. Hannafin looked up from his last and said, "Well, if it isn't the hard O'Neill."

"How's the form, Jimmy?" Dermot asked.

Dermot watched as Hannafin skillfully filed around the edges of a new sole he had just nailed on a shoe. He took out a box of matches, lit a small candle that was beside him and replied, "First, I'm alive and there are billions dead; second, I'm healthy and there are millions not and third, I've eaten and there are thousands hungry."

"God Jimmy," Dermot laughingly complained, "you never give a straight answer to anything."

"That's because there never are straight answers to questions," Hannafin answered. He withdrew the hot iron from the flame of the candle and applied it to a stick of black wax. Drops of the wax fell on the heel of the shoe and Hannafin pressed the iron over the heel, smoothing the wax into the tiny holes and crevices.

"What do you think of the letter that was read off the altar last Sunday?" Dermot asked.

Hannafin looked up shrewdly at Dermot. "Is that letter giving you trouble?"

"No, not at all," Dermot quickly denied. "I'm curious what you think of it."

Hannafin blew out the candle and set aside the iron. "Dermot, the Church is also a political institution," he said. "In order to survive it must play politics. And survival is of great importance to the Church. To minister to souls it is necessary to be active and strong. Therefore the Church's first concern is political power; the acquiring of more power to enable it to administer more effectively to the faithful; the consolidation of power to keep its present effectiveness and to fight against any loss of power because it would weaken its ability to preach the word of God and to save souls. Do you understand that?"

"I understand the words but I don't know what you're getting at."

"Simply that the activities of the I.R.A. may cause the Northern government to restrict the freedom of the Catholic Church. Therefore the Church has decided to officially disassociate itself from the I.R.A. We make the mistake of thinking that the Church is concerned with the political independence of Catholics. Political freedom or national independence is sought by people because they believe it's a more just political arrangement and more conducive to individual happiness. But the Church is not particularly worried by political justice or happiness. This world is strife, a vale of tears, and true justice and happiness are to be found only in the next world: 'Seek first the Kingdom of God.' The Church is concerned with political systems because of their relation to the Church's power. If necessary it will accommodate itself to a dictatorship as it is doing today in several countries."

"Ah now listen, Jimmy. You can't say that the Church didn't support the rising in 1916."

"They didn't, as a matter of fact. When the rebellion first broke out the Church was against it because they thought it was a lost cause. And it appeared to be in the beginning. It was only in 1918 and 1919 that the Church officially began to lend its support to the I.R.A. and it was obvious then that the I.R.A. had a good chance of freeing Ireland. What would have happened if the Church had remained antagonistic to the independence movement? Simply that when Ireland became free the Church would have found itself in the position of having little political influence. In 1916 the chances of a successful rebellion appeared to be hopeless and the Church was against the rising. Then for a few years the issue was in doubt and the Church did not lend its support to one side or the other. When it became clear that the independence movement was liable to succeed, the Church switched sides. I'm talking about the Catholic Church as a whole. There were individual priests who were in favor of the I.R.A. from the very beginning. But the official attitude of the hierarchy went through these three stages."

"Then the reason for the bishop's letter is that the Church is afraid of being associated with the I.R.A. because they think it will fail?" Dermot asked.

"That's the main reason. As it happens the Church also has strong moral reasons to condemn the I.R.A. Reasons which I personally believe in."

"But the Church has always been for Irish freedom. Throughout our whole history it has always supported independence," Dermot protested.

"Not always. In 1800 the Catholic bishops supported the Act of Union which abolished the Irish Parliament and left Ireland completely dominated by England. When they did support independence for Ireland it was because it also meant greater freedom for the Church. I wonder what would have happened during the rebellion if England had been a Catholic country instead of a Protestant one. I'm willing to wager a pretty penny that the Catholic Church would have remained strongly against the independence movement for fear of losing political influence in England. As it happened, Catholicism is practically nonexistent there, and the Church could lose little by supporting Irish claims.

"You're twisting everything around."

"I'm not. To the Catholic Church freedom simply means freedom to practice the Catholic religion. If the Church could do so with impunity, it would close every Protestant church in the world tomorrow. If it had the temporal power it would be under a moral obligation to do so because the Protestant Church is heretical. As for freedom to vote, freedom from arrest without warrant and freedom of the press— these things don't concern the Church. Do you think the Catholic Church cares about freedom to vote in Spain? On the contrary, the Church is quite happy with Franco and will do everything it can to prevent elections being held in Spain in case that Franco is booted out and the Church lose some of its power. Again I have to remind you that the Church is power-conscious because the more power it has the better able it is to go about its business of saving souls—and saving souls is the end for which the Catholic Church exists."

"What an answer I get to a simple question," Dermot complained.

"I suppose it does sound confusing. You asked me what I thought of the letter?"

Dermot nodded.

"I'm afraid that I think the Church is right. Although mind you I'm against partition. I'm against it because it deprives Ireland of its richest one-sixth. But if we're ever going to solve the problem it'll be with the help of the Protestants and not by antagonizing them. The trouble is that we Irish, we Irish Catholics, are an emotional breed and we think too much of our past glories and heroes. We've got to forget a thousand years of Fenian memories. We've got to kill and bury our

Fenian dead. We've become ridiculous in the eyes of the world. We've kicked the pedestal out from under ourselves. We're the laughingstock of the universe. Sitting around our hearth fires, serving up a comic-opera revolution every twenty years. Why aren't we like Denmark, or Switzerland, or New Zealand? All small countries but all prosperous. We'd rather daydream about our glorious past than get our bottoms off the dungheap of the present. We'd rather blame our laziness and shortcomings on the Battle of the Boyne and Cromwell, weep about the Treaty of Limerick and the Black and Tans, than make an honest effort to look ourselves in the face. I'm not an old man, nor a wise one, but as far as I'm concerned the whole of bloody Ireland isn't worth the life of one sick, scrawny Orangeman."

"If I didn't know you better, I'd think you were serious."

"I am serious. I don't want to see any Orangemen killed. I think they can be the salvation of Ireland. We need them. If anyone is going to make Ireland prosperous, it's the hard-headed businessmen of the North. The Free State government has done a damn poor job of making Ireland a fit place to live in. The Protestants are a more practical people and they can teach us many things about how to make the country richer and stronger. We need their practicality to balance the emotionalism in our national character. We need them also as a bulwark against the power of the Catholic Church. I have to warn you that the Church is not a democratic institution and I believe in democracy."

"Jimmy, I don't know whether you're a bad Catholic or a bad Irishman."

Hannafin put the other boot down on the floor and brushed off his apron. "And you. Which are you going to be?" he asked Dermot.

Dermot frowned. "I'm both. A good Catholic and a good patriot."

"To be a good Catholic you'll have to drop out of your organization. To be a good patriot, you'll have to defy the Church," Hannafin challenged.

"You're fishing, Jimmy. You don't know whether or not I'm in the I.R.A."

"Perhaps I am. But I'm willing to wager that I can name every man in Duncrana who's in it.

"Go on," Dermot scoffed. "You're sitting all day there on your wee stool dreaming fairy tales."

Hannafin slid a boot over the last and looked up. "You want me to name them? Not only that but the sergeant knows too."

"Why doesn't he do something then?"

"He's hoping he won't have to. He doesn't want to see any young fellow in jail for several years."

"He's awful soft then," Dermot said.

"No. The sergeant's trouble is that he's a decent man and there's little thanks for being that."

"I'm going home, Jimmy. I can't listen any more to your blathering," Dermot said. He opened the door and walked out into the street.

FOURTEEN

Dermot, Sean and Corrigan were escorted into the cattle shed by one of the Brigade men. Most of the men had already gathered and in the dull glow that came from a lantern hung on the hay rack, Dermot recognized his companions from the ordnance raid. He also noted a supply of arms neatly laid out on empty feed bags: Bren guns, rifles and a box of grenades.

A youth approached and Sean said to him, "The hard Terence! Is everything ready for the grand military ball to-night?"

"So far. The two withdrawal detachments are ready. Your man Corrigan is with one of them, isn't he?"

"That's right," Corrigan answered. "I'm with the detachment that covers the Enniskillen end of the county road."

"Good. Johnny over there will give you a Lee-Enfield and some ammo. He's in charge of your detachment."

Corrigan left the group and went over to the man that Terence had indicated.

For a moment Dermot felt lonely as he watched Corrigan walking away. Then he turned to Terence, "What time will the withdrawal detachments go out?"

"In about fifteen minutes," Terence answered. "We'll leave in about an hour. Laverty's gone already and at midnight he'll cut the phone wire. We should be getting over the wall by then."

"What kind of arms are we taking?"

"Bren guns and two grenades apiece for the assault group," Terence answered.

Several others arrived and low greetings were exchanged. Someone came over to Dermot and Sean and handed each a burnt cork. They began to rub the cork over their faces. Dermot remembered the last time he had rubbed cork on his face, a Halloween night some eight years previous, when a group of young lads had stolen a fowl buyer's cart, taken it apart and left the body in the churchyard and the wheels on top of the creamery roof. He smiled when he realized that he felt no different than he did when he was twelve years old. There was the same air of hysterical determination, the same delicious feeling of impending danger and the same comradeship. He lit a match and held it under his cork. He let the cork cool and then rubbed it briskly over his hands.

"Am I well covered?" Sean asked.

Dermot took his cork and gave a few strokes to the side of Sean's nose. He grinned at him. "I'd hate to meet you anywhere tonight. You're a holy show."

"I'll be a holy show to those tender British lads when they see me," Sean answered. "They'll think the Old Boy's come for them."

One of the withdrawal detachments started to leave and

Dermot whispered good luck to Corrigan as the three men filed out of the shed. He said to Sean, "A good man, Corrigan."

"A corker, not a drop of fear in him," Sean agreed.

Presently the Brigade O.C. arrived with another four men. In the soft, indistinct light of the lantern he appeared younger than the last time Dermot had seen him. The O.C. greeted a few men and then called for silence. "Right now, men, let's have your attention here. I'll briefly run over the plans again. The two withdrawal detachments have gone out to their posts on the Applebridge road, one detachment on each side of the barracks. Ten of us will go over the wall. The demolition squad will put the power plant out of order and then go to the arsenal and lay explosives for blowing it up. The assault group will take up positions opposite the guardhouse. As soon as the lights go out this group will open fire, pinning down the guard and preventing them from coming into contact with the demolition group. Tim, who is in charge of the assault group, will give the word to retire and his men will go out the main gate. To the right of the main gate, about fifty yards up the road, there'll be a black Vauxhall to evacuate the assault group. I'm in charge of the demolition group and we'll go back out over the wall at the same spot we came in. I want to remind you that tonight we're carrying out an offensive action. We're not worried about getting arms. We want to prove that the I.R.A. is able to attack a British army barracks, inflict casualties and cause a certain amount of damage. We have to prove that we're an army, not a bunch of sneak thieves as the Orange press has called us." The leader gave a slight cough and called, "Coughlin?"

"Aye?" a middle-aged man answered.

"As soon as you put the lighting system out of order you'll go to the wall where the rope ladder is and wait for the rest of my group. You're to hold your ground at all costs. If you can—take cover, but don't leave the rope ladder till we arrive."

"Right," Coughlin answered.

"Tim, hand you out the weapons and ammo," the leader continued. "Remember to keep the safety catches on your firearms till we're over the wall. I want no accidents happening."

Tim came over with two Bren guns for Dermot and Sean. "You've handled this gun before?" he asked them.

"Aye," Sean answered.

Dermot hefted the gun in his hand and asked, "It's loaded?"

"It is then. There's a full clip and you'll not be issued another one. It's set for single shot firing and keep it at that unless you have to fire a burst. If you're attacked, switch it to burst-firing but for the guardhouse, single shot is enough. Here." He handed Dermot two grenades.

Dermot inspected the grenades. He held the lever down and pulled the ring out to see that it wouldn't stick. He replaced the ring, repeated the operation with the other grenade and then put one into each jacket pocket. He checked the ammo clip and the safety catch on the Bren gun.

The Brigade O.C. came over and asked, "Everything all right with you Duncrana men?"

"Right as rain," Dermot replied.

The leader inspected them to see that their faces were properly blackened. He tapped the white triangle of Dermot's neck and said, "Button up that shirt before you go over the wall."

Dermot nodded. The leader checked his watch and then called to the rest of the men, "There's time for a cigarette, but remember, no smoking from the time we leave here until the whole operation's finished."

Several men lit cigarettes and Sean offered one to Dermot.

Dermot smiled as he thought of how tight Sean ordinarily was with his cigarettes. He took one and lit it and glanced around at his companions. One man leaned against the wall, slightly apart from his companions, his arms folded, his eyes closed and a concentrated, almost grim, look on his face. He was tunelessly humming "The Boys of Wexford." Another man sat on an upturned box and Dermot could make out the loop of a pair of rosary beads that dangled from the man's clenched hands. Dermot wondered how the man could pray when what he was going to do was supposed to be a mortal sin.

Close to the door Hugh and the O.C. were talking. Dermot gave a humorous snort as he noticed Jonathan, slung across Hugh's back. From a group of men at the other end of the shed Dermot heard a voice ask, "Peter, did you bring any more of that yellow fuse?" The voice sounded lower than normal yet still above a whisper as if the speaker were unsure of how loud he ought to talk.

The minutes passed and Dermot and Sean put out their cigarettes. Finally the leader lifted down the lantern and blew it out. He spoke softly to the men. "All right—single file the whole way. No talking and no smoking."

Dermot and Sean followed Tim out the door of the shed. The file of men started across the country, following a thorn hedge. Once the headlights of a car on a nearby road threw a soft splash of light over the field and the men melted into the shadow of a hedge. They waited a moment and then continued their journey through more fields and over a stone wall. For about ten minutes they walked in an old lane before again cutting across the fields. They came out on the brow of a little hill and the leader gathered the men around him and said, "There's the barracks below us." He indicated a compact group of stone buildings encircled with a high stone wall.

The night was clear and soft and heavy with growth. High

in the air a plane labored and a dog at the nearby farm-house challenged it. The muffled sound of the barks reminded Dermot of Tone and for a fierce lonely moment he wished he were back home. He could almost see the dog, his paws out, staring sphinxlike at the fire. And he saw Bella too and heard the accordion. Deep in his mind the tune formed and the words came whispering to him. "We may have good men but we'll never have better."

The leader checked his watch and motioned to the men. They went over the brow of the hill and started descending. When they reached the bottom of the hill they turned right, again following a hedge. A few hundred yards away Dermot could see the black bulk of the barracks. They stopped at a gap in the hedge and the leader pulled out the thorn bushes that had been placed in it. Dermot noticed the spear-shaped ends of the recently cut bushes and knew that the gap had been specially made for the night's work. It somehow comforted him and gave him a feeling of confidence in the organization.

They filed through the gap and the man ahead of Dermot bent low as he crossed the open field. Dermot followed his example. In a moment they were all in the shadow of the barracks wall. They followed the wall until they came to an angle and the leader turned and beckoned to Tim.

Tim came forward and two men, their hands joined, made a foothold for him and lifted him up. His hands searched the wall and a small piece of mortar broke off and fell, bouncing on Dermot's shoulder. The sound of Tim's heavy breathing and the rasp of his clothes against the wall came with a loudness that made Dermot hold his breath. He watched as Tim swung his legs up and straddled the wall. Then he heard the light clink of metal as a hook was fitted into a crack. A rope flipped down and the leader grabbed it and gave a steady pull, testing its hold. Then he swung up, his body arching away from the stone, his boots searching for footholds. On top of the wall

Tim had fitted a second rope and the leader went down the other side. Another man went up the rope and then it was Sean's turn. Dermot stood with his back against the wall and with his cupped hands guided Sean's foot to a projecting piece of rock that served as a foothold. As Sean neared the top of the wall, his slung Bren gun hit a piece of rock and made a tremendous clunk in the ears of the men. Everyone froze in a listening attitude while Sean crouched low on top of the wall. Several seconds passed before Sean started easing himself down the other side.

Someone caught Dermot by the arm to indicate that it was his turn. He reached for the rope and started pulling himself up. A hand caught his foot and guided it on the wall. As he neared the top, Tim stretched forth a hand and Dermot caught it and was silently helped to the top of the wall. Tim handed the other rope to Dermot. His boots slithering against the stones, Dermot came down the rope in short awkward drops. He felt his legs being caught as he was lowered to the ground by Sean.

Ten yards in front of him Dermot could barely see one of the huts in which the soldiers slept and he marveled that no one had heard their entry.

Another man dropped to the ground and Dermot moved down to give him room. Presently all the men were over and Tim himself came down the rope, his agility surprising in a man so large. The leader and Tim held a whispered consultation for several seconds before Tim motioned with his arm and five of the men, including Dermot, followed him.

The men filed silently between two buildings and halted on the edge of a small square. A thin chink of light showed from beneath a door in one of the buildings and Dermot wondered why Coughlin had not yet put the power plant out of commission. Across the square stood the guardhouse and from the wire enclosure that surrounded it came the sound of heavy boots. Dermot heard and counted the fifteen steps of the sentry, the halt, a right turn, another right turn and fifteen more steps. The pattern of sounds had a peculiar beauty of its own: the precise implacability of each steel-shod pace; the authority of the crashing halt; and Dermot felt a wondering fear of the awesome order and discipline of their opponents.

Bending double, Tim moved cautiously over to a wall and along the wall until he was directly opposite the guardhouse. He waited until the men caught up with him and then motioned them down a short flight of steps that ran parallel to the wall and led to a storehouse. From behind the steps the men had a clear field of fire across to the guardhouse. Tim positioned the men, one to each step. Dermot was on the second last step and had to kneel to get adequate cover.

"Peter, as soon as the lights go out," Tim whispered, "I'm going to throw a grenade. After that we'll fire a few rounds at the guardhouse door. As soon as we stop, you jeuk down along the wall and open the main gate. It opens outward. Stay outside the gate and wait for us. We'll give you time to reach the gate and then we'll open fire again."

Tim pushed his Bren gun up and left it laying on the parapet. Drawing back, he moved closer to the men and whispered, "Listen, as soon as the grenade goes off, fire three rounds apiece at the guardhouse. Then stop and don't resume firing till I tell you."

Tim went back to his place and the men crouched down on the steps and waited. Fifty yards away the sentry paced, unaware of the raiders. Dermot kept his eyes on the chink of light that showed from beneath the guardhouse door and wondered what was keeping Coughlin from putting out the lights. He looked across at Sean who was crouched on the step below him.

When he looked again at the guardhouse the thin band of light had disappeared. He crouched lower, getting his head below the level of the ground. From the bottom of the stairs he heard the rustle of clothing as Tim threw a grenade, and a second later the metallic clunk as it bounced on the concrete. From the sentry came a loud, wild "Halt" followed immediately by the explosion of the grenade. A brief, orange flash was thrown across the square. Dermot swung his gun up on the parapet and pushed forward the safety catch. From his right came a flurry of spitting shots. He squeezed off a round and felt the solid punch of the gun into his shoulder. Twice more he fired before he pulled in the Bren and crouched down again behind the wall.

From across the square Dermot heard the shouts of a soldier as he turned out the guard. Someone fired back and he heard a bullet slam the wall behind him and another go whining off in a ricochet. Two quick shots followed and then a silence fell on the square. From the barracks to the left of Dermot came several shouts as the soldiers woke up. A flashlight came stabbing from one of the huts. A single shot ripped out from the guardhouse and then from the main gate came the drawn-out squeal of a bolt sliding back.

"Fire away at the guardhouse," Tim shouted. The men resumed firing and Dermot let off two quick rounds at the door of one of the huts. The probing flashlight went out and Dermot swung his gun around and fired again at the guardhouse. He saw the winking flashes as the fire was returned. His excitement spilled into anger and he let out a wild yell as he methodically kept pulling the trigger. Close to him he heard the angry thunk of a bullet and felt the sharp sting of a chip of stone that was kicked into his face. He ducked behind the wall and felt his cheek. Then ashamed of his momentary cowardice he eased himself up and fired four more rounds at the guardhouse. Suddenly, from the direction of the arsenal, came the stuttering of a machine gun as the demolition squad ran into trouble. Dermot wondered if they were withdrawing.

Tim reached up and caught him by the arm. "Myself and McRory and Devlin are going out now. Once outside the gate we'll keep up a fire until yourself and Sean get out. Keep whacking away at the guardhouse."

Dermot nodded and squeezed off a few more shots. He sensed the disappearance of the three men. Activity came again from the sleeping barracks and Dermot shifted his position and fired in that direction. Beside him Sean kept firing at the guardhouse.

For a second Dermot felt an awful loneliness as he realized that he and Sean were probably the only two left in the barracks. Outside of the one burst of fire there had been no further action from the demolition squad and Dermot supposed that they had gotten out safely.

He was about to suggest to Sean that they withdraw when he heard a confusion and running footsteps from the guardhouse. He snapped off another shot at the guardhouse and then heard a heavy squeal as the main gate was closed. As the sound died he felt in his stomach a slow expanding balloon of fear. In his sudden panic he grabbed Sean by the arm and hissed, "The bastards have closed the main gate—we can't get out." Swiftly anger overcame his fear and he flipped the gun to burst, aimed at the gate and pulled the trigger. The shots went rocketing out, sluicing into the gate. Then Dermot heard a high scream that descended into a moan from a soldier that had been hit. He reached up and pulled down the butt of the gun and swore as he realized that he was out of ammunition. He turned to Sean, "Come on! We'll go over the wall."

The two men left the shelter of the steps and sprinted across a corner of the square. Rifle fire followed them and Dermot heard a grunt from Sean and felt him catch his arm for support. "God-o-God, I'm hit!" Sean yelled. Dermot pulled at his companion and half-dragged, half-forced him over to the opposite wall where they stopped for a moment. Dermot reached into his pocket and took out a grenade. He looked over in the direction of the guardhouse and saw several flashlights playing over the square. He pulled the pin from the grenade and hurled it onto the square. He heard the bounce and roll and then the loud crump of the explosion. The flashlights snapped out and Dermot grabbed Sean and whispered, "The ropes are here somewhere. The first angle we come to." The two men moved cautiously along the wall. From the direction of the square came the sound of running footsteps and a shout. Suddenly they were at the angle and Dermot felt for the rope. He placed the rope in Sean's hand and boosted him up the wall. Sean had left his gun against the wall and Dermot wondered if he should try to carry both guns. He decided against it, slung his own gun and swarmed up after Sean. At the top he looked back over the square. A dozen flashlights made crossing beams as they laced from one building to another and a welter of confusing orders arose. Dermot realized that it was only a matter of moments until a light would be played on the wall. Sean had already made his way down the other side and Dermot grasped the rope and half-slid, half-jumped after him. As he landed on the ground, he caught Sean's arm and asked, "Are you hurt, Sean lad?"

"I've a bullet in my leg."

"Can you walk on it?"

"I'll have to," Sean replied.

"Let's go then," Dermot said. Holding Sean by the arm he detained him for a moment. He reached into his pocket and took out the other grenade and pulled the ring. Wheeling his arm back he lobbed the grenade over the wall and then started off through the field. The muffled thud of the grenade explosion came to him and he grinned dryly. Suddenly the sky was lit up as a tremendous explosion rocked the ground. Both men dropped to their knees with the unexpectedness of the noise.

"It's the arsenal," Sean cried exultantly.

"Boys-a-dear, but that will keep them busy for a while."

They got to their feet and made it to the shelter of a hedge. "Are you bleeding bad?" Dermot asked him.

"The pants are soaked. I can feel it running into the boots."

"Can't do anything here. We've got to get farther away. Every inch of this land will be searched before morning. We can make for the Cross Wood but I'm afraid of getting stuck there and they'll have it cordoned off as soon as it gets light. The best thing is to make a swing around the barracks and head south toward the Free State border. If we can get into the glens we have a good chance of giving them the go-by."

Sean got to his feet. Both men looked behind them at the barracks. A thin shoot of flame came from the arsenal and several trucks could be heard slamming gears as they left the barracks. The men turned and continued through the fields.

FIFTEEN

The pearl-gray edges of the dawn found the two men sheltering on the lee side of a hedge. They had traveled all night, a fatiguing journey through hedges, plowed fields, flax holes and bogs. Owing to the numerous turns and detours they had made, Dermot was no longer sure of the direction in which they were headed. Several times during the night the furious barking of dogs had warned of their approach to farmhouses and more than once Dermot had been tempted to seek refuge, hoping to find a family that would not give them away. Now that the dawn was breaking, he was glad that they had waited. In the light of day it would be easier to find a Catholic farmhouse. The fact that a house was thatched was almost a sure indication of a Catholic owner as Protestants, because of their better land and higher incomes, usually had slated houses.

Gradually Dermot began to make out their surroundings. Looming across in the next field, he noticed the dark bulk of a shed. He urged Sean to his feet and they made their way over to the building. Inside it was dark and Dermot unslung his Bren and left it standing in a corner. He scrounged around and found a few old bags which he laid on the ground. Sean sank gratefully down on the bags and grinned up at Dermot. "What are you going to do?" he asked. "Winter me in the shed, the way I'll come out fat and prancing for the May Fair?"

"I'm going to have a look at your leg," Dermot answered.

Sean opened his trousers and pulled them halfway down. Dermot lit a match and closely inspected the wound. On the inside of one thigh there was an ugly red tear and the rest of the leg was caked with dried blood. Dermot took out a handkerchief and tried to wipe away the encrustations. He had been expecting to see a small round hole instead of the rough piece torn out of the thigh.

"It's not a bullet that done that," he said. "It's either a piece of grenade or a ricochet. Anyway it seems to have stopped bleeding. How do you feel?"

"I'm most discomfortable," Sean grunted.

"Are you fit for more walking?"

"You little fart. I could walk the legs off you!"

"Listen to me now. I'm going outside and look around for a wee while. We can't travel till that leg's looked after. I may be gone a right while so don't stir till I get back."

"Bring back some grub with you. I'm historical with hunger," Sean said as he twisted on the bags, his hand searching for a pack of cigarettes. He took one out and lit it. In the flare of the match his face appeared, still covered with the black soot he had put on the night before. Dermot gave a short laugh as he remembered that his own face was also blackened.

Dermot stepped outside the shed. The drizzle had stopped and the day was well broken. Fretful gusts of wind came hedgehopping over the fields, shaking the swollen drops of rain from the bushes. A dark brown ribbon of earth meandered away from the shed and gave evidence of a much-used cattle path.

Dermot took his handkerchief and wet it on the dew-heavy grass. Scrubbing vigorously he tried to remove the cork black from his face.

Presently, his toilet finished, he put his hands in his pockets and looked around. A quarter of a mile away, beneath the fold of a hill, he noted the thin, climbing plume of smoke that came from a farmhouse. He watched as the smoke scattered with the wind and then, in a still moment, began to ascend again. He headed in the direction of the house.

He crossed several fields and came to a lane and followed the lane until it emerged into a farmyard. Here he stopped and stood at the gable-end of an outhouse while he glanced around. A yellow and black farm cart was heeled up in the yard, its twin shafts pointing at the sky. Dermot read the neat lettering on the near shaft of the cart—"Michael McGurk, Terraslin." Thank God, he thought, for Gaelic names. A man called McGurk could be nothing but a Catholic.

He looked around searchingly. A long low wall formed one side of the yard, its whitewash flaking off and discolored a streaky yellow with the rain. To his left stretched the house itself, thatched and whitewashed. A few hens were huddled under the eaves, their feathers wet and plastered in close to their bodies.

From inside the kitchen he heard the rattle of a bucket and then the front door opened. A young lad came out carrying a bucket of mash and started walking up the yard. Dermot stepped from behind the gable-end and into view. The youth stopped and gravely eyed him. Dermot had not been successful in getting all the black off his face and traces of it still ringed his neck and ears. The youth wonderingly set the bucket on the ground and continued staring.

"Is your Da in?" Dermot asked.

The lad nodded.

"Tell him there's a man in the yard that wants to see him. That's a good lad."

Dermot remained at the gable-end while the lad went back into the house. Several seconds passed and presently a big raw-boned man stepped out of the door and looked up the yard. His hair was uncombed and he wore an old pair of blue serge trousers and a rough flannel shirt. One half of his braces hung down the side of his pants.

"Well now, what is it you want?" the man shouted in a half-irritated, sleep-heavy voice.

Dermot walked down to meet him. He stopped a few yards away and said softly, "I'm in trouble."

The man whistled in amazement as he recalled the news he had just heard on the wireless. "Get in the house," he ordered, jerking his head in the direction of the door.

Dermot entered the kitchen, followed by the man and his son. He walked over to the fire and turned his back to it, warming his legs. "I'm sorry to be troubling you," he said apologetically.

"No trouble, no trouble at all," the man answered absent-mindedly and raising his voice, shouted, "Martha, we've company. Hurry out and make a wee sup of tea."

A middle-aged woman came out of the bedroom and into the kitchen. She had been combing her hair and the long gray strands lay down over each shoulder. Giving a quick twist she rolled up her hair and pinned it to the top of her head in a bun. Bending down, she lifted the tongs and jabbed at the turf fire, sending the flames shooting up around a kettle that hung on the crook.

"Sit down," the man told Dermot.

Dermot sat down and spread his hands to the fire.

"Are you alone?" the man asked.

"No," Dermot answered. "I've a friend in a cattle shed back of the house a ways. He's hurt."

"You're one of the boys who was out last night?"

Dermot said nothing and the man continued quickly, "You've nothing to fear. You're as safe here as in your own house. I heard about the raid on the wireless just a few minutes ago."

"What did they say?"

"They said you blew the barracks up."

"Was anyone captured, did they say?"

"No, nothing about that. Four British soldiers are in the hospital—one of them's critical."

Dermot remembered the high scream that had come from the gate of the barracks. "I hope he doesn't die," he said.

"Wouldn't be a great loss," the man dryly replied.

Dermot noticed the woman putting two eggs into a saucepan of boiling water and told her, "Just a wee drop of tea, mam, and we'll be on our way. Don't be making a feed for us."

The man lifted the loose brace and slipped it over his shoulder, "Your friend, he's not badly hurt?"

"He needs a doctor," Dermot answered.

"A doctor!" the man exclaimed. He noticed his son standing at the fire, taking everything in, and he gruffly ordered him, "Away out with you Jimmy and feed the calf." He turned to Dermot, "Why didn't you speak up sooner?"

"It's a bad business and I don't know if you'll want to help."

The farmer looked hurt. "Man, anything I can do."

"How am I going to get him to a doctor?" Dermot asked.

"Aye, that's a question. The bloody police and B-men will be blocking all the roads and turning everybody inside out. We'll have to get a doctor out to him—and that's as dangerous. If the police see a doctor coming out anywhere in this direction they'll be out along with him."

Dermot pulled his stool over to the table and began buttering a piece of soda bread. The farmer drew up a chair opposite him and asked, "Where's your man hurt?"

"In the leg," Dermot continued between mouthfuls, "I don't think he has a bullet in him. There's a dollop torn out and it looks like a piece of grenade done it. It's been bleeding all night and he's lost a great deal of blood."

"You're sure it's not a bullet?" the farmer asked.

"I can't be sure of anything. It looks like someone took a spoon and scooped a chunk out of his leg. If it was a bullet it was a ricochet that took a piece with it."

"Do you know what we could do?" the man said thoughtfully. Dermot cracked the top off an egg and dropped a pinch of salt on it. "We could send for the veterinary," the man continued. "O'Brien's an old friend of mine and the police would take no notice of a vet coming out here. If it's a flesh wound, O'Brien could take care of it and I think he could even take a bullet out."

"My man wouldn't be in any danger from a vet?" Dermot asked.

"Damn the danger. O'Brien's a better doctor than half the surgeons in the county."

"How could we get him word?"

"Our Jimmy will be heading for school in half an hour. I'll have him leave a message at O'Brien's."

Dermot turned over the possibility in his mind. If the vet could bandage up the wound perhaps Sean would be fit to travel and they wouldn't have to involve anyone else. "How far is it to the Free State border?" he asked.

"By road it's a little over twelve miles." The man pondered a moment and then suggested, "If you're thinking of trying to make it over the border it would be better to keep to the fields and follow the railway line. It's maybe three miles farther but you'd stand less chance of getting nabbed. The roads will be hiving with police and B-men."

Dermot pulled in the second egg and began to eat it. He was surprised at the powerful hunger he had and how tired he suddenly was. If they could get one good feed into them, he thought, they might be able to make it over the border that night. "I don't want to get you into any trouble," he said to the farmer.

"Trouble is it!" the man protested indignantly. "Sure I'd be out myself if it wasn't for the wife and children."

"Could we stay in the shed until evening?"

"Certainly, man."

"Once it comes near dark, if my man's fit to travel, we'll head towards the border and maybe get over tonight."

"There's no one in Applebridge you could get word to?"

Dermot quickly rejected the idea. There was too much police activity to risk involving anyone from Brigade. They would have to find their own way out. He shook his head and replied, "No, it's too dangerous."

The lad came back into the house and the man called him over to the table. He laid his arm on the boy's shoulder and said, "Jimmy, I want you to stop in at O'Brien's the vet, before you go to school. Tell him I've got a sick cow out here. Tell him," the man's head lifted to the ceiling and he thought for a moment as both Dermot and the lad watched him, "tell him that a cow tried to break out of a shed and has a bad cut on the leg where she was wounded getting out. Can you remember that?"

The lad nodded seriously and the father continued, "Repeat the message for me now."

"I'm to tell O'Brien the vet that we've a cow that tried to break out of the shed and it's hurt badly on the leg."

"No, not hurt, Jimmy. Wounded on the leg."

"And it's wounded on the leg," the lad repeated.

"Good lad! Mind not a word to anyone about it except O'Brien. And go straight to school after you deliver the message and no talking to any of the lads at school. If you do this wee job right I'll let you take the cart and mare in next Saturday for the feeding stuff."

The boy turned and picked up his school bag from a chair. "Will I go now?" he asked.

The farmer smiled at his son's eagerness. "Better you'd wait for the lunch your mother's making ready," he said. He looked over at his wife and added, "Make a wee bit to eat for the other lad."

"I'm doing that," the woman replied, a faint note of irritation in her voice.

Dermot stood up. "I'd best be getting back out to the shed. I don't like to leave my friend alone too long. You'll send the vet when he comes?"

"Aye, I will. I'll be out in a few minutes with something to eat for him. Go you along."

Dermot thanked the woman for the breakfast and left the kitchen. He walked quickly back through the fields and entered the shed. Sean had been sleeping and he awoke with a start. "Is that you, Dermot?" he called.

"Aye."

"What news?"

"There's a doctor on the way out to treat you. He should be here in an hour or so. Ever hear of a Michael McGurk of Terraslin?"

"No. There's a young McGurk plays football for the Monyvale team. I think he's from Terraslin."

"Wouldn't be the same family. This man's only got a young cub about the place. How do you feel?"

"I'm that hungry I could eat a bull between two breadvans."

"How's the leg?"

Sean shrugged. "It's no worse."

Dermot began gathering handfuls of clean straw from the floor and corners of the shed. He gathered an armful and brought it over to Sean. "Here, sit up for a minute and stick this under you."

Sean sat up, groaning as he did so, and Dermot pushed the straw back under him. He took out a pack of cigarettes and offered one to Sean. "I had the grandest feed," he said. "Two boiled eggs and a mountain of fresh soda bread. And the tea!" Dermot gave a sigh and a click of his lips, "Man-dear, it was that strong you could have danced on it."

"You wouldn't bring any back for me, you miserable bugger," Sean protested.

"The farmer's on his way out with a feed for you. Now be damn quiet or I'll have you handed over to the peelers."

Sean gave a short laugh. Dermot thought of the news on the wireless and exclaimed, "Declare to God, I near forgot. The raid was on the news this morning. Four British soldiers are hurt. One of them's critical."

"Only four? I thought we slew the whole battalion!"

Dermot heard a noise outside the shed and went over quickly to the door and peered out. A dog came romping up to him and halfway across the field Dermot saw the farmer carrying a bucket.

Presently the farmer entered the shed and placed the bucket on the ground. He lifted out a teapot and a tin mug and set out the tea. Sean began to wolf down the food and the farmer maintained the traditional courtesy of not speaking to him while he was eating. Instead he addressed himself to Dermot, "I think the wisest thing is to rest here until evening and then make for the border. I'll bring some tea again in the afternoon and have my woman make something for you to take."

"We don't want to get you into any trouble," Dermot said.

The farmer snorted his depreciation. "If the police come searching around the place, I'll still have time to send you word," he said.

The men fell silent and the dog came over and smelled at Dermot. Dermot reached down and scratched the dog behind the ears and the animal wagged his hindquarters in ecstasy. Dermot continued scratching the dog as he wondered what his parents, and especially his mother, would think when he didn't show up. He realized they would know the reason for his absence as soon as they heard of the raid. He knew too that Neeve would be worried.

Sean finished eating and the farmer gathered up the tea things, replacing them in the bucket. "I'll be back when O'Brien gets here," he told them. He was about to leave the shed when Dermot caught him by the arm and said, "We've a gun we can't take with us." He pointed to the far corner of the shed.

The farmer looked over and frowned. "Throw an old bag over it and sometime tonight I'll pick it up and stuff it away in the thatch of the roof."

"It's empty," Dermot said, trying to make the gun sound less dangerous.

"I'll take care of it and you can tell your men where you left it. When the police get over their fever, your friends can come out for it." The farmer called to the dog and left the shed.

Sean gave a sigh of contentment and stretched out full length on the ground. "Man, that feed was powerful," he said. "Stand guard there private, while the adjutant catches a little sleep."

Dermot grinned over at him. "Sleep away. You'll need it before this night's out."

Dermot walked over to the door of the shed and squatted along one wall in such a way that he could see out through the half-opened door. He tried to cat-nap, closing his eyes. He dozed fitfully and once woke with a start when a shadow fell athwart the threshold. He looked out and then relaxed as he stared into the perplexed face of a black cow. After what seemed like hours, he heard voices and again peered out. Coming across the field were the farmer and a small fat man with a black bag. Dermot called across to Sean, "Hey wake up! Here's the doctor."

The vet came first into the shed. He looked at Dermot and jovially asked, "Now then, where's this wounded cow?"

Dermot motioned with his head to the corner where Sean was sitting up, tenderly rubbing his thigh. The vet went over and reached down to count his pulse. Then he loosened Sean's trousers and pulled them down.

"We'll have that fixed in no time," he said cheerfully.

He straightened and took a package of cotton wool from his bag. Pulling off a small quantity, he held it to the neck of a bottle. Working surely and quickly, he carefully washed away the crusted blood from around the wound with the saturated cotton wool. The hydrogen peroxide bubbled up fiercely in a white froth and the cotton wool came away pink and red from the leg. The vet finished washing the wound. He poked it experimentally with his forefinger and asked, "Does it hurt much?"

"Like the hammers of hell," Sean answered.

The vet reached again into the bag and took out a scalpel. Sean looked away when he saw the knife and closed his eyes. Spreading the wound wide with his fingers, the vet began to scrape gently, periodically wiping the scalpel clean on a wad of cotton wool. He doused it again with the hydrogen peroxide and once more started to scrape it. Sean had his face screwed shut, and Dermot winced in unison with him. Again the vet cleaned the wound with peroxide. Straightening, he said to Sean, "You're lucky. There doesn't seem to be any foreign body in there."

"Thank God for that," Sean replied.

"As soon as you can, have another doctor look at it. I can't do much except sterilize and dress it. You should have an X-ray taken."

Sean nodded and Dermot interrupted, "As soon as we're across the border, I'll have him in a hospital."

The vet spread a white salve on the wound and started to bandage it. He worked quickly and in a few minutes had the thigh completely covered with white wrappings. He tied the bandage and stood up. Sean pulled up his trousers and started buttoning them.

"What's the charge for that?" Dermot asked.

"If he were a cow I could charge a quid. You see I'm a vet and if I charge you anything, I'll lose my license. I'm only supposed to treat animals."

Sean looked in astonishment at Dermot. The latter laughed and said, "Sean, I always said you were a horse of a man."

"A vet," Sean repeated wonderingly.

The vet closed the bag and said to Sean, "Try getting up now and putting your weight on the leg."

The farmer helped Sean to his feet. Sean went pale when he put his weight on the leg. His face tense, he pushed the farmer away and tried a few steps across the uneven floor of the shed.

"Do you feel a sharp pain anywhere?" the vet asked.

"No," Sean answered doubtfully.

"You'll be all right. Rest up for the remainder of the day. When you start out this evening, go slowly for the first hour or so. If it starts to bleed, you'll have to rest for a while."

"I'll cut a good strong ash plant for him," the farmer interrupted. "That will help some."

"He'll be all right," the vet assured them.

"Thanks a lot for your help," Sean said to the vet.

"Not at all. I had the same disease myself twenty years ago."

The vet and the farmer left the shed. Dermot walked outside with them. He drew the farmer aside and said, "If the vet charges anything, let us know and I'll make it up to you."

"There won't be any charge. Try and get some sleep—both of you. You needn't worry about being disturbed or anything. I'll be back around four with another feed for the both of you."

Dermot re-entered the shed to be met with an angry comment from Sean. "By God, it's a hard neck you've got—getting a vet to treat me."

"I could have gotten a doctor, complete with an escort of the R.U.C. Would that have pleased you?"

"By Jesus—if you ever tell a soul about this, I'll scuttle you," Sean threatened.

Dermot laughed as he realized that Sean was more afraid of the story getting out than he was of the police. Though he had no intention of ever saying a word about the vet, he knew that in some mystic way the story would eventually become public property, to be told and retold at wakes in the future.

"Rest yourself," he ordered Sean. "It's a hard night we have ahead of us."

"A bloody vet," Sean grumbled to himself.

SIXTEEN

The men rested as the day slid by. In the early evening the farmer returned, bringing a bucket with the tea things. He laid a clean bag on the floor of the shed and started to set out the mugs and spoons, bread and hard-boiled eggs.

"How's the leg?" he asked.

"Middling," Sean answered. "It's a wee bit stiff. Any more news about the raid?"

"The police have lifted seven men in Applebridge under the Special Powers Act. They say that whether or not they get proof of them being on the raid, they'll intern them for the duration," the farmer answered.

"Anybody lifted in the other towns?" Dermot asked, thinking of Duncrana.

"Over thirty in Belfast and fourteen in Derry City. They claim that some of the raiders were wounded."

"Don't know where they get several from," Dermot answered. "Far as I know, only Sean was hit."

"Sure I'm worth any two men," Sean said.

"Well, that's what they say," the farmer reiterated. "They've thrown a cordon around the Cross Wood. Some of the men are supposed to be hiding there."

Dermot swallowed a mouthful of tea. "A damn good job we didn't shape into that place. We'd never get out."

The farmer indicated several sandwiches wrapped in a white cloth. "There's some bread and a couple of hard-boiled eggs for tonight." He reached into his pocket and took out a small flashlight. "You'd be the better of this along with you."

Dermot took the flashlight and put it in his pocket. "You've been shocking good to us. Mind we won't forget it."

"Good?" the man repeated in a questioning tone. "You should leave in about an hour," he continued. "It will start darkening then. Come out till I show you."

The two men stepped outside and the farmer pointed, "Do you see that wee bit of a hill—the other side of the row of aspen trees?"

"Aye."

"Make for the crown of that hill. From there it's half a mile to the railway tracks. They cut through a valley there. Follow the tracks to your right—but keep to the fields. It wouldn't surprise me but they'd have some sort of patrol on the line all night."

"How far would it be to the border?"

"About fourteen miles. It'll take you all night going through the fields. If you lose the tracks, listen for the trains. There's six or seven that go through in the night."

"How will I know when I'm across the border?" Dermot asked.

"About half a mile on the Free State side there's the Gortcallen customs station. It's a small station but it'll be lit up because there's no blackout in the Free State. The road that goes through to the coast runs close to the station. Get on that and you'll get a lift with someone. Keep away from the Free State police; I wouldn't trust them too far. I hear DeValera is cracking down on the I.R.A."

Dermot looked across the fields with a professional eye. He noticed a plow standing lonely at the end of a furrow. "You're not finished with the plowing yet?" he asked.

"Just that half field and I'll finish it tomorrow. It's purty land and won't need much work."

"We've got all the work done," Dermot said.

"And the corn?"

"It too."

"Your land would be earlier than ours?" the farmer asked, a slight uneasiness in his voice as though the question were a delicate one. It was the first mention he had made of where the two men came from.

Dermot hesitated a second and then replied frankly, "I live close to Duncrana."

"Aye, that land around there is a wee bit earlier than ours," the farmer said.

The conversation stopped and Dermot and the farmer went back into the shed. Sean was on his feet, walking unsteadily with the help of a stick the farmer had brought.

"You'll be ready for the pension any day," Dermot joked.

"How does it feel?" the farmer asked.

"A wee bit stiff but I'll be fit to travel." Sean leaned against the wall and took the weight off his leg.

The farmer gathered up the mugs and spoons and replaced them in the bucket. He lifted the bag and slapped it against the wall several times to shake off the wisps of hay and dirt that were sticking to it. He walked over to the far corner of the shed, laid the Bren gun down flat and placed the bag over it.

"I'll come for it when it's dark," the farmer said.

"Whatever suits yourself," Dermot answered.

The farmer lifted the bucket and walked over to the door.

He turned and asked, "Is there anything you might need before you go?"

"Not a thing," Dermot assured him.

"Well in that case, I'm away. God bless."

"Bless you too," Sean and Dermot answered in unison.

Dermot closed the door and the shed grew dim in the failing light. "Rest yourself, you'll have a rough night of it," he said.

Sean limped over to his corner and sat down on the pile of straw. "We're the great pair of bloody idiots," he remarked as he settled himself.

"Is it just now you're finding that out?"

"Will I be able to go home again after I do get into the Free State?"

"I doubt it," Dermot answered. "If the police pick you up and see that leg it would give the whole game away."

"I'll have to stay in the Free State until the fluking war's over?"

"Probably."

"I could say I got it falling off a tractor or something," Sean mused. "I don't see how they could prove it came from a bullet."

Dermot picked up a wisp of straw and started chewing on it.

"You could do that but you'd better not chance it. If they see the wound at all they'll connect it with the raid and if they can't try you, they'll at least intern you under the Special Powers Act."

"And you, what are you going to do?" Sean asked.

"I've got an aunt in Donegal. I'll say I was visiting her for a few days."

"Suppose the police check on it?"

"How can they check? They can't cross the border into Donegal and the Free State police won't give them any information."

"They could pick you up and intern you anyway," Sean argued.

"They could but I don't believe they will. They won't be expecting any of us to head back into the North. Anyway, they won't have any idea that I was on the raid. It's not like your wound."

"I suppose you're right," Sean answered.

The men lapsed into silence and gradually the shed grew dark. Outside the rabbits hopped forth from their burrows, little gray stones, sitting sculpture still along the hedges. A fox came noiselessly padding in from the mountains, his red flag of a tail bobbling gently through a rushy field. From a hedge emerged a badger, backside first, as he waddled into a ditch and then turned and lifted a sharp-pointed head, sniffing at the night air. A pair of curlews came wheeling low, their wings slicing purple circles from the dusk, their mournful cries keening the death of the day.

The two men emerged from the shed and stood for a moment at the door, getting their bearings. They struck out across the fields until they came to the row of aspen trees and then to the brow of the hill. Below them they could see the narrow defile and the barely perceptible roadbed of the railway line.

"We follow the tracks to the right," Dermot remarked. "He said we shouldn't go down on the railway, but it would be a lot quicker. What do you think?"

"The police will be watching the railway stations, but I doubt they'll patrol the line. They may at the border, but not this far back," Sean answered.

"Right-o then, let's chance it."

The men made their way down the hill and started to walk on the narrow path on the outside of the rails. An hour later they heard the sounds of a train in the distance and they scrambled away from the line and lay in a little wrinkle of land. The train drew near, its blacked-out carriages swaying, the engine lit with a soft red glare from the firebox. It rocketed past and for several minutes longer they lay on the wet grass listening to the dying sound of the engine. Then they got to their feet, made their way back to the rails and resumed their march. They walked for another hour before deciding to take a rest.

"How far have we come?" Sean asked.

"Between four and five miles. How's the leg?"

"It's very stiff and shocking sore but I can keep going for a while yet."

They lay beneath the cover of a whin bush that grew on the embankment. "I wonder if the rest of the men got away?" Sean said.

"Chances are that some of them were picked up by the police in Applebridge. The whole question is whether the police can find any evidence of them being on the raid. If they can try them and give them a jail sentence they'll be treated as common criminals. If they decide to intern them for the duration they'll have to treat them as political prisoners."

"What's the difference?" Sean asked.

"Well, political prisoners can wear civilian clothes and they don't have to do any work in the jail. There's also a difference between being a convicted prisoner and being a political internee."

"How are we going to continue our work if they arrest all the leaders?"

"They won't get all the leaders and even if they do, new leaders are always cropping up."

Sean rolled over on one side and lifted his leg into a more comfortable position. "You know if I don't get back from the Free State, the company will need a new adjutant."

"Who do you think will be appointed?"

"Either you or Corrigan—probably you. For some reason Brigade H.Q. thinks you're the whole cheese."

Dermot wondered why the news left him flat. A month ago he would have been delighted at the thought of being company adjutant. Now he wasn't so sure. "Maybe McGinnis wouldn't hear of me," he objected.

"McGinnis will go along with Brigade's recommendations."

Dermot gave voice to his thoughts, "Maybe I wouldn't want the position."

Sean sat up suddenly. "You daft? There's no maybe about it. If they pick you—you're the new adjutant. What's the matter? You getting the wind up or something?"

"Something," Dermot answered as he stood up and stretched himself. He looked down at Sean and asked, "What happens if that British soldier dies? Are we guilty of murder?"

"It's war I tell you. What do you mean murder?" Sean said heatedly.

"The Church says it's murder. I'm beginning to wonder if we have the right to shoot British soldiers."

"This is the great time to be getting doubtful about it. It's always been war between us and the British and it always will be war until every square inch of Ireland belongs to the Irish people, until the tricolor flies over the city hall in Belfast. They know it's war; another battle in a seven-hundred-year war."

"We'd better start again," Dermot said.

Sean let a groan out of him as he got to his feet. "Trouble with you is that you're always thinking. And if you think long enough you'll twist yourself into joining the British Army."

"No fear of that," Dermot laughed.

They made their way back to the railway line. Sean complained frequently about his leg and Dermot was forced to slow the pace.

Several times they stopped for brief rests, sitting a moment or two on the ties. Once they stopped where the railway ran through a low marshy field and the roadbed was built up about eight feet. As they were about to resume their journey, Dermot heard a slight noise from the direction they had come. He grabbed Sean and rolled with him down the embankment. The slope was flanked with a ditch full of running water and both men slid into it. Dermot caught Sean and pushed him in against the tall weeds that grew on the steep slope above them. Both men were up to their waists in the water of the ditch, their heads and shoulders pressed in tight to the bank. From down the rails, an open diesel car came plupping along. It carried a driver and four police armed with rifles, a pair facing forward and a pair facing the rear. The two lead police carried powerful flashlights and the beams probed out over the surrounding land. Dermot lay still, his arms over Sean's shoulders, pressing him in against the ground. The car drew abreast of them and Dermot heard a harsh cough from one of the police. Then the sound advanced as the car passed and Dermot raised his head and looked after it. The twin beams of light were slicing at the darkness in long sweeping arcs, pulling in close to the rails, sweeping out over the surrounding fields and playing at the bottom of the embankment. The lights disappeared in the distance and Dermot sighed, "Phew, Mother of God but it's the purest fluke yon boys didn't see us."

"I've hurt my leg. I think it's bleeding again," Sean said.

"We've got to get away from the line. Those buckos will be coming back."

Dermot went back up the embankment and got Sean's stick. He handed it to him and said,"Let's get away from the tracks and then we can rest a while and look at your leg."

Sean grunted as he got to his feet and scrambled out the other side of the ditch. He hobbled painfully a few steps. "I must have caught it on something. It hurts like hell."

"Here," Dermot offered. "Sling an arm around my shoulder and we'll manage that way."

They made their way across a marshy field, full of potholes and tough islands of rushes, sometimes sinking to their calves in soft places. Their passage was made more difficult because Dermot was afraid to use the flashlight. Finally, they emerged from the swampy meadow and came to a sloping plowed field, the furrows ribbing out in front of them. They crossed the field and took refuge in the next one, behind a potato pit. Sean sat down and leaned back against the side of the pit. He sighed gratefully and said, "Whew! I'm punctured. You wouldn't have a bottle of whiskey lurking in one of your pockets?"

"You'll live," Dermot answered. "If you're hungry we could eat the eggs and bread but I think it's better to save them till later. It's early enough yet and we've still eight or ten miles to go."

Sean did not reply and Dermot, hunkered down beside him, twisted around and tried to peer in the direction of the railway. He started rummaging through his pockets for a packet of cigarettes. The packet was wet from the water in the ditch and the remaining two cigarettes crumpled in his hand as he tried to withdraw them. He felt the soppiness on his fingers and threw them away in disgust. He nudged Sean, "Hey, give us a cigarette."

Sean made no reply and Dermot asked again, "Sean?"

When Sean didn't answer the second time, Dermot reached over and shook him by the shoulder. He felt his comrade's body topple over on its side. Dermot got up anxiously and propped Sean into a sitting position again. "God above! The bugger's fainted," he said in a whisper. He pushed Sean's head down between his knees and began to massage the back of his neck. After a few seconds he felt the pressure on his hand as Sean tried to raise his head.

"I started to get sick," Sean said weakly.

"You fainted," Dermot said accusingly.

"Away out of that. I didn't faint. I just felt sick for a second."

"I was talking to you for five minutes and damn the word you heard!"

"I'll be all right in a tick."

"Take a couple of deep breaths," Dermot ordered.

Sean started breathing deeply. Dermot took out his handkerchief and bent over him, rubbing his forehead. "You think we
should take a look at your leg?" he asked.

"What good would it do?" Sean said. "Better to leave it
alone. Let's rest for a wheen of minutes and then I'll give it
another try."

"You got a cigarette?"

"Bloody moocher," Sean replied as he reached into his jacket
pocket and pulled out a packet. He handed the cigarettes over
and Dermot lit two of them, shielding the match with his
jacket.

"My backside is wet," Sean complained.

"Old cold backside! Oh, it's great heroes the country is pro-
ducing, complaining of wet backsides," Dermot taunted. He
began to sing softly, "As down by the glenside, I wet my old
backside."

Sean grunted, "How far are we from the border?"

"It must be another ten miles and at the rate we're going the
war will be over before we get there."

"Well then, let's be moving," Sean said. "If I feel bad, sure
we can rest again."

The two men got to their feet and continued their journey.
As best they could, they followed the roadbed of the railway.
Several times they went astray and while Sean rested, Dermot
ranged out until he located the railway again. They used the
flashlight sparingly, mainly on the hedges to locate gaps and
gates.

For the most part they traveled in silence as both men began
to feel the effects of the past two days. Once their path was
blocked by a bog and they had to go down to the railway and
walk on the ties until they passed it. Fearing the police car's
return, they took to the fields again as soon as possible. During
one of their frequent rests, they ate the bread and hard-boiled
eggs. Sean found the going increasingly difficult and Dermot

had to keep nagging at him with the result that they fell out and wouldn't speak to each other for a space of an hour. It was during this estrangement that Dermot, walking ahead of the hobbling Sean, came across a donkey in a field. He waited until Sean had caught up with him and said, "With a bit of luck, you'll be riding in style."

Dermot walked slowly over to the animal, talking away to it. "Here fella, oh what a lovely wee donkey, at'a a fella." The donkey's ears flapped forward as he watched the advance. Dermot stretched out his hand and cautiously scratched the donkey on the neck. The animal lowered his head and dunted him on the shoulder. Dermot craftily slid an arm around the donkey's neck and with the other hand began to scratch him between the ears. He called to Sean, "Take the leather thongs out of both your boots. Can you make a halter?"

"If they're long enough," Sean answered as he stooped and unlaced his boots. He took out the two thongs, tied them together and began to fashion a rough halter. He handed the makeshift halter to Dermot and the latter slid it over the donkey's head. The animal stood patiently while the halter was tied. Dermot gave an experimental tug and the donkey moved forward.

"Here, hold the halter a minute," he told Sean.

Sean took the halter and Dermot swung himself onto the donkey's back. The animal made no objection other than putting his head down. Dermot slid off. "Up you get," he said to Sean.

Sean, with Dermot's help, managed to mount the animal. He straightened himself. "Let's hope he doesn't take a notion to balk when we're leaving the field," he said.

Dermot led the donkey off and they continued through a succession of fields: plowed fields and harrowed fields, meadows and brushy pasture land, all the time trying to follow the railway. At one point they were fortunate in coming across an old lane that roughly paralleled the railway for a mile and a half but finally they had to abandon it when it turned sharply, striking off at a right angle to the rails.

They made steady though erratic progress as the night wore on. Several times Sean dismounted and rested while Dermot kept hold of the donkey. They had no way of knowing how far they had traveled and both kept looking for signs that they had crossed the border. The few farmhouses they encountered were dark, without signs of life, except for the querulous barking of a dog.

Toward morning, as the blue-white curtain of the night was lifting, Sean fell off the donkey. They were going down an incline and the donkey stumbled. Sean, either from carelessness or fatigue, fell off the animal's back. In the confusion Dermot lost his grip on the halter and the donkey trotted away. Dermot stopped first to see that Sean was all right. Then he called to the animal and tried to follow him. For half an hour he tramped through the field and around the small slope they were traversing, but finally had to come back and confess that the donkey was lost.

Sean treated the matter lightly, remarking, "I'll have that ass court-martialed."

They started again but had not gone a dozen steps when Sean had to call a halt. "I can't keep my boots on," he complained.

Dermot unlaced his own boots and cut each thong in two with his penknife. He gave Sean one pair of the shortened laces and they proved long enough to tie each boot. Dermot relaced his own boots with the other half pair.

They continued walking and the dawn shyly began to break. First the dim outlines of hedges appeared, followed by the ridges of the hills, crowned with an odd tree standing sentinel against the skyline. They had come into a mountainy area and all around them stretched the hills, the lower halves aproned with whin bushes and stunted fir trees, and above them looming the peaks, proud, bare and stony. Gradually the sun flung forth its golden fingers, awakening the sky, and hundreds of feet below them the railway lines and sleepers emerged.

They sat down on a small hummock of grass and shared Sean's last cigarette. From off to their right came the challenging crow of a cock. At the same house, a farm dog was rhythmically barking in a deep authoritative tone. Faintly from the distance answered the excited yelping of a younger dog.

A quarter of a mile away they made out a low cabin tucked in against the side of a hill, flanked by a turfrick and a small haystack. The people of the house were still abed, no plume of smoke announcing a lit fire.

"Could you not take a run over there and ask how far we are from the border?" Sean asked.

"They're not up yet."

"They'll probably be up by the time you get there."

"Even so. Suppose they realize who we are and go for the police?"

"Hell to your soul, I was only asking," Sean answered crankily.

Dermot looked over and was suddenly shocked at Sean's appearance. His hair was tousled and hanging down in loose cords and his face was splotched with black patches. The eyes were red-rimmed and narrowed with fatigue. His mouth had a petulant droop that reminded Dermot of a small boy about to cry. "How do you feel?" he asked sympathetically.

"Ah God above, I'm scundered!" Sean answered. "I think to myself—I'll take five more steps and then ask for a rest. I go five more steps and then think—ten more. And then five more and I'll ask." He placed his head down on his knees and his voice came in a mumble, "When we rest I think how wonderful it is to be sitting down. But after a minute I start to get cold. I'm cold all the time and if I sit more than a minute my teeth start boxing with each other. And the hunger that's on me! I'd nearly give myself up for a breakfast of rashers and eggs and a couple of strong mugs of tea and to sit at the fire after it . . ." His voice trailed off.

Dermot picked up a small stone and began to roll it around in his hand. He began to think of the British soldier and wondered whether or not he'd live. For some reason he tied in their flight with the soldier's recovery. His mind equated the two things until he felt that if they got across the border, the soldier would survive. He remembered vividly the soldier's scream when he cut loose with the Bren. It was funny he had never known that kind of a rage before. At the moment of firing the gun he had wanted to kill as many soldiers as he could. He shivered and flipped the stone away. The first thing was to get some life into Sean. "Listen Sean," he said. "You come from a hardy race of people. Your ancestors were big strong men who had this to do many's the time. The fact that you're alive, a descendant of a race that was persecuted and harried by the British for hundreds of years, proves you're a tight man. Think of your ancestors."

"Screw my bloody ancestors!" Sean answered grumpily.

"Come on. It can't be more than a mile or two to the border, maybe not even that. If we made a mistake now, with the border so near, it wouldn't be nice to sit on our backsides in his majesty's guest house in Crumlin Road, thinking if we'd have gone another half mile we'd have been free. Let's jeuk around till we're at the top of that wee hill yonder."

Sean got unsteadily to his feet. Dermot went over to him and said, "Here put your arm around my shoulder and it'll ease you a bit."

"I wouldn't mind the leg so bad, nor even the cold. It's not knowing how far we have to go."

Dermot urged him forward, "Well, let's travel this wee bit to the hill and then maybe we'll know."

They moved to the top of the hill, Sean shuffling along, his arm around Dermot's shoulder. At the top they sat down again while they looked out over the surrounding country. Dermot caught Sean by the arm, "Look, here comes a train!"

They watched as a train came slowly puffing through the hills. Clouds of smoke billowed from the engine as it crawled over the track. They watched as it drew abreast of them and then passed. About a mile ahead it stopped and Dermot could make out the low buildings of a railway station.

"I wonder if that's on the Free State side?" Sean said.

"It's impossible to tell," Dermot answered. He looked around intently and then noticed a narrow road that girdled the base of one of the mountains. "There's a bit of a road down there," he said. "I could skite down and maybe find out where we are. What do you think?"

"Aw God above, don't leave me here," Sean protested. "I'd perish if anything happened to you."

"Don't worry, nothing's going to happen. At the worst I'll be gone an hour," Dermot reassured him.

"Go then," Sean said irritably, "but for God's sake don't get picked up by the peelers. If you do, not a word about me. I might still be able to make it alone."

Dermot got to his feet and moved off down the hill. He encountered the dirt road and followed it for a short distance until he rounded a curve and saw that the road led into a broad tarred one. He went forward cautiously until a green roadside sign caught his attention. In Gaelic lettering it informed that the side road was not an approved one for border crossings. As soon as Dermot saw the Gaelic lettering, he knew they were across. He went over and patted the sign several times. Then he walked out boldly onto the tarred road and waited. Ten minutes passed before a lorry came bouncing along. He stepped into the middle of the road and stopped it.

The driver, a small lean youth wearing a black beret, looked down from the cab, "What's up?" he asked.

Dermot explained the situation and the youth immediately

agreed to help. Dermot got in the lorry and they drove up the side road. When they reached the top of the hill, they found Sean stretched out on his stomach, asleep, his head pillowed in his arms. Dermot stared at him for a second and a warm feeling of friendship slipped over him when he thought of their journey through the night. He spat and said to the youth, "There's a horse of a man. He's lost a barrel of blood and he's been walking all night, at least thirty miles, and the hills reeking with police and dogs and not a word of complaint did I hear from him."

Their voices woke Sean and his head swiveled around in fright.

"We're in the Free State," Dermot said.

"Thank God," Sean said simply. "How far are we from the border?"

"You crossed it a mile back," the youth replied.

They got Sean to his feet and helped him down to the lorry. As they drove into the nearest town, both Dermot and Sean fell asleep. The youth knew who they were, having read of the raid in the local newspaper. He began making up a story to recount to his companions. They were staggering along through the fields when he spotted them. Could he say they had guns, he wondered. It would sound a lot better. One of them was bleeding, something shocking, the blood running out of his trousers. They were real I.R.A. men—no doubt about that— hard chaws from the Black North.

The lorry slowed down and stopped in front of a small store. The three men got out and the youth showed Dermot a doctor's office. They went into the office and while Sean was having the wound treated, Dermot fell asleep in a big armchair. He was awakened by the youth who had returned. "You're to come to our house and have a feed," the lad told him. "I'm to wait and bring you," he further explained as he sat down.

Sean and the doctor came out of the office. Dermot stood up and asked, "Well, what's the damage?"

"He's as right as rain," the doctor answered. "All he needs is a few days' rest. That last doctor did a good job of treating it. Come back again tomorrow and I'll have another look at it."

"How much do we owe you, doctor?" Dermot asked.

"Nothing at all," the doctor answered uncomfortably.

"No listen, doctor. We can pay a little at least," Dermot said.

"Mind I don't approve of your clique at all," the doctor answered. "But I can't take anything from you. I did nothing for it except change the bandage." The doctor's mood changed and he smiled wryly, "There's nothing wrong with that boyo that a good woman couldn't cure."

The three men broke out laughing and the doctor walked out to the front door with them.

They followed the youth to a house where breakfast had been prepared. They washed up, ate, and then went to sleep in the beds that had been readied for them.

About six in the evening, Dermot woke up. He and Sean had been sleeping in the same room. Dermot swung his legs out of bed and started pulling on his trousers. He noticed that the trousers had been dried at the fire as had the socks and boots. He moved over to the other bed and woke Sean, "Listen Sean, I'm going back to the North tonight," he told him.

Sean sat up in bed, pulling his jacket off a chair and draping it over his shoulders. "You don't think there's any danger?"

"Oh, there's a wee bit. If they ask I have an excuse ready for where I was. I don't think they'll arrest me though. If I were leaving the North it'd be a different matter. You'd better stay here until the wound is healed. Even then it might not be safe to come back, but I can find out and get word to you."

"You'll make a report to McGinnis?"

"Right." Dermot finished dressing himself. "If you need money, send word to us and we'll arrange it."

"I'll manage," Sean answered. "You'll drop in at the house and tell them I'm all right? And not a word about the leg."

Dermot stood up, leaned over the bed and ruffled Sean's hair. "Keep away from these Free State women. They say they're a terror for marrying."

He turned and left the room. Sean stared at the door a moment and then removed his jacket, slid down into the bed and went back to sleep.

SEVENTEEN

Dermot settled back in the train compartment and opened the newspaper. He was about to start reading when the train gave a jolt and slowly began to move. He laid the paper down on the seat and looked out the window. On the receding platform two big electric bulbs were burning, throwing interlocking circles of light over the ground. A railroad employee, walking slowly and carrying a wrapped up flag, crossed the platform and disappeared into the station house.

Inside the carriage a dim yellow light was burning. Seated across from Dermot was an old man. He had a sere, corrugated face and white mustache ends that looped down over a puckered button of a mouth.

"It's nice to see a place lit up for a change," Dermot said to the old man.

The man looked over and grunted indignantly, "The buggers oughtn't be allowed to have the place lit up like that. Damn well they know it's a perfect guide to the German bombers. The whole Free State border is a carnival of beacons, pointing the way to the shipyards in Belfast."

Dermot smiled inwardly as he realized that he had trod on the tail of an Orangeman. He wondered if he would talk so loud traveling the other way, into the Free State instead of the North. He decided that he probably would, having reached the age when he knew that no one would lift a hand to him.

Dermot dismissed the old man from his mind and opened the newspaper. He started skimming over the story of the raid. ". . . daring foray by I.R.A. Four British soldiers wounded . . . one critical in Applebridge Military Hospital . . . believed to be twenty raiders . . . raiders completely destroy arsenal . . . no arms taken . . ."

Dermot could not resist dropping a remark to his companion, "Looks like they've had a wee bit of excitement in the North since I've been away."

The old man glowered back. "'Tis a great pity them tinkers aren't rounded up and hung," he growled.

His courage rises the nearer he is to the border, Dermot thought. He went back to the newspaper. ". . . raid is regarded as significant . . . a new phase . . . direct military action instead of raiding for arms . . . the prime minister threatens wholesale arrests of sympathizers . . . thirty have been interned . . ."

A railway porter came in and lowered the blinds on the train window and Dermot realized that they were approaching the border.

The train slowed down and panted to a stop. Dermot lifted the blind and looked out. He could hear a shout or two and saw a flashlight throwing a dancing beam on the ground as the black bulk of a man followed it. Seconds later the door of the compartment opened and two R.U.C. men entered. The taller of the two, a sergeant, carried a flashlight in his hand and the other had a small clip-board with a piece of paper on it.

"Identity cards," the sergeant requested.

Dermot felt a quick lance of fear as he reached into his jacket pocket and pulled out his card.

The old man handed his card over and remarked, "Brave night, sergeant."

"It is that. A lot of growth in that weather," the sergeant replied, as he glanced at the card and handed it back.

He turned to Dermot and took his card. "Name?" he asked as he started reading.

Dermot thought with a quick touch of anger that if he had a nice Anglo-Saxon name like Bobby Reid or Billy Partland, the sergeant wouldn't have asked that question. "It's on the card," he replied dourly.

"I know it's on the card but how do I know that the card is yours?" the sergeant asked.

"Well, the name's O'Neill." Dermot's words twisted with nervousness as he continued, "the name same as Shane O'Neill, as Phelim O'Neill, as Art O'Neill, as the Hugh O'Neill who beat Elizabeth to her knees."

"I didn't ask for the history of your tribe," the sergeant said curtly. "What were you doing in the Free State?"

Dermot was tempted to say that he had been breathing the air of freedom. Instead he replied, "Visiting friends."

The sergeant continued looking at the identity card. Insistently he asked, "The name of your friends?"

"An aunt."

The sergeant turned the card over. "The name of your aunt?"

"O'Neill," Dermot answered untruthfully.

"Where does your aunt live?"

Dermot thrust his hands in his pockets and scrounged down into the seat. He knew what was going to happen next before he had the words out of his mouth. The old stubbornness swept over him. He had experienced it often—in grade school, in the Christian Brothers High School, at home when someone with authority pressed him too far. He did not look up at the sergeant as he doggedly replied, "That's none of your business."

To his surprise, the sergeant merely warned, "You'd do well to keep a civil tongue in your head." He turned to the other policeman and said, "O'Neill, Dermot."

The constable ran his pencil down a list of names on the sheet of paper. He shook his head slowly and Dermot, seeing the gesture, relaxed. The sergeant wordlessly handed back the card.

The two policemen left the compartment and Dermot again picked up the newspaper. The old man coughed several times and Dermot looked over at him.

With an outraged look on his face, the old man complained, "Here-by-God! You're the brazen tinker!"

Dermot leaned over and said confidentially, "I'm the adjutant-general of the I.R.A."

The old man drew back. "I don't give a hoot if you're the Pope of Rome. You're a cheeky gat!"

"I hate the peelers," Dermot said. He extended his right hand, thumb up and forefinger pointing, "Koosh! Koosh! I'd like to shoot all the bloody peelers in the North."

"God but you're the great blackguard!" The old man began to shake with excitement. "It's in jail you should be—you impudent pup!"

Dermot continued in a dreamy tone, "And after I get all the peelers," abruptly his face hardened. "I'd like to shoot the king. Koosh! Koosh! and that'd be the end of old stuttering George."

The old man was scandalized. He reached up to the rack and clapped his bowler hat on. Dermot shifted his forefinger until it pointed at the old man's vest. A fierce look came over his face as he hissed, "Koosh! Koosh!"

The old man glared wildly, "Bloody papist! Bloody kiss the Pope's bloody feet!"

Dermot kooshed again and the old man fled, slamming the door of the compartment. Dermot leaned back and started laughing.

An hour later the train arrived in Duncrana. Dermot walked up from the station. He wondered if the police in Duncrana knew of his absence and whether they would question him.

He was going to stop in and talk to McGinnis but the shop was closed and he remembered it was Sunday. As he stood outside, wondering whether he should go to Hannafin's, he heard McGinnis' peculiar walk coming up the street. He backed in against the door of the bicycle shop and waited. When McGinnis was about five yards away, Dermot stepped out and said, "Hello Don."

McGinnis stopped. "Mother of God, where did you come out of?" he asked in a surprised voice.

"I just got back on the nine train."

McGinnis caught him by the arm and together they went down the alleyway and entered the repair shop by the back door. McGinnis switched on the light and lifted himself up on the bench. Dermot sat down on a box.

"Where's Sean?" McGinnis asked.

"In the Free State."

"He's hurt?"

Dermot said quickly, "Nothing serious. A ricochet hit him on the leg. He'll be as right as rain in a week or so."

McGinnis' dark eyes lit up as he began talking. "Boys, you've no idea of the sport we've had. That night the sergeant and two policemen raided eight houses here in town. Of course they found nothing. The B-men had roadblocks up all over the place. You could hardly stick your nose out the door without being stopped by them. The next day the police lifted the Brigade O.C. and the Brigade adjutant and four other men in Applebridge."

"The Brigade O.C. and adjutant were on the raid," Dermot said.

McGinnis scornfully answered, "Aye, but the police don't know that."

"All the same it'll be a loss with the Brigade O.C. interned."

"It will to be sure, but in another way it'll be a blessing. We couldn't turn a hand here without the approval of Brigade. Yesterday I got a message from them to act on our own." McGinnis smiled grimly and continued, "I've already planned two raids. Both of them on police barracks. The police need a touch now after them lifting the boys." He leaned forward and asked eagerly, "But here I am blathering away. What was the raid like? What happened that Sean got hit?"

Dermot related the story of the raid and their flight to the border. When he had finished, McGinnis said, "That was great work, great work. You were lucky you got away over the border. They even had planes and dogs out the next day, looking you."

"We didn't travel during the day—only at night."

"Who shot the soldier?"

Dermot hesitated a moment before replying, "It was hard to tell. There were half a dozen of us firing away."

"But couldn't you tell if you were aiming at somebody or not?" McGinnis insistently asked.

"It was dark and we were shooting in the general direction of the guardhouse." For some reason, even in front of McGinnis, Dermot did not want to admit shooting anyone.

"All the same it was great work. I'd have given my right arm to be with you."

Dermot thought about Sean and asked, "Can you get word to Sean's family that he's all right? I'd be the better of not going anywhere near them."

"I'll get word to them tonight. We'll have to see about getting some money to him too. I'll get in touch with Brigade and they can send him some."

"God knows how long that will take," Dermot objected. "Couldn't you send him some from here?"

"I could but the raid was carried out by the Applebridge crowd. It's their responsibility—not ours."

"For the love of Moses! We're all working for the same cause. Send him a few quid. At least enough until Brigade can get some money to him."

A quick frown of annoyance crossed McGinnis' face. "I'll see what can be done," he said indefinitely.

"I'd better be getting back home. I don't know what in under God I'm going to tell them."

"Don't worry about that. Listen Dermot, can you come down tomorrow night? I'll need some help in planning one of these raids. Now that Sean's gone, you'll be acting adjutant until we get word from Brigade as to who'll replace him. It'll probably be you anyway."

Dermot stood up and stretched himself. "I'm so tired I could sleep till Easter Sunday," he complained.

"Take a run in tomorrow evening. I'll be in the shop the whole time."

Dermot said nothing and buttoned his jacket. He walked over to the door. "'Night," he called to McGinnis.

As Dermot came up the lane to his house he heard the strains of the accordion and he smiled. From inside came a questioning bark from Tone. He pushed on the latch and walked into the kitchen. Bella stopped playing when she saw him and his mother blessed herself quickly. For a moment there was silence as he pulled a chair up to the fire and sat down.

"Have you had tea?" his mother asked and reached forward, placing the kettle on the crook.

"I'm brave and hungry," Dermot replied.

Ned was seated in the corner, cleaning his nails with a penknife. He scraped under the thumbnail, looked at the dirt with interest and then wiped the blade on the leg of his trousers. He asked Dermot, "Have a nice trip?"

"Brave trip," Dermot answered reticently.

Bella wriggled out of the straps of the accordion and hung it over the fireplace. She turned and asked indignantly, "Where in the name of God have you been?"

"Away."

"Away? God in heaven, what an answer. Away where?"

"If anyone asks, I was visiting Aunt Josie in Donegal."

Patrick wanted to ask his son about the raid but was afraid of bringing down the wrath of his wife. He compromised by saying, "The sergeant was here asking for you. We told him you left early Saturday morning and didn't say where you were going."

"Saturday morning?" Dermot repeated.

"Aye, we thought the raid being Friday, it would be better to say Saturday morning."

"You won't fool the sergeant," Bella interjected. "Yon boy's not as green as he's cabbage looking."

Kathleen came over and looked down at her son. She didn't know whether to laugh or cry. "Sit over to the table there and eat something," she said. She shook her head pessimistically and added, "You're a terrible lad."

Dermot sat over to the table and started to eat. His mother sat down across from him and her hands started nervously playing with the salt shaker. "Listen Dermot, I want you to stay away from that crowd."

Dermot looked over at his mother. The upper part of her mouth was slack and he felt a twinge of annoyance that she had taken out the upper half of her false teeth. Usually she waited until bedtime before removing them. Sometimes her false teeth bothered her and no matter how often she was told that she looked better wearing both sets, she still persisted in occasionally taking out the upper one. Dermot, still tired and irritable from his exertions of the past two days, felt a mean desire to hurt her and replied, "I can't."

"What do you mean, you can't?"

"I just can't. I can't leave the organization just because I want to. I'm in it now and I'll have to do what I'm told."

His mother shook her head, "To think I've reared a son who could say to my face that he can't leave an evil thing."

"There's nothing evil about fighting for your country," Patrick interrupted.

Dermot wished that his father would keep quiet. He knew from experience that Patrick usually managed to make things worse.

"There's evil in shooting people," Kathleen answered. "Shooting young men and them not knowing what's happening, not even knowing they're in danger. There's evil in killing, killing in the secret dark of the night. There's evil in ignoring the teachings of the Church."

"The Church be damned," Patrick grunted. "So long as the Church gets its money in dues that's all the teaching it's worried about." The time for the Easter dues was drawing near and the thought of paying them was rankling in Patrick.

Mechanically Dermot continued to eat, hoping that the subject would blow over.

"Did you shoot any of the soldiers?" his mother asked.

"No," Dermot lied easily. "I wasn't even inside the place. I was guarding one of the roads to the barracks."

Kathleen looked searchingly at her son and wondered whether or not to believe him. She went over to the fire and came back with the teapot, refilling Dermot's cup. From the kettle she poured hot water into the pot, sloshed it around and opened the kitchen door. With a vigorous sweep of her arm she scattered the water and tea leaves over the yard. The cat sneaked in and slid along the wall, its tail erect. Kathleen came back and set the teapot down on the table. "I'd rather," she said to Dermot, "I'd rather see my son in jail for five or six years than to think he's shot someone—killed someone."

"I haven't shot anyone," Dermot said wearily as he pulled his chair around to the fire. Bella moved over to make room for him. He looked across at her and asked, "How's the courting?"

"You've got a neck," Bella snapped. "Coming back here and making jokes and everybody astray in the head wondering what's happened to you."

Dermot sighed and called Tone over and began to pat him on the back. The dog's tail drummed slowly on the floor. Kathleen came to the fire for hot water and found her way blocked by the dog as she tried to get in to the kettle. She thumped Tone in the ribs with the back of her doubled fist. "Get back out of that, Tone," she said crossly and the dog slunk away from the fire and started to crawl under the table. The cat saw him coming and tried to skip away. Tone darted at her with his mouth open and she let a quick spit out of her and jumped to the side. Backing against the wall, she arched her body and looked indignantly at the dog. Tone made a wry face at her and thumped his tail in quiet satisfaction.

"I'm going to bed," Dermot announced, as he got off the chair.

He left the kitchen and went into the bedroom he shared with Ned. For a moment he sat on the edge of the bed as he unlaced his boots. Then he took off the rest of his clothes and hung them on a nail. Flinging back the heavy coverlet, he stretched himself out in the bed with several convulsive jerks, his body tensing with the shock of the cold sheets. He pulled the coverlet up over his head.

A few minutes later his mother came into the room. She stooped down and felt his socks. "Those stockings are damp," she said accusingly. She picked them up and held them in her hand. "Did you say your prayers?" she demanded.

"I'm saying them," Dermot answered from beneath the cover.

"Wonder you wouldn't say them on your knees like a decent Christian."

He turned over on his side. "Ah Mother dear, I'm desperate tired."

With a precise gesture she smoothed the coverlet at the foot of the bed and sat down. "You'll have no more to do with them?" she said pleadingly.

"I wish to God I wouldn't, but I'll have to."

"You don't have to at all. You could go to England or the Free State."

He looked at her over the edge of the coverlet. "Is it you that's telling me to go to England? Why don't you let Bella go?"

"Bella's just a wee slip of a girl. That's different. God knows I'd rather see you in England, or even Australia, than mixed up with that wild bunch. No good will come of it." Dermot looked away from his mother. His glance rested on the lamp that hung on the wall. The oil was getting low and the flame from the half-dry wick was starting to flutter, projecting erratic shadows in the room. He closed his eyes. "I'd never have gotten mixed up in it, had I known that the Church was against it," he said. As soon as the words were out he knew that he meant them. He thought he should ease his mother's mind and he added, "Don't worry too much. They've interned most of the leaders and that means there won't be anything doing for a good while."

His mother stood up. "I'll leave you alone. Finish your prayers."

"Take the lamp with you. It needs oil," Dermot told her.

Kathleen lifted the lamp from the wall and left the room.

Dermot lay still, grateful for the sudden darkness. It would be nice, he thought, to go to England. In a few years—two or three—he could save enough to come home and get married to Neeve and open some sort of a business. A nice handy wee business with none of the dirt and muck of a farm. But could he run out and leave the Duncrana crowd? They would say he was cowardly, he realized. By the time he came back maybe the whole business would be dead, though as long as the border existed there would always be trouble and bitterness. They would always hold it against him, unless he could find a way of leaving that didn't look like desertion. He thought about McGinnis. That was the great blood and thunder man, planning a couple of raids. He would have to talk soft to him, try to get him out of the notion of being another Mick Collins. He wondered whether McGinnis loved his country as much as he loved the idea of being a gunman.

The murmur of voices from the kitchen became lower and he drifted off to sleep.

EIGHTEEN

The district inspector tapped the floor with his cane. Then he placed it behind him, rocked back on it and asked, "You've had no trouble in Duncrana?"

"None yet," the sergeant answered as he played with a sheaf of papers on the table in front of him. "At the same time I believe there's a company of the I.R.A. here. So far they've been inactive but I don't know how long they'll stay that way."

The district inspector walked over to the window of the day-room and looked out through the bars at the street outside. The sergeant closely watched the spruce-looking figure and knew that the D.I. was adopting a pose of profound meditation. He noted the correct Guards' mustache and the black and gleaming Sam Browne belt. "By these signs shall you know them," came filtering through the sergeant's mind. Authority and a thousand years of police stability emanated from the D.I. He was the culmination of a millennium of rule by appearance and around the world millions of black and brown, white and yellow people paid tribute to authority synthesized in a Sam Browne belt and a Sandhurst bearing; whole continents conquered with a Guards' mustache and a swagger stick.

The D.I. turned and said the expected thing, "A quiet village, Duncrana."

"Quiet enough," the sergeant answered with a wry smile. "A good little place too. If it weren't for this I.R.A. business we'd have no trouble at all."

"You have a copy of the list of suspects you sent to county headquarters?" the D.I. asked.

The sergeant went over to a cabinet and pulled out a drawer. He came back and handed a piece of paper to the D.I. "You'll notice there are two lists," he said. "The first list is of those I'm reasonably sure are in the I.R.A. As sure as a man can be without direct evidence. The second list are possible suspects."

"You've only five on the first list," the D.I. commented.

"Yes, that's all. It's difficult to estimate the strength of the I.R.A. here. I would say from ten to thirty men."

"Do you think that some of the locals were involved in the Applebridge raid?"

"It's possible."

"Could you name them at all?"

"No. Beyond saying that they're more likely to be found in the first list than in the second."

The D.I. read aloud the names on the first list: "McGinnis, Don, age twenty-four, bicycle mechanic; O'Neill, Dermot, age twenty, farmer; Reilly, Sean, twenty-two, farmer; Malone, Peter, twenty-eight, unemployed; Corrigan, Dan, twenty-two, carpenter's helper. You've checked the whereabouts of these men on the night of the raid?"

"They're all accounted for except Reilly. I couldn't check all the men on the second list."

"And Reilly?" the D.I. asked.

"He disappeared the night of the raid and hasn't been seen since."

The D.I. pursed his lips, "Quite significant. Take him in for questioning when he returns. That is if he returns."

"I plan to do that," the sergeant said.

The D.I. walked over to the sergeant's desk. "You know," he said, looking thoughtfully at the sergeant, "we should lift those five men."

"I'd rather you wouldn't," the sergeant answered.

"I won't over your objections," the D.I. stated. Loath to leave the matter at that, he continued, "You know what my answer is for this trouble. Intern the most likely suspects from each district and we'll break the back of the organization."

"It may, but I'm looking beyond the present," the sergeant replied. "If these men are interned, they'll come out after the war, and they'll be the seed of future disturbances. The local people get on well with the police. If I lift these men the town won't blame police headquarters, or me, Sergeant Crawley, they'll blame the police and future sergeants coming here will find an embittered village."

"I shouldn't worry about bitterness. We're concerned about laws—not emotions."

The sergeant went over to a small washbasin and turned on the tap. He let the water run and then filled a cup and took a drink. He set the cup down and said to the D.I., "I realize that I shouldn't be saying this, but I don't believe in lifting men under the Special Powers Act. I know it's wartime—I have a son myself in North Africa—but so far we've adopted constitutional means. Wholesale arrests without trial will justify the I.R.A.'s contention that we're an undemocratic government."

The D.I. made a small face. "Sergeant I could understand your reasons for not wanting the men interned if you thought there'd be no trouble with them. But the reason you've given is not relevant to your duties as a police sergeant. I should leave the political aspects of the matter to the government."

"And keeping bitterness alive isn't a political aspect?" the sergeant asked.

The D.I. ignored the question and his cane came up for a second, the end of it pointing at the sergeant. "You realize that if anything happens here both myself and the Tyrone police commissioner will take a rather dim view of your judgment?"

The D.I. lowered the cane to the floor as the sergeant replied, "I'm too old a man and too long a policeman to guide my actions solely by what my superiors might think."

The D.I. suddenly became brisk. "Right then, for the moment we'll hold off. However, should Reilly come back, question him regarding his whereabouts and take a set of prints and forward them to the police lab in Belfast. I'll have the Border Section keep watch for him. We have a set of prints from the Bren they left behind."

"Do you want me to notify you if he returns?"

"Not unless his prints match those on the Bren. In that case we'll have something to proceed with."

The D.I. lifted his hat from the hatrack. "Well sergeant, I must be going," he said.

Sergeant Crawley accompanied him to the door. "Don't worry about Duncrana, sir. There'll be no trouble from here."

The D.I. walked out to the street and his driver opened the door of the car for him. He settled back and put the proper condescension into the wave he gave the sergeant as the car drove off.

Later that afternoon, the sergeant took a pair of boots around to Hannafin. He entered the shop and placed the boots on the counter.

Hannafin looked up, his black eyes probing, saying, "The law; steady, implacable, unrelenting." He fell silent, picked up the boots and looked at the worn heels with interest.

"Go on," the sergeant requested laughingly, "it sounds interesting."

Hannafin took the leather knife and scraped a piece of dirt from beneath the arch of one of the boots. Musingly, he continued, "But sometimes a fever grips the body that directs the law. A shiver or two passes through it. The nerves stumble, the whole corpus agitates, the heart panics, the legs weaken, the feet shuffle and the boots wear. And I, James Hannafin, Caucasian, Celt, Catholic, cobbler—I see the evidence. The right heel worn down more than the left, where Sergeant Crawley has been standing on the stone floor of the barracks, thinking and worrying, spinning slowly on the heel of the right boot to the tune of that little weakness, the slight sickness that has upset the functioning of that greatest of British institutions—the law."

The sergeant laughed, "Tell me, Jimmy, if you didn't know about the Applebridge raid, what interpretation would you have put on the worn heel?"

Hannafin placed the boots on a shelf. "Another one just as good." Abruptly the ruminative mood left him and he rubbed his hands together briskly. He stood up and gave a little jig, singing as he did so, "Oh, you and me in the one bed'll lie; and you'll lie next the wall." He looked over at the sergeant and asked, "How's Derek?"

"The best. No complaints from him."

Hannafin sat down again. "That's good," he said. "Tell me, sergeant, will Britain win the war?"

"Britain always wins the war—even when she loses," the sergeant replied.

"There's been one long war she's never won."

"Ireland?"

"Aye. She's managed to hold the good will of America, of

Canada and Australia and New Zealand—but what a defeat in Ireland."

"You're wrong, Jimmy. The fact that we're speaking English is a proof of England's victory. And it was a victory for Ireland too, because it was England that brought civilization to this country. English common law, universal suffrage, parliamentary procedure, were all taken from England. The Irish were in what Captain Boyle calls 'a state of chassis' and the English came over and governed them, disciplined them, showing the Irish how to govern themselves."

"But it took a 1916 to force England to allow the Irish to govern themselves," Hannafin protested. "And any country that forces another into the awful terror of a revolution can hardly be called the greengrocer of civilization's fruits."

"I think," the sergeant said pensively, "that England's mistake was in not recognizing the emotionalism of the Irish people. I wonder if England's civilization is the result of the awesome English serenity, the rationality, the ability to compromise, or if the Englishman's reserve, his stiff upper lip, his lack of emotion is due to a thousand years of continuing civilization?"

"If the average Englishman is the result of a thousand years of civilization, then God keep me happily savage," Hannafin answered.

"Jimmy, you're a terrible man."

"I am that," Hannafin replied. "I who am bald and bent and blind, with a heavy heart and a wandering mind."

"Yeats?"

"'The Wanderings of Usheen.'"

At that moment the front door opened and Dermot O'Neill entered the shop. He looked in surprise at the sergeant.

"Have a nice trip?" the sergeant asked.

"Middling," Dermot answered, after a moment's hesitation.

"Sean come back with you?"

Dermot wondered if the sergeant knew that both he and

Sean had left the town together. Again he hesitated before answering, "No, he didn't. Why, is he gone somewhere?"

"He isn't in Duncrana—hasn't been for a couple of days. I thought he went away with you."

Dermot laughed, partly in relief and partly for effect, "Now what would Sean be visiting my Aunt Josie for?"

"Perhaps for the same reason you wanted to visit her," the sergeant answered enigmatically. He picked up his cap and placed it carefully on his head, pulling down the visor. "I'm afraid, Dermot, you're going to get into trouble," he said. "It would vex me to see you locked up for a few years."

"Don't worry about me, sergeant. I can take care of my own affairs."

"Can you take care of your friends as easily?" the sergeant asked.

"Aye, I can handle them too."

The sergeant turned to Hannafin, "They'll be ready on Saturday?"

"Saturday evening."

"Good night Jimmy, good night Dermot," the sergeant called as he left the shop.

"What was he doing in here? Was he asking about Sean and me?" Dermot demanded in an intense whisper.

"Don't get your water hot," Hannafin replied, motioning toward the shelf. "He left in a pair of boots. Anyway, he'd know better than to try and get information out of me."

Dermot lifted himself up on the bench and sat with his knees drawn up. Hannafin looked over at him and said, "You be to have great sport on your vacation."

"What do you mean? I was with my aunt in Donegal."

"Aunt how-are-ye. You're as nervous as a May trout," Hannafin scoffed.

Dermot relaxed and smiled, "Aye, I had rare sport in a way." He continued in a low tone, "I shot a man." He sighed and felt the tenseness leaving him.

Hannafin paused in the act of hammering in a nail, "One of the British soldiers?"

"Aye," Dermot looked at the ceiling. "I thought of what it would be like to shoot a man. I thought it wouldn't bother me one way or the other. Last Friday night I was in a rage. I enjoyed shooting and I felt a wild joy when I heard the screel of your man getting hit."

Hannafin snorted sarcastically, "Like shooting a fox?"

Dermot continued in a wondering tone, reliving the moments of the raid. "I aimed the gun and fired. I wanted to kill everyone. It wouldn't have mattered who I killed. I could have shot the men who were with me. I didn't think of Ireland, or that I was righting the wrongs of seven hundred years. I only thought of what a strange power was on me. I could have slaughtered a hundred men." He suddenly sobered as he added, "I'm afraid the one I shot is in the hospital."

Hannafin laid aside the hammer and took the boot off the last. "Don't worry your head about him. Young Annie McCourt was in this morning. Her sister works at the military hospital and she says that the soldier is going to get well. They must be listing him as critical to keep the Orangemen all worked up."

"Thank God for that. I wouldn't like to be the cause of any man's death."

"And Sean?"

"He was shot but it's nothing serious. He's in the Free State."

"You must have had a wild time."

Dermot shook his head. "To tell the truth I was more worried over the British soldier than I was over us."

"You're a rare turn."

"I don't know what's right any more."

"That's when life begins to get awkward. When we start worrying about the right and wrong of things instead of doing what the neighbor is doing, or what he expects *us* to do."

Dermot lifted himself down from the bench. "McGinnis inside?" he asked.

"I don't think so," Hannafin replied.

"I'm away then," Dermot said and left the shop.

On his way up the street he stopped in to see McGinnis. Several men were in the shop and Dermot waited until they had left. The light was turned off and they both went into the empty kitchen. McGinnis sat down at the kitchen table and said, "I've been working on a raid. I want to know what you think of it."

Dermot cracked a knuckle. "I don't think we should attempt anything for a while," he replied. "Not until the police activity dies down."

"No," McGinnis objected sharply. "We have to prove that the I.R.A. isn't affected by the police raids."

"Why?"

"If we stop our activities now—the men will lose heart."

"Go ahead," Dermot acquiesced.

"You know the police barracks at Trilarran? It's a small country barracks with three policemen and a sergeant. It would make the ideal place for a quick raid."

"Hold on," Dermot objected. "We haven't started to raid the police yet. Does Brigade know you're planning this raid?"

"Amn't I after telling you before that Brigade has given me authority to plan raids without referring to them," McGinnis said impatiently.

"I know, but so far we haven't touched a police barracks. After all, the policemen are Irishmen. They aren't part of the British Army."

McGinnis stared curiously at Dermot. "They might as well be," he answered. "Anyway, after the police lifting the boys in Applebridge, it's time they were given a touch. As for their being Irishmen, they shouldn't be helping England. If they're Irish, they're traitors to their country."

He reached over to a little alcove under the window and

pulled out a piece of paper. Taking a pencil he began to make a rough sketch. "Pull up a chair," he ordered.

Dermot sat down at the table and watched as McGinnis sketched in details of the proposed raid. Inside him something kept warning that he would have to find a way out of going on the raid, but he said nothing and appeared to be in agreement with his commanding officer as the latter unfolded his plans.

NINETEEN

Spring came to the land of the O'Neills with the quickening caress of a lover. The harshness of March was left behind and a new softness, a perennial tenderness enveloped the land. It was the time of conception, of the sprouting of seed in the uterine earth and spring's swollen ecstasy touched everything. Trees began to bud, the oats to braid, grass to shoot and the cat got pregnant.

Staid old cows began to flirt, calling lugubriously to the legendary bulls of their memory. Matronly working mares laid back their ears, rolled their eyes and delicately stepped around like fillies. Dogs were riotous, traveling miles at night to come wearily home in the morning, battle-scarred and content. At no time did roosters harangue the sun with such impudent brashness and never were hens more coy.

Old men felt a new briskness in their bones and the resigned, winter-weary thoughts of turning over the farm to
someone else evaporated as they noted with surprise that they
could work as well as ever, though the following day seemed
to bring more aches and pains than usual. Girls coming home
from the dances found the lads more insistent and their own
defenses somewhat weakened. If brawling March was puberty
—then April was a courtship: tender, complete and joyful.

Bella felt it and her playing of the accordion took on a
deeper beauty. Kathleen performed her own peculiar spring
rite, a highly problematical budget that allowed the purchase
of a set of Beleek China by Christmas. Tone, usually a good
cattle dog, forgot the dignity of his calling and on several oc-
casions exuberantly chased a couple of amused young rabbits.
Patrick remembered old sea songs, forgotten all winter, and
slurring over the unnautical lines, chanted his way around
the farm. Ned began to think wistfully of a new girl working
in Duncrana and went about his work holding involved, im-
aginary conversations with her.

Hannafin took the notion that he was a young man again
and his wife, half laughing and half serious, wanted to know
what kind of an old cod he was anyway, at his age.

Billy Gilkinson got drunk the April fair day and wept
beautifully in Devlin's pub over a favorite dog that had been
poisoned some five years previous.

Father McCory shocked the housekeeper by singing a song
about a man who had a dozen wives. For several weeks he
neglected Aquinas and Newman and went for long walks in
the country. He even astonished Father Sheehy, borrowing his
fishing rod one evening and coming back with an eight-inch
trout.

Father Sheehy himself felt the change. His disciplined, cor-
ner-cutting morning Mass became slower and more sedate.
For years the daily churchgoers had been accustomed to a

twenty-minute Mass and they felt vaguely resentful when the parish priest suddenly sprang this more measured, thirty-minute ceremony. But Father Sheehy paid no heed and his Latin was stately, clear and perfectly pronounced. Never was the consecration more reverent or the "Dominus Vobiscum" more benign and no longer was the prayer for peace cut short at the end of the Mass.

Sergeant Crawley put in a new bed of rose bushes and began leaving the barracks an hour earlier in the evenings. Police discipline slacked off and the constables on town patrol spent most of their time in Moran's pub, shifting to the kitchen when closing time came.

Even the shuffle of McGinnis' leg became lighter and several times he was heard whistling.

Dermot thought of Neeve and Neeve thought of Dermot.

And Sean Reilly, remembering the dances and girls of Duncrana, let homesickness defeat his caution and returned from the Free State.

Dermot heard the news at home. All morning he had been drawing manure with the mare and cart to one of the meadows. He was standing ankle-deep in the doughal, graiping the manure into the cart when he heard Finnegan's lorry coming up the lane. He stepped out of the dungheap, the steam rising from his rubber boots, and led the mare and cart into the garden. The lorry turned around in the yard and backed up to the kitchen door. The driver unloaded a bag of flour and brought it into the scullery where he placed it on a wooden box. Dermot was standing in the yard, cleaning his hands with a bunch of hay when the driver came out, offered him a cigarette and asked, "Hear about Sean Reilly?"

Dermot felt a tiny splash of fear. He dropped the handful of hay, took the cigarette and shook his head.

The driver was full of the news. "He was lifted by the police last night. They have him in the Crumlin Road Jail.

They say he was with the I.R.A. and the police claim they found his fingerprints on the Bren gun the raiders left behind."

Dermot closed his eyes for a moment as he inhaled. With all the excitement of their flight and Sean's wound, they had never thought of fingerprints on the Bren. "Are they going to try him?" he asked.

The driver stepped up on the running board and opened the door of the cab. "I suppose so. What will the I.R.A. do now?"

"Be damned if I know," Dermot answered.

"Boys-a-dear, but they'll give poor Sean twenty years," the driver said as he slammed the door of the lorry. He waved to Dermot and drove down the lane.

Dermot brought the mare out of the garden and backed her into the doughal. He lifted the graip and continued loading the cart. With fingerprints and a half-healed wound, they had more than enough evidence, he realized. He wondered if they had gotten his own fingerprints too. It was stupid to have left the gun behind and worse for Sean to have come back. Now they would have to try and get him out and the police weren't likely to be careless with the only suspect they had found. He would have to go in that evening and see McGinnis. They couldn't let Sean go on trial.

He stuck the graip near the tailboard and called to the mare, "Get up Tessie, come on." The mare lowered her head, hunched her forequarters and leaned into the collar.

That evening Dermot went in to see McGinnis. The latter sent word to Quinn and Malone to meet at the shop at ten o'clock.

At ten the four men were gathered together. The news had come as a shock. Dermot explained, "I told him to stay in the Free State until we sent word it was safe to come back."

"Did they lift him at home?" Malone asked.

"They pulled him off the train as soon as it crossed the border," McGinnis replied.

"What does it matter how he was arrested," Dermot said impatiently. "We've got to get him out."

McGinnis shook his head. "We don't have to do a thing. I don't see what we can do. He's in Belfast and we can't try a rescue there. The Belfast companies have enough of their own men interned without trying to free one of ours. The whole point is that he disobeyed orders. He should have stayed in the Free State. I can't risk losing any more men because of Sean's carelessness."

Dermot ran his tongue over his lip. "For pity's sake, Don! That's no way to talk. He's one of us. We can't let him stay in jail for maybe ten or twenty years." Dermot appealed to Malone, "What do you think, Peter?"

"We can't do anything until they bring him to trial," Malone answered. "If they try him here in Duncrana, there might be a chance."

McGinnis abruptly threw out his hand and said, "As long as I'm commanding officer of this company we'll try no rescue, here nor anywhere else. He's one man. The organization has lost him. We can't ditch our work and plans because we've lost one man. He shouldn't have been so bloody careless leaving the gun behind."

Dermot thought of their long flight and their hardships together. A quick temper boiled as he replied, "You weren't there. What do you know about it? The man was wounded— the blood was pouring out of him. Was he supposed to climb a wall in that shape, lugging a machine gun around with him? Oh, we're a grand bunch of comrades, we are!"

McGinnis looked sharply at Dermot. The tic on his cheek started jumping. "Don't forget, it's me that's the O.C. of the company and I'll make the decisions," he said. "We'll have no more talk about it now. Quinn, let you find out when he'll be brought to trial and where. Until then the matter's finished."

Dermot stared bitterly at his O.C. and said, "I hope if you ever find yourself in that position, you'll still be as concerned about the organization."

McGinnis answered pompously, "I'd go out tonight and die if I thought it would help in any way to end partition."

"Aye, you're the great bloody hero," Dermot remarked sarcastically.

McGinnis was about to reply when Quinn interrupted, "Let's let it drop for now. Maybe we can do something later."

TWENTY

Several weeks later Sean was brought to trial in Duncrana. The town was packed as the special sessions coincided with the weekly market day. Lorryloads of police arrived from Belfast to prevent any demonstrations or a possible rescue of the prisoner by the I.R.A. The public houses did a roaring trade as the sessions, Sean, the I.R.A., the government and the price of feeding stuffs were cussed and discussed furiously.

The event drew photographers and reporters from both English and Irish newspapers. Early in the morning an English reporter with a passion for getting his story direct from what he called "the little people" was manhandled in a nationalist pub for referring to the accused as a terrorist instead of a patriot. The police managed to restore calm and escort him off the premises.

Catholics and Protestants, normally good friends, refused to speak to each other. Old Billy Gilkinson got drunk and from the steps of Devlin's pub challenged any "whore's son of a Papish" to fight but as even the Catholics liked old Billy, nothing happened until eventually the police led him away, swaggering down the town, leering at his Catholic neighbors and defiantly singing "The Boyne Water."

Two Catholic boys from the parochial school placed an Irish tricolor on top of the ball alley and heaved stones at the sorely tried police when they attempted to remove it.

Hannafin didn't do a stitch of work and spent the whole day circulating from one pub to another, stirring up arguments.

The trial was to start at twelve o'clock and at half past eleven the courthouse was jammed. Dermot had managed to squeeze in at the back and find standing room.

At a few minutes past twelve the judge and the clerk of the court arrived and the prosecutor, a king's counsel, took his seat at the proper table.

Being uncomfortable in the press of people, Dermot had maneuvered his way until he stood with his back against the rear wall. He had felt trapped in the crowd and even yet was trying to shove his way, along the wall, to the back door. He came across an elbow of piping that stuck out about a foot above the floor, the pipe leading straight up the wall. By hooking one foot in the elbow and grasping the pipe, he found that he could lift himself above the rest of the crowd. He noticed that the front of the courtroom was liberally sprinkled with policemen and among them he recognized the sergeant.

At that moment two constables came shouldering their way through the people at the back of the courthouse. Following them came Sean Reilly, handcuffed between two more policemen. A final pair of constables brought up the rear. Sean noticed Dermot and flashed him a quick grim smile. Dermot closed his eyes and shook his head. Sean was marched up to the prisoner's dock, a bare table with a wooden railing in front of it.

From his position Dermot watched as the clerk of the court consulted with the judge. The judge rapped his desk and announced that the court was in session. The clerk stood up and read out, "The crown versus Sean Reilly."

The king's counsel began to present the crown's case. In a flat confident voice he charged treason-felony as "Sean Reilly, in company with persons unknown, conspired to stir up and levy war against his majesty's government in that he provided himself with a machine gun and journeyed to Applebridge in preparation for an attack; entered, disguised and armed, a building of the war department; was within the building, a military barracks; and attacked the guard with gunfire, wounding four soldiers."

Sean was directed to take the stand. After the customary questions concerning his identity, he was asked how he pled. He replied in a loud, controlled voice, "As a member of the Irish Republican Army, I refuse to recognize the legality of a British court on Irish soil and, as an Irishman, I refuse to admit allegiance to a British king."

A murmur ran through the crowd as Sean's admission of membership in the I.R.A. was tantamount to a confession of guilt. Despite this, the judge ordered that a plea of "not guilty" be entered.

The fatigue of holding onto the pipe caused Dermot to lower himself to the floor. A strange uneasiness pervaded him and although he knew his fear to be irrational, he was frightened that someone in the court would point him out as Sean's accomplice. He nervously eyed the back door, a few feet away from him.

Meanwhile the trial moved swiftly. Sergeant Crawley swore that the accused had never before been in trouble but that on the morning following the raid, he had gone to the house of the accused and had been informed that the accused was away on a vacation.

A doctor gave evidence that he had examined the accused and found a triangular shaped wound in the right thigh, that had been of recent origin and probably caused by a bullet or piece of grenade.

Several soldiers gave evidence of being in the barracks on the night of the raid and hearing machine gun fire and the explosions of grenades.

Four soldiers, one of whom had his arm in a sling, gave evidence that a body of men had attacked the guardhouse with grenades, rifles and machine guns and that the guard had returned the fire.

A military policeman testified that he found a Bren gun inside the wall, near the place where the raiders had made their entry and escape by means of a rope.

A ballistics expert testified that six empty cartridge cases had been found inside the barracks and that it appeared that these cases had been fired in exhibit A, whereupon he pointed to the captured Bren gun.

A fingerprint expert gave evidence that the prints found on the gun matched those of the accused.

There was no defense as Sean, in refusing to recognize the court, neither employed a defense counsel nor cross-examined prosecution witnesses.

Dermot again hoisted himself on the pipe and watched as the prosecutor summed up the case, laying special emphasis on five points: Sean's fingerprints had been found on the captured gun; six cartridge cases had been found inside the barracks and proven to have been fired from the Bren; a large wound, not yet healed, had been found on the leg of the accused; the accused was missing from Duncrana the day after the raid and, finally, the accused admitted to being a member of the I.R.A.

During the K.C.'s summation, Dermot had become increasingly nervous with the strange feeling that he himself, and not Sean, was on trial. He stepped down to the floor and noticed that his hands were wet and heavy with sweat. He felt a moment of weakness and a faint wave of nausea swept over him. As he strove to control the sickness, his ears caught the judge's voice, the phrases seeming to drop down from the wall behind him. "In this, as in all other cases . . burden on the prosecution to prove their case . . . finding a verdict in accordance with the evidence . . . the crown seems to have proved . . . it would appear that the accused . . . attack planned with deliberation."

There was a stir in the courtroom as the judge finished his speech and the jury retired. The court was not recessed and the spectators sensed a quick verdict. From the head of the courtroom came a commotion as two policemen started to leave. Dermot glimpsed the black figures making their way down the aisle. They seemed to be looking toward the rear wall and Dermot had the sudden feeling that they meant to arrest him. He started pushing and shouldering his way along the wall, half sick and sweating with fear. The crowd, seeing his face drained of color, made way for him and he stumbled out the door and into the street. He crossed over and went down an entry into Mulgrew's yard and took refuge in an old stable. There he sat on the floor and waited for the weakness to pass. A vague sense of shame came over him as he realized that he either should have tried to free Sean or should have given himself up and gone on trial with him. And he knew that however long a sentence Sean would serve, he would always feel a guilt, a sense of failure.

Feeling better, he got up and walked out on the street. The crowd had started to leave the courtroom but the fear still burdened Dermot and he walked up the town, away from the people.

"Were you at the trial, Dermot," a shout followed him. Dermot turned to see one of the McIntyres, a member of the company, hurrying to catch up with him.

"I was a wee while," Dermot answered.

"Sean got ten years."

"Ten years," Dermot echoed softly. "And we won't lift a finger to help him, John?"

"No," McIntyre said awkwardly, defensively. "But some day soon we'll get a chance to free all the lads."

"That's what McGinnis says," Dermot said angrily.

"If there wasn't a chance, sure we wouldn't be fighting," McIntyre countered.

Dermot felt impatient at McIntyre's lack of understanding. He said to him, "John, I was with that man. I should be with him now."

"Ach man I know how you feel," McIntyre replied. "A few drinks is what you need." McIntyre felt uncomfortable and seeing his brother standing on the steps of Devlin's pub, took advantage of it and said to Dermot, "There's Tom. I have to see if he bought any plants." He turned and hurried down the street.

Dermot continued up the town, his mind a disordered riot of thoughts. Ten years; ten summers and ten springs. Sean would be thirty-four, his youth gone, his life half over. A horse and cart passed him. Longer than the lifetime of a horse, he thought. But the horse was a prisoner too; a prisoner of the farmer and he had to work at the farmer's whim, although there was a difference. The horse didn't know he was a prisoner and Sean would know. Was it worth it? Did the people of the Free State appreciate the freedom that the men of 1916 had given up their lives for? Or were the people in the Free State any freer? They could fly the Irish flag but what was a flag? Why was it so important to fly a particular flag? They were citizens instead of subjects and lived in a republic instead of a kingdom but these were mere differences in words.

A youth came walking down the street, holding out from his body a pair of hens. Their feet were tied together and they hung down from the youth's fist, neck feathers ruffled out. Two more prisoners, Dermot thought, or were we all prisoners? But again hens wouldn't know the difference. A squawk came in answer as one hen tried to lift her head. They know something is wrong. They know they cannot move and they want to, Dermot thought. But all this wondering was foolish. He should decide what was right and then do it. Should he try to free Sean? And perhaps kill a British soldier and lose his own freedom? No, that wasn't the answer. What should he do about the I.R.A.? Should he leave it? Was it right or wrong? Always he had thought that Ireland should be free but now he didn't know what freedom was—or what absence of freedom justified a rebellion. Who could he ask? McGinnis? But he was afraid that McGinnis was a rebel because of something inside him, something that had nothing to do with freedom or the lack of it. In any country McGinnis would be a rebel, against state or Church or family. He would like to ask the sergeant but the sergeant had to give the answers the law gave and these he didn't trust. Not the laws that were passed by the Northern government. He would ask Hannafin, although Hannafin never gave answers—that was the trouble with him. A great man with questions but no good with answers. Still he could ask him. Ask him whether he was right in being in the I.R.A. and if it was wrong, what he should do.

The people were starting to leave the town. The circus was over. They had seen a man sentenced to ten years in prison and each one was happy that it had not happened to him. Secretly some of them thought it was the proper medicine for Reilly. Why could he not be like the rest of his neighbors instead of trying to make a bloody hero of himself? Others thought hard and bitter thoughts about England and viewed the trial as the latest in a litany of injustices. Some of the young girls felt aggrieved that a good man and a potential husband had been withdrawn from circulation—Sean had always been great sport.

A cautious English reporter went into a Protestant-Orange pub and, mindful of the morning's difficulties, diplomatically referred to Sean as a patriot. He was promptly assaulted by a furious Orangeman who mistook the timidity of the newsman's speech for a Dublin accent. The police again rescued him.

The sergeant released a sober Billy Gilkinson and he made a nuisance of himself, going around to everybody and apologizing. Billy felt bad when he heard that Sean had been given ten years.

Ned O'Neill worked himself into a slow anger against the government until it grew fierce enough to be used as an excuse for getting patriotically drunk.

Sean's mother and father went home to their farm, closed the door of the house and began wordlessly to set about the evening's tasks.

TWENTY-ONE

Dermot tossed uneasily in his sleep. He was dreaming and he found himself in a box. The box was so small that Dermot had to kneel. Through the box from top to bottom ran a cable and Dermot could tell by his body that the box was swinging in huge arcs. At the end of one of the arcs, when the box was slightly tilted, a burst of light came down on him and he looked up and saw that the top of the box had disappeared and overhead there was nothing only a deep blue. Not the clear blue of a sky but the turgid heavy blue of a storm-roiled sea. The box swung through two more arcs before one of the sides fell away. He cowered against the cable, grasping it with his hands. He tried to look over the side but his fear pulled him back. Slowly the box swung through space and another side fell away. Dermot could see over the edge and for miles below him there was nothing but space that melted away, and he knew that if he fell he would hurtle forever through the blue depths. He looked at the cable and followed it up through the space overhead to where it disappeared into the blue thick sea. Another side fell and now there was only one side left and the bottom platform. He watched and counted the swings of the arc and at the end of each swing expected to see the fourth side fall. It fell in the middle of the next swing and Dermot grasped the cable with both hands and watched as the side floated away from him, slowly turning over and over, until his eyes could no longer follow it. He started trembling and tried to shout but his voice came out in a whisper and he knew that no one could hear him. He could not bear to look out any more and he closed his eyes and crouched on the platform, hanging onto the cable. He held it tightly with his hands, and his legs were twisted around it. Suddenly there was no cable, only the platform and it was dropping swiftly. He screamed.

The sound woke Ned, who slept in the same room, and he went over to his brother. "In the name of God, what's wrong with you, Dermot? You've been squealing and shaking like a stuck pig."

Dermot made out the dim form bending over him. He sat up in bed and stared fearfully at Ned. The tail end of the dream was still vivid in his memory.

"I was dreaming," he said.

"You were nightmaring," Ned answered disgustedly. "You'd better get hold of yourself!" Ned went back to his own bed and struck a match and looked at his watch that hung from a nail above the bed. It was five-fifteen and he thought what a shocking thing it was that a man could not get a decent sleep with a brother that took to roaring like a bull in the small hours of the morning.

Dermot felt a vast relief flood over him. It felt good, he thought, to sit in bed in the quiet of the early morning and hear the heavy breathing of his brother. He looked out the window and noted the bluish tinge of the coming dawn and heard the vainglorious arpeggio of an early blackbird.

Somehow he knew that life had changed, a corner of the blanket of fear had been lifted and when the time came he would throw off the whole blanket and do the thing that was right, and not the thing that he wanted to be right. He didn't know why the dream made any difference but sitting up in bed he felt the change. He lay down again and slept the rest of the night like a child.

The following morning at breakfast, Ned sconced him about the nightmare and Bella wanted to know what the dream was about but Dermot could not remember. He remembered it as a terrifying dream that somehow was good for him but he could not remember what it was or why it was good.

That evening, after the cows had been milked and the work all finished, Dermot went into town. He entered the cobbler's shop and found Hannafin facing the radio, a pencil in his hand. He had his head bent slightly and with the pencil was conducting the music that filled the room. He was so intent on his task that he did not hear Dermot come in and for a full five minutes Dermot watched him unobserved. The single electric bulb that hung from the ceiling threw the shadow of Hannafin's arms on the wall. His body was slightly hunched, his makeshift baton tracing arabesques in the air. Sometimes his left hand, half-clenched, would hook upward as he implored the orchestra to higher efforts. The music took a softer tone, a more measured rhythm in three-quarter time, and Hannafin's head started to sway as his pencil gently rose and fell in figure eights. The mood of the music changed, became more imperative, and the pencil stabbed sharply, calling in the brass. The left hand shot out, palm downward, restraining the strings. Rapidly the music came to a climax and finished as Hannafin brought both hands down, as if he were driving a stake into the ground with a rock. Exhausted, he stood motionless for a moment.

Then his ears caught the tumultuous applause of the audience. He turned and humbly bowed to Dermot, bowed again to the buffing machine in one corner and bowed for a third time to the holy calendar of St. Anne de Beaupré.

Dermot's presence finally registered and Hannafin straightened. "I didn't do very well," he said sheepishly. "I had a lot of trouble with the strings."

Astonished, Dermot stared back at him. "You're daft, Jimmy!" he said challengingly.

The soft mood left Hannafin as he briskly replied, "Daft? Not at all. What happens when you hear Irish music? You tap your foot, isn't that right?"

Dermot nodded and Hannafin continued, "Instead of tapping my foot I wave my arms. Now what's daft about that?"

"Nothing," Dermot replied as he turned the thought over in his mind. What was the difference? Dermot used his feet and Hannafin used his hands. That was the thing about Hannafin. His talk had a daft ring but he could always explain himself. Dermot felt good about his decision to come and see him.

"What did you think of the sentence that Sean got?" he asked casually.

Another piece of music came over the radio. Hannafin cocked his head and listened a moment. Then he walked over and switched off the wireless. He came back and answered, "What can I say? He was guilty. He as much as admitted it and the law took its course."

"I know, but do you think the law was right?"

"Whether the law is right or not, it's wrong to take up arms to change the law. Violence is on another level, the level of savagery, and the law is on a civilized level. Sean paid the consequences of attacking the law from a level that the law does not recognize."

"Well then," Dermot affirmed, a little exasperated, "Sean was wrong and the law right?"

"I didn't say that. I think Sean was wrong but only his Creator can answer that question."

"If violence is wrong," Dermot said slowly as he thought, "then both England and Germany are wrong for fighting this war?"

"Yes, I think so. However, when it reaches the level of disputes between nations it becomes another matter. In reality, law is not recognized between nations. There are such things as international law and the League of Nations but the truth is that only the very weakest of nations are prepared to accept international law. The rest of the countries ultimately depend on their national strength and the strength they obtain through alliances. Statesmen say that their nations will accept peaceful means of settling disputes, but in their hearts they know that in matters affecting the interest of a country, it is the number of planes and tanks a nation can command that decides its course of action. To get back to the North—we accept, Catholics and Protestants, the rule of law. Therefore, having accepted the rule of law, we should abide by it."

"But the Catholics in the North don't accept the rule of law. The fact that the I.R.A. is fighting is a proof of that," Dermot objected.

"The strength of the I.R.A. is about one percent of the total Catholic population of the North and of the Catholic and Protestant population combined, it is less then one-half of one percent. Why should this small group defy the rest?"

"You're not being fair, Jimmy. In the first place the I.R.A. is an army and only the able-bodied serve in an army. By and large, the Catholics in the North support the I.R.A."

"Do Catholic women support the I.R.A.? Ask Sean's mother if she supports it. Does your mother? Does Bella? Or Neeve? At a political or patriotic rally both Neeve and Bella would undoubtedly cheer and sing, "God Save Ireland," but let it come close to them, let it affect their men and they want no part of it. You don't hear them protesting but that's mainly because they let the men talk. As long as freedom to practice the Catholic religion is allowed, the women of the North won't support rebellion. How many married men do you have in the organization? Damn few because their wives and children stop them. The women may not roundly damn the I.R.A. but one way or another they see that their husbands don't get mixed up in it."

"So rebellion's not the answer?" Dermot asked.

"No," Hannafin shook his head slowly, "not in the North."

"But the I.R.A. has to keep trying. They have to keep the question alive. If it weren't for the I.R.A. the people of England and the rest of the world would think that the Irish have accepted partition."

"There are other ways besides the gun."

"Not with the Orange government we have. They have the political districts sewed up and fixed through gerrymandering. How about Derry City where thirty thousand Catholics elect eight members to the city council and eighteen thousand Protestants elect twelve members? How about discrimination in jobs and the letting of county council houses? What are we supposed to do when the prime minister of the Northern government recommends to a large Protestant audience that they hire no Catholics; or when another minister of the government boasts of never having employed a papist? Is it not strange that in a country with a Catholic population of forty percent, there has never been a Catholic minister in the Northern government since it started?"

"You don't eliminate an evil by substituting another for it," Hannafin said.

"You know as well as I do that the Northern government is founded on fraud and exists through fraud. What good are constitutional means with such a government? In 1922 there was supposed to be a boundary commission to take a plebiscite whether we wanted to stay in the North or not. What happened? The Northern government refused to consider the findings of the commission. Both Tyrone and Fermanagh would be in the Free State today only for political trickery."

"You still can't change a man's mind by shooting him. Anyway even if such a plebiscite were held and Tyrone and Fermanagh did go into the Free State, would the I.R.A. accept that? You know they wouldn't. There would still be four counties partitioned off from the rest of Ireland."

"All right," Dermot said wearily. "Let's suppose that rebellion isn't the right answer. But we Catholics of the North want union with the Free State. Historically, economically, geographically, Ireland is one nation."

"Agreed."

"Right. We Catholics want to unite with Southern Ireland. We have tried constitutional means and they have failed. What other way is open?"

Hannafin sighed, "We haven't tried constitutional means. We have elected representatives who have refused to sit in either Stormont or Westminster. Is that trying constitutional means? Have the nationalists in the North at any time tried to cooperate with the Unionist government?"

"What answer can you give?" Dermot asked.

"There are several other answers. One way is for the Catholics of both the Free State and the North to drop the religious question and drop this chant of 'end partition.' To approach the problem from another side, the Free State government should ignore the border: do away with border customs; allow elected representatives from the North, whether Catholic or Protestant to sit in the Irish Dail. Such representatives could be restricted to voting only on matters that affected the North. The Free State government should offer scholarships to Catholic and Protestant students from the North. They should attack the border psychologically by considering it to have no importance. And the Free State government would have to ensure that the Protestant religion had adequate safeguards. Divorce should be legalized. Protestants accept divorce as morally admissible. So long as divorce is outlawed in the republic we are trying to establish Catholic morals on a Protestant minority. The Free State government should strike out the clause in the constitution about Catholicism being the official religion in Ireland. That's a big stumbling block to Protestants, even though in practice it means nothing. The Southern government should also economically ignore the border. They should do away with duties and tariffs against Northern goods despite the economic loss involved and even though Northern Ireland does not reciprocate. They should extend to the Northern government, as far as possible, all the benefits and advantages feasible instead of treating it as a deadly enemy."

"Aye, and how much would it cost them?"

"It would cost money but the economic loss would be small and easy to bear if it meant the reunification of Ireland. Eventually the Protestants in the North would lose their fear and see the economic advantages of joining with Southern Ireland. There's only one appeal to Orangemen—appeal to their pockets. That's where they keep their principles."

"And do you think the Free State government could afford to keep losing money on such a proposition?" Dermot asked.

"They could because as long as the North is cut off from the rest of Ireland, the whole country will be economically weak and never develop her full potential."

"Let's suppose this program is followed. How long would it take to do away with the border?"

"Legally it might take a century. But such a policy would start doing away with the border tomorrow. If the Free State government started to ignore the border in matters of trade and travel, the Northern government would look foolish having a whole border administration in a country where ninety percent of the population ignored the existence of that border."

"It makes some sense but I don't think it would work. You said there were other answers," Dermot suggested.

"There is another way that has an even better chance of working. The birth rate in the North is higher for Catholics than for Protestants. Eventually, the Catholics should outnumber the Protestants."

"Aye but they won't. The Northern government and Protestant businessmen won't give work to Catholics and they're forced to emigrate."

"I know that," Hannafin agreed, "but wait a minute. We're not trying to hold the Catholics in the North. If the Free State government would pay a small unemployment benefit to Catholics in the North it would, along with the regular unemployment benefit, be enough to keep them at home. The Irish in America should invest money in the North through buying farms and businesses, providing employment for Catholics. If such a campaign were started, there are enough Irish all over the world who could invest small sums to start Catholic industries and businesses in the North. Eventually the Catholics, through their higher birth rate, would outnumber the Protestants."

"The Protestants wouldn't sell farms or businesses. What happens when an Orangeman wants to sell his farm? He tells the local Orange lodge and they make sure they get a Protestant buyer for it. They won't sell to Catholics."

"We may not be able to buy many farms but we could always compete in business. I don't mean bakeries and grocery stores but new industries that would employ Catholics and keep them at home. Why doesn't the Eire government organize a special fund for investment in the North?"

Dermot laughed, "That wouldn't work either."

"It could work, but the Irish won't let it. The blunt truth is that we can't take a long view of anything. We are not yet fully civilized. We are not the English or the French who use reason. We use emotions and our emotions are too tied to the past. The old traditions, the old slogans, the old answer of taking up the pike and gun, still rule us. Another fifty years and perhaps we'll be able to view the border objectively—not as a clarion call to revolution. We're still haunted by a fear of Britain, of British domination. Take any political speaker today who attempts to criticize our shortsightedness and he's labeled as being pro-British and anti-Irish. Even our artists have suffered from this. O'Casey is an example. O'Casey was a giant with a poet's voice and he handed us our weaknesses, wrapped in verse and shrouded in laughter. And for a while we laughed. Until the professional patriots started whispering and we turned on him. 'What can you expect from a Protestant?' we asked. 'He's anticlerical, an atheist, anti-Irish,' we said. We got the reliable emotions going and a mob tried to break up his plays in Dublin. We loved our neighbor to such an extent that he followed the example of Shaw and Joyce and fled his native land, fled the narrow-mindedness and bigotry. And when O'Casey praised the communists—how self-righteous we were. When a man has suffered so much from nationalism we shouldn't be surprised if he turns to a political system that at least gives the appearance of being international."

"They say he went to England because he could make more money there," Dermot observed.

"Oh aye, they say that too. He sold himself for British gold. But what are the British paying for? Has he written any plays praising England? Far from it; his plays attack the most sacred of British institutions, the church and political system. Is this what they're paying for?"

"I don't know," Dermot answered apologetically. "I'm only saying what I hear."

"They're quick to condemn O'Casey. Quick to forget the long years that O'Casey worked and starved in Dublin for an Irish republic. He tried to tell us a few things. What happened in 1922? We fought and beat the British Army with old sticks and pitchforks. The treaty was signed and then we started to fight each other. And the English government sat back and laughed and shouted, 'Oh! what a lovely bunch of coconuts.' And O'Casey tried to tell us some of these things. But let no one criticize the Irish. We're all saints and scholars." Hannafin shook his head good-naturedly, "Now, how did all this come about?"

"I just asked a question," Dermot replied.

Hannafin looked up at him sharply. "You're beginning to doubt now. You don't know what's right and what's wrong any more. You want me to tell you to get out of the organization. And I won't do that. Someone told you to get into the I.R.A. and you got in and now someone will tell you to get out—and out you'll get. But don't think about it."

"You're wrong, Jimmy. I am thinking about it. But I have to have something to guide me," Dermot explained.

"That's not too difficult. Ask yourself what Christ would do if He were faced with the same problem. But only ask this question with the very difficult problems. If you try to live your life the way Christ lived His, people won't like you and one way or another they'll try to get rid of you."

"Yes, but it wasn't hard for Christ to tell right from wrong because He was all-knowing. I'm not."

"We can still do what we think Christ would have done, facing the same problem. That's the only advice I can give," Hannafin replied.

Dermot jumped down from the bench, walked over to the door that led into the kitchen and opened it. He looked in at the clock on the fireboard, nodded to Jimmy's wife and came back. "Jimmy, I've got to be going. Some day we'll have another wee talk."

The serious look left Hannafin's face and his black eyes gleamed, "Tell her to keep away from Byrne's hayshed."

"Jimmy, you must have been a terror in your younger days."

"Damn the that. I was a lamb in wolf's clothing," Hannafin answered as Dermot bid him good-by and walked outside.

For a few seconds he looked down the Back Street. Someone was getting water from the pump at the foot of the hill and he could hear the splashing sound as the bucket slowly filled. The bobbing headlight of a bicycle drew near and a voice called from the darkness, "Night."

"Night," Dermot answered as the bicycle went on past and down the street. He heard the quiet echo of the "night" from the bicyclist as he passed the woman at the pump and her equally soft answer.

He turned and walked around the square and down the Main Street to Neeve's shop. He knocked softly on the front door and in a few minutes Neeve came out. She had on a heavy woolen coat with the collar up, and in the little light there was, Dermot could see the white bell of her face. Impulsively he reached out and touched her cheek, "Hello wee angel," he said.

"Hello, my warrior bold," she answered. She linked arms with him and they walked down the street and out the Rathgiven road. They reached their tree and Neeve stood with her back to it. They looked at each other for a moment and then hungrily kissed. Neeve sighed. Dermot reached out, patted the trunk of the tree and said, "I wonder how many couples have courted under this tree?"

"It's a poor substitute for a hearth of our own," Neeve answered.

"I know," Dermot said as he laid his face down into her hair. "Poor wee Neeve, poor wee Dermot," he said in mock sorrow. He drew back and looked into her eyes. Leaning forward, he bent and kissed her eyelids. "Listen Neeve, I'm going to get out of the I.R.A."

"Oh thank God for that," Neeve said fervently. "You don't know how worried I was when you were away those few days. I don't want to see you where Sean is."

A darkness crossed Dermot's conscience. What would Sean think of him leaving the I.R.A.? And he that was serving ten years for his country. What would McGinnis and the rest of the men think? He would have to leave Ireland for a while. They would give him no peace.

"I'll probably go to England as soon as the summer comes," he said.

"It'll be a dark day that you leave but I'd rather see you away out of Duncrana, and know that you'd be back in a year or two, than run the chance of seeing you in prison for the next ten years."

"If I do well in England, maybe start a little business or get a good job, could you come over?"

"Not for a while," Neeve answered. "If my brother Jim was home out of the Free State Army, he could look after Mother and the girls but, until he's back, I'll stay in Duncrana. But sure maybe the war will be over shortly."

They stayed under the tree for half an hour. A growth-heavy breeze courted the budding leaves about them and set the branches to swaying in a slow rhythm. The hedges rustled with the slight movements of the night creatures. The air was humid and thick with the smell of growing things. They held onto each other and kissed periodically and overhead the massed banks of clouds moved unconcerned across the vaulting heavens. A shower fanned out from the tail of a rain-heavy cloud and drops hit the big tree. They pressed in closer to the trunk.

"Neeve, wee pet," Dermot said, his voice low and serious. "I've something to tell you."

She looked up expectantly. "What?" she whispered.

"The angels are making their water on us."

She pushed him away roughly. "God in heaven, but you're a terrible lad." She became a little angry and started to walk out on the road. He pulled her back and as she struggled he pinioned both her arms behind her back and held them there with one hand. With the other he tilted her head and kissed her on the chin. "I love you," he said simply.

She lowered her head and burrowed her face into his coat. Her arms went around him and one hand moved up and rested on the back of his neck. Overhead the rain-heavy cloud moved on and the drops stopped falling on the tree.

TWENTY-TWO

It was Sunday night and four men had gathered in a little room at the back of Duncrana Parish Hall. The room was used for storing stage props and backgrounds for the Duncrana Dramatic Society. The society itself had ceased to function some time ago over a dispute with Father Sheehy. Hannafin, one of the leading members of the society, and several others had wanted to put on O'Casey's *Shadow of a Gunman*, but Father Sheehy had forbidden them because O'Casey was nothing but a "godless atheist," a remark that caused Hannafin to wonder what the difference was between an ordinary atheist and a godless one. Father Sheehy then suggested another play by a "Catholic author," but Hannafin had tried to talk the society into going ahead with rehearsals on the O'Casey play. For a while they continued rehearsing but when Father Sheehy told them he would not allow the use of the parish hall for the play, they had quietly surrendered and Hannafin had resigned from the society in disgust. With Hannafin's resignation the society fell apart and since then the scenery and props had been gathering dust in the little storeroom.

High on the wall a hurricane lamp had been hung, outlining the four men who were waiting the arrival of McGinnis.

Dermot stood leaning against two horses that were drinking from an idyllic lake in the middle of a painted pasture. "I wonder what's keeping McGinnis?" he asked.

No one answered. Quinn, the intelligence officer, sat reading a British Army handbook entitled, *Explosives: Their Manufacture and Use.* Malone and Corrigan were seated on a ladder that was stretched out between two boxes.

"Here young Quinn, is that the New Testament or the Old?" Dermot asked.

Quinn looked up from the booklet. "It's the New Testament," he replied tartly. "In fact the latest testament." Dermot noted the short edge of his tone and wondered what he was annoyed about. He looked over at Corrigan and Malone and asked, "I wonder if McGinnis is still going ahead with the raid on the police barracks?"

"Why shouldn't he?" Quinn demanded.

"Don't get your rag out," Dermot warned. "I only asked a question."

Quinn put the book away in his pocket. "It seems to me that you've been trying to take over the company ever since you've been on those two raids. You're always criticizing McGinnis."

"I'm not trying to take over anything," Dermot answered.

"You're a soldier. We're all soldiers and McGinnis is the commanding officer and we're supposed to obey his orders."

Dermot laughed dryly. "Ah go back to your schoolbooks," he said, referring to the fact that Quinn was still at school. Dermot realized that Quinn was repeating something that McGin-

nis had told him and he wondered if McGinnis had been complaining. Well, after tonight there'd be no more complaining.
He'd just drop quietly out of things and get away.

A low knock came to the door and Malone went over and
opened it. McGinnis came shuffling in and looked around.
"We all here?" he asked.

"Aye, *we're* all here," Dermot answered.

McGinnis opened his coat and sat down on an upturned
box. He pushed his bad leg straight out in front of him and
asked, "Did you get that information, Quinn?"

Quinn stood up smartly, "I did. There's only two constables
and a sergeant in the barracks. There's another constable but
he's sick and in the county hospital. So far they haven't replaced him."

"Good," McGinnis answered. "One less to deal with.
Where are the arms kept?"

"In the dayroom downstairs. They have six rifles, a couple of
revolvers and some ammo."

"And the files?"

"All their files are in the one filing cabinet, also in the dayroom."

"What's upstairs?"

"Two rooms; one of them is a sleeping room with four cots.
The sergeant's wife and child are staying in this room. They
moved out of Rathgiven to be near the sergeant but so far they
haven't found a house close to Trilarran and they're staying
temporarily in the barracks. The other room is an old storeroom—full of rope, petrol tins and stuff like that."

McGinnis frowned, "The woman and child are going to
complicate things. We'll have to be careful."

Dermot began thinking. A woman and child; here was his
opportunity to get out of the organization. He interrupted Mc-
Ginnis, "Wait a minute, surely you're not going to carry out
this raid with a woman and child staying in the barracks?"

"Why not?" McGinnis asked. "They'll be upstairs and we

don't intend to go up there. Just burn the files and capture the arms."

Dermot shook his head. "Oh no. In the first place you don't know what's going to happen when you set off the explosives. It's all very well talking about breaching a hole in the wall, but we're not experts with that stuff. The charge may not loosen a single brick and it might blow the whole bloody barracks sky-high."

"I know what I'm doing," Quinn interrupted. "I've studied this whole thing. There'll be just enough explosives to blow a a hole in the wall of the dayroom. There's a weak part, where a door has been bricked up." Quinn's voice grew pedantic as he continued, "Guncotton takes the line of most resistance and the effects of the blast will be felt mainly on the wall. Practically no force will travel upwards through the air. That's the way guncotton works."

"There's still a danger with the explosives," Dermot insisted. "Anyway, what's going to happen when we breach the wall? The constable on night duty, if he isn't knocked out by the blast, will start shooting at us. If we take care of him, the sergeant will come running down the stairs and we'll be shooting up at him. You mean there's absolutely no chance of a stray bullet hitting the woman or child?"

"You're terribly concerned about them and not a bit about us," McGinnis complained.

"I didn't join the organization to make war on women and children." Dermot appealed to Malone. "What do you think, Jim?"

Malone pondered a moment before replying, "Aye right enough, women and children are a different matter. I wouldn't like to think I had a hand in the shooting of a woman or child."

Dermot had not expected any support from Malone and he realized that for his own purposes it would be better to alienate the group rather than have them withdraw from the raid. McGinnis gave him another opening when he said, "I'd shoot any woman in Ireland if I thought it would help end the border."

"Would you now?" Dermot asked quietly.

"I would," McGinnis answered truculently.

"You'd shoot our Bella if it would help end the border?"

Corrigan broke in, "Ah for God's sake, where's that taking us to. You know bloody well Dermot, that shooting Bella couldn't help to end the border."

"I asked a question," Dermot said as he stared challengingly at McGinnis.

The tic started pulsing on McGinnis' cheek. He drew in the bad leg and stood up. "Is it trouble you're looking?" he asked.

Now, Dermot thought, this was the moment to stick to his guns. "I'm not looking trouble, nor will I bring it on innocent people. As long as the sergeant's wife and child are staying in the barracks, I'll have nothing to do with the raid."

"You know this is insubordination?" McGinnis asked.

Dermot felt his temper slipping as he curtly answered, "I don't give a frig what it is. I'm not shooting at any women or children."

McGinnis flushed as he looked around at the others. Both Malone and Corrigan avoided his gaze while Quinn stared intently at Dermot. McGinnis looked again at Dermot and said coldly, "We won't need you. You're dismissed." He jerked his head in the direction of the door, signaling Dermot to leave.

For an anger-filled moment Dermot felt a deep humiliation. He wanted to argue with McGinnis but the fact that he had won his point, had managed to get out of the raid over an argument that seemed halfway sincere, prevented his saying anything. He held in his anger and walked out the door, slamming it behind him.

With a set face, McGinnis stared at the door. Then he turned around and asked, "Anyone else with the same notion?"

No one spoke and McGinnis sat down again. "We'll need a total of ten men. Corrigan, you'll take O'Neill's place . . ."

The men listened quietly as McGinnis continued explaining the details of the proposed raid.

Dermot felt a curious freedom as he walked up the road to his home. Tonight, he knew, could be used as an excuse for not attending any more meetings. In about a month he could get everything arranged to go to England and wash his hands of the whole mess. He would have to make sure that he had a good excuse for the night of the raid. McGinnis had said a Sunday night. Every Sunday night from now on he'd make certain he was in some public place.

He began to do a little mental arithmetic. At any sort of a job in England he could save at least two quid a week. In a year that would be over a hundred quid. Enough to get married and to buy a few sticks of furnishings. A hundred quid was even enough to take him to America or Australia, if England didn't suit him.

He turned up the lane to his house. To get away he'd need about ten quid. There'd be no getting it from the old man. The most he could get out of his father was ten shillings at a time and he had to twist for that. Maybe Bella had some money. His mother had some but she'd have to know why he needed it and he'd rather not tell her he was leaving till the last moment.

Tone met him halfway down the lane, rearing up and wagging his tail. The dog walked ahead, turning his head now and then to see that Dermot was following. Dermot watched the faint white patch on the dog's back and continued thinking. The fare over would cost two quid and he should have enough to keep him two weeks—that would be another eight pounds. He could sell his bicycle for two quid and either ask Bella or his mother for the rest.

He opened the door and walked into the kitchen. His mother was bending over a steaming pot of potatoes. A pounding stick was thumping vigorously as she made a mash for the hens. On the table a dress had been laid out and Bella was sprinkling it, dipping her hand in a bowl of water and shaking the drops from her fingertips. She lifted the iron out of its holder and her mouth tightened into a cherry as she spat on the face of it. The angry white spittle hissed back at her.

"You're home early," his mother said as she carried the pot out to the scullery.

"Where's Ned?" he asked.

"They're gone over to Loy's," Bella answered as her arm went up and down in a slow caressing motion over the dress.

Dermot went over to the table and quizzically eyed his sister. He softly began to sing, "Oh, I had a true love if ever a girl had one."

Bella laughed and pushed him away with her free arm. "Get out—you big calf!"

"Who are you chasing now?" he asked.

"Not chasing anyone," she replied as she continued ironing.

"How about little Johnny what's-his-name? The lad with the quiet talk? Did you get any courting at all from that wee fella? He looks as if a good night's courting would be the end of him."

Bella set the iron down and turned to her brother, "At least there are more ducks than one in my pond," she haughtily replied.

"Aye, but it's a swan I have," Dermot answered.

Kathleen came out of the scullery. "Don't you two ever stop?" she asked.

Dermot sat down by the fire. "This country would grow years on a man," he said in a doleful voice.

"Grow ears on you and you'd be the picture of Rafferty's ass," Bella said.

"I said years," Dermot objected as Bella smiled in quiet satisfaction at her pun.

"What's wrong now?" Kathleen asked.

He looked over at her and replied, "I think I'll go to England." Suddenly he felt uncomfortable, as if he had said something shameful and to hide the feeling he bent down and lifted a few turf from the hob and placed them at the back of the fire.

His mother came over and asked, "You're not in trouble?"

Dermot straightened, "No," he replied doubtfully.

"Do you want to go to England?"

"I'm afraid I'll have to go. I told them tonight I was through with them."

"Thank God foi that," his mother said.

"It's about time you got some sense," Bella chimed in from the table.

"Hush, be quiet," Kathleen ordered. "When will you be going?"

"I'll need to go soon. Inside a month."

"You're in a desperate hurry," his mother said suspiciously.

Dermot sighed, "Look, you don't know what it's like. They'll give me no peace. If anything at all goes wrong they'll think I informed and they'll be watching me all the time."

"You'll need money. How much will you need?" his mother asked.

"I was counting up coming home from town. About ten quid."

"You needn't ask Daddy for it," his sister said. "If he hears you're for England, he'll take a fit."

"We'll not say a word to him about it, or Ned either," Kathleen said. "Ned gets a wee sup of drink somewhere and he's liable to drop a remark or two."

Kathleen got up and went over to the dresser. She lifted down an old teapot and brought it over to the table. She reached inside, spread out the contents and started to count the banknotes. Her fingers smoothed out several pound notes and stacked the silver coins. "I have just enough," she said. "There'll be no set of Beleek this year, but what harm." She swept up the money and replaced it in the teapot.

Dermot felt a pang about the Beleek. Every year she saved

for a set and every year something happened. "I'll send it back as soon as I get work," he promised.

"I know you will," his mother answered.

"Did you tell Neeve?" Bella asked.

"She's been at me a good while to go over," Dermot answered.

"Neeve's a sensible wee girl," his mother remarked. With the tongs she flattened a few turf coals from the fire and placed the teapot on top of them. She went over to the dresser and set out a cup and saucer.

Bella gave a few last minute touches to her dress and carried it gingerly to her room.

"Here, sit over," Kathleen called to Dermot as she poured out a cup of tea. Dermot stood up and carried his chair over to the table. His mother took off her apron and rolled it up. She sat down opposite Dermot and said to him, "It'll be hard to see you leaving but you don't know how my heart's been scalded with the thought of you, like poor wee Sean, in prison for God knows how many years. I'd rather than anything you'd leave the country than ruin your life that way. What did they say to you?" she asked.

"They didn't say much. What can they say after me being on two raids?"

"Who's in charge of it?"

Dermot buttered a piece of soda bread. He glanced over at his mother, closed his eyes and shook his head.

A quick hurt flickered in his mother's face. "Never mind," she said. "I thought if anything happened, I'd know who to go to."

"If anything happens," Dermot said as he methodically chewed on the bread, "go to either Hannafin or the sergeant."

"Surely Hannafin's not mixed up in it?"

"No, he's not. But he'll know what to do."

Presently Patrick and Ned returned. Patrick sat in his usual chair, on the other side of the hearth from Dermot. He lit his pipe, his face sucking in sourly as he made little popping sounds. He twisted his head and spat in the fire. Giving Dermot a calculating look, he remarked, "They were just saying over in Loy's that the I.R.A. is done for, now that they've lifted so many of them."

Dermot said nothing, refusing to be drawn into a discussion with his father over the I.R.A. Perversely, he replied, "It'll soon be time again for the Easter dues."

"Easter dues—how-are-ye," his father grunted. "It'd take a body working from the crack of dawn to the fall of night to keep the dues paid. That and the taxes and tobacco three and six an ounce." As he thought of the appalling price of tobacco he looked at his pipe, much as a man might look at an old friend whose unexpected treachery has just come to light. He reached up and set the pipe on the mantlepiece. "There was great crack over there tonight about Saint Patrick. Here boy," he said, motioning to Dermot, "you're the scholar around this house. Where was Saint Patrick born?"

Dermot nearly said Downpatrick but then he remembered that Downpatrick was Saint Patrick's burial place. "I think he was born in northern France," he replied.

"France? Boys-a-dear, did you ever hear the like of that?" Patrick shook his head in wonder. "The marvels of this world will never cease. Bill Henderson said over in Loy's that Saint Patrick was born in England and that he was a Protestant saint. Of course, being a Protestant, you'd expect a wee bit of ignorance from him. Old Paddy Loy, he give him the queer answer. 'Here-by-God,' says Paddy, 'you'll be claiming DeValera on us next.'"

Dermot and Ned laughed. "What did Henderson say to that?" Dermot asked.

"Mind there's no flies on Henderson," Patrick replied. "He said that DeValera was a great man all right because anybody could drive a horse but it took a great man to lead asses."

An appreciative gust of laughter greeted the remark. "Aye, there's something to that," Kathleen remarked dryly.

Patrick looked over sharply at his wife. She stood up and walked over to the table in front of the wireless. "It's time we were getting to bed," she said as she picked up the alarm clock and wound it.

Dermot started unlacing his boots. Bella reached down and with the tongs began to rake the fire. She pulled the ashes over the glowing coals until they were completely buried. In the morning, in the bottom of the ashy mound, there would still be several lit coals to start the new day's fire with. Although no one would say so openly, letting a fire go completely out was a sure way of bringing bad luck on a house. In a throwback to the Druidic ceremonial fires, people raked their fires every night and in some of the older houses the hearth fire had been kept continuously burning for over two hundred years.

They all knelt down and Kathleen started the nightly rosary. "The Five Joyful Mysteries. First the Annunciation. *Our Father* . . ."

Their voices rose and fell as they prayed. Patrick slid back on his heels and made himself comfortable. Ned had his head bowed, arms up to his face, as he mumbled into the palms of his hands. Bella knelt erect, holding her rosary over the edge of the chair and responding in a loud clear voice. Dermot propped his folded arms on the seat of his chair and leaned his head against the back of it. On his stockinged feet he could feel the pleasurable warmth of the fire. His *Holy Mary*, strong at the beginning, trailed off into a whisper at the end.

Underneath the table Tone gravely contemplated the group. From outside came the sound of a rattling chain as the wind rose and started tormenting the haggard gate.

TWENTY-THREE

Don McGinnis got off the bus in Applebridge. McGinnis had always hated the county capital. It was a symbol of English rule and all the more offensive because of its unobtrusiveness. In the seventeenth century it had been a small fort and King James, on his way to defeat at the siege of Derry, had watered his horse at the river and camped a while on the broad acres that surrounded the place. Later an English gentleman had molded an estate around the fort; a neat patch of Essex stitched into the savage fabric of O'Neill's province; rows of apple trees, clipped hedges and a sloping lawn in front of the Big House.

In 1803 it had been made the county capital, largely because it had remained loyal during the Rebellion of 1798. A short time later it became the home depot of the Fermanagh Fusiliers, a regiment that had distinguished itself in Wellington's Peninsular Campaign.

Even the name grated on McGinnis' ears. An Anglo-Saxon name for an Anglo-Saxon town. Applebridge was in a valley, a weak placid place where the River Foyle sliced its way through yielding meadows. It epitomized the English virtues: broad utilitarian streets; an orderly, almost fastidious park; the solid Gothic county courthouse; the discreet statue of Lord Kitchener opposite the post office. It had none of the wild strength of Duncrana, the lean eagle that plumed itself on top of a peak. Duncrana was Irish, Irish the cut-stone houses that grew out of the hungry flanks of the hill. Applebridge was a courtly English sentence, a Shakesperian sonnet, a legal phrase. Duncrana was a Gaelic war cry, the wild keen of a banshee, the fearful sluagh-ghairm of an Irish kern. Applebridge was the present indicative, Duncrana the past subjunctive. McGinnis hated Applebridge.

He spent an hour walking around the town: looking into shop windows; watching the British Army recruits drilling in the field beside the recently-raided military barracks; listening to the rude, vigorous bargainings of the men who bought and sold in the weekly pig market.

Finally he made up his mind. He left the pig market and limped up Irish Street, past the almost apologetic Lord Kitchener, past the twin spires of the Catholic Church, until he came to a large grocery store. He looked up at the windows above the store, at the neat golden letters that read, "Fitzgerald—Dentist."

He went into the hall and up the stairs. Opening the door, he walked over to the girl at the desk and asked, "Could I see Christy?"

"Do you have an appointment for today?" the girl asked.

"Appointment? No. He's a friend and it's a personal matter."

The girl got up from the desk and went into a room that led

off the office. In a few seconds she returned, followed by a tall young man in a white smock. "Don," he said and offered his hand.

McGinnis shook hands with him. "I've something important to talk about," he said.

"Come on in." They went into the dentist's workroom and Christy walked over to the window and sat on the ledge beneath it. He pointed to the chromium chair with its brooding tree of dental instruments. "Have a seat," he said, an amused expression on his face.

McGinnis grimaced. "Not bloody likely. I hate those things." He walked over and leaned against a steel cabinet. "You're the new Brigade O.C.?" he asked.

"That's right."

"I'd like Brigade permission for a job that the Duncrana Company has planned."

"What is it?"

"A raid on a police barracks. Actually the old Brigade O.C. gave us authority but I thought it better to check again since he's been interned."

Christy spread his hands, "You know what the situation is here. We've been disorganized the past few weeks. If you already have authority for it, I don't see that you need to get it again. Where is it?"

"Trilarran, about five miles from Duncrana." Having considered that there was no need to complicate matters, McGinnis did not mention the sergeant's wife and child.

"What's the raid for?"

"Arms and destroy their files. And the company needs a little action. It's hard to keep them tuned up on weekly drills."

"Aye, that's a problem," Christy agreed. "I would say to go ahead with it."

"I was planning to but I had to come up anyway. I need a few things."

"What?"

"Three-o-three ammo and a half dozen detonators."

"Can't get them for you today. If you send a man up this Saturday, I'll have them ready."

"I'll send Corrigan up."

Fitzgerald leaned back against the window. "That was a bit of bad luck—about Reilly."

"Aye, he was the adjutant of the company and a damn good man. It was queer the way he was lifted." McGinnis almost began to believe that Dermot had something to do with it.

"What do you mean, queer?"

"Why did they only lift Reilly and not O'Neill? They were both together and the police must have known they were both missing on the night of the raid."

Fitzgerald shook his head. "It doesn't make sense, Don. If O'Neill had anything to do with Reilly being lifted, surely he'd have managed it when they were trying to get out of the North, just after the raid. As far as I know, if it hadn't been for O'Neill, Reilly would never have made it to the border. What brought him back, anyway?"

McGinnis shrugged his shoulders. "I suppose he saw that the police didn't bother with O'Neill and he thought he'd be safe too. If O'Neill had wanted Reilly lifted for some reason, he couldn't do it when they were escaping. It would have been too obvious. Everybody knew they were together."

"What makes you suspicion O'Neill?"

"I don't know, odd wee things. He's changed this last while. He hasn't been coming to meetings lately and when he does he's twisting with everybody. There's just something odd about him."

"Ah no," Fitzgerald objected. "I know that whole family as well as you do. I used to play football against his brother Ned. You'd never find an O'Neill informing. However, you're the O.C. of the company and perhaps you'd better keep an eye on him."

"Maybe I'm wrong," McGinnis said doubtfully.

"I'm sure you are. How are things about Duncrana?"

"The police have been fairly quiet. The B-men are as active as ever. A week ago they nearly killed a British soldier. It was a dispatch rider on a motorcycle and the B-men signaled him to stop. I don't know whether he didn't see them or thought they were the I.R.A., but damn the stop he did and the B-men fired a couple of rounds after him. The soldier went roaring down the road at eighty miles an hour. The Duncrana B-men called the Rathgiven police and they set up a barricade on the road. When the dispatch rider came to the barricade he practically fell into the arms of the police telling them the I.R.A. had tried to ambush him."

Fitzgerald started laughing. "God, but that's the rare one. If we can get the B-men to firing at British soldiers, we won't have a thing to do but sit back and enjoy the sport. By the way, did you know that another battalion has been posted to the North?"

"No. When was this?"

"Night before last. A battalion of the Argyll Highlanders disembarked at Larne."

"Where are they being posted to?" McGinnis asked.

"We don't know yet. Anyway, it's another battalion weaker they are in England. The Germans will be delighted to hear that piece of news."

"Aye, the government's got the wind up. A few more raids and maybe we can draw another battalion or two. We have to keep hammering at them. We can't let up." McGinnis' face clouded as he continued, "Please God, this summer the Germans will invade and we'll finally get our freedom."

"You know that we lost an intelligence man last week?" Fitzgerald asked.

"Aye I heard that. Are they bringing him to trial?"

"I don't know. They must have got their eyes opened when

they saw the intelligence reports he was bringing into the Free State. Next day we had copies of everything sent over again to headquarters in Dublin."

"There's no danger of him informing?" McGinnis asked.

Fitzgerald laughed dryly. "Not a bit. They could try for a hundred years and get nowhere with that laddy. His father was killed in 1920, during the riots in Belfast."

McGinnis said somberly, "Aye it takes a lot to square that kind of an account."

Fitzgerald stood up. "When's this raid?"

"I'm not sure yet. Probably two or three weeks from now. We still haven't got everything arranged."

Fitzgerald walked over to the door with McGinnis and shook hands with him. McGinnis went down the stairs and out into the street. He felt relieved now that he had permission from Brigade for the raid. That would clear him if anything went wrong. It would also be an unanswerable argument for anybody who might be influenced by O'Neill in the matter of the sergeant's wife and child. Probably the sergeant's family would find a house by the time the raid was carried out and even if they didn't they'd be safe enough upstairs. He couldn't let anything interfere with their plans. They had to keep hammering at the British Army and the Northern government. They needed more arms too. He knew the lessons of 1916. When the Germans invaded and the I.R.A. went out, the British would execute a few of the leaders and there'd be no containing the fury of the nationalist North. If they had the arms there'd be no trouble in raising an army. It all depended upon whether or not they could keep the organization going strong until the invasion. As soon as the rising started, there'd be plenty of work for men like him. Like Dan Breen, he'd take the Duncrana men out to the hills and make a flying column out of them. And with England caught between an invasion at home and a rebellion in the North, they'd probably let the North go and concentrate on fighting the Germans at home. If England withdrew her troops it wouldn't be hard to talk the Free State government into occupying the North and if they did, the I.R.A. would see that the British never got in again. If Britain tried to hold onto the North, there was a good chance they'd be defeated in England and Germany would know how to be generous.

He caught the two o'clock bus back to Duncrana.

That evening McGinnis met Dermot in Hannaflu's. When he was ready to leave, he asked Dermot, "How about walking up the street a ways with me?"

Dermot nodded and followed McGinnis out of the cobbler's. As they rounded the church wall, McGinnis said in a friendly tone, "I hope there's no ill will over last Sunday night?"

"Not at all," Dermot answered.

McGinnis stopped and put his hand on Dermot's arm. "I was up today in Applebridge talking to the Brigade O.C."

"So?" Dermot answered cautiously, his body tensing at the touch of McGinnis' hand.

"I got their full agreement to the raid."

"Did you tell them about the sergeant's wife and child?"

McGinnis hesitated a moment and Dermot noticed it. "I did. They said that by the time the raid was carried out, the wife and child would be out of the barracks. If they weren't we couldn't let it hold us up."

No, Dermot thought, it wasn't good enough. He would hold his ground. It was possible that they'd allow him scruples over the raid but if he gave in now, he didn't know when he'd get another opportunity to get out of the organization. "I'm sorry Don, but as long as there's a doubt about the sergeant's wife and child, I won't have hide nor hair to do with the raid."

McGinnis dropped his hand. "You're no bloody good," he said bitterly and walked away.

Dermot watched the limping figure go up the street. He wondered if McGinnis would still go ahead with the raid. Even though, Dermot admitted to himself, his own concern was only an excuse to get out of the I.R.A., still it was undoubtedly wrong to endanger civilians in their raids. He wondered if McGinnis had really talked to the Brigade O.C. He wouldn't put it past him to tell a lie to get his own way; especially if he thought it would help the cause. He watched McGinnis move up the street: the curious bending shuffle of his good leg as it bore the whole weight of the body; the heel of his bad foot as it buckled out, canting upward, never touching the ground. He suddenly felt a terrible pity for McGinnis and also a terrible fear. That twisted pathetic walk had an inevitability of its own. The street was deserted and for a moment Dermot felt that there was no one in the town but himself and Don. McGinnis disappeared around a corner and Dermot continued to stare after him. Then he turned and went back to Hannafin's.

Hannafin had finished work for the evening and was sitting on his stool reading the newspaper. He looked up as Dermot entered.

"Anything fresh in the paper?" Dermot asked.

"Nothing much," Hannafin answered as he folded the paper and threw it over on the bench. "A German plane crashed in the Free State. The pilot was picked up and interned."

"Well, the war's over for that man," Dermot remarked.

"When's your war going to be over?"

"It's over already. I'll probably be going to England soon."

"So, you've given them the go-by?"

"Aye, I told them I'd have nothing more to do with them."

Hannafin grunted. "I'm sure they took it sportingly. Did they have a farewell dinner and present you with a silver watch and talk about the years you devoted to the cause?"

"Who's inside?" Dermot asked.

"The wife and old Biddy Kerr."

"Not a word about this, Jimmy. They're planning a raid on a police barracks. The sergeant's wife and child are living in the barracks and I told them I'd have nothing to do with a raid where women and children were involved. Wasn't that a fly thing to do? It gave me a damn good excuse to get out."

"But they're going ahead with the raid?"

"Aye, they said they couldn't help it about the sergeant's family and that they'd be careful. But I'll have nothing more to do with it. Wasn't I right, Jimmy?"

"'Wasn't I right Jimmy?'" Hannafin mocked him. "You're only interested in finding someone to tell you that you're right. And now you're making your plans to scoot off to England."

"Well, what should I have done then? Go along with them on it?" Dermot asked defensively.

"Remember what I told you—what your guide should be? What do you think Christ would have done?"

"He'd have done the same. Refused to have anything to do with it," Dermot uneasily replied.

"Deed then you have a remarkably poor view of the Savior. You know better than that Dermot. He would have stopped them."

"Well, I'm not the Holy Ghost. What can I do against twenty men?" Dermot pleaded.

"You haven't even considered what you can do. It's easy to see that. You can't say that you're not responsible because you're not taking part in the raid. You are responsible. You're as much responsible as anyone else around Duncrana for this raid. You were on a couple of raids yourself and approved of these policies. Your exploits," Hannafin said the word mockingly, "helped to encourage other young men in town to do the same. Now you say—'I'm tired of it all. I'm getting out.' And that's your responsibility finished? No, it's not Dermot."

Dermot got a little angry. "You're the great saint yourself. Why don't you stop them?"

"I'm not a saint," Hannafin protested. "I'm a sinful old man. Why don't I stop them? I'm not in a position to stop them and you are. You're not trying to prevent an evil which you yourself are partly responsible for."

"Why should I get myself into a lot of trouble over people I don't even know?"

"I've already told you why you should. It's you that's in the position to stop this raid. It's an evil; these activities have been condemned by the Church; innocent people are liable to suffer and you're partly responsible for the whole thing."

"How can I stop them? What can I do against twenty men?"

"Go to the police," Hannafin said quietly.

"Go to the police!" Dermot echoed in an astounded voice. "God help me, I'm not an informer, Jimmy. That's the one thing I'd never do."

Hannafin sighed, "You wanted to know the right thing to do, but you're not willing to consider some of the things you could do."

Dermot protested, "Oh no, Jimmy, not that. An O'Neill turning informer?" He closed his eyes and shook his head rapidly at the thought.

Hannafin leaned over the counter. "Look Dermot, if you told," he nearly said McGinnis but checked himself in time, "your leaders that you were going to tell the police all about the raid, it would soon stop their plans. You wouldn't even have to go to the police."

"They wouldn't believe I'd do a thing like that," Dermot objected.

"Still, they couldn't take the risk."

Dermot looked at him suspiciously. "You're not working for the police by any chance?"

Hannafin threw back his head and laughed. "Have I asked you any questions at all about the organization? Have I asked you the names of any of the members? Have I asked where the police barracks is that's going to be raided? Don't be daft, Dermot."

Dermot turned his back to the older man. "I don't know what in under God's holy name to do," he said despairingly.

Hannafin got up and began tidying the shop, putting away

his tools and placing a pair of boots on the shelf. He got a broom from the kitchen and started to sweep the floor. In a few moments he had a small pile of litter in the middle of the floor: leather shavings, old ripped-off soles, worn steel shards, nails and sparables, pieces of waxed thread and tiny puffs of dust. Once or twice he looked over at Dermot but the latter was staring moodily at the doorway. He emptied the sweepings into a small box to be later picked over for pieces of usable leather. He finished the sweeping and took off his apron and hung it on the nail that supported the calendar of St. Anne de Beaupré. He came around to the front of the counter and said to Dermot, "Why don't you talk it over with one of the priests?"

"Which priest?"

"Either of them. Although Father Sheehy is an ardent nationalist, if you pinned him down on a question like that, there's only one answer as a Catholic priest he could give. Father McCory would be easier to talk to though. The parish priest would never forgive you for putting him in that sort of a position."

Dermot looked sourly at Hannafin. "I wonder what you'd do if you were in my shoes?" he asked.

"God help me, I don't know," Hannafin answered. "I don't know if I'd be man enough to do what I think you're going to do," he said sympathetically.

"Aye, I'm the great old idiot that ever got mixed up with that gang."

"I know one thing," Hannafin remarked. "You remember that after the raid on the Applebridge barracks you were worried? Afraid that the soldier might die?"

Dermot nodded.

"Well if this raid is carried out and a policeman is killed, or if anything happens to the woman and child, you'll never forget it the rest of your days."

Dermot reached out and lightly pushed Hannafin's shoulder.

"You'll be the death of me yet, Jimmy," he said as he turned to leave the shop. Hannafin called a good night and switched off the light and went into the kitchen. He drew up a chair to the stove.

His wife looked at him questioningly, "Who were you talking to?" she asked.

"Young O'Neill."

"A right lad."

"The best—a darling lad. I wish I could learn to leave other people's problems alone and take care of my own."

"Dermot has problems?"

"Mountains of them. At twenty a young fella lives from one crisis to the next. You know sometimes I mourn the days of my youth. Tonight I'm very thankful to be over fifty."

"Now what kind of talk is that to be coming out with?"

"Here! Don't be asking so many questions and put me on a cup of tea. Is a body to starve to death around here?"

His wife got up and lifted the poker and punched it between the bars of the grate, rattling it up and down to get a good fire going again. She filled the kettle and placed it on the stove. On her way out to the scullery, she stopped at her husband's chair and placed her hand lightly on the back of his neck. "You're an old cod, Jimmy," she said affectionately.

"I'm a harum-scarum, devil-may-carum, Irish country boy," Hannafin recited as he reached back and caught his wife's hand.

TWENTY-FOUR

Father McCory was working on a report in the rectory study. His long legs were spread out under the table and his blond head bent over a sheet of paper. A small lamp splayed a cone of light over his shoulder but beyond that space the shadows fuzzed indistinctly, losing their edges, until they merged in the penumbra of the corners of the room.

The curate was filling out the report of births, deaths and marriages that had to be forwarded every month to diocesan headquarters. Most of the clerical work of the parish fell on his shoulders, and although he was by no means a bookkeeping sort of man, he rather liked the compiling of reports. Usually he had the help of Father Sheehy but the parish priest had left earlier in the evening to visit several members of the dramatic society in an attempt to revive that body. Father Sheehy felt somewhat guilty because the society was no longer functioning.

It had been a healthy community enterprise, much to be praised for its Christian spirit and the contributions, both financial and cultural, it had made to the parish. The parish priest felt that enough time had passed to make the members of the society again anxious to put on a play. He was prepared to let them produce any play they wished, trusting to their good sense not to jeopardize his friendship for the society by again attempting a controversial one. He had, in truth, been rather startled at their insistence on doing O'Casey, though he well realized that in any parish body there were always one or two members, no matter how subservient they might be in their own homes, who insisted on showing a rebellious attitude to the spiritual counsel of their priests.

Father McCory heard the front door slam and moments later the parish priest entered the study. He looked over at the curate and asked, "What's that you're at?"

"Births, marriages and deaths," the curate replied. "Did we have any funerals this month?"

Father Sheehy took off his coat and hung it on the hatstand. He walked over to the fire and stood with his back to it. Bending his head slightly, he absent-mindedly patted his white hair. "There was old Sally Greenhart, but I think that's the only one," he replied.

"Aye right enough, old Sally, Lord have mercy on her," Father McCory said as he wrote her name in the death column of the report. "What age would she have been?"

"Arrah put down seventy—that's a nice age for her," Father Sheehy suggested.

Father McCory put down seventy. "What did old Sally die of anyway?"

"What did she die of?" Father Sheehy repeated. "Well, if you'd have heard young Doctor Donnelly telling me what she died of—Lord save us—it sounded like a papal encyclical. It's no wonder she died. I don't see how she lived as long as she did with all those things at her."

"No odds, I was just wondering," Father McCory commented.

"I mind my father telling me," Father Sheehy continued, "that in the olden days, people died of only two things: the cramps or the fever. If they had pains it was the cramps; if they had a sweat, it was a fever. That way everyone in the country knew what each person died of. Now the doctors have a hundred different names for the two things—but mind you, at the heels of the hunt, they die with either pains or a sweat."

Father McCory was going to point out that sometimes people died in their sleep, without either pains or sweat, but he decided to hold his tongue because he had something else to mention. He had noticed that the parish priest had forgotten to wipe his shoes on the mat at the front door and had tracked in a few pieces of mud with him. The curate pointed to the floor. "You'll have me in trouble again with Martha over those tracks. Every time there's muck on the floor she comes to me about it," he grinned at Father Sheehy. "She says she's kept house for you for eight years and she knows that it isn't you that does be tracking in all the dirt."

Father Sheehy chuckled. "Aye, she used to blame the last curate too. Though he wasn't as soft as you are. He'd tell her it was me that was doing it. Martha would shake her head and say no more in case she'd be responsible for a priest telling a lie."

Martha had been housekeeper in the rectory for nearly eight years. She was well over the minimum age of forty prescribed by the Council of Trent. Always she referred to the two priests as "saints" though she might admit, in privacy, that housekeeping for saints could often be more difficult than housekeeping for ordinary mortals. She revered Father Sheehy and although she grudgingly admitted the sanctity of Father McCory, she was suspiciously distant with him. For one thing there was his reading all the time, and for another his playing football with the town team. Martha had her own notions of what was right and proper for the priesthood and the idea of a priest "galloping up and down in shorts and a jersey" was definitely not one of them. Martha never went to confession to Father McCory.

Father Sheehy was still thinking of his efforts to resurrect the dramatic society. He had talked to several of the members but had sensed a lack of enthusiasm and, rightly or wrongly, had blamed Hannafin for it. Realizing that he would have to win over the cobbler, his mind was industriously searching for a lever to use. "Does Jimmy Hannafin ever go to confession I wonder?" he asked the curate.

Father McCory looked up in surprise. "Not to me at any rate."

"Nor to me," Father Sheehy added thoughtfully.

"Perhaps he goes in to Rathgiven," Father McCory suggested.

"I think I'll have a talk with my bold Hannafin."

Father McCory wondered what was going on between the parish priest and Hannafin. He realized that Father Sheehy was not solely concerned with saving an errant soul. "Hannafin's a funny man," he said, keeping the subject open. "He's not what you'd call very religious but I doubt if you'd find a better, a kindlier man in the town."

"He's a whelp, that's what he is," Father Sheehy angrily answered. Remembrance of their difficulty over the O'Casey play came back to him. "Do you know what he told me when we fell out over putting on the last play? He said it was priests like me that caused the French Revolution. He's got a neck, throwing French history in my face."

Father McCory laughed and the parish priest looked over sharply at him. "What's so amusing?" he asked.

"It sounds exactly like Hannafin. And you needn't argue history with him, French or Irish, or even the history of the Church. He's a very well-read man."

"That gives him no license to be insulting." Father Sheehy hunted around in his pockets for his pipe. He liked an odd draw on the pipe, although he did stop every Lent to show good example to the rest of the parish. Lent was a trying time for Father Sheehy. He allowed himself an odd moment of crankiness or sarcasm but during Lent he was always afraid that the loss of the pipe was tempting him to contrariness and therefore he was unusually mild during the Lenten period. As soon as Lent was over he went on a self-righteous splurge of giving vent to his tongue and the sermon for the first Sunday after Easter usually had the congregation squirming.

He lit the pipe and carefully drew on it. "You know, the people don't have the same respect for the clergy they used to have."

"You mean," Father McCory said slyly, "it's not as easy to give them good advice."

Another thought filtered into the mind of the parish priest. "You mind the sermon I preached last Advent about the girls sitting on the fellas' laps at the dances and how they'd have to put a stop to it? Well, I went to the ceili in the hall last Sunday night and there was a dozen of them, showing not an ounce of shame, perched on the knees of their men. And not a one shifted when they saw me come in. I hold you I soon shifted them. I've a good notion to take a look in at all the ceilis in the future and make sure they put a stop to that nonsense!" The priest glared as he thought of all the evil in young people. "And a Christian can't walk down the town after a dance with the couples plastered up against the doorways, giggling and carrying on with the devil's work. Old Laura Tully complained to me a few weeks ago. You know her house that has the wee doorway to it? The night of a dance she says she can't get a wink of sleep with some couple or other in the hallway. I told her to throw a basin of cold water down on them—nothing like cold water for dampening the ardor. It's getting to be a shocking sinful town." He sighed and pessimistically added, "Aye and God knows how many are laying out around the haystacks."

"I wonder what has Laura Tully up at four in the morning?" Father McCory replied. "I'm inclined to doubt that any young couple would make much noise under those circumstances. Mind you, old people can be curious sometimes."

"All the same, the young ones are making a proper Paris out of this wee town. The next night there's a dance, I've a good notion of sashaying down the street with a flashlight and a blackthorn stick and chasing them all away home."

Father McCory knew the futility of trying to argue with the parish priest on that particular subject. He came over to the fire and warmed himself for a moment. "No marriages this month?" he asked.

"None."

"And no births?"

"No births either. Don't know what's coming over the people in this parish," Father Sheehy grunted.

From the hall door a knock reverberated and both priests looked at each other. "It's a sick call," Father Sheehy said, shaking his head grimly.

Father McCory got up, went out to the hall and opened the door. Dermot O'Neill was standing on the stoop. When he saw the priest he pulled the black beret off his head and placed it under his arm. "I'd like a word with you Father, if it's not too late," he said.

"Not at all. Come on in, Dermot," the priest replied.

Dermot entered the hall and Father McCory shut the door behind him. He said to Dermot, "We'll just go into the kitchen and that way we'll not disturb Father Sheehy."

The two men entered the kitchen and Father McCory switched on the light. He walked over to the stove. Lifting the poker he vigorously stabbed at the fire until the tiny live coals cascaded through the bars of the grate. Then he went over to the barrel in the corner and broke several pieces of turf in two and brought them back to the fire. He lifted the lid of the kettle and peered inside and set it over the hot part of the stove.

Dermot was awkwardly standing at the entrance to the

kitchen. The priest noted his discomfiture. "Sit down Dermot, and take the weight off your legs," he said.

Dermot stuffed the beret into his coat pocket and looked around at the heavy wooden chairs that surrounded the kitchen table. He picked a chair along the wall and sat down stiffly, his hands resting on his knees.

"It won't be long till the season starts again," the priest remarked.

"No deed it won't, Father. Another few weeks."

Father McCory pulled over a chair and sat down opposite Dermot. "Do you think we'll have a good team this year?"

"As good as last year. We'll miss Boyce, he's away to England, but some of the younger lads are nearly ready."

"We'd need to do better than last year. We were a bit of a flop against Rathgiven and Applebridge," Father McCory complained.

"We'll have to get in more practice, Father. That's all that's for it."

"Aye practice, that's what we sorely need."

The priest gave Dermot a quizzical look and Dermot edged his chair back until it rested against the wall. He ran his tongue over his upper lip, cracked one knuckle and said, "I've come to you about a serious matter, Father."

The priest smiled. "Sometimes things don't seem as serious when we talk them over with someone. A load shared is a load lightened."

"You know, Father, that there's a company of the I.R.A. here in Duncrana?"

"I suspected as much," Father McCory replied quietly.

"I've been in it since it started, Father."

"You know it's a mortal sin?" the priest asked.

Dermot nodded his head. "I didn't know it at the start," he said. "It was after I joined that the bishops' letter was read. Anyway Father, the Duncrana company is planning a raid on a police barracks. I told them I wanted no part of it because the police sergeant's wife and child are staying in the barracks and they'll probably be there the night of the raid."

"You were right, Dermot."

"I tried to talk them out of it but they wouldn't listen to me." Dermot leaned his elbows on the table and covered his face with his hands.

The priest stood up and walked over to the dresser. He took down a teapot and measured out two spoons of tea from a packet. "Do you like your tea strong, Dermot?" he asked.

Dermot looked up and nodded.

The priest set the teapot down beside the kettle and asked, "Why did you come to see me?"

"I don't know what to do. Somebody told me to talk to you."

The priest came back to the table and looked down at Dermot. "What do you want me to do?"

"Nothing Father. I just want advice."

"Do you want me to talk to them?"

"Not at all, Father," Dermot hastily said. "Anyway, they wouldn't listen to you. They're very bitter over that letter from the bishops."

"The letter had no effect then?"

"Not that I know of," Dermot answered.

The priest shook his head. He stood up and went back to the dresser and took down two cups and saucers. He poured out the tea and brought it over to the table. Dermot put some sugar in his cup and stirred mechanically. "If the Church gets dragged into this, it'll only make things worse," he said. "The O.C. of the company is a shocking stubborn man. If you went to him he'd consider it a direct challenge from the Church and he'd go ahead with the raid just to show that the priests have no influence over him in regard to his patriotism." Dermot laid a sarcastic emphasis on the last word.

Father McCory finished his tea and pushed the cup and saucer aside. "I could talk to the rest of the men. Perhaps they'd listen to me."

"They'd listen all right but that's all, Father," Dermot replied. "The O.C. would have a sure argument against you. He'd say they were backing out because they didn't love Ireland. He'd say that the clergy never supported the rebels and never would but that some day the clergy would thank them for their freedom. He'd say they were afraid and were using the clergy as an excuse. You know what the young men of this town are like. They'd have to follow him because of that."

"Apparently then they won't heed me," the priest said. "I'm sure even if he wanted to, Father Sheehy would have no better luck. There are only two places in town strong enough to stop them—the Church and the police. If the Church can't, that leaves only the police."

"I can't go to the police," Dermot said dourly.

He pushed back his chair and walked over to the stove and stood in front of it, his back to the fire. Above the kitchen door hung an oleograph of the Sacred Heart. A cross had been lightly superimposed over the picture and Dermot read the words at the end of each arm of the cross: love, honor, reparation, IHS.

"Why should I have to stop them?" he asked. "Is it my duty to? Would it be a sin if I didn't?"

Father McCory was watching him closely. "I don't know, Dermot," the priest replied. "We're all enjoined to obey the civil laws where they don't conflict with Church dogma. According to the laws of the state you're duty bound to tell the police. There might possibly be some justification for the I.R.A. to ignore the civil laws and rebel, but I doubt if they're justified in jeopardizing the lives of a mother and child. Anyway the bishops have condemned the I.R.A."

"All I want to know is the right thing to do," Dermot said.

"I think you should probably go to the police," Father McCory answered slowly, his tone conveying a certain measure of doubt.

Dermot jammed his hands into his pockets and appealed to the priest. "But how can I go to the police? If it were myself I wouldn't mind. It would kill my father. To have everyone in the country saying that an O'Neill turned informer and my father on the run in 1916 and my uncle Vincy killed by the Black and Tans. The whole country would go against us. You know what the people are like around here."

The priest answered thoughtfully, "You could go to the police and tell them about the raid without mentioning who was going to take part in it. Then go to your O.C. and tell him you've gone to the police and warned them. He daren't carry out the raid with the police knowing all about it."

Dermot thought for a moment and then objected, "But would my O.C. believe me? You know Father, I was one of the men on the Applebridge raid and I was on the ordnance barracks raid too. He'll find it hard to believe that I would go straight to the police and inform."

"I'm afraid it's the only way open. You'll have to convince him that if he goes ahead with the raid, you'll tell the police."

"What's to stop him from telling me they're calling off the raid and then going on with it?" Dermot asked.

"Nothing. Which means that you'll have to go to the police anyway. You'll have to make sure your O.C. knows that the police have been informed."

Dermot took out a cigarette and lit it. He grinned ruefully at the priest. "And I used to think I had worries," he said.

"Going to the police is only one answer, Dermot," Father McCory said. "Do what you think is right. We can't slip out of the way of our consciences. As a priest I can advise you as to what I think your duty is, but I can't foresee everything. I don't know what the I.R.A. is liable to do to you—if you go to the police."

"I'm not worried about that," Dermot said.

"Or the effect on your family," the priest added.

Dermot suddenly felt restless. He took his cap out of his pocket and said, "I'm sorry to have troubled you, Father. I'm in such a stew over the whole business that I don't know which way to turn."

"What are you going to do?"

"I don't know."

"Have you made your Easter duty yet?"

"I was at communion last Christmas," Dermot answered.

"And you haven't been since?"

"I've been in the I.R.A. since then."

"Well, you're out of the I.R.A. now—aren't you?"

"I am and I amn't. I don't know if anyone ever gets out of it," Dermot complained.

"Come and see me again when this thing settles itself," the priest said. "At all events, I want to see you out for the first football practice."

"I doubt if I'll be out for football this year. Either way I'll have to leave Duncrana sometime in the next few weeks."

They walked down the hall to the front door. "Whatever you do, Dermot, see me before you leave. Won't you now?"

"Don't worry, Father, I'll drop in some evening."

Dermot put on his beret and buttoned his trench coat. He said good night to the priest and walked down the gravel driveway. Father McCory stood watching for several seconds and then went back into the house. He entered the study and Father Sheehy asked, "Who was it?"

"Dermot O'Neill," the curate answered.

"You were a right while with him. Anything important?"

"We were discussing the national pastime." Father McCory smiled at the older priest and walked over to the shelves and took down a volume of Suarez.

Father Sheehy grunted and stretched his legs in front of the fire. "This town's football mad," he grumbled to the other chair.

TWENTY-FIVE

The following evening Dermot went into Duncrana. As he was passing the bicycle shop, on his way to Hannafin's, he impulsively stopped. He stood looking at the shop window for several seconds and then opened the door. The outer store was empty but McGinnis was busy in the workshop and looked up as Dermot entered.

McGinnis bent again to his work. He tightened a nut on the rear wheel, straightened himself and slung the spanner onto the bench. Elaborately, he began drying his hands on a rag.

"Keeping hard at it?" Dermot asked.

McGinnis answered with a grunt, his face set.

Dermot awkwardly brought the subject into the open. "Surely you can wait until the man's family have found a house?"

McGinnis gave a derisive laugh and lifted himself up on the bench. "Why?" he asked.

"Because it's not right and you know it, Don. Don't be hard-headed. There'll be other chances to do work for the organization. Why involve a woman and a youngster?"

"Don't try any of that talk with me," McGinnis answered. "I know what you're after. You're not a whit concerned over the sergeant's family. You've been at this a long time, I'm the commanding officer and I've planned this raid and I'm going to carry it out." McGinnis looked contemptuously at Dermot and continued. "You got rid of Reilly nice and handy but you're not going to get rid of me."

Dermot's face tightened with anger. "What do you mean, I got rid of Reilly?"

"Why was he lifted the minute he stepped back across the border and not a hand's been laid on you?"

"I had nothing to do with him being lifted," Dermot protested.

"No, you didn't," McGinnis said slowly and insultingly. "I've noticed you lately. Everything I do is wrong. You were the great playboy on two of the raids and now you think you can step in and take everything over. But there's one question you can't answer. How was it Reilly was picked up and you weren't?"

"I had nothing to do with it," Dermot shouted. His face turned pale as he lost his temper. "I don't want to take anything over and you bloody well know it. I know what's wrong with you. Your head is full of plans of being a great hero—another Dan Breen. You don't give a hoot about Reilly rotting in jail, or about a woman and child being shot. The only thing you want is to be the rebel on the run. You can't wait until you're the genuine I.R.A. man; until you're dragging yourself all over the mountains with your trench coat and a revolver in the pocket. Well, I'll have no part of it. If you won't call off the raid I'm going down to the barracks. I won't give the names but I'll bloody well let them know that Trilarran is going to be raided." Dermot was shaking with anger as he finished.

McGinnis reached over and picked up a wrench. "You tell the police a word of that raid and I'll have you killed," he shouted. "Now get out of here before I cleave your head open." He slid down awkwardly off the bench, the spanner lifted over his head. Dermot backed away a few steps.

"I'm going," Dermot said. "But you'd better think the whole thing over. This Saturday at twelve I'm heading for the barracks and if I haven't had word that the raid's been called off, I'm going to tell them about it."

McGinnis lurched forward a step and raised the wrench. "Get out of here, you bloody informer," he shouted, his face contorted with rage.

Dermot, to show his lack of fear, turned his back on McGinnis and walked slowly out of the store. He went down the town until he came to the church wall. He had a headache and was trembling with a mixture of fear and anger. He slid down on his hunkers, along the wall, and turned up his coat collar. The night wind soughed in the trees behind him. He was afraid of them, he thought bitterly, as he lowered his head onto his knees. Afraid of the name they'd give his family; of what they'd say to his father and Bella and Ned. And he was afraid too of what they might do to him. With a terrible clarity he knew what was going to happen next. McGinnis wouldn't back down and he'd go to the police and the company would start hunting for him.

He got to his feet and walked down the street to Neeve's house. He tapped lightly on the door and in a few moments Neeve came out. "Is there anyone in?" he asked.

"No. Why, what's wrong?"

He pushed past her and into the shop. She closed the front

door and switched on the light. "My God!" she exclaimed. "You're as white as a sheet."

"Could you make me a wee cup of tea?" he asked.

"Surely," she answered and went into the kitchen. Dermot sat down in one of the leather chairs.

Neeve came back from the kitchen. "It won't take long," she said. "I've put the kettle on to boil."

Dermot reached up and caught her by the arm. "I'm in a wee bit of trouble."

"Not the police?" she said, her eyes wide with shock.

"No," he replied calmly and began to tell her of the proposed raid on Trilarran barracks.

Meanwhile, back in the bicycle shop, McGinnis had rounded up four men and was talking to them. Quinn, Malone, Big John McIntyre and his brother Tom were listening as McGinnis heatedly spoke, "You all know the trouble I've had with him. He was always criticizing and since those two raids there's been no reasoning with him. Now he says that he'll go to the police if we go ahead with the Trilarran raid."

"Why's he so concerned?" Pat McIntyre asked.

"I don't know why, but I've got my suspicions," McGinnis replied. "He either wants to take over the company or he's afraid of getting interned. We can't let him stand in our way. He's got to be stopped or the company is finished. And I won't let that happen." McGinnis' voice rose as he continued, "For hundreds of years there's always been an O'Neill somewhere when Irishmen have tried to free their country. There's always been one miserable, cowardly Irishman who'd back out or go running to the police. It's not going to happen here. Never had we a better chance to clear the British out of the North. For centuries they've been lording it over us with their 'Ulster is British' routine. You can't go down the road for a walk of a Sunday evening without having a B-special stick a rifle in your gub and insult you. We can't fly our national flag or sing the national songs. I'm browned off with it." He placed his hand on his cheek for a second to control the tic that started beating. Then he sat down on a box and thrust out his bad leg.

He spoke almost in a whisper, the words hissing out, as his dark face screwed up in anger. "You know what the Tans did to my father? They took him out of the house, in front of my mother and tied him to a tree. Then they used him for bayonet practice. They cut him to ribbons in front of my mother's eyes."

His voice rose with passion as he looked at each man in turn and each man looked away. "Do you see that foot? That poor twisted foot?"

The men self-consciously looked at the foot and quickly glanced away again. "I got that foot that same night," McGinnis fiercely said. "That's one thing I owe the British government. My mother was carrying me at the time and she tried to stop the Tans from killing my father and they knocked her down and kicked her. They're the kind of people that Dermot O'Neill doesn't want shot. They're the ones he's trying to protect."

McGinnis wearily stood up and clutched at the edge of the bench for support. They all watched him intently. He drew a deep breath and continued, "Well, we have them now. Germany has them beat and they know it. It's only a matter of months till the invasion, and we've got to do our share. We've got to keep hitting them, give them no peace, make them put a Tommy on every square yard of Ulster soil. We've got to avenge the deaths of the men who died in '16; the Irishmen and women who have been murdered down through the centuries. We've got to avenge the priests whose heads were shaved and tar poured over them and set alight. We've got to avenge the men who were shot and hung and tortured, the thousands that Cromwell slaughtered at Drogheda. We've got to avenge the broken promises of the Treaty of Limerick.

If we fail now, Ireland will never know another chance and Ireland's dead will never sleep in peace."

"What do you want us to do?" Quinn asked, a rapt expression on his face.

"We've got to stop O'Neill."

"How?" Quinn asked as the others listened closely.

"By showing him what will happen if he goes to the police. We've got to get him and give him a good working over; beat the be-Jesus out of him; mind, not enough to put him in the hospital, but enough to make him realize that if he informs against us he'll be killed. Enough to put the fear of God in him."

Quinn shook his head doubtfully. "He's a husky lump of a man."

"My God," McGinnis said scornfully. "You mean to say that five of us can't handle him?"

"We'll handle him all right," Malone answered grimly.

"Bloody sure we will. He's still somewhere in town. Quinn, go you down to Hannafin's and see if he's there. If he's not there, try Neeve Donnelly's. If he's not in either place come back and let me know."

"You don't want me to tell him anything?" Quinn asked.

"No. Just find out where he is. If he's not in Hannafin's, ask Jimmy. Maybe he'll know where he's gone to."

Quinn left the store. For several minutes the men were silent until Tom McIntyre asked, "Just how much of a hiding do we give this boyo?"

"Enough to put the wind up him," McGinnis answered. "Don't hit him in the face. We don't want to leave marks on him. Whack away at the belly and ribs. It would be best to have two men hold him. Tom, let you and John hold him from behind and Malone, Quinn and I will take care of the rest."

McGinnis looked at his watch. "It's nearly news time," he said as he walked over to the wireless and switched it on.

Dance music came stealing out and the men fell silent. Presently the program ended and the dry, slightly bored voice of an announcer came on. ". . . British troops counterattacked yesterday in and around Benghazi and took some German prisoners. . . . In daylight raids over the French coast, Royal Air Force light bombers claimed the destruction of shipping in the channel ports of Dieppe and Dunkirk. . . . German bombers raided London and Dover again last night . . ."

"Did you hear that?" McGinnis asked. "About destroying shipping in the channel ports? That means that Germany is gathering a fleet, getting ready to invade England. They're concentrating their shipping. I'll hold money before the end of June, they'll be in England."

"What happens to us here in Duncrana if they invade?" John McIntyre asked.

"We go on the run," McGinnis answered. "We become a flying column, ambushing British troops and destroying communications. We'll have our work cut out for us then."

McGinnis reached over and switched off the wireless. Again a silence came over the group. Malone took a shilling from his pocket and flicked it with his thumb. The spinning coin rose and winked in the light. It came down with a soft slap in his palm and he flipped it again. The two McIntyre brothers stood leaning against a bench, John with his long legs crossed and his head slightly lowered. He was nervously rubbing the palms of his hands up and down his thigh. His brother, Tom, was watching Malone flipping the coin. Tom reached one hand into his pocket and started to handle a few coins. He plunged the hand up and down several times, making the coins rattle. McGinnis looked over in annoyance and he stopped.

McGinnis picked up an oily rag and reached high over his head to a rack and lifted down a stainless-steel bicycle wheel. He set the wheel between his legs and began to run the oily rag around the rim. Then he started to wipe the spokes, doing each one separately. He kept working on the wheel until a noise at the front door broke through the heavy silence in the room.

"That's Quinn back," Malone said. McGinnis started for the door but Malone called to him, "Stay where you are. I'll get it."

Malone returned with Quinn and McGinnis asked, "Did you find him?"

"Aye, he's in Neeve Donnelly's," Quinn replied. "I didn't see him but I could hear them talking away inside."

"Good man. Here's what we'll do. Go you down Quinn and stand opposite Donnelly's until O'Neill comes out. As soon as he shows, you scoot around by the back of the church and come out again on the Main Street like you're coming from Hannafin's. Tell O'Neill that I was looking him. Tell him I have important news. He'll think I've changed my mind about the raid. If he asks you where I am, let you say I was in Hannafin's but that I left and that I'm probably at home. Walk you on up the street with him and when the both of you come to O'Connor's shop, say to him, 'Let's go down by the back, I think McGinnis has locked the front.' Then head down O'Connor's entry with him. When you come to the corner that turns into our place, we'll grab him. Have you got all that?"

"I have surely," Quinn answered. "But suppose he doesn't want to come?"

"He'll come, don't fret yourself about that."

"Right then, I'm away," Quinn said and left the shop.

"We'll be waiting at the end of the entry," McGinnis called after him.

The men looked at McGinnis for guidance. He left the shop and went into the kitchen and returned a moment later, buttoning his trench coat. He picked up a short stick that he used in prying tires off bicycle wheels and nodded to the men. "Might as well start."

The others left the store and waited at the front door until McGinnis had switched off the light and locked the door. They walked the short distance down the street in single file and turned into the entry. McGinnis brought up the rear.

Back in Donnelly's, Dermot was standing with his back to the big mirror and Neeve was facing him. She said heatedly, "Dear God Dermot, is it not enough trouble you're in without getting in trouble with the organization too?"

"I've told you," Dermot said patiently. "I was wrong to have joined the I.R.A. I was wrong to have been on the ordnance barracks raid. I was wrong to have shot the soldier in Applebridge. I'm not going to stand back and be wrong any more. I'm going to stop them because I'm the only one who can and because I'll never be at peace with myself if I don't."

Neeve sighed, making a little click with her tongue. "If you go to the police on Saturday, you'd better plan on leaving Duncrana the next day. They're liable to shoot you."

Dermot laughed, trying to reassure her. "Damn the shoot me they'll do."

Neeve stepped forward and laid her head on his chest. "Listen to me, Dermot. You can leave before the raid. Forget about going to the police. You're doing the right thing in getting out of the organization and you can't be responsible for what they do after that. But don't inform on them. That's the one thing they'll never forgive and it's the one thing, no matter how right you are, the people will always remember. You'll never be able to come back to Duncrana."

Dermot reached down and caught her hands, doubling them up inside his own, "I'll think about it, wee lamb. I'll think between now and Saturday."

She looked up at him. "Don't get yourself into any more trouble," she pleaded.

He disengaged himself and said, "I'd better be getting on home. Thanks for the cup of tea."

She put one arm around him and they left the shop and walked out into the narrow hallway. There they stood for a minute and kissed each other. In the semidarkness of the hall, Dermot could barely see her face. He reached over, smelling her hair, and caught a faint tang of vinegar. Then he bent down and kissed her softly on the chin. "Good night, wee pet," he whispered.

She gave him a final hug and opened the door. "Good night," she said as he stepped out into the street.

A slight drizzle had started to fall. The harsh outlines of the buildings were softened with the wisps of fog that were creeping up from the meadows and curling in and around the town. Dermot shivered slightly and turned up the collar of his coat. As he was walking past the church he heard foot steps approaching and he waited to see if he would have company on the road home. The figure loomed closer and Dermot finally recognized Quinn.

"Hey Dermot," Quinn called. "McGinnis was looking you."

Something in the tone of Quinn's voice gave Dermot a slight uneasiness. He instinctively recognized something odd about a person who shouted after dark. "Was it long ago?" he asked.

"No," Quinn answered. "He was in Hannafin's, asking for you. He's probably back in the shop by now." Quinn edged closer and threw a nervous look at Dermot. "Come on," he said, catching Dermot by the arm. "I'm going up that way myself."

The two men continued their walk up the street. Dermot began to feel sorry for his outburst at Quinn the previous Sunday night, during their discussion of the raid. "Tell me," he asked, "are the boys still intending to go on that raid?"

"As far as I know," Quinn answered, almost apologetic.

"Listen, why don't you wait until the sergeant's wife and child have found a place to stay?"

"I'm not in charge of the company," Quinn replied defensively.

"Forget it," Dermot said. He knew it was no use talking to Quinn as the latter would do whatever McGinnis wanted.

A big, wet drop of rain came floating down off a roof and landed on Dermot's face. He pulled his beret out of his coat pocket and put it on. They came abreast of O'Connor's entry and Quinn stopped. "Let's go in the back way. The shop's closed by now," he said as he started to turn down the entry.

Dermot hesitated briefly, troubled by a vague feeling. Then he stepped out and caught up with Quinn. They walked in silence for a few steps until Dermot complained, "What's your hurry? You're nearly running."

"No hurry at all," Quinn answered, slowing his pace slightly.

They reached the end of the passageway and Quinn turned the corner first. Dermot was right behind him and as he turned into McGinnis' yard, he was roughly grabbed and held. "Uuuf?" he grunted, "what's wrong?"

His arm was caught from behind and twisted up his back. Another man had an arm around Dermot's neck. Dermot saw McGinnis, Malone and Quinn standing in front of him.

"You're still going to the police this Saturday?" McGinnis stated.

Dermot felt the bubbles of fear in his stomach and uneasily replied, "Listen Don, let's cut out this carry-on."

McGinnis replied by stepping forward and giving Dermot a swinging slap across the face. Dermot's head jerked back. Malone stepped in and drove a fist into his stomach and another into his ribs. Dermot's breath whistled out with the blows but he quickly recovered and struggled against the men who were holding him. He lashed out viciously with his foot but McGinnis avoided the kick. Quinn reached in and slapped him twice across the face but Dermot barely felt the slaps and realized that Quinn was afraid to hit him hard. Quinn's fear somehow lent him courage and the thought of Quinn's treachery sent a rage tearing through him. "I'll kill you, Quinn!" he shouted.

The grip around his neck tightened, cutting off his speech. He straightened with the agony in his throat and a fist sank again into his stomach, causing a sharp explosion of pain. A sudden barrage of blows caught him in the sides and ribs and he lost his wind and started to slump. A stinging slap across the mouth brought his head up sharply. Again he tried to kick out but someone whacked him across the shins with a stick and he moaned with the knifing agony in his legs.

From the distance, the voice of McGinnis floated in. "O'Neill, you're a bloody traitor—an informer!"

"I think he's fainted," one of the McIntyres said.

Dermot heard the comment and felt their hold on him loosen. The pain seemed to stab at him from all over his body. Hazily he decided to let his head hang and his body remain limp. Without meaning to, he braced his weight on one leg and the pain came lancing up from his shin. Again he groaned.

"He's all right," McGinnis said.

Dermot lifted his head slightly.

McGinnis continued, his voice an ugly, controlled shout. "Listen O'Neill, this is only a sample of what you'll get if you go to the police. If you know what's good for you, you'll stay away from the barracks."

Dermot lifted his eyes and located the pale blob of McGinnis' face. He spoke softly to it. "You poor wee gimpy bastard."

McGinnis leaped in and drove a fist into Dermot's face. Dermot felt the burst of pain on his cheekbone and the hard feeling that something was tearing his nose off. McGinnis shuffled back and Dermot started to cry with rage, "I'll kill every one of you. There's not a man among you."

He again felt the pressure on his throat. He lunged wildly

and managed to free one arm and swing it clumsily behind him. Then he started to lose consciousness.

"The bugger's fainted," Quinn said.

"Good," McGinnis replied. "We've taught him a lesson. Sit him up against the wall."

The McIntyres dragged Dermot back to the wall and eased him down.

"Right," McGinnis called to the rest. "We'll go home now and not a word of this to anyone."

Tom McIntyre looked back at Dermot and asked, "Will he be all right?"

"Come on," McGinnis said impatiently. "That frigger's as strong as an ox."

The men left the yard.

Dermot sat against the wall, his head down on his knees, breathing in big gulps of air. He stayed motionless for several minutes and then raised his head and blew the hair out of his eyes. He opened his coat and gently started to massage his stomach and chest. His hand went up and began stroking the tender part of his cheekbone. "Bastards," he said aloud.

He leaned wearily against the wall and thought that now he would have to go to the police or they'd think that he was afraid. And Quinn, wasn't he the raging fighter? All the size of him with the soft baby face and the thin, ferrety nose. That was a boyo to be dancing around, slapping his face. And McGinnis, he had fairly shaken him with the gimpy remark. It was worth a cuff or two to throw that in his face.

He reached down and with both arms levered himself to a standing position. Groaning with the soreness that waved through him, he took a deep breath and winced as a sharp pain stabbed his side. He stood for a few seconds, leaning back against the wall.

The drizzle had turned heavier and a light rain was now falling. He lifted his face to it. He smelled at the night and thought of the land and how it needed the rain. He reached a hand up to his head and felt for his missing beret. Moving slowly around the area, he searched for it with his foot. When he finally located it, balled up and heavy with mud, he rolled it up and stuck it in his pocket.

He rested a short while and thought of the long walk home and wished that he had brought his bicycle. He decided to go to Hannafin's and ask for the lend of his. He made his way up the entry and went walking slowly down the town and around to Hannafin's. The shop was shut but he caught the thin glimpse of light that ribboned out from under the door. He opened the door and found Hannafin with his feet up on a box and reading a newspaper.

Hannafin looked up as Dermot came over to the counter. "You're late coming on your visit," he remarked. Then he noticed the dark red bruise on Dermot's cheek and the disheveled hair. "What happened to you?" he asked, as he set the paper down.

"I had a wee accident," Dermot answered. "I'm as stiff as a tombstone. You wouldn't lend a fella your bicycle by any chance?"

"Come here till I get a good squint at you," Hannafin ordered.

Dermot came around behind the counter and grinned crookedly.

"The organization?" Hannafin asked.

Dermot nodded.

"It could have been worse," Hannafin consoled him.

Dermot eased himself back against the inside of the counter and lifted the legs of his trousers. A purply welt ran across both shins.

"A kicking too?" Hannafin asked.

"Somebody belted me with a stick."

"How do you feel?"

"Not bad now, but for a while I passed out."

"Ireland forever," Hannafin's voice took a tone of mocking

bitterness as he continued, "land of saints and scholars. The green soft hills and the warm open hearts of the people."

"Do I look bad?" Dermot asked.

"No. There's a wee bruise on your cheek, but that's all that's noticeable."

Dermot sat down gingerly on a stool.

"Would you like a shot of whiskey?" Hannafin asked.

"I'm a Pioneer," Dermot answered automatically.

"Damn the Pioneers. I'll have the wife make you a wee drop of punch."

"I broke my pledge about a month ago," Dermot added.

"Good lad, there's hope for you yet," Hannafin said. He went into the kitchen and told his wife to fix a glass of punch. He returned and laid a hand on Dermot's shoulder. "It was me that got you into this," he said, with a shake of his head.

"No deed, it wasn't," Dermot protested.

Hannafin went back into the kitchen and returned with the punch. "It's a pity to waste good whiskey on a man who doesn't appreciate it," he said, as he handed the glass to Dermot.

Dermot took a sip and set the glass down on the counter. "I'm going to the police this Saturday," he said. "I'm going to tell them that the I.R.A's planning a raid on Trilarran barracks. I won't give the names of the men but at any rate I'll stop the raid. Then Monday I'll head for England."

"Did you tell your friends this?"

"Aye, I did."

"And they thought they could change your mind by bashing it in," Hannafin commented. "Deed then, I know you a damn sight better than they do. Listen, the organization meets in Corr's barn, in Nally's barn, in Rafferty's cattle shed. Where else?"

Dermot looked up in surprise. "How do you know where they meet?"

"Those three were easy. What I have to know are the other places."

"Why?"

"Never you mind why. Don't worry, I won't be giving the police any information."

Dermot shook his head doubtfully. "Sometimes in the shop," he said and glanced at Hannafin to see if he caught the meaning.

"Right," Hannafin said.

"Sometimes in the little shed at the back of the hall," Dermot continued. "Sometimes in the railway shed at the Rockcutting Bridge. They have a key for it. Do you want the fields they drill in too?"

"No. Just the buildings."

"That's all then." Dermot finished the punch and set the glass down on the counter.

"Come on out to the yard," Hannafin said. "I'll get you the bicycle. You can bring it back tomorrow evening."

The two men left the shop and went through the kitchen and down the steps into the yard. Hannafin wheeled the bicycle to the gate and handed it to Dermot. He opened the gate to let him out.

"I'll have it back tomorrow," Dermot promised.

"Don't worry about it and be careful on the way home."

"Night, Jimmy," Dermot said as he mounted the bicycle and cycled awkwardly into the street.

TWENTY-SIX

In the waiting days that followed, Dermot continually thought of his problem. More than once he was tempted to back down on his threat of going to the police but as Saturday drew near he realized that he would have to follow his original decision. Behind all his reasoning lay the knowledge that he could not allow anyone to think that he had backed down through fear. He knew that whatever an O'Neill might do, an O'Neill could not show cowardice. His name came to him burdened with the honor of a thousand years and he feared that honor more than he feared pain or ridicule or even death.

He thought of all the fears that he had ever known; of the fantasy-embroidered fear of the banshee that had caused him to whistle with all the pitiful bravado that his eight years could muster, as he went about his nightly chore of closing and locking the two fowlhouses; of the long tick-tocking fear of the school clock when a challenge had been passed or accepted and he knew that at three the ring would form in the schoolyard and his opponent would have a head as thick as a gatepost and arms that flailed continually and tight, knobby fists as hard as rocks; of the dry-throated fear of walking the parapet of the railway bridge as the train came thundering down the rails and the heart-stopping moment when the locomotive's noise tore through his ears, down to the soles of his feet, and the hot explosion of steam hid his companions and he knew with an awful clarity what hell was—a wild, roaring noise, clouds of steam and a firebox to fall into. And in thinking over these fears, Dermot realized that at bottom they all had the same basis—the fear of being afraid when the moment came, the fear of showing fear in front of others, the fear of letting down his name.

Saturday morning found Dermot in Duncrana, standing on the steps of Devlin's pub. From there he could see down to the police barracks and up to McGinnis' shop, while across from him was the church and the road that led into the Back Street and Hannafin's.

A fair sized crowd had gathered in the town. There were farmers in to sell neatly built-up cartloads of hard, black peat. There were black-shawled women, carrying baskets of eggs and cloths of home churned butter, moving graciously with that peculiar rhythm of people whose lives are regulated by seasons rather than hours. To McGuone, the fowl buyer, came little boys with sad limp rabbits they had caught in snares, and McGuone in the dealing, treated each youngster with an adult dignity because in his youth he had courted their mothers and fought their fathers and he knew that his own sons would do the same to their brothers and sisters. Old men, hitching along on a cane, gathered with their cronies at the church wall to damn the younger generation as a pack of lazy blackguards, to suspiciously examine each other for signs of failing health and to let a few drops of tobacco juice dribble quietly over their waistcoats.

From the steps Dermot watched it all while the fear inside him mounted and his name kept him rooted. Presently he noticed Malone walking down the street. Malone glanced briefly at him as he passed Devlin's and continued down the town until he came to a telephone pole, four houses up from the barracks. Here he stopped, folded his arms and leaned against the pole.

Ten minutes later Dermot saw McGinnis, dressed in his old trench coat, leave the shop and come shuffling down the pavement. At that moment a girl came walking up the street, wheeling her bicycle, a shopping bag slung from the handlebars. She stopped opposite Dermot and called, "Dermot, are you going to the dance in Loughbeg tomorrow night?"

"I don't know," Dermot answered as he watched McGinnis draw near.

"It's McCarran's band. There's a carload going from here."

Dermot noticed that McGinnis had stopped across the street from him. He looked down at the girl and answered absentmindedly, "I think maybe I'll go."

"Ah now Dermot," the girl laughed. "Sure there's no need for you to go to Loughbeg for a wee bit of courting." She leaned her ample backside against the saddle of the bicycle.

"It's not that," Dermot said as he looked over at McGinnis and pondered the significance of the trench coat which had come to be an unofficial uniform in the company.

"Is Neeve going?" the girl asked.

"I don't know," Dermot answered. The coat could mean nothing, he thought, or it could mean that McGinnis considered himself on duty.

"Haven't you asked her?"

"No. I mean we haven't talked about it." He carefully scrutinized the pockets of the coat, looking for the bulge that meant a gun, but McGinnis had his hands balled up in the pockets in such a manner that Dermot could make out nothing.

"What are you looking at?" the girl asked, puzzled by Dermot's preoccupation.

"Nothing." Dermot shot a glance down at Malone.

"You're poor crack today," she complained. "Well, I must be getting on home. Good-by, Dermot."

"Good-by, Kitty." Dermot stepped away from the wall as McGinnis crossed the street and stopped at the bottom of the steps.

"Well?" Dermot asked.

"You can't go through with it," McGinnis warned.

"Are you calling off the raid?"

"No, we're not. But before you go down to the barracks. You see Malone down there?" McGinnis jerked his head down the street.

Dermot's mouth tightened into a thin line as he answered, "You should have known better. Malone can't stop me."

"A gun can," McGinnis said menacingly.

"He might have a gun but he daren't shoot me in the middle of the street."

"He has orders to shoot the minute you come abreast of him." McGinnis looked down the street toward Malone who was carefully watching the scene on the steps.

"Why don't *you* shoot me, Don?" Dermot asked, his voice carrying the implication that McGinnis was afraid to.

"You go down that street and you'll be shot. Make no mistake about that," McGinnis answered.

"Listen Don, I wasn't afraid of a few guns on the raid on the ordnance barracks, nor at Applebridge. I'm an O'Neill, Don, and nobody threatens an O'Neill."

Dermot started down the steps of the pub. McGinnis stepped back a few paces and watched him. When Dermot reached the bottom of the steps he stopped and forced himself to look McGinnis full in the eyes. Then he turned his back and started walking slowly down the street. He was in mortal fear of being shot by McGinnis but he continued his slow walk, fervently hoping that his deliberate show of nonchalance wouldn't provoke McGinnis into shooting where he hadn't meant to. He wondered whether he would first hear the shot or feel the bullet. He made up his mind, at the first sound of a gun, to break into a zigzag run down the street. With each passing step, however, the feeling grew that McGinnis was bluffing and he knew that if McGinnis wouldn't shoot, Malone wouldn't either. He nearly laughed in relief as he drew even with Malone and noted that he made no move.

A constable was on duty when Dermot entered the barracks. The policeman looked up from the desk. "The hard O'Neill," he said. "I never thought I'd see you in here without a pair of handcuffs on."

"Is the sergeant in?" Dermot asked, his voice quavering slightly with a nervous reaction.

The constable was in a bad mood and felt like baiting his visitor. He took his time in answering, pretending to busy himself with some papers on the desk. Finally, he looked up and asked, "Would I not do you?"

"No, you wouldn't. It's a private matter."

"You'll have to wait for him," the constable replied. "He's gone home for dinner and won't be back till one. What do you want him for?"

"I'll tell him that when I see him. In the meantime I'll have a seat," Dermot answered as he sat down on a chair.

The constable ignored Dermot and went back to the papers. After a few minutes had passed, Dermot asked, "Tell me, how did they get Reilly?"

"You heard the evidence in court," the constable replied.

"I heard the evidence all right but why was he lifted the minute he crossed the border? They didn't know whose prints were on the gun till they picked him up."

"I wouldn't know about that. Anyway, he's where he belongs. You weren't mixed up in that business by any chance?"

"A loyal citizen like me?" Dermot scoffed.

"I'd like to get you in a dark corner somewhere." A slow rage was growing on the constable. "I'll hold money I'd get some information out of you."

Dermot sneered insolently as he answered, "You'd need to eat another few bags of oatmeal before you'd jig with this O'Neill."

"I'd go through you like a dose of Epsom salts!"

Dermot indolently stretched his long legs and slumped out in the chair in a manner to indicate his composure. He quietly answered, "It takes more than that snot rag of a uniform to make a man out of a child." Immediately he felt sorry for the remark and quickly added, "What wrong with you anyway? I'm here on a peaceful errand and you're acting like I just blew up the Houses of Parliament."

"The sergeant's too damn soft with you fellas. I'm getting sick of the whole bunch in this town." Months of resentment spilled over as the constable bitterly complained, "Every time one of you passes the barracks, you spit. There's never a kind word for a policeman in this town. If we say hello to any of the girls, they won't speak to us. What wouldn't I give for a transfer to some good Protestant town like Portadown," he concluded.

Dermot felt a twinge of sympathy for the policeman and showed it by remaining silent.

Presently the sergeant returned. He nodded to Dermot and said to the constable, "I'll take over the dayroom for a while. Would you run out to Evishanoran? Somebody drove into a cow belonging to Simy Boyd."

The sergeant opened the neck of his tunic and sat down on the desk. He waited until the constable left the room and then asked, "Now then Dermot, what's your difficulty?"

Dermot stood up and walked over to the sergeant. For a

moment he stared at a framed portrait of a frozen-faced King George the Sixth. He ran his tongue quickly around his lips and shifted his gaze from the king to the sergeant. "Sergeant, I've got some information for you."

"Good man," the sergeant said encouragingly.

"Don't ask for more than I can give."

"That's all right, Dermot. Go ahead."

"The I.R.A. is planning a raid on Trilarran barracks. It's to be sometime within the next month, probably two weeks from tomorrow, on a Sunday night."

The sergeant pulled in a piece of paper and wrote on it, "Trilarran, Sunday night. Go ahead," he said to Dermot.

"That's it all," Dermot answered nervously.

The sergeant looked up. "That isn't it all," he said sternly. "How did you find this out?"

"I don't have to tell you that. You know how I found out."

"How many men on the raid?"

"About twelve."

"Who are the men responsible?"

"I can't tell you," Dermot answered.

The sergeant walked over to the window. He stood with his back to Dermot and said, "I'm not a very good policeman. Many's another man would get the rest of the information out of you."

"No, they wouldn't. I'm shockingly thickheaded," Dermot replied.

"Perhaps they wouldn't at that." The sergeant smiled briefly and turned around. "Why do you tell me this much?"

"The sergeant at Trilarran has his wife and youngster living in the barracks with him."

The sergeant pursed his lips, letting out a silent whistle. "That's right. They're staying at the barracks until they can find a house. Do your friends know this?"

"They do and they're going ahead with the raid," Dermot answered.

"Do they know, by any chance, that you've come here?"

"They know that too."

The sergeant shook his head. "There'll be no raid on Trilarran then."

"I doubt it. I had to come because they wouldn't listen to me."

The sergeant sat down wearily and asked, "What kind of men are they, Dermot? What kind of hate is in these people that they'd shoot at women and children? Do you know that it hasn't been a month ago that I argued the D.I. out of lifting and interning five men from Duncrana? It was just after the Applebridge raid. Mind you the D.I.'s not a bit slow. It turned out that at least one Duncrana man was on that job—Reilly."

The sergeant got up and went to the files and pulled out a folder. He brought it over to the desk and took out a sheet of paper. He started reading the names: "McGinnis." He looked at Dermot but Dermot's face remained expressionless. "O'Neill," he read and looked again at Dermot. "Reilly, Malone and Corrigan." He threw the paper down on the desk and angrily said, "If it hadn't been for me those five would be in the Crumlin Road Jail today. As it is, one of them's in for ten years."

"I have to thank you for not lifting me."

"Don't thank me too soon. I might take a notion and have the four of you lifted yet," the sergeant grimly answered.

"If you do, make sure you put me in a separate jail," Dermot said dryly.

"What am I going to do about you now?"

"I'm going to England soon."

"But in the meantime, what will the I.R.A. do?"

"Aye, that's a question and a half," Dermot replied. "I told them I wouldn't give any of the names. Only the fact that they're planning a raid on Trilarran."

The sergeant noticed the bruise on Dermot's cheek. "What happened to your face?"

"Fell off the bicycle," Dermot lied.

"That's the queer old two-legged bicycle that did that," the sergeant said caustically. "Do you think they're liable to make another raid instead?"

"I don't honestly know, sergeant. I'm sure they won't consider Trilarran after knowing that I came here. I know that Brigade . . ." Dermot hesitated, aware that he was about to reveal information that he shouldn't. "That in other places they're disorganized since the last police raids. It'll take them a little while to get over it."

"Why don't you tell me the names of the local men?"

"Whatever I do, I'd rather go to jail myself than give away any of the men. That's the one thing I can't do."

"Do you have your identity card with you?"

Dermot pulled out his wallet and handed his card to the sergeant. The sergeant took the card and went over to his desk. He sat down and wrote on the blank last page, "Restricted to Duncrana, County Tyrone." He signed his name and stamped the entry with the official police seal. He handed back the card and explained, "I have to do this. I'll have to let the D.I. know about this information and he'll probably want to know if I restricted the inform . . ." The sergeant nearly said informer and Dermot smiled weakly as the former quickly corrected his mistake. "The informant to the town here. In fact, he may want to see you himself."

Dermot replaced the card in his wallet and asked, "How am I going to get to England with a card like this?"

"When you're ready to go, come and see me and I'll cancel the restriction."

"God above sergeant, I may want to go on Monday," Dermot protested.

"So soon?"

"Depends on what the boys will do. I may have to leave Duncrana very sudden."

"If you think it would help any, I can arrange to have you

lifted and sent to Belfast, and then after a week or so you'll be released on the understanding that you get out of the North," the sergeant offered.

"No sergeant," Dermot replied. "The less I have to do with the police—the better. Anyway, I'll be getting out of Duncrana shortly."

The sergeant shrugged his shoulders. "All right, but there's one thing I want you to do. Drop in here at the barracks at least once a day. If you don't show up every day, I'm going to lift McGinnis, Corrigan and Malone. Will you do that?"

"I suppose so. Any particular time you want me to come?"

The sergeant considered for a moment. "It would be better to drop by in the evening."

"Right, I'll do that. I'd best be going now."

The sergeant walked out with Dermot. At the door he detained him and said, "Be careful, Dermot."

Dermot was uneasy about being seen with the sergeant at the door of the barracks. He stepped away from him, into the street, and started up the town. He kept watching for Mc-Ginnis or Malone but saw neither of them.

All the way up the street he had the feeling that the whole town was watching him. He nodded to those people who spoke to him and hurried on. At the door of the church he hesitated, wanting to drop in for a minute, but a nameless fear made him anxious to be at home. And all the time he felt that he had done something shameful and he knew that his visit to the barracks had changed his life, had divorced him from his people and that once he left Duncrana, he would never again come home.

TWENTY-SEVEN

Dermot slept late the next morning and did not rise until eight-thirty. He swung himself over the side of the bed and sat for a moment contemplating the bruise marks on his legs and ribs. He pulled on his trousers, swam into his shirt, padded over to Ned's bed and looked at the watch that hung from a nail in the wall. Going over to his bed, he got on his knees and groped around for his Sunday shoes. He dug his feet into the shoes and trailed on into the kitchen.

His brother was sitting motionless at the fire, his head in his hands. Dermot pulled up a stool and started lacing the shoes.

At the kitchen table, Bella was rattling around setting out the breakfast things. "Do you want two eggs?" she asked Dermot.

"Aye, two," he replied.

"That playboy," she said, nodding at Ned and making a face to show her disgust, "wants nothing to eat this morning."

Ned looked up and Dermot noted the redness of his eyes. "Be to be brave crack last night in Devlin's," he said to his brother.

Ned gave a prodigious yawn. He slid around sideways on the stool and stretched his legs out in front of the fire. "Aye, right crack it was," he answered as he screwed one eye shut and peered hopefully out of the window with the other.

Bella's arm whipsawed through a loaf and the fresh slices built up neatly on one side. She laid the knife down and walked over to the fire. Her mouth tightened into a grim curve as she looked at Ned's legs stretched in front of the hearth. He sheepishly pulled them in and she took the tongs and poked at the fire several times, sending the flames spearing up around the saucepan that hung from the crook. Reaching over, she ruffled Dermot's hair and he pulled away protestingly.

"Daddy and Mom have gone to first Mass," she told him. "The cows are milked already."

"What took the old one out to the byre?" Dermot asked.

"I don't know what came over him. He took a notion and milked them himself."

"Lo, the day of wonders has not yet passed," Ned said solemnly.

Bella set out plates, saucers and eggcups on the table. She walked over to the fire and lifted off the saucepan with the boiled eggs inside. She spooned them out and placed them on a plate. "Here you two, sit over," she called to her brothers.

Dermot and Ned rose and came over to the table and sat down. Bella poured the tea into three cups and pulled over a chair, sitting down with them. She looked at Ned with an amused smile. Ned grinned back at her and made a face, "Can't stomach anything except tea," he complained.

"You could fairly drink a bottle of stout this morning, couldn't you?" Bella asked.

"A bottle? I could drink a bloody barrel," Ned replied.

"Wee darling, why don't you switch on the wireless?" Dermot asked.

"I'm running from morn to night, waiting on the pair of you," Bella complained as she got up.

"Offer it up as an act of mercy," Ned suggested piously.

"Deed then it'd be the great act of mercy if you'd take the pledge," Bella scolded as she walked over to the small table. She switched on the wireless and they listened in silence as the weekly farm bulletin was read. Following that came the weather report and finally the news.

The announcer read the news with a controlled excitement in his voice. "Early this morning German troops invaded the Russian half of Poland. First reports say that German divisions have driven twenty miles into the Russian Zone and that Russian troops are falling back in an orderly withdrawal. The Finnish Army is in a state of full mobilization and it is believed that they will join in the attack. The Turkish prime minister has declared that his country is following a policy of strict neutrality." The announcer went on to give fuller details of the fighting.

Dermot set down his cup. "England's saved for another year," he said.

"It's great to have a scholar in the house," Ned remarked dryly.

"Germany will have to beat Russia before she'll invade England," Dermot explained. "She won't fight a war on two fronts if she can help it, and it's going to take all of a year to beat Russia, that is if Germany's fit."

"Don't they ever stop talking politics in this house," Bella complained to the dog.

"That's going to give the I.R.A. some trouble too," Dermot continued thoughtfully. "They're all set on a rising this summer, thinking Germany will invade then. But it'll be over a year now, or maybe longer. With the police on both sides of the border cracking down on the I.R.A., I don't see how they'll keep the organization going."

"It would be a great blessing if they couldn't," Bella said caustically.

The men finished breakfast and went into the bedroom to change their clothes before going to Mass. Bella washed the dishes, fed the hens, scolded the dog, swept out the kitchen and had everything tidied up by the time her mother and father came back from Mass.

At ten-thirty the three young people left the house to go to second Mass. At the door of the chapel they separated, Dermot and Ned going to the men's side and Bella to the women's.

After Mass, Dermot went around to Hannafin's and found him seated in the kitchen, drinking a cup of tea. "What Mass were you at, Jimmy?" he asked as he sat down and spread his hands to the fire.

"First, with that darling man Father McCory."

"Well, what did he have to say?"

"A grand sermon on the Sixth Commandment. I don't know why, but that's the only commandment that seems to be broken in Ireland. Impure thoughts," Hannafin snorted.

"Impure thoughts lead to impure actions," Dermot remarked pedantically.

"But why is it a sin to think of breaking the Sixth Commandment and not the rest?" Hannafin demanded. "Is it a sin to think of disobeying our parents? Is it a sin to plan out a bank robbery in our minds and gloriously spend the gains? Is it a sin to think of saying a bad word instead of saying it? Some day I'm going to confession and I'm going to confess all the thoughts I've had about breaking the commandments. I'm going to confess unkind thoughts, dishonest thoughts, disobedient thoughts, pagan thoughts, murderous thoughts. I'll give one of those priests the queer old working over," Hannafin threatened.

Dermot laughed. He bent forward and tore off a piece of

paper from an old newspaper. Folding it into a long spill, he stuck it between the bars of the grate. The end caught fire and he withdrew it and lit a cigarette.

"It's time for a reform movement in the Catholic Church," Hannafin stated.

"What kind of reform?" Dermot asked.

"A reform for them that's only mildly interested in religion." Hannafin chuckled as he thought of the hundreds who would fit in that category. "There ought to be," he continued, "a wee interval in the middle of the Mass so we could all go out for a smoke. And cushions on the seats for the bony ones. Boys, I do feel sorry for them. It must be torture on Vinegar Ryan to kneel for an hour."

"And no more sermons while we're at it," Dermot said, falling into the mood.

"We'll have no more sermons whatever. Instead we'll have public confessions. Wouldn't that be lovely? To hear some of the saintly old women in this town wailing and keening their sins?"

"And the men and women sit all through-other. No more separation," Dermot added, thinking of Neeve.

"And no collections or prayers after Mass."

"And we'll cut the Holy Hour down to a Holy Fifteen Minutes."

"And the Forty Hours Devotion down to four."

"We'll have to do something for the altar boys," Dermot said, thinking of his own days on the altar.

"Aye, we'll take them out of those bloody frocks they wear and give them football stockings and jerseys."

"How about abolishing the bishops?" Dermot asked.

"Ach we'll need an odd bishop to keep the deans in line."

"Well, we'll do away with the Pioneers and the Legion of Mary," Dermot said.

"Away with them!" Hannafin cried.

"And no fast days."

"Or Ember Days or Holy Days or Days of Awful Abstinence," Hannafin concluded.

They finally ran out of reforms and for a few minutes they joyfully contemplated the havoc they had wrought with the ritual of the Holy, Roman and Apostolic Church.

"Are you over the effects of your patriotism?" Hannafin finally asked.

"My patriotism?"

"Well, the patriotism of your friends."

"I feel all right today."

"Did you go to the police yesterday?" Hannafin asked.

"Aye," Dermot answered unwillingly.

"You'd better be careful."

"I will. If I get through today, I don't care. I'm leaving in the morning for England."

"You going anywhere tonight?" Hannafin asked.

"No. When I go home I'll not set foot out of the house until tomorrow morning."

"You're taking the nine train?"

"Aye."

"You'll drop in before you go?"

"I will surely." Dermot stood up. "I'm off. I'll see you in the morning, Jimmy."

Dermot left the shop and walked slowly around by the back of the church. The town was deserted and had that curious flatness of an Ulster Sunday. Dermot thought that he could always tell what day it was by the set of the town and he could never mistake a Sunday. Life seemed to suspend itself on that day. All the shops were closed, no cars or lorries were on the streets and what few people were about, were slowly and decorously taking the traditional Sunday walk. Dogs did not fight on Sundays and cats remained primly seated in armchairs, foregoing their usual forays into the gardens of the town. Little boys knew what awaited them if they dared to whistle and little girls did not giggle as much. The town went into a trance and did not waken until evening when the hackney cars gathered their loads for the dances.

Dermot walked past Devlin's pub and thought of all the fair days that he had stood on the steps and watched the throngs of people eddying about the town. He moved up the street and stopped again at Flanagan's entry and recalled the night they had hung a kid goat by the heels from the latch of Flanagan's back door. The bleats of it could be heard for miles. For weeks afterward old Jimmy Flanagan claimed that he and Maggie were soon for the sod because he had heard the banshee, screeling away in the wildest keen and scrabbing at the back door itself.

He walked past the grade school and remembered his fight with Timmie Murphy and the erupting crowd of boys, ringing him in, shouting and dancing around for a better view. He could almost see the hard head of Timmie, bent low and ramming in and he, Dermot, his stomach full of empty, backing away and pumping blows into the bundled up head and face. And Timmie got a split lip and for weeks Dermot swaggered his way around the school until one day on the fair green little Petey Begley punched him back into proper perspective.

He passed the priests' rectory. The three gooseberry bushes were still there and he remembered the night that he and a group of others had raided the garden and ravaged the gooseberry bushes. For weeks afterward they had debated whether it was a mortal sin or venial sin, and how they were ever going to confess to Father McDonald that they had raided his own garden. Finally they had gone to confession in Rathgiven and the priest there had told them that they would have to make restitution and offer to pay for the gooseberries. Dermot had been frightened out of his wits by the idea of going up to the rectory and offering to pay Father McDonald for the theft. He had mollified his conscience by putting a sixpence in an envelope and mailing it to the parish priest along with a cryptic note that read, "For the gooseberries."

His reveries were interrupted by the sound of a car which overtook him and stopped. The front doors sprang open and McGinnis, Malone and the two McIntyres got out. Dermot looked around, thinking to run, but dismissed the thought as cowardly. In a moment he was surrounded by the four men.

"In the car," McGinnis directed, giving him a push. His arms were tightly gripped and he was marched to the car and shoved into the back seat. Young Quinn was driving and he wheeled the car around and started back toward town.

"Another kicking?" Dermot asked.

McGinnis twisted around in the front seat. "You're being held for trial," he said.

"Now listen fellas, all I did was tell them that Trilarran was going to be raided. I didn't give the names of anybody," Dermot protested.

"You'll have an opportunity to explain that at the trial," McGinnis answered.

"When will the trial be?" Dermot asked.

"Tonight," Malone replied. "We have a couple of men coming down from Brigade around midnight."

Dermot wondered if he should tell them that McGinnis, Malone and Corrigan would be lifted if he didn't show up that evening at the barracks. He decided against it, fearing they would think that he had given the three names to the police.

The car drove around to the back of the parish hall and stopped. The men got out and opened the little storehouse and escorted Dermot inside. Malone brought a length of rope with him. They pulled Dermot's arms around behind his back and tied them tightly at the wrists.

Dermot was determined not to show fear and to keep his courage bolstered, he threatened them. "You'd better shoot me after this, because if I ever get loose I'm going straight to the barracks and give the names of every man in the company and where the arms are stored and the names of everybody I know, including the Brigade men."

"You've already done that," McGinnis said scornfully.

"I haven't," Dermot replied. "Damn fool that I was."

"You've done enough already," Quinn said.

They finished tying his arms and made him sit down. They stretched out his legs and tied them at the ankles. Then they ran a piece of rope from his wrists, twice around his waist and down to the ankles. Dermot sinkingly realized that he would never get out of the ropes unaided.

McGinnis made a quick inspection of the knots. Satisfied, he looked at Dermot and said, "We'll bring some grub before night."

"Bloody decent of you," Dermot sarcastically replied.

The men left the shed. McGinnis was last to leave and he shut the door behind him. Dermot heard the rattle of a lock and the sound of a key turning.

He stretched out, trying to make himself comfortable, and began to wonder how he could break out of the shed. Presently he tried to get at the rope around his ankles with his teeth but no matter how he strained his head wouldn't reach that far. He grew tired of his efforts and gave up in disgust.

He had been a fool, he thought, to get in the car so easily. His best chance was to have made a run for it, even though he doubted that he could have escaped. He wondered if it would do any good to shout. By chance someone in passing might hear him. He started to shout, feeling silly at the racket he was making. Methodically he roared as loud as he could and after each roar he listened for a while. After a minute or so he heard the lock being opened and for a moment hope flared. A square block of light slid into the shed and John McIntyre stepped inside. "No good shouting, Dermot," he said. "If you keep it up I'll have to put a gag on you."

"You're outside all the time?" Dermot asked.

"Aye and there'll be somebody on guard till the Brigade men arrive."

"You're not taking any chances, are you, John?"

McIntyre shook his head. "Don't blame me for this, Dermot. It's all your own fault."

"Listen John, there's cigarettes in my coat pocket. Be a good lad and take them out and light one for me," Dermot asked.

McIntyre came over and reached into Dermot's pocket and took out the cigarettes. He put one in Dermot's mouth and lit it. Dermot inhaled gratefully and said, "Take one yourself, John."

"Thanks," McIntyre replied in an embarrassed way as he took one out and replaced the cigarettes in Dermot's coat. He walked over to the door and pulled it to and came back and sat down against the opposite wall. The two men looked at each other for several seconds in the dim light of the darkened shed.

"You don't think they'll shoot me?" Dermot asked.

"I don't know what they'll do. If McGinnis had his way you'd get shot without any trial. Malone made him send to Brigade and get some of their men down."

"Malone did? Well, there's some good in that little shit," Dermot said.

A silence fell on both men. They sat and smoked and each was uneasily aware of the other and each one loath to reopen the conversation.

Finally, Dermot spit the butt out of his mouth and remarked, "It's a rare world. It isn't so many years ago that you and I were altar boys with old Father McDonald. Do you mind the time that Timmie Murphy pushed you down on top of a pile of holly in the vestry and the both of you fought and Father McDonald came in the middle of it?"

McIntyre laughed. "Aye, and Mass was ten minutes late that day with Father McDonald refereeing."

"A shocking man for fighting, Timmie was."

"He couldn't fight for his breakfast either, but he was forever at it."

"I beat him one day," Dermot said.

"Aye, I mind that. And after the fight was over Timmie threw a big rock at you and you into the chasing of him."

Dermot sighed, "Aye, we had great sport then. But what are we doing now, John? Shooting at women and children and talking about murdering one of your old comrades."

McIntyre looked away self-consciously. "Listen Dermot, don't blame me for this," he said. "I'm only obeying orders and you can't say you weren't warned." He stood up. "I have to go out again. We're being relieved every two hours until the Brigade men come and I was given orders to stay outside all the time." McIntyre's voice had an undercurrent of embarrassment.

"Go on out and be a good soldier, whatever you do," Dermot said bitterly.

McIntyre walked outside and locked the door.

Dermot, enveloped in gloom, thought back on his schooldays; the way John McIntyre used to fall asleep in class; the day he was sleeping and they tied his legs to the steel support of the desk and when the master called on him to recite, he had startled up, dragging desk, books, himself and his seat companion over in a heap. And the set of him trying to explain to the master how his legs happened to be tied. He had always been a good-natured devil, Dermot thought, without harm or hate in him.

It was dusky in the shed and Dermot could barely see the details of the painted landscape that leaned against the opposite wall. He felt a curious lassitude and wondered why he wasn't more concerned about his situation. He realized that they might have him shot but somehow he wasn't too excited over it. If they sentenced him to death, would they let him have a priest? Probably not, for fear the priest would try to talk them out of it. Where would they bury him? Who would shoot him? How? The questions went racing through his mind as he alternately thought of Neeve and his family and prepared his arguments for the trial. After what he had done for the organization he could expect some understanding from them. They knew up in Brigade how much he had worked for the cause. Surely they wouldn't allow him to be shot? If he told them he was going to England, would they not allow him to leave? Where was the sense in shooting him?

He let his head fall on his chest and tried to sleep but his head was full of thinking. From outside he could hear the chirping of spring-intoxicated birds and the lonely whine of an odd car that passed on the county road. Inside the gloom deepened as the sun cut slowly down the sky.

TWENTY-EIGHT

As the day wore on both Bella and her mother started to worry over Dermot's absence. Dinner was served and eaten in an unusual silence. Patrick went over to Loy's in the afternoon and came back again at teatime. The cows were milked, the hens fed and the creamery can left at the end of the lane for the milk lorry.

The day slowly failed. Tone went on his afternoon prowl through the garden and haggard; Bella started knitting a cable-stitch pullover for Dermot and Patrick sat in omnipotent silence at the fire.

Kathleen made a pot of tea and the three of them sat over to the table. She looked at the clock for the hundredth time and asked, "I wonder where that cub's gone to?"

"Don't be worrying over him," Patrick replied. "He's well able to look after himself."

"I suppose the other one's in Devlin's?" Bella conjectured.

"More than likely," Patrick agreed.

"I've a great pair of sons," Kathleen complained, "That none of them would come home of a Sunday. One of them drinking the whole day away and God only knows what trouble the other one's getting into."

"If it'll ease your mind any, I'll go in after the dishes are done and see if I can find Dermot," Bella offered.

"Would you do that, like a good girl?" her mother asked.

"Leave the lads alone," Patrick scolded. "They do their work around the place all week without being hounded on Sundays."

Kathleen sighed. "It's not like Dermot to stay away of a Sunday. He's always home for dinner."

Patrick thought that his son was away on another job for the I.R.A. and although he was secretly proud of him, he was at the same time vexed that his wife should be worrying. He decided to go to Loy's again, fearing that Kathleen and Bella would press him into looking for Dermot. He finished his tea and left the kitchen.

Bella lifted a scrap of bread that Patrick had left on his plate and threw it to the dog. Tone trapped it with his mouth and his tail thumped a thank you. "Don't worry about him," Bella said. "He's probably gone to a football game somewhere."

"There are no football games today or he'd have mentioned it," Kathleen despondently answered.

"Well, don't worry. I'll go into town and find him." Bella filled the kettle with water and took down the big dishpan from the dresser.

Her mother sat at the table, gazing blankly at the row of hooks where the coats were hung. Her hands played slowly, nervously, twisting her cup round and around. "Don't bother with the dishes," she said softly. "Go you on into town."

Bella was about to object but she realized that her mother

would be more content if she went to look for Dermot. She walked over and lifted down her heavy woolen coat. She distastefully hefted the weight of it and said, "It's too warm to wear this but I'm afraid it'll rain."

"Take Dermot's raincoat," her mother sugested.

Bella replaced the woolen coat and took down Dermot's trench coat. She turned up the sleeves. The coat flopped loosely around her, reaching almost to her ankles. "Mother of God, I'm drowned in this thing," she complained. She caught both flaps of the coat and tightened them in around her body.

"It's better than dragging that heavy coat in with you," Kathleen said. "Take it off and tie it around the handlebars and then if it rains you can put it on."

Bella unwound herself from the coat and took it off. She said good-by to her mother, dipped a finger in the holy water fount that hung on the kitchen wall and went out to the shed. She folded the coat over the handlebars and tied it with the belt around the front fork. Then she mounted the bicycle and cycled down the lane.

Going first to Hannafin's, she leaned the bicycle against the shop window and knocked softly on the door. Jimmy's wife came out and invited her in. Bella walked into the kitchen, somewhat self-consciously, half expecting to see it packed with men. However, it was still too early in the evening for visitors and no one was there except Hannafin and the wife.

Hannafin sat at the kitchen table, doing a crossword puzzle. He looked up and asked, "One-eyed Irish god—five letters?"

Bella studied for a moment before replying, "Balor."

"Good for you. Balor it is." He filled in the blanks neatly. "One more hard one. Unit of weight? Four letters?"

"Ounce? No, that's five. Let's see. Dram?"

"No. It doesn't fit. This one ends with an O."

"Kilo!" Hannafin's wife answered triumphantly.

"Boys-a-dear but that's the smart woman I've got." Jimmy shook his head wonderingly. The truth was that Jimmy knew both items but could not resist asking others for the answers. He folded the paper and pushed it to one side. "Whose heart are you breaking now?" he asked Bella.

"There'll be few hearts broken over me," Bella answered, mock-modestly.

"Boys, if I were twenty years younger, I'd give you the queer old run-around," Hannafin threatened.

"Was Dermot in at all today?" Bella asked. She sat down on a chair and smoothed her skirt over her knees.

"He was in after second Mass for a while. He said he was going home." Hannafin looked at her, his bushy eyebrows tightening down. "He left here about twelve-thirty and said he was going home," he repeated.

"He hasn't been at home at all, all day. Not for dinner or tea," Bella explained.

"Maybe he went away somewhere with the boys," Jimmy's wife suggested. "Are there any football games anywhere?"

"Not that I know of," Hannafin answered. "Anyway it's too early yet for regular football games."

"Why don't you try Neeve Donnelly's?" Mrs. Hannafin asked.

"That's where I'll go next," Bella replied. "Maybe he's with her or maybe she knows where he is. I'm worried over him; it's not often he doesn't come home at all of a Sunday." She stood up and with the back of her hand brushed the hair up from her brow.

"Will you stay for a wee drop of tea?" Mrs. Hannafin asked. "It's not often we have you."

"I'm just after tea this minute at home," Bella answered. She turned to Hannafin. "If he happens to wander in, tell him I was looking him."

"I'll do that," Hannafin answered as he walked her to the door. He came back to the kitchen and sat down at the table. His fingers started drumming on the newspaper.

"You'll be looking for him next," his wife complained.

Hannafin pessimistically shook his head, "The lad's in trouble."

"Don't go getting mixed up with that crowd, Jimmy," his wife advised.

"If he doesn't show up in another half hour or so, I'm going to look for him," Hannafin said as he stared out the window.

"Arrah sit where you are and don't be bothering your head with him. Like as not he and Neeve are in some hayshed."

"Hayshed, how-are-ye," Hannafin said shortly. Then he lifted his head in a listening attitude, "It's raining," he remarked.

"Did you ever know a Sunday yet that it didn't rain?" his wife asked.

They both sat quietly and listened to the rain. It hit the pavement outside with soft irregular plops. The tempo increased and the wind flung a handful of drops against the window. It spotted, collected in little islands and streaked sadly down the pane. From the yard they could hear the trickling gurgle of the rainspout as it emptied into a barrel in irregular spurts.

Hannafin's wife got up and went into the scullery and came back with an empty feed bag. She folded it once and placed it just inside the front door where visitors coming in could wipe their feet.

Hannafin felt a sudden uneasiness and moved from the table over to the fire, spreading his hands to the dull red glow in the stove. Another rattle of rain hit the window and Hannafin looked over and grimaced.

From the scullery came the melancholy drip-drip of a leak in the roof. He mentally made a note to see about getting the roof fixed and called to his wife, "Better put a bucket under that leak in the scullery roof."

His wife went out to the scullery and the sound of the drop changed to a heavy metallic clang. Hannafin went out to the shop and came back, carrying the radio. "That sort of a night needs music," he explained as he plugged in the set.

He switched it on and waited for the current to warm up. His hand fiddled with the knobs until he got a station that was playing music.

He went back to the stove and sat down. His head went back and his eyes closed. The orchestra was playing the third movement of a Tchaikowsky symphony and the haunting loveliness of the piece grew a strange sadness in Hannafin's heart.

His wife, looking over at the closed eyes and the relaxed mouth, realized anew how little she knew her husband. His hands lay folded in his lap and one forefinger was strenuously conducting. She smiled, watching the lively jauntiness of the finger as it seemingly controlled the music.

A drop of rain fell down the chimney and sizzled briefly on the inside of the stovepipe. Faintly, from outside the house, came the heavy sough of the wind as it sowed the night with rain.

The music ended and Hannafin opened his eyes. "Make me a wee cup of tea like a good woman," he said. "I've got to look for that omadaun."

His wife pulled the kettle over on top of the stove and poked at the grate. She rose and prepared the tea and Hannafin sat over to the little table. He listened to the rain; to the drumming of it on the window and the plunking of it in the bucket, and tried to figure out where Dermot could be.

He finished his tea, stood up and put on his raincoat. "I'll be back in no time at all," he told his wife.

"Let you not stay out too long in that or you'll catch your death of cold," his wife scolded.

Hannafin opened the door and stepped out into the night. The slanting rain slammed at his face and the force of it made him draw his breath. Walking quickly, he made his way around the church and down the town. He went in the back entry of Neeve Donnely's and knocked on the back door.

Mrs. Donnelly came out. "Jimmy Hannafin!" she exclaimed.

Hannafin stepped inside, shaking himself vigorously and a

shower of raindrops fanned out on the stone floor. He wiped his head and face with a handkerchief. Neeve, her three younger sisters and Bella were seated around the kitchen fire. Hannafin nodded to them and said, "There's a touch of damp in that night."

"There is indeed," Neeve answered. "It's not often we have you over, Jimmy. And such a night too!" Neeve shook her head in wonder.

"Here sit up to the fire, Jimmy. You must be foundered," Mrs. Donnelly said.

They made room for him at the fire and he sat down and slowly rubbed his thighs. "Man, the fire's the place on a night like that," he commented.

"What takes you out tonight?" Neeve asked.

"It's not for a walk," Hannafin answered and then turned to Bella and asked, "Did you find your brother?"

"No, not yet," Bella answered. "Neeve said she hasn't seen him at all today. I decided to wait here a wee while in case he shows up."

"I was on my way down the street and thought I'd drop in and ask," Hannafin said. He stood up and the others looked at him in surprise. "I hate to be running off like this, but I have a wee call to make and I don't want to leave it too late," he explained.

Neeve and her mother protested but Hannafin belted his coat and turned up the collar. "If Dermot shows up, let me know," he said to Bella.

Bella walked over to the door with him. As he was about to leave, she reached out and caught his arm. "You know something about Dermot. Where is he?" she asked urgently, her face tightening in concern.

He caught her arm and lowered it. "Don't be getting all fussed up," he said. "Your brother's all right." He turned and walked down the steps and out through the entry.

He stopped as he reached the street and looked down the town. The rain was slicing the night to shreds, bouncing off the street and pavement. He saw the yellow bulb outside the police barracks and in the dim, orange light he noted the dark bulky shadow leaning in the doorway. He walked down the street and stopped when he came to the barracks. "That's a raw night," he said.

"It is that." The sergeant made room for him in the doorway. "You're out in bad weather," he commented.

"I'm looking for a wee fella. His folks are annoyed about him. He hasn't been home to dinner or tea." Hannafin looked up shrewdly at the sergeant.

The sergeant shifted his position slightly to avoid a steady drop of rain that was falling from the lintel of the doorway. "I might be looking the same man myself. Would it be young O'Neill?" the sergeant asked.

"The very man. It's shocking how popular that lad's got lately. Everybody's looking him." Jimmy hunched his shoulders and looked out at the hurrying army of raindrops.

For several seconds neither of them spoke. Then the sergeant said, "He was supposed to come here for a wee visit tonight but he hasn't showed yet." The sergeant's tone invited confidence.

"Mind that fella has other friends and he might be with them," Hannafin said meaningfully.

"These other friends—they wouldn't like to see him out in this weather? They'd probably keep him a while?"

"The very I.T. That's just what they'd do. They're a shocking hospitable crowd," Hannafin replied.

"Didn't he have a notion of going away tomorrow?" the sergeant asked.

"I heard him say something about England," Hannafin answered.

"If he's with friends, he might be hard to locate?"

"No. I can find him," Hannafin asserted. "I might have to go around a few places but eventually I can find him. That is if his friends haven't invited him out of town."

"Aye, that's the point. I wanted to give him a wee note. I have a brother that owns a bakery in England and if our boy went there he'd have no trouble in getting a job; at least until he gets on his feet. I wrote to this brother telling him all about him."

"Well now, sergeant," Hannafin said, "You could give me that wee note and I'll see that it's delivered. That would save him the trouble of coming here."

"It would at that. Wait a moment, Jimmy."

The sergeant disappeared into the barracks. Presently, he returned with a white envelope which he handed to Hannafin. "There's my brother's address in there and a new I.D. card," he told Hannafin. "Tell your man to destroy the old one. This one has no restriction on it, so he'll have no bother. If you don't find our friend, bring back the envelope."

"Would tomorrow do?"

"Tomorrow would do grand," the sergeant agreed. "But if you locate him and he doesn't have a chance to drop around to see me, come yourself. I'll be in the barracks till midnight and in the house after that. I won't be going to bed till two or three."

Hannafin slid the envelope into the inside pocket of his jacket. "Good man, sergeant," he said. He buttoned up his raincoat and looked out at the rain that slanted through the yellow reflection from the bulb. "I'm away now, sergeant. I'll see you later tonight or in the morning."

"Wait a tic, Jimmy," the sergeant said. "You don't think you'll be needing help?"

Hannafin seemed embarrassed as he replied, "Ah now sergeant, I do and that's the truth, but I'd be the better without police help. I'll bring his brother along."

"Aye, I know what you mean. But listen, don't be afraid to send me word if things go wrong."

"I'll send for you sergeant if I have to, but I'm hoping there'll be no need."

"Mind take care of yourself, Jimmy," the sergeant warned. "That's a bad night to be abroad."

"I'll be all right, sergeant." Hannafin stepped out of the doorway and started up the street.

He went past the church and around to Devlin's back yard. He knocked quietly on the back door of the pub. For several minutes he waited and then knocked again. From inside the pub he heard footsteps in the hall and the muffled question from the other side of the door, "Who's there?"

"Jimmy Hannafin," he answered.

A bolt drew back and the door opened. Mrs. Devlin filled the hall, barring his passage. "Did you see the police at all, Jimmy?" she asked fearfully.

"Ach now you're all right, wee love," he lied fluently and easily. "The sergeant's gone home and McVey and Harris are drinking in Moran's."

Mrs. Devlin shuffled beside him. "They've been bad lately, God's curse on them. This I.R.A. nonsense is turning all the police contrary."

They walked into the kitchen and Hannafin stood opposite the fire. Thin wisps of steam started rising from his coat. "What will you have?" Mrs. Devlin asked.

Jimmy cocked his nose in the air, savoring the smell of stale porter and Irish whiskey. Sniffing delicately he answered, "I'll have some of that."

"Porter is it you want?" Mrs. Devlin asked.

"I'll have a wee shot of Bushmills."

"Would you not like a bottle of porter? I dread going out to the bar and wracking around."

"Would you have me drink porter on a night like this?"

Hannafin impatiently demanded. "Get me a shot, woman dear, I'm foundered."

She padded out of the kitchen and Jimmy heard the cautious turn of the key in the bar door. He listened intently, wondering if any of the snugs in the bar were occupied. He caught the murmur of a male voice followed by the scrape of a shoe on the floor.

Mrs. Devlin returned with a shot glass of whiskey and Hannafin handed her the price of it. The money disappeared into the heavy pocket of her blue apron. Hannafin watched her, an amused glint in his eyes. "There's a pocket that needs relining brave and often," he remarked.

She looked suspiciously at him and answered, "Ach Jimmy the wee bit of business I do after hours would hardly keep body and soul together."

"Well anyway, here's to your health, mam, may you never be raided this year." He lifted the glass to his mouth and drank half the whiskey.

Mrs. Devlin threw up her hands. "Don't be talking about raiding. The police have the heart put crossways in me. Twice this past month they've come after hours."

"Is Ned O'Neill in the bar?" Hannafin casually asked.

"Who's looking him?" Mrs. Devlin demanded from behind the blue apron.

"The bloody king of Portugal's looking him," Hannafin answered sarcastically. "Tell him to come out to the kitchen for a minute."

Mrs. Devlin slid out of the kitchen grumbling away to herself.

Ned came walking out of the bar, carefully placing one foot after the other, holding a glass of stout in his hand. He looked at Hannafin and a wide smile split his face. "Oh the lovely man Hannafin. Listen Jimmy, let us sing a song about Ireland."

"Ireland be damned. You're stocious."

Ned stood up straight and rocked back slightly on his heels. "Oh the devil he hoisted her up on his back," he sang softly. "He was seven years going and nine coming ba-a-a-ack."

"You sing like a bloody goat," Hannafin said disgustedly. "Listen Ned, your brother's in trouble." He noticed Mrs. Devlin listening to the conversation and he ordered her brusquely, "Get me another one."

She gave him a sour look and padded out again.

"My lovely brother," Ned mumbled. "The lovely wee brother that wouldn't drink a bottle of stout with me." Ned drew closer and Hannafin decided that he wasn't too drunk to help him.

"What kind of trouble is it?" Ned asked.

"He's in trouble with the organization and if we don't find him tonight, you're liable to be waking him in the next day or two."

"Waking him!" Ned suddenly became serious. "Name of Jesus, what are you talking about?"

"The organization has him locked up somewhere. He's in trouble with them. I can't explain everything here but we've got to find him tonight."

Ned lifted his drink, his lower lip nestled the rim of the glass and a great draught of porter disappeared. "The I.R.A. has him? Where are we going to find him?" He set the empty glass down on the stove.

"I know a few places he might be, but I'll need help. I need a man who isn't afraid of a wee bit of a scuffle."

"Deed then if Dermot's in trouble, here's one man who isn't afraid of king or pope," Ned declared, raising his clenched fist in a threatening way.

Mrs. Devlin came back into the kitchen with Hannafin's drink and Ned pulled out a pound note. "Here," he said to her. "Take Jimmy's out of that and bring me a half pint of whiskey. It's a long cold night and I haven't the strength of a new dropped calf." Mrs. Devlin pocketed the money and went out to the bar.

Ned gave an expansive smile. "Oh but you're the lovely one Jimmy. A decent man to think of me brother. That's a deluge outside," he said warningly.

"It isn't that bad. As soon as you finish that drink we'll be moving. It might take us half the night to find him."

Ned walked over to the stove and sat down on the coldest part of it. His speech slurred a little as he said, "We'll make a great circle. From Devlin's to Rafferty's to Byrne's to Moran's and back to Devlin's." He named the four biggest pubs in the village.

Hannafin grunted. "I'll great circle you. You won't find Dermot in any of those places."

Mrs. Devlin came back with the half pint of whiskey and Ned eagerly reached for it. He contemplated the bottle for a moment and then with a slow deliberate motion, stuffed it into his pocket. "Aye, but that's the rare holy water," he said.

Hannafin tugged him by the arm. "Come out of that with you. It's time we were moving." Hannafin linked one of his arms and gently urged him in the direction of the hall. Mrs. Devlin accompanied them with worried little shuffles. She opened the back door for them and peered out into the yard. "Be quick," she whispered, as the two men sidled out and into the rain.

TWENTY-NINE

The two men stood in the middle of Main Street. The night was black with a hard lacing rain, the drops pelting into their coats as they bowed their heads to the storm. From a score of rainspouts came a symphony of water: the main spouts disgorging themselves with a heavy, drumming sound; the smaller drainpipes splashing erratically in a brassy gurgle while individual drops pizzicatoed all over the pavements.

Hannafin hunched his shoulders. "Let's go down the town and try Rafferty's shed."

Ned shook his head impatiently, the drops flying off, the way a dog shakes water from his back. "Oh for the feathers of a duck," he mourned. He glanced longingly at the rear entrance to Moran's pub as they were passing it. Hannafin, interpreting the look, caught him by the arm and complained, "We've no

time for that now. When we find your brother the two of us
will have a few together."

Ned walked unsteadily, grumbling in a monotone. "He
might have picked a nicer night to get in trouble. The heavens
are emptying. I'm wet to the marrow. My boots are full. My
poor wee toes are swimming around in two bogholes . . ."

They continued down the Rathgiven road and turned
through a gate and into a field about a quarter of a mile from
the town. Both men sloshed their way through the wet-heavy
grass until they came to the opposite side. Hannafin stopped
Ned. "Let you stay quiet here a moment," he whispered.
"There might be someone with him."

Hannafin peered intently, trying to pierce the blackness of
the night. Finally he noticed the shed and the blacker oblong
of an opening. He stepped closer and saw the open door. "He's
not here," he called to Ned. "Come on and we'll take shelter
for a minute."

Ned came tramping up to the shed. Both men went inside
and Ned walked over to a corner and wearily sat down on the
dirt floor. Hannafin lit a match and peered around. He
grinned at Ned and eased down on his hunkers beside him.

"He's not here and he hasn't been here," Hannafin said.

Ned grunted.

"The next place," Hannafin continued, "is the little shed
behind the hall. Then we'll go up the top road and try the railway shed at the Rockcutting Bridge."

Ned reached into his pocket and withdrew the half pint of
whiskey. He pulled out the cork and tilted the bottle, swallow-
ing a mouthful. Reaching over, he hit Hannafin on the arm
and put the bottle into his hand.

Hannafin took a drink and returned the bottle. "Bowls of
barley, honey and wine," he said to Ned.

"Ach Jimmy, you're the lovely fella with poetry," Ned
sighed. "I'm no good. I only know the one poem." He began
to recite in a schoolboy, sing-song voice. "My Aunt Gin she

took me in, she made me tea in her wee tin, half a bap and a big cow-clap and three goat's pills from her wee shop."

Hannafin snorted his disgust. "Oh Tara, the things they do to your harp," he complained. He shook Ned by the arm. "Let's be moving. We'll be all night finding Dermot at this rate." Ned rose unsteadily and both men left the shed. They started to re-cross the field. Somewhere above them a cloud ruptured, spilling a lake of rain. They started running for the gate and tho shelter of several oak trees that grew along the road. Together they huddled under a large tree until the shower passed and the rain returned to a steady relentless drizzle.

They left the tree and walked back to the town. As they passed Devlin's, Ned thought of the good fire in the kitchen and hopefully suggested a drink but Hannafin urged him on. They went past the bicycle shop and walked over the little road that led to the parish hall. As they walked quietly to the storehouse, a voice called to them, "Is that you, Don?"

Hannafin stopped Ned and whispered to him, "Shuush, that's young Quinn!" On tiptoe they moved another few steps.

Quinn's voice came with a thin edge of fear to it, "Who's that?"

Suddenly they saw Quinn leaning back against the door of the storehouse. He stood facing them and Hannafin could tell by the crouched posture and the outstretched arm that Quinn was pointing a gun.

Quinn bent a little lower and asked nervously, "What do you want?"

"Dermot O'Neill," Hannafin answered quietly. Ned was rooted still, staring at Quinn in bewilderment.

Quinn made a gesture with the arm that held the gun. "Dermot's staying here," he warned them. "Don't come any closer."

Hannafin was about to start reasoning when Ned stepped forward. Quinn backed away a step and shouted, "I'll shoot you, Ned!" Ned said nothing and implacably walked forward until only a yard separated the two men. Then he reached out and caught Quinn by the wrist and twisted hard. The gun dropped to the ground. Ned said slowly as he looked into Quinn's face, "You weren't going to shoot Dermot?"

"They will Ned," Quinn babbled on the verge of tears. "They will because he's informed on us." Ned looked in wonder at him.

Hannafin came up and seized Ned by the arm. "Don't touch him Ned. He's just a lad. Come on, we've no time to waste." He looked over at the door and noticed the padlock. Holding out his hand, he tersely commanded, "The key!"

Quinn reached with his free hand into his pocket, pulled out the key and handed it over. Hannafin inserted the key in the lock and opened the door. He stepped inside and Ned dragged Quinn in with him and closed the door. Hannafin struck a match and glanced around. He saw Dermot sitting down against the wall, his arms behind him. "There's a lamp on the wall," Dermot called. Hannafin lit another match and peered around until he located the lamp. Lighting a third match, he lit the lamp and brought it over close to Dermot. "You all right?" he asked.

"I'm frozen and stiff as a board. Is that Ned with you?"

"Aye," Ned answered and approached his brother, pushing Quinn in front of him.

Hannafin bent down and untied the ropes. Dermot weakly stood up and began to massage his wrists and ankles. "I've got a raging headache," he complained.

He stamped around for a minute and then reached into his pocket, pulling out a pack of cigarettes. He lit one and remarked, "This town's getting to be a shocking place." He grinned wryly at Hannafin.

"What were they going to do?" Hannafin asked.

"Try me or something. They're waiting for men to come down from Brigade for the occasion."

Dermot seemed to notice Quinn for the first time. He walked over and stared at him. Quinn tried to draw back but Ned thrust him forward. "This is the great little gamecock," Dermot said sarcastically. "What are we going to do with him?"

"We'll just lock him in here," Hannafin answered. "What time were they supposed to come for Dermot?" he asked Quinn.

"I don't know," Quinn answered. "Someone's supposed to relieve me at ten-thirty," he replied, his voice unhappy.

Hannafin took a watch out of his pocket. "It's a little after ten now," he said.

Ned shoved Quinn forward, releasing him. He reached into his pocket and took out the half pint of whiskey. Tilting the bottle to his mouth he took a quick drink before offering it to Hannafin. Hannafin took a swallow and in turn offered the bottle to Dermot. Making a tight face, Dermot screwed his eyes shut as the whiskey caught his throat.

"That's not Dermot drinking whiskey?" Ned asked incredulously.

Dermot handed the bottle back. "It is indeed." He grinned at his brother. "You got any spare money?"

Ned reached into his pocket and took out a five-pound note. "I've that if it's any good to you."

"I'll need it," Dermot said, taking the note and pulling it into his pocket.

"Let's leave this place before someone comes," Hannafin suggested, moving toward the door.

The three men left the storehouse, locking Quinn inside. Hannafin slipped the key into his pocket. He started feeling around the ground with his foot. "Where's that gun?" he asked.

The other men also started looking and finally Dermot located it. He began to put it in his pocket but Hannafin stretched out his hand, "Here give it to me," he said. "I'll take care of it."

Dermot handed the gun over. As they were walking away from the hall, Dermot asked, "What will the I.R.A. do to you two boyos now?"

"They'll not do a thing," Hannafin answered. "The I.R.A's finished for another generation. The Germans attacked Russia today and that means no invasion of England for a long time yet."

Ned sentimentally draped an arm around his brother's shoulder. Now that the moment of danger was past, his drunkenness was coming back. "My wee brother, God help him," he said. "What's my poor wee brother going to do now?"

"I'm going to England tomorrow; first thing in the morning," Dermot replied.

They went around to the Back Street and entered Hannafin's house. Inside the kitchen they backed up to the fire and the heat started the steam wreathing up from their clothes. Hannafin told his wife to get something to eat for Dermot and she went out to the scullery to prepare a meal.

Ned set the bottle on the kitchen table and Hannafin found three glasses and poured out the remainder of the whiskey. He handed the drinks around and solemnly raised his glass. "Here's to the next rising in 1961."

"This one's not over yet," Dermot warned.

"It is indeed; it's punctured," Hannafin answered. "Our national folly won't be repeated until the next generation."

Dermot finished his drink and said, "I'll need to be getting on home. I'll have to gather up my clothes and get some money. I want to see Neeve too before I leave."

"You'll not go home, or to Neeve's either," Hannafin said sharply. "As soon as they find you're gone, they'll be looking you. You'll leave Duncrana tonight. Go down the back gardens and take the railway line to the blacksmith's bridge. When you come to the bridge, cut across to the road and walk on into Rathgiven from there. There'll probably be a B-man patrol out on the Rathgiven road tonight and you don't want to be stopped by them either. You'll be well past the patrol when you come out at the bridge. When you get into Rathgiven wait around the square until four o'clock. Red O'Connor leaves at four with a load of milk for the creamery at Portadown. He'll give you a ride as far as there. You'll get a train from Portadown around nine-thirty for the city. When you get to Belfast go to a picture house or somewhere but keep away from the docks, until it's time to leave. At about a quarter to nine get a taxi and make him take you straight to the Liverpool dock—the night boat leaves at nine. There'll be police around the docks and you'll be safe by then."

"Listen Jimmy," Dermot objected. "I'll have to go to the barracks. My I.D. card has a restriction stamp on it."

"I've got a new I.D. card for you and an address in England where there's a job waiting. The sergeant gave them to me," Hannafin explained as he took out the envelope and handed it across to Dermot. Dermot opened the envelope and glanced at the card and the address. He withdrew his wallet and held up the old I.D. card. "What do I do with this?" he asked.

Hannafin took the old card and read the restriction stamp on the back of it. He turned around and opened the front of the stove and pushed the card into the fire. He reached for his glass and asked, "How about money? Do you need more?"

"I'm afraid so. I should have another fiver."

"I'll give it to you and you can send it back to me when you're working."

"Not at all," Ned interrupted. "Give him the fiver and I'll pay you back tomorrow."

Hannafin went out to the shop and came back with a small cash box. He opened it, counted out five one-pound notes and handed them over to Dermot. "I don't care who pays me back," he said.

"Thanks Jimmy," Dermot said as he pocketed the money. "Ned will see that you get it."

Ned nodded his agreement. Mrs. Hannafin set the tea out on the table along with some cold meat that was left over from the dinner. "Here, sit over," she called to Dermot. "It's not much but it'll hold you for a while."

"It's grand, mam," Dermot answered as he pulled a chair over to the table and sat down. He was ravenous with hunger, having eaten nothing since breakfast. Hannafin and Ned remained silent while Dermot was eating. Twice Mrs. Hannafin refilled the plate with bread. Dermot finally pushed back the chair. "Man, that was powerful," he said thankfully.

"You poor thing, you must have been starved," Mrs. Hannafin commented as she cleared away the dishes.

Dermot went over to the stove and lit a cigarette. "Well Ned," he said to his brother, "God only knows when we'll see each other again."

Ned shook his head sorrowfully. "It's a hard thing to see you leaving. I'd nearly rather it was myself."

"You're a better hand with the land than I am," Dermot said, as if in explanation.

"I am indeed," Ned replied scornfully. "I'm nothing but a hired hand around the place, trotting at the old one's heels all day long."

"You know how he is. He has to do everything himself."

"If it wasn't for herself, I'd be away with you," Ned threatened. "Listen, if you run short of money, don't be backward about writing."

"There's plenty of work in England. I won't be needing money."

Hannafin spoke up. "You'll need some sort of a coat, Dermot. I've got an old raincoat you can have. It has a rip in one of the pockets but sure you'll not be too particular, so long as it keeps the rain off you."

"I'll have to pay you for it," Dermot said.

"None of that. When you're coming back from England with your pockets lined of money, you can bring me a new one."

Dermot sat down opposite the stove and gave a contented sigh. "I hate the thought of shaping out. That's a wild night to be leaving home."

"You'll have to see Neeve tonight too," Hannafin said.

"Do you think it's safe to go over there?"

"No I don't. I'll go over and send her here," Hannafin said as he buttoned his coat. "Ned and I will send her over. As soon as she leaves here, go you down our garden, across the car lane and down the back gardens to the railway line. I think you'll be safe enough."

Dermot looked at Ned and asked, "You'll not be back here?"

"Do you need me at all?"

"No. It would be better for me to go alone down the gardens." Dermot suddenly felt an overwhelming surge of tenderness for his brother. He stood up and went over to Ned. "Say good-by to them at home for me. Tell Mom that I'll send her the price of a set of Beleek China as soon as I can. Tell Bella that once I get settled, I'll find out about nurses' training. Maybe they'll let her go over, now that I'll be there."

"Do you have any message for the old one?" Ned asked.

"Just tell him that I couldn't help it. Tell him that I was always an O'Neill; that when the moment came I wasn't afraid, neither of the I.R.A. nor of the British soldiers."

Ned lowered his eyes and fumblingly shook hands with his brother. He wanted to say something warm, something that would let Dermot know the love he felt for him. "You need a shave," he said lamely.

Dermot felt his chin. "I'll do bloody well until I get to Belfast," he replied. Dermot suddenly remembered something. "Listen, when Loy's bitch throws her pups, be sure to get one for us. Tone's the father of that litter."

"Aye, I'll pick one out."

"And give my football togs and boots back to the club."

"Aye, I'll do that too."

"And yourself, don't go hitting the bottle too much," Dermot advised.

"What the hell else is there to do in this kip?" Ned's voice had a bitter ring as he continued, "I wish to God it was me going instead of you."

Hannafin interrupted the conversation. "Let's be off. The sooner you get out of town, the better, Dermot." He reached out and shook Dermot's hand. "I'm sorry about this. It's a hard and a cruel thing I've done to you. But it was the right thing and you're the kind of man who can't deceive himself. You'll write me once in a while?"

"I will to be sure," Dermot replied.

Hannafin moved out into the hallway and Dermot and Ned again shook hands, this time silently. Dermot pushed his brother affectionately on the shoulder and Ned turned and joined Hannafin at the door. They turned up their collars and stepped out into the street.

Mrs. Hannafin closed the door behind them and took Dermot into the kitchen. Dermot sat down on a chair and began to cry. He smiled at Mrs. Hannafin. "I'm a bit of an old cod," he said, ashamed of his emotion.

Mrs. Hannafin started to sniffle a little herself and to hide it she went out to the kitchen and began to tackle the dishes.

Hannafin, Ned and Neeve stood in a little knot at the entrance to Donnelly's kitchen. "Have you found him?" Neeve asked.

"We have," Hannafin replied.

"He's all right? Where is he?" Neeve demanded impatiently.

"He's over in our house," Hannafin answered. "Let you go over to him now but remember he can't stay too long in town. Don't keep him more than ten minutes or so."

"I won't," Neeve answered. She looked over at Ned and said, "It's a pity you didn't come a wee bit sooner. Bella decided not to wait any more and she's away home. You should go on home and tell your mother, Ned. I'm sure she's astray in the head, worrying about Dermot."

"I'll be going home in a minute or so," Ned answered sheepishly.

Neeve turned around and called into the kitchen, "I'll be back in a wee while. I'm going over to Hannafin's." She put on her coat and walked out with the two men. When they reached the square, Hannafin said to her, "We won't be going over with you. Mind now, don't keep him back too long."

"I won't," Neeve promised.

Hannafin and Ned left her and walked around to the back entrance of Devlin's pub.

Neeve continued across the square and down the back street. She knocked on Hannafin's door and Mrs. Hannafin came out. "Is Dermot in?" she asked.

Mrs. Hannafin nodded and Neeve stepped inside. Just then Dermot came out and caught her by the arm. "I have to leave tonight," he said.

"I know," she answered simply.

Still holding her by the hand he drew her into the shop. He put his arms around her, pulling her in close, and began to kiss her. She sighed and laid her head on his shoulder.

"You'll never come back," she said.

"I'll be back in a year."

"No. You'll never come back. If I want you, I'll have to go over after you. Whatever you do, promise to write me."

"I'll write at least once a month," Dermot said. He tilted her head back. "I'll never forget you, Neeve."

She reached up and ran her finger down his cheek. Then she gently drew it across his closed mouth. He made a kissing motion at the finger and it slid around to the back of his neck and she pulled his head down. He kissed her and she laid her cheek against his. He felt a wetness on the cheek and for a moment he did not know if he was crying again or if it was Neeve. He tried to lift her head away but she resisted. He raised his head slightly and buried his face in her hair. There was the faintest smell of vinegar from it and he knew he would never again smell vinegar without thinking of her. He moved his head slowly from side to side, letting her hair brush his lips. He felt a desperate need to tell her exactly why he loved her, so that she would always remember. "I love you," he whispered into the strands. "I love the way you walk and I love your hands. I love the little mole on your cheek and I love the way you say 'convenience.' I love the way your eyebrows meet and your head tilts to one side when you're serious." He stopped for a moment, thinking, and then added. "I love you because you want to make something of me."

Neeve was quietly sobbing, unable to speak. "Don't," he said. "The night has cried enough." He slowly tried to disengage himself but she held on tightly to him. Again he bent and kissed her, tenderly, on the bridge of the nose and on each eyelid. On his lips he could taste the salt of her tears.

"Be good, wee angel," he whispered and pulled away from her. He turned, opened the door and blindly walked through the kitchen and out the back door.

Neeve laid her head down on the counter and wept.

THIRTY

McGinnis was sitting on the bench in the workshop reading Dan Breen's *My Fight for Irish Freedom* when an urgent knock bounced off the door. He slid down from the bench and went over and opened it. Malone stepped inside quickly.

"O'Neill's gone," he said in a low worried voice.

"Gone?" McGinnis echoed, his brow furrowing in bewilderment.

"Aye gone," Malone repeated. "I went over to the hall and couldn't find Quinn. Then I shouted through the door of the storehouse and he answered me from the inside. I broke the lock and he came plowing out. He said that Ned O'Neill had let Dermot out. Quinn and I were on the way over here when he took to his heels and disappeared. He's got the wind up over something—the little bugger."

McGinnis' face tightened in scorn. "That's the reliable man, Quinn," he said sarcastically.

"We've got to get O'Neill. He swore he'd go to the police," Malone said, his voice high and excited.

"Shsssh, for God's sake, they'll hear us," McGinnis warned, nodding his head in the direction of the kitchen. He got down on his knees and pulled out a big tool box from under the counter. Lifting the lid, he took out two revolvers wrapped in oily rags.

"Here," he said, handing one to Malone, "he's liable to try to hook away on the eleven train to Applebridge. Go you to the station and hide behind the water tower. If you see him at all," McGinnis made a clenching motion with his hand to indicate the pressing of a trigger. "If he's not at the train," McGinnis continued, "then go to the barracks and keep an eye on it for a while. He might take a notion and go there. If you don't run across him, report back here at twelve o'clock."

Malone unwrapped the gun and stuck it into his jacket pocket. "What are you going to do?"

"I'm going to O'Neill's house. He may go home tonight and plan on leaving in the morning. He's not afraid of us. He's thickheaded and he'll take his own time. Listen, before you go to the station get hold of Corrigan and tell him to come here and wait for the Brigade men. I'll be back myself at twelve, whether or not I find O'Neill."

McGinnis looked at his revolver and then shoved it into his coat pocket. He went into the kitchen, picked up his trench coat and told his mother he was going over to Hannafin's. He and Malone left the workshop together. McGinnis took his bicycle from the yard and the two men separated when they reached the street. Malone walked on down the town and McGinnis mounted the bicycle and rode in the opposite direction.

The rain had slackened into a misty drizzle and in the light of the bicycle lamp it had the appearance of fine snow. McGinnis cycled slowly and purposefully, his body dipping awkwardly each time his bad foot put pressure on the pedal. As he rounded the first curve in the road he saw, fifty yards ahead, a red light making small circles as a signal to stop. He swore softly and wondered whether he should turn back. He decided against it and cycled to where two B-specials stood in the middle of the road. He dismounted a few yards away and wheeled his bicycle forward. A powerful flashlight threw a beam in his eyes, temporarily blinding him. The white circle slid down his body to his feet and jerked up to his face before it was lowered. As his eyes adjusted, he recognized the black-uniformed men as Farland and Ranley, two local Orangemen.

A voice lashed at him, "What's your name?"

McGinnis felt a quick gouge of anger but prudently contained it. "For God's sake fellas, you know me. It's McGinnis."

There was no hint of either recognition or friendship as the voice demanded, "Your identity card!"

"Listen Billy Farland, it's me, McGinnis who has the bicycle shop."

"Less of your guff and give me your card," Farland ordered.

McGinnis leaned the bicycle against his body and reached into the inside pocket of his jacket. His anger showed as the little tic on his cheek started agitating. His hands shook as he fumblingly extracted his identity card from a bunch of papers and handed it to the B-special.

"Where are you going?" Farland asked.

"Up to Taylor's on a visit."

"Your bloody late going on a visit. Where are you going?"

McGinnis sighed exasperatedly, "I'm going to Taylor's. I told you already. Where else would I be going—a night like this?"

Ranley stepped forward. The B-special was carrying his rifle at the port and as he drew near to McGinnis he reached out and tapped him lightly on the side with the barrel of the gun.

"What are you doing?" McGinnis demanded.

Ranley remained silent and tapped him on the other side.

The rifle hit the revolver but the clothes prevented the gun from making a noise. McGinnis felt a sweat break out on him. "For the love of God fellas, what are you doing to me?" he said pleadingly.

"Hold your bloody tongue," Farland ordered. "You're damned quiet now when you're up against men with guns. You papists need to be taught a little civility." Farland swung the light up into McGinnis' eyes and the latter, though blinded, could not prevent the beginning of a sneer from showing. The B-special handed back the identity card and pushed McGinnis so that the latter fell back a step or two. "Get away on now about your business," he ordered.

McGinnis was trembling with anger and for a wild hate-forced moment he wanted to take out the Smith and Wesson and start shooting. He grabbed the bicycle and wheeled it around the two men. They played the light on him as he was walking on up the road. He continued walking for a hundred yards or so, determined not to give them the opportunity of laughing at the awkwardness of his clubfoot when he was cycling. When he felt that he was far enough away, he hobbled the leg over the bicycle and started cycling.

It was a good job, he thought, that they didn't search him and find the revolver. They were the great pack of heroes, them and their bloody rifles. He should have plugged the both of them. That's what was wrong with the country. For too long they'd let the Orangemen lead them by the nose without fighting back. And now it looked as if there'd be no invasion this year. How was he going to hold the company together? Already Quinn had the wind up. It was all O'Neill's fault, he knew. He'd have to show he was capable of dealing with O'Neill or they'd all leave the company and drift back to the old ways. Well, he'd get the informer and after that they'd make new plans. They'd put the fear of God in the police and B-specials if they had to shoot the half of them. All this talk about constitutional means was nonsense. The only thing Ireland ever got from England through constitutional means were the Penal

Laws. The gun was the only answer Ireland needed; the only answer England ever listened to. And it was time that the Loyal Orange Lodge and the B-men had a taste of it. But first he had to get the informer. He had to show that no one could inform on the I.R.A. and get away with it. O'Neill was no good, and every group of Irishmen had it's O'Neills and they had to be weeded out. One bad Irishman could undo the work of a hundred patriots. Since O'Neill had turned contrary, nothing had gone right with the company. He was almost sure that O'Neill was behind the lifting of Reilly. And Reilly would be revenged before the night was out.

He cycled steadily until he arrived at O'Neill's lane where he dismounted. Looking back along the hedge that bordered one side of the road, he saw a wooden gate leading into a field. He opened the gate and left the bicycle lying on the grass under the shelter of a clump of blackberry bushes that formed part of the hedge. Then he started walking toward the O'Neill house. He went through two fields and into the haggard at the back of the house. Crouching low, he limped halfway across the haggard, taking refuge behind a haystack. From his position he could see through the back window of the house and into the kitchen.

He was still a good thirty yards from the window and he wondered if he could be sure of hitting Dermot at that distance. Lying full length on the grass, he took steady aim through the window, supporting his right wrist with his left hand. He realized that he wouldn't get more than one shot at Dermot before the latter could take cover. If he moved much closer he ran the risk of being caught or recognized before he could reach the bicycle, not being able to run fast with his club-foot.

The only one to be seen in the kitchen was old Patrick, sitting on a chair beside the fire and reading a newspaper. McGinnis waited about fifteen minutes and then saw Mrs. O'Neill cross the visible part of the kitchen and go to the fire.

The steady rain had soaked through his trench coat and he

was beginning to shiver with the cold. Another ten uncomfortable minutes passed before he decided that Dermot had not yet come home.

He's still in town, McGinnis thought, as he retreated from the haggard. He went back through the fields and took up a position behind the hedge on the other side of the road. Cautiously he lit a match and looked at his watch. It was still only eleven. He'd wait another hour and if Dermot didn't show up he'd go back to town and get the Brigade men to help him. It was possible that Dermot had already left but from the look of the parents, he didn't think so. They didn't seem upset in any way and likely knew nothing of what had happened during the day.

From over the hills came floating the sound of a train whistle. He wondered if Dermot was on the train. Malone would probably be at the barracks by now. The whistle wailed again and McGinnis felt an irrational desire to be on the train himself, a thought that he recognized as a form of weakness and quickly dismissed.

The rain kept falling in a steady drizzle, punctuated now and then by brief gusts of wind. Periodically he stamped his feet trying to keep warm. The rain, soaking through his clothes and into his boots chilled him and his foot began pulsing with the rhythmic pain that came with wet weather.

He was standing in the field opposite the end of O'Neill's lane at the point where the lane led into the county road. He could see the county road for a considerable distance on either side of the lane and to make his task easier, anyone entering the lane had to dismount to open a heavy iron gate.

After half an hour's waiting he heard the sound of a motor approaching. He peered out through the hedge and saw the black car go hurtling past, its tires throwing out a bellying skirt of rain. The car was going into Duncrana and he wondered if its occupants were the men from Brigade headquarters.

Presently he heard a faint hum and saw the light of a bicycle coming from Duncrana. He changed his position so that he was facing the end of the lane, withdrew the revolver from his pocket and waited. The light came closer and bobbed to a stop as the person dismounted from the bicycle. McGinnis held his breath as he recognized Dermot's trench coat. The collar was turned up and above the collar McGinnis thought he saw the black beret that Dermot usually wore. The gate was slowly swinging open when McGinnis extended his arm and pointed the gun through the hedge. He swore inwardly at the way his arm shook. Then he stiffened and took careful aim at the middle part of the coat. He kept wondering if he would actually have the nerve to fire as his finger slowly squeezed the trigger. The sound of the shot crashed on his ears to be followed, almost instantaneously, by a drawn-out grunt that rose to a half-scream and stopped. McGinnis heard the clatter of the bicycle as it fell to the ground and saw the dim shape clinging to the gate for support. He raised the gun again and in a sudden shame-driven rage, shouted incoherently while he fired four more shots.

He forced his way through the hedge, limped across the road and looked down at the figure that lay sprawled in the lane. The bicycle lamp threw a soft splash of light over a luxuriant head of red hair that lay, flowered out and mud-stained, in a small puddle.

As he stared in disbelief, Bella's eyes opened. She looked up at him and her features contorted while a lonely hurt-filled whimper broke from her.

He shook his head quickly and started running in a sideways scrabble out to the county road. He violently threw the gun away and it bounced on the road and slid into the grass verge. "Mother of Christ, have mercy on me. Mother of Jesus," he sobbed as the pained whimper that came from Bella still rang in his ears.

THIRTY-ONE

Kathleen and Patrick had both run out of the house on hearing the shots.

As they came running down the lane they saw ahead of them the sprawled figure and the fallen bicycle. Kathleen gave a great sob as she recognized the long red hair. "My God! It's Bella!" she moaned.

Patrick reached down and tenderly lifted his daughter. "Hush, wee angel," he said, trying to still the agonized whimpers that came from Bella. He started up the lane with her, Kathleen alongside urging him to hurry. His face was lifted and the rain settled gently on the lips that were praying aloud, saying the Act of Contrition for his daughter. "O my God, I am heartily sorry for all my sins . . ."

He brought her into the bedroom and laid her down on the

bed. Then he turned and went back down the lane where he lifted the bicycle and began cycling into town for the doctor and the priest.

Back in the bedroom, Kathleen stared at her daughter in bewilderment. The coat and dress had been removed and she felt a rising fear and horror as she looked at the splotchy bloodstains all over Bella's slip.

Kathleen went out to the kitchen dresser and took down a small bottle of rum. With shaking hands she tried to force her daughter to drink some of the rum but Bella had lapsed into unconsciousness and the liquid mixed with the thin trickle of blood that came from one corner of the mouth.

Kathleen set aside the bottle and took down Bella's rosary beads from a nail on the wall. She knelt down beside the bed, her head resting against her daughter's legs. Sinking her face into the bed, she began praying, the *Our Fathers* and *Hail Marys* automatically coming out in a pattern, while underneath, forming a background, were the continual entreaties. "Our Father, Who art in Heaven . . . Please God who did so love the world, don't take Bella . . . Thy Kingdom come, Thy will be done . . . Blessed Mother of the Seven Sorrows, don't take Bella . . . on Earth as it is in Heaven . . . Holy Saint Brigid intercede for me . . . give us this day our daily bread . . . O Sacred Heart of Jesus, ask anything in Thy Name, don't take my daughter . . . and forgive us our trespasses . . . Blessed Saint Joseph, don't let my Bella die . . . Hail Mary full of Grace . . . not O Mother of God, my only daughter . . . Holy Mary, Mother of God, pray for us sinners . . ."

Deeper still in the mind, in the region where thoughts are not given shape, the memories stirred and were thrown, lightning-clear, into the prayers and supplications. Bella, her head to one side, playing the accordion . . . Glory be to the Father, to the Son and to the Holy Ghost . . . O Blessed Saint Anne, who knew the pains of childbirth, don't let my daughter die . . . Bella seven years old, freckled and redheaded, riding the

mare in from the fields with Patrick holding the bridle . . .
Our Father Who art in Heaven . . . don't ask this of me . . .
Bella, nine years old, coming into the kitchen, flushed and ex-
cited with the news that she had found a hen's nest in the
hedge with eleven eggs and a brooding angry hen . . .
Blessed art Thou amongst women, and blessed is the fruit of
Thy womb . . ."

Outside the rain kept falling, a steady slant that pierced the
ground. The oats bent with the rain and thrust their shoots
deeper into the soil. The tubular roots of the potatoes sucked
at the moisture and fed it to the sprouting stems.

In the byre the cows lay still, contentedly chewing their
cuds. Now and then one would twist its head and listen wisely
to the rain that splattered against the door.

In the mountainy field behind the house, a fox uneasily
curled in a hole with two cubs, her long tail wrapped around
them, a maternal tongue licking the fur of her offspring. From
a hole in a sandy ridge, a lonely rabbit hopped forth and then
froze. It felt the rain and distastefully turned around and
hopped back into its warren. In the tangled roots of the blackberry bushes, the field mice nervously burrowed deeper amid
the roots and grass, trying to escape the trickles of water that
seeped down through the bushes. In the big oak tree near the
well, an owl sat in the black hole that was the door of its house
and philosophically surveyed the night outside, uttering every
now and then a lugubrious comment. A weasel flowed between
the rocks in a loose built stone wall, its tapering nose scenting
the hiding places of mice.

Inside the house Tone padded around in the kitchen. He
went to the door that looked in on Bella's bedroom and
gravely contemplated Kathleen, on her knees beside the bed.
Then he turned and resumed his restless prowling. Under the
table the cat delicately whipped her tail back and forth while
her eyes unblinkingly followed the dog.

Presently the door of the kitchen opened and Patrick entered with Father Sheehy and Doctor Kelly. They went directly to the bedroom, where the doctor made a brief examination of Bella and then stepped back and looked over at the priest. Almost imperceptibly he shook his head. Father Sheehy took the stole from his pocket and slipped it around his neck. He unscrewed the top of the bottle of holy oils and bending over Bella, began administering Extreme Unction.

Kathleen broke out in a wild uncontrollable sobbing on seeing the priest anoint Bella on the lips with the holy oils. She was about to rush over and tear the priest away from the bed when Patrick, sensing her intention, caught her by the arm and led her out into the kitchen. She went over and leaned against the kitchen table, her gaunt body heaving with sobs. From the bedroom she could hear the low Latin murmur of the priest. The doctor came into the kitchen and stood beside her, wondering how to comfort her. Patrick went back into the bedroom, feeling that his wife was safe with the doctor watching her. In between the sobs, Kathleen desperately listened to the murmur of the priest, expecting it to stop at any moment.

Suddenly, for the space of a second, a terrible stillness petrified the kitchen. The voice of Father Sheehy had stopped. For one full second a strangeness was in the house and even the dog felt it. He stood stock still, his ears pointing forward and the hair on his neck bristled out. Kathleen bowed her head, "God be good to my only daughter," she murmured. The doctor hurried back into the bedroom.

She heard Father Sheehy's voice and the low murmur of her husband as he answered the priest. Presently both men came into the kitchen, the priest taking off his stole and folding it.

Patrick came over to his wife and gently touched her on the arm. She wrenched violently away from him. Her rid-rimmed eyes narrowed and the lips pulled back over her teeth in a sharp half-grin. "Mother-of-God," she shouted, pointing to her husband. "Look at him! Look at the evil soul of a man who didn't love his family. Who never loved anyone but a brother that's dead this twenty years."

"Hush now, Mrs. O'Neill," the priest interrupted. "That's no way to be talking at a time like this."

Kathleen whirled on Father Sheehy and cried bitterly, "And you—the man of God; the holy priest who encourages the young lads in their shooting and killing. Oh! but you've been the great sower of hate and it's ourselves that's gathering the crop, this night."

Father Sheehy stared at her, terrified by the passionate accusation. Then the long years of his ministry came to his aid and inwardly the prayers began to form.

Wild-eyed Kathleen looked in turn at each of the men. "Where are my sons?" her voice keened. "Where's Dermot? Is he lying in a ditch somewhere, his body filled with the Christian charity of his comrades? The charity they showed to Bella?"

The doctor spoke soothingly to her. "Here now, Mrs. O'Neill, this is no good at all. I've a wee pill here that will help you. It won't take a minute." He started searching through his bag.

From outside the house came the faint echoes of a song and the four of them lifted their heads in astonishment. Someone was coming up the lane singing. They listened to the words of "The Bold Fenian Men" and as the chant came closer they recognized the alcohol-slurred voice of Ned.

"We may have good men, but we'll never-r-r-r have better, Glo-o-o-o-ry O! Glo-o-o-o-ry O! to the Bold Fenian Men."

The voice stopped and they heard the lifting of the door latch. Ned stepped into the kitchen and lurched a little as he looked around the gathering.

"Some died by the wayside," he recited, putting his hand against the wall to steady himself. Suddenly his befogged brain took in the fact that something was wrong. He saw his father spring across the floor and felt the smack of a fist against his cheekbone and heard the fierce hysterical voice of Patrick, "You drunken scut! Bella's dead!"

Tone, unaccustomed to the shouting, began to whine and crawled under the table where the cat made room for him. Ned stumbled over to the fire and sank down on a chair. "Bella dead?" he repeated stupidly.

Kathleen turned her back on the men and looked out through the kitchen window. Her voice was low and quiet again as she began to pray, "Mother of God, who did so love the world as to give up for its redemption her only-begotten Son . . ."

THIRTY-TWO

Sergeant Crawley was sitting at the fire, reading Spinoza's *Ethics* when a knock came to the door. He laid the book face down on the chair and went over and opened the door. Don McGinnis stood on the threshhold, his eyes wild, his clothes soaked with rain.

"Come in," the sergeant said.

McGinnis limped in and stood in the middle of the room. The sergeant shut the door and asked, "What's wrong?"

"Wrong? I . . ." McGinnis hesitated and stepped closer to the fire. He turned and hurriedly spoke, "I shot someone. Bella O'Neill."

"Bella O'Neill?" the sergeant asked incredulously.

McGinnis' voice took a pleading tone. "I didn't mean to. I

was trying to get Dermot and Bella came up the lane." He grimaced and leaned his weight against a nearby table, placing the bad leg conspicuously out in front of him.

The sergeant strode across the room and caught him by the shoulder. At that moment the phone rang. He crossed to the wall and lifted the receiver. "Hello? Yes. Yes. Dead! God save us! Of course. I'll be at the barracks in ten minutes. Yes." He replaced the phone and turned around.

"I didn't know," McGinnis said in a low voice, talking to his clubfoot. "I thought it was Dermot. It was Dermot's trench coat she had on."

The sergeant frowned as he stared at his visitor. "I could have had you in the Crumlin Road Jail two months ago," he said reflectively. "I'm as responsible for her death as you are." He walked over to the closet and took out his tunic. Swiftly he buttoned it and jerked the belt tight. He lifted down his raincoat and placed it cape-fashion around his shoulders. "Why?" he demanded. "You knew that Dermot didn't give the names of any of the men in the organization. Only that Trilarran was being raided. Why?"

"He was a traitor to the cause," McGinnis mumbled to the floor.

"The cause! The bloody, blasted, bleeding cause! For the cause you'll murder and thieve and shoot women."

McGinnis started sobbing, his self-control gone. "I did it for Ireland. It wasn't her I meant to shoot. I only wanted to free Ireland." He lifted his head and glared wildly at the sergeant. "My father was shot by the Tans. This leg I got from the Tans."

The sergeant caught him by the arm and shook him roughly, "The Tans are gone now!"

McGinnis' dark eyes were hate-filled with the memory of the B-men who had stopped him. "Aye, the Tans have gone, but now we have the B-specials." He made a pushing motion at the sergeant. "But we'll clear them too. The way we cleared the Tans. The only argument the British understand—the gun!"

His face contorted in self-pity as he remembered Bella. "Oh Sacred Heart of Jesus, have pity on me," he moaned.

"Come on," the sergeant said gently and led him out the door.

Inside the church Father Sheehy knelt at the communion rails. Over and over in his mind, Kathleen's accusation turned and lanced and probed. He remembered his stormy speeches to the Gaelic League. Had that been partly the cause of Bella's death? Bowing his head he wondered why he hadn't followed up the bishops' letter with a sermon condemning the violence that was gathering. Why had he not been more of a priest and less of an Irishman? Where had he begun to go astray?

The cold and the damp seeped into the church. Sheets of wind-bearing rain slammed at the stained-glass windows on the west-side. Hanging from a long chain at the head of the nave, a small red lamp burned in flickering fits, throwing barely enough light to reveal the wooden crucifix and the suffering compassionate face of a Celtic Christ.

Father McCory sat reading in the parlor of the rectory. Idly he wondered where the parish priest could be. Father Sheehy had left at eight o'clock to visit Doctor Kelly and had not yet returned and it was now past midnight. He stirred and slid a little lower in the chair. Turning to the sports page, he read the review of the challenge match between Cork and Dublin. Duncrana would be playing next Sunday and they'd probably be without O'Neill. He hoped that Dermot would come again to the rectory before he left. He wondered why it was that in spite of playing football on the town team, in spite of being more available to the people, he knew less of what was going on than Father Sheehy. He supposed that with the years their confidence would grow. It was a disadvantage being a young priest—though not as far as playing football was concerned. If they could get young Murphy to play left halfback and switch McKey to the midfield it would plug the vacancy left by O'Neill. He folded the newspaper and dropped it to the floor.

His eyes wandered around the room and he noticed the mud-traced print that came as far as the hatstand. Martha would be blaming him again tomorrow.

Over in the Back Street, Hannafin sat listening to a continental station on the wireless. He had a pencil out and was conducting a symphony orchestra as they played Ravel's *Pavanne pour une enfante défunte*. His wife was watching him, an amused smile on her face. There was no doubt that he was a bit of a cod, but that man of hers had courage. That queer little man with the bald head and the paunch had his own peculiar type of courage. Suddenly feeling a great warmth for her husband, she got up and lightly tapped him on the cheek, "It's time for bed," she said softly.

"He's not a bad conductor, but mind I'd bring in the woodwinds a little stronger near the end," he complained. "It's just a wee bit off balance."

In his majesty's prison on the Crumlin Road, Sean Reilly uneasily lay on an iron cot. He was dreaming and in the dream he was walking through the fields. He had set several snares for rabbits and in each snare a cat had been caught. The cats had tried to scratch and bite him when he had attempted to set them free. At one snare, a particularly big cat was scratching and spitting so ferociously that he was afraid to go any closer. Then Dermot came walking down the field with a pitchfork and solved the problem by killing the cat with several stabs of the fork. He started arguing violently with Dermot and Dermot lunged at him. He woke up. For half a second he expected to see Dermot there. He blinked his eyes in the absolute darkness of the cell and then an aching loneliness swept over him when he realized where he was. He would like to see Dermot again. He would like to tell him that nothing in the world was worth the loss of ten years' freedom. He turned wearily on his side and tried to go back to sleep.

In the bedroom she shared with her sisters, Neeve lay staring at the ceiling. In her mind she was walking with Dermot down the railway line and into Rathgiven. Hardly conscious of it, she felt now and again the salty scald of a tear.

Dermot O'Neill was nearing Rathgiven. Weary now with the walking and the misery of his wet clothes, he trudged up the little hill that led into the town. He walked past the silent and darkened houses until he came to the square and saw the big bulk of Red O'Connor's milk truck. He tried to open the cab but both doors were locked. Grabbing one of the sides he swung himself up on the platform of the lorry and began to unfold the canvas tarp that was lying there. He let the rain puddles run off the tarp and sat down and arranged it around himself. Lighting a match, he looked at his watch—three-ten. There was still an hour to wait. The rain came slanting down, somewhat lighter than it was earlier in the evening, and Dermot thought how good the rain would be for the land.

From somewhere in the town came the dim sound of music and Dermot guessed that an all-night party was in progress. He listened intently, trying to discover what tune was being played, but all that came to him through the confusion of the rain and the wind were the unmistakable notes of an accordion. The dark and the distance lent loneliness to the sound. It came intermittently, helped or hindered by the wind—at times muted and barely heard, at times a clear passage of several notes. The music tantalized him and he tried to ignore it, pulling the edge of the tarp up over his head. Then all he could hear was the dancing pattern of the rain on the canvas. The sound made him drowsy and he began to fall asleep.

Too long a sacrifice
Can make a stone of the heart.
O when may it suffice?
That is Heaven's part, our part
To murmur name upon name,
As a mother names her child
When sleep at last has come
On limbs that had run wild.
What is it but nightfall?
No, no, not night but death;
Was it needless death after all?
For England may keep faith
For all that is done and said
We know their dream; enough
To know they dreamed and are dead;
And what if excess of love
Bewildered them till they died?
I write it out in a verse—
MacDonagh and MacBride
And Connolly and Pearse
Now and in time to be,
Wherever green is worn,
Are changed, changed utterly:
A terrible beauty is born.

From "Easter, 1916" by W. B. Yeats.